Chris Petit is a filmmaker and writer. His previous novels are *Back from the Dead* and *The Psalm Killer*. He lives in London.

THE HUMAN POOL

Chris Petit

Scribner

First published in Great Britain by Scribner, 2002
This edition published by Scribner, 2003
An imprint of Simon & Schuster UK Ltd
A Viacom Company

1 3 5 7 9 10 8 6 4 2

Simon & Schuster UK Ltd
Africa House
64–78 Kingsway
London WC2B 6AH

Simon & Schuster Australia
Sydney

www.simonsays.co.uk

A CIP catalogue record for this book
is available from the British Library

ISBN: 0–7432–3119–8

Typeset by M Rules
Printed and bound in Great Britain by
Bookmarque Ltd, Croydon, Surrey

For Emma

Vaughan, Twenty-nine Palms, California, The Present

Here's the problem. I wrote this book once the way I was told to, as fiction, to a formula: sex by page such-and-such, with guns to follow. 'Tell it like it was,' my then editors urged. 'Make the reader stand next to you.' The thing is, nobody else's description, or the movies, prepare you for what it's like when it happens to you, and as for the one-liner that sold the story – *My Trip to Genocide Hell* – it belittles the facts and leaves me feeling ashamed. What they wanted was unimportant compared to the near invisible details which do the real damage.

The first time, I wrote it in the third person, cutting out the history and the shuttling between different characters. Unfortunately, it meant losing most of Hoover's diary. Being both old and a messy organiser, Hoover was regarded as an embarrassment and worth no more than a cameo as a Deep Throat. Hoover sprawls: old man's time. What they really objected to was that he is too cussed and remembers too much. He understands that life lacks narrative organisation, that it feels like something other than a story.

For my part, most of the time I felt as though I was in a rush of drowning. Also I have never read anything in fiction so chilling, or inadequate, as a transcript of a real torture interrogation, for its simultaneous ability and failure to convey what was going on. By what mental process does someone decide to write, *Subject screams. Statement incomprehensible?*

History misleads us, I have discovered, thanks to Hoover. We are taught that it is about things ending and beginning, that it is sequential, a progression of dates down the years, when in reality it is all about connections. The stuff that really scared me didn't even make it as footnotes in the version they wanted me to write – like what was the real purpose of the sale of a large consignment of wooden huts by a construction company in neutral Switzerland to the Waffen SS in 1942? Or look at the word 'neutral': during the Second World War German goods trains were allowed to pass through Switzerland only so long as the contents were not armaments, which, of course, Italy's Jews were not.

Which leaves the patient stitching together of multiple details: for example, how the death of an enemy agent in Lisbon in 1942 indirectly connects to the disappearance of a container-load of illegal immigrants sixty years later. I am reminded of the beginning of the old Robert Redford picture *Three Days of the Condor*, which asks why a book that hasn't sold in its original market should be translated into half a dozen Middle Eastern languages. After which Redford goes to fetch breakfast and returns to find everyone in the office shot dead.

I also find myself thinking of that game about the film star Kevin Bacon and how many moves it takes to connect him to any other actor in the history of Hollywood. It is frightening how few (frightening because of the viral shadow that hangs over the game), frightening too when applied to other areas. How many moves from George W. Bush to Osama Bin Laden? One. Bin Laden's brother Salem was a partner in George W's oil firm which went belly-up. A wise American poet whom I met once, Ed Dorn, dead now, always maintained that the Gulf War was a Bush family affair about offshore oil leases; when it comes to politics *always* look for the vested interest. Also of relevance to the several secret histories which follow is Dorn's remark: 'Listen. Just because the record isn't there doesn't mean it's lost.'

How many moves from face cream to ethnic cleansing? One, as it turns out, thanks to the pharmaceutical industry.

As it is Hoover's story, I will begin with him. Without him I wouldn't be here, so I owe him a formal thanks for that, as well as for permission to use his files, which form the spine of what follows. Further assistance was provided by documents previously belonging to Hoover's former associate – Obersturmbahnführer Karl-Heinz Strasse of the SS – and papers generously provided by Beate von Heimendorf. 'Begin' is not a straightforward word in Hoover's book. For him past and present co-exist: 'They bleed into each other, nephew.' Calling me 'nephew' was his condescending way of being affectionate. Or perhaps he meant something more calculated. I wonder if by giving me his files he intended an act of classic transference. Having wrestled with them so long – as I sit here in the high desert, holed up in the Harmony Motel – I find my own writing starting to impersonate his.

Hoover told me that May 1945, was *his* obvious starting point, because it was then that he first realised how much was (and remains) invisible. But you can cut the pack anywhere – 1942, 1945, 1999, this year, next year – it all links up in the end, not necessarily in the order that it happened. And thanks to the factor known as human error, there may be no closure, ever, maybe no resolution either. Just another cut of the pack, with death the only solution.

Hoover, Washington

It is hard to recall exactly how the end of the war had been, or what I felt in May of 1945, now nearly a lifetime ago. The justification of our cause was plain for all to see: in our equipment, in our rations and in our sense of being a young country whose time was still ahead. We had no history to appeal to and, given the mess the Nazis had made of their Thousand Year Reich, most Americans were content with surface, and the idea of being able to lead lives unburdened by other people's yesterdays.

Many of our troops arrived late enough in Europe to see only the exhaustion of defeat, and to take advantage of fraternisation and the barter of our superior US rations. Everyone wanted what our soldiers had. Their lives had a shine to them, or so it seemed. They were only there to finish a job before going home to America's better lives, bigger skies, and more energetic, plain-speaking ways. That we might have been naive did not occur to us (in the face of so much exhausted irony). To most of us, anyway.

Now I am a first-generation American. In those days I

was still in the process of becoming one. Part of me remains untouched by, and resists, this assimilation. In speech I retain some of my native accent. Not that I keep any other connection to my country of origin, which I left in 1940, with the desire never to return. In fact, that is not entirely true, and I must be careful to get this right. All my life has been bounded by a homesickness, and the paradox that I never made an effort to go back. Perhaps there was no home: Liège lies in my memory beyond a dream.

A night or two ago on a satellite channel, a German film director talked about being a small boy in 1945 watching the first American troops arrive in his village, and how he cried in fright at the strange and novel sight of a black GI eating a banana. I offer this story for two reasons. Because of the odd, roundabout way coincidence works, it is possible I was a witness to this scene, though this was a common fright for German children that spring. There were a lot of black men and enough bananas. The story also demonstrates that tensions among ourselves – the flaws in our own argument – were ignored. We were liberators. Our policies were not under scrutiny.

On matters of coincidence: the older I get the more I discover unexpected connections. I have led a busy life, full of people and unusual conjunctions, so I should not be surprised, yet I am. This might be a fretful mind looking for meaning where there is none or censoring everything except what it registers as having an obscure significance. I am equally surprised by how often I see people I know on television and read in the papers of their deaths, the count getting closer. I am even starting to see the dead. I glimpsed Willi Schmidt on a TV news item, and he has been dead getting on sixty years. For a moment I was sure. The incident unsettled me. My war memories cut out Willi Schmidt. That's what I mean about it being hard to recall how the end of the war had been. They were not straightforward times.

That May and June of 1945, Germany was a bewitched countryside, whole swathes untouched by war, picturebook villages with their half-timbered houses and blossom, in which, of course, not a single Nazi could be found, not even the schoolteacher with his upper lip pale from a shaved-off Hitler moustache. He, like the rest, claimed he had been awaiting Liberation. All the paraphernalia of the Third Reich – swastikas, Nazi street names, pictures of the Führer – had miraculously vanished, taken down in the night, like the decorations from some festive season cut short, leaving everywhere looking strangely denuded. Like the local teacher's shaven lip. After a dozen years of hierarchy, and all the propaganda, and what my daughter Naomi with her college education would call 'iconography', there was nothing.

Though the larger fear had vanished, our unease persisted. Behind the open friendliness of the normal greeting between soldiers who didn't know each other – 'Hey, buddy, how ya doin?' – lay a real anxiety. Stay-behind units of crack Nazi troops, of wolf-like savagery, were rumored to be disguised as American soldiers and hiding in woods, ready to start a rearguard action. Germany was still a haunted and untamed landscape, in which the improvised informality of American signs – 'Bring in your jeep, we never sleep' – took on the appearance of hastily assembled superstitious relics. There was the realisation too that what had been fought had been more than just a war. 'Hey, Grabowski, those dirty Kraut bastards murdered a million Yids, what do you think of that?' I remember what Grabowski answered. 'Yeah, ain't that a pisser,' he said, as he whittled a piece of wood, sitting by the roadside, with the resigned air of a man who had just realised that no one would ever learn, least of all the victor.

I subscribed to the euphoria and simplicity of victory despite my own war which had been clandestine, grubby and morally compromised; having done nothing to stop the screams of the tortured; having dined with 'dirty Kraut bastards' who had negotiated the deaths of millions. But I believed I had acted out of necessity, for a greater good, for security and stability. Now I suspect the joke was on me.

Since Mary died last November I find myself thinking more about the time before her, since the raw scar of her absence is too painful. I feel blurred now she is gone. Florida, where we had lived and being a place where people go to die, is not conducive to mourning. I am not close to the children, and am reluctant to be parcelled out for them to take turns to put me up (and put up with me). The grief I felt was very different from the one the children projected on to me. I no longer wanted or needed company. It was enough to get through the day that I had my conversations with Mary – sometimes aloud, sometimes in my head. The void left by her is more attractive than the life on offer without her. In these long, drawn-out days – time's equivalent to dull tundra – I find myself eager to settle accounts. Secrets need airing in the end.

Like many men who have led dubious lives I was sentimental about my marriage, and despite my lapses, told myself I should try to keep things straight in affairs of the heart. Another joke at my expense: Mary's journals reveal that my marriage was more complicated than she had led me to believe.

The weeks after my wife died were full of watery November afternoons spent walking on an empty beach, entertaining thoughts of getting a dog, stalled by the morbid fear that the dog would one day find me dead. I could imagine the children worrying about me among themselves. I held out until falling and spraining my wrist, which resulted in strapping. Yes, I had been drinking. I had always been extra-careful to give the glass table a wide berth – being mindful of how the actor William Holden had died, gashing his head in a fall and bleeding to death – but tripped over the chair leg. On the subject of actors, I have been told by my children that I look like a dead TV actor, Richard Boone.

Foolishly, I mentioned the sprain to Naomi on the phone. There followed immediate summonses from all the children. It took until Christmas to winkle me out of our home in Englewood, with invitations issued in the names of the grandchildren – Tom and Mickey, Dwight, Hannah, Mo (for Monica) and Joe Junior – the unspoken implication being that I wasn't going to be around much longer to enjoy their company.

My power book has become my lifeline. It lets me spend the mornings alone, writing or pretending to write. The family makes joking references to my memoirs, even though they have no idea what I did beyond something boring for the government. I have never discussed the real nature of my work, except once with Naomi, late one night when we had a bottle of red wine to finish. But Naomi simply shrugged: so what? So much for unburdening. Most children, I have noticed, remain incurious about their parents. Josh, my eldest – Mary had a penchant for Biblical names; there's David as well – jokes that my mornings consist of endlessly typing the same sentence: All work and no play makes Dad a dull boy.

Josh lives in Iowa, of all places. I managed three weeks there before pleading that it was too cold, and moved down to David in Phoenix. David's wife is an insistent over-pleaser and within days I was plotting my escape. The stay lasted a month before I could extricate myself without appearing ungrateful.

The point of coming to Naomi was that I was supposed to look up old Washington contacts; except what do you say?

Naomi has always been my favorite, perhaps because of her late, unplanned conception and a wilfulness shown as a child, a propensity for disobedience, long since lost. I'd had hopes for Naomi, and I still like her the best, but she married a dope and her children are spoiled. Her even good cheer and politeness are very different from how I remember, and both act as distancing devices; I wonder if she isn't on Prozac. In the evident unspoken dissatisfaction of her life I see my own parenting mistakes. Our failure to talk, even when one of us makes the effort, is sad.

Naomi has a shed in the garden with an oil heater, where I work. The grass is lustreless and muddy after a late snowfall. My arrival in Washington had been greeted by raw February winds and one or two early spring flowers that were trying to push their way up: the high-suicide weeks, the ones that did for Sylvia Plath. The shed heater was efficient enough but Naomi, on finding me at the desk wrapped in a blanket, always tried to persuade me to work in the house, where there is no room. The truth is, I have nothing to do, except brood, and wait. So I write.*

A couple of weeks ago, a TV program about life changes invited the viewer to write an obituary as a form of self-assessment. I had snorted at the time, and argued with Naomi who is increasingly susceptible to the panaceas of

*Hoover's papers for this period consist of several formal and informal diaries, computer files of draft chapters of different parts of his 'memoirs', in no particular order, as well as other notebooks and files of thoughts and jottings. This chapter is an organisation of that material, much of it undated, and takes its cue from a note of Hoover's: *Start always with the past.*

experts, yet I see that my log-on file for the next day contained the paltry offering:

> Born Liège 1919. Army conscript, 1939. Nazi invasion, 1940. Captured. Escaped on bicycle, dressed as paysan, traveled through France, uneventfully, until chance meeting with Belgian fascist. His stolen papers used for passage from Brittany to French West Africa. There involved in an historical footnote following the Dakar Raid (Sept 1940), interpreting for German agents organising the retrieval of Belgian gold reserves, forwarded after the fall of Belgium and France.

I have just realised. This gold, in all likelihood, I saw again, five years later in Frankfurt, with Allen Dulles. I also note that I omitted to mention that I'd had to kill the Belgian fascist for his papers.

For a long time now I haven't known where to begin. Do I begin at the beginning? If so, where is the beginning? That boy, born Joseph van Hover in Liège in 1919, who exists now only in a solitary black and white photograph showing a lad in suspenders and short trousers, with a defiant gaze and a pudding-basin haircut, seems irrelevant to this. The children had the photograph enlarged recently and treated by computer to remove the creases and faults of age and fading development. In its newly smooth state the boy who was me has taken on a strangely ironed-out and lifeless appearance. At what point did Joseph van

Hover turn into Joe Hoover? Perhaps that is my beginning.

As it is, most days are spent avoiding the issue. It is as though – as though is a frequent and annoying phrase of mine, but in its combination of suspension and correlation (and wishful thinking) it is an accurate enough summary of my life – as if I could enter my past through the back door and, by coming at it from an unexpected angle, find the moment which illuminates everything before and after.

Kafka wrote that there are many places of refuge, only one of salvation. But the opportunities for salvation are as many as the places of refuge. I understand what he means, I think. Each line I take back into my own life leads to a dead-end. Connections I expect to be made don't happen.

Bad days are spent writing Mary painful letters she will never read, saying everything I should have said when she was alive. I took to writing her as a way of confronting my failures as a husband and a father, and those of my children. The letters were brutal in their assessments and I wasn't sure why I was doing it.* The worst days are wasted playing Eric's Solitaire on the computer.

I live among the dead more than the living, find myself in increasing acceptance of death. The grandchildren were channel-hopping – an irritating habit for anyone old enough to remember having to get up to switch stations – and jumping up and down on the settee, when that once

*Hoover, elsewhere, on the subject of his wife: *Another story; another life, another book (!)* Hoover's letters to his wife have since been deleted.

familiar figure, taller than the rest, stooping now, pushed the camera aside, refusing an interview. TV as resurrection machine: dead Willi Schmidt come to life again.

It *had* to be coincidence, I told myself. The man looked too young. Nor am I comfortable with the notion that Willi might be alive. I am aware that in my writing I avoid mention of those who haunt me most – men like Willi and Karl-Heinz.

The kids changed channels again and lost the item. I yelled at them. They snitched on me, which resulted in Naomi working to contain her anger as she said, 'Don't you ever raise your voice to my children.' I wanted to push her until her resentment came bursting out, to have the flat-out row that would let her show her bitterness at my indifference and put us in touch. But she backed off, because she knew I would have forced her to admit that she had married a dope.

What I am trying to record in these pages is what I once believed. I believed I was working for change. I deluded myself, that the system I supported was better than its alternative. I believed that enemies were there to be defeated, and once that was done, progress would be made. What I did not see, and see only dimly even now, is that there was and is a whole other set of connections, a whole other way of working, where these beliefs do not apply. (I delude myself still: I watched men working those connections throughout the war. Dulles. Himmler. Eichmann.)

Most of all I believed in a future, even though that

future would be betrayed by those who inherited it. Which was their right. That was part of the belief too. I didn't believe that what had been fought for would be dismantled and discarded quite so unceremoniously, nor that such idiocy would prosper. Today I see purposelessness everywhere, in the frenetic activity of the aimless, and a world bereft of ideals. This is what we fought for: the right of those who followed to pursue lives of gratification and self-destruction.

Vaughan, Frankfurt

The Krauts do banter. We drive around, bored, thrash-metal white supremacy on the tape-deck, doing vigilante runs into the Turkish quarter. They talk tough-boy, kick shit out of the Schwarzers. Pasty boys rule. Kraut pasty boys. Frankfurt pasty boys. Five men in a car, old enough to know better, on edge and off-guard from early cans of beer, gazing hungover at the morning street, looking for trouble.

When they find none they turn on you, because you're not one of them and you're sitting next to them and tolerance is running low, seeing how far they can go before they start sticking the knife in. Thin beery farts and giggles, then they ask: What are you doing in Frankfart, man? More farts, more laughs. The driver cracks the window, in a tiny gesture towards civilisation's progress.

They speak invasive English, learned from music lyrics, and display an insatiable appetite for slang: dipstick, dog-fuck, dildo. Tomorrow we do the letter 'e'. They call everyone wanker. Black wanker. Brown wanker. Yellow wanker. Cunt wanker. Jew-wank. They call each other Kraut-wank, fixing you with a look, daring you even to think it. It's funny between themselves.

They teach you to see the way they do. Stupid shops. Stupid rich-clothes consumer shit. American shit everywhere: Coca-Cola and McDonald's shit. Love your neighbour shit. Advertising shit. Stupid big company sign shit: the corporate asshole. Smug suits. It's a dog's world. The Krauts do barking. They have learned to call everything a ditch. Frankfurt's a ditch. You start to wonder what the executive suits would look like on all fours, picking their teeth up off the pavement.

The line between acting and believing gets thinner. It would take a rash man to call the Neos' bluff, jumpy as they are and afraid of penetration.

Some days they tolerate you. Others they're suspicious. Today is one of those days. You hit them with your Nazi spiel, the one that goes Daddy got himself a Kraut bride in the 1960s – Mummy Kraut. Mummy Kraut's dead Daddy was a big Nazi. Cool uniforms, attitude, good scrapbook. The Krauts want to believe me. Grandpappy an SS General, dead in the war.

But, hey, how do we know you're not an undercover guy? Or a Jew? Let's see if he's got a Jewish dick. Come on, or why do you hang around with deadheads like us? Hey, cophead, you wanna suck some real dick? Hey, man, we're just fooling around. German sense of humour.

So why *would* a nice English boy hang around with a

bunch of Neos? Of course there is an ulterior motive – but it's my business to show them there isn't.

They eventually tire of the Grandpappy line and you own up – just kidding, boys – and tell them how you spent a long time in South Africa and your sister got gang-raped by Schwarzers with thirty-five-inch dicks. Eeeech! go the skinheads. But they're not buying that either. We want proof, man. So you tell them: Look up the *Tooled* website. *Tooled* is a fanzine for racial invective. Let's go check it out, man.

Internet café. Computer geeks go cold sweat when we walk in. I show the Krauts stuff I wrote three or four months ago, standard hate riffs dressed up as jokes.

They believe me now, but they still don't like me. You're a real funny guy about the Germans ha ha. We're gonna make you eat Krautdick, teach you to be nice to us.

Trashing a Turkish grocery store, throwing tins on the floor, playing for laughs, pissing on the counter: See, boys, I am on your side.

To clarify: this is what I do for a living, pretending to be an unpleasant person, hanging out with unpleasant people, winning their trust. The problem is, hang around too long – we're not even talking weeks here – you forget what nice is. You start to get off on that spurt of fear you see in people's eyes when they realise you might hurt them. You start thinking Neo, applying their thinking back onto them. You end up thinking Neos are no better than animals: fascist cunts, all of them. Argue your way out of that.

Hoover, Florida

I am back in Florida, in disgrace, after falling out with Naomi, who told me I was no longer a welcome house-guest. I left straight away – with some relief – without waiting for the grandchildren to return from school. Naomi insisted on driving me to the airport, to give me the full benefit of her silent disapproval.

The strangest sight greeted my return. The outside walls of the house had grown black with what looked like a mold or fungus, until I noticed it squirming. Having watched *The X-Files* with the grandchildren – and been amused by their rampant paranoia and conspiracy; if ever there were a vehicle in search of a cold war – I thought I was witness to an alien invasion. Which in a way I was: millions of dark caterpillars were writhing over the concrete back wall of the house but, for some reason, avoiding the wooden surfaces.

By now, Naomi has no doubt told her two brothers of my banishment. As they all take after their mother in their lack of forgiveness, we will soon be entering our own

Cold War, with massed ranks of grandchildren exercising along the family border.

The house feels lifeless after being shut up for so long. Walking in, I had the strongest premonition of its contents having used up nearly all their allotted time – the books, too many still unread, the sofa which I had always thought was in the wrong position, the sagging matrimonial bed we never got around to renewing. By Floridian standards the house is overdue for demolition. It stands on a key near Englewood, one of the less fashionable parts of the Gulf, another old people's colony full of too many well-pensioned, bright-coloured, romper-suited senior citizens too old to jog and down to a shaky power-walk by way of exercise. The house was built in the 1950s by an international architect of minor repute, mainly out of dark wood and glass. For all the window space it has always been gloomy inside. My neighbours consider my neglect of it disrespectful to the value of the area. In the weeks after Mary died I had contemplated selling, and one realtor – a vivacious woman whose cheer was, I suspect, chemically enhanced – described it to me, without meaning offence, as 'just a shack'.

As all the children experience money difficulties they are no doubt hoping I will sell and settle with them to avoid death duties. Which means that sooner or later they will make their peace with me and suggest I move somewhere more manageable and nearer one of them.

The problem was the bad stuff I wrote about them on my computer – David, shiftless; Josh, dull; Naomi, disappointingly conformist. The offending passage made reference to my adulteries, previously unknown to Naomi, who said, 'It desecrates Mom's memory.'

As for these infidelities, they happened a long time ago. The shadow lives of the war, the secrecy, the false identities, the fear, and excitement, of discovery had been hard to shake off, and had been replayed in the bedrooms of adultery.

It was Naomi's kids who undid me. Deciding they wanted a preview of Grandpa's memoirs, they printed a batch.* Computer literate they may be, at a frighteningly young age, but their reading skills are limited, and they needed Mom for help. Naomi had at first told them not to go interfering with Grandpa's private business, but once she had taken a look herself she couldn't stop, and had ended up screaming, red-faced, 'How can you even *think* this stuff? I see now I don't know you at all!'

My post was all mailshots and bills, apart from one package. In it was an old book with no indication of who had sent it or why, other than the book-dealer's receipt, which listed an address in Missouri I had never heard of and stated that the dealer, Richard W. Dean, traded in modern first editions and collectibles. The book's title was *Watcher in the Shadows*, the author Geoffrey Household. The copy posted was the English first edition, published 1960.

*File subsequently deleted by Hoover or his self-righteous family. No record exists.

I had no idea who sent it, or why anyone should think I would be interested.

According to Richard W. Dean, whom I called, it was me who ordered the book, by post and paying with a credit card whose details matched mine.

The story summary on the book's wrapper noted that the hero was, like me, foreign, that 'it was so long since the war that [he] had forgotten his past and former nationality'. That he was pitted against 'a ruthless and highly intelligent murderer whose motive is neither political nor criminal, but straight revenge'. The back cover, publicising new fiction by the same publisher, included Richard Condon's mind-control thriller *The Manchurian Candidate*: was *that* a clue? For the first time in as long as I could remember I felt uncomfortable being alone.

On page 8 the postman knocks to deliver a package. Boom! He gets blown up and, 'On the path lay the upper and lower halves of the postman, joined together – if one could call it joined – by the local effects of the explosion.' On page 16 the man for whom the bomb was intended receives a photograph of Buchenwald concentration camp with a small cross in the corner marking the officers' mess, which he takes to mean, 'You do not appear to be worried. That is a pity. I wish you to be worried.'

It was 9.32 A.M. when I saw the postman coming, carrying the packet. My bomb disposal skills are nil. Everything felt so normal – the day, the weather, the man's uniform – that it seemed absurd to tell him to put down the parcel and run, so I was left holding it, wondering if I was the chump.

The label was neatly typed and correctly addressed, the packet almost snug in the hand. It seemed too late in life for any of this. I placed the packet carefully in a pail of water and phoned the local chief of police, who was more of an acquaintance than a friend. He did not sound convinced by my explanation and I was messing up his day. The occasional case of geriatric jogger rage was about as tough as it got round here. The chief wasn't sure of his procedure and said he would have to call back.

While waiting for him I dropped and smashed the glass jug for the coffee-maker – thanks to what an old aunt of mine, who had been a governess in England, would have called 'butterfly fingers'. (Mary's things had taken to ambushing me whenever I strayed into what she regarded as her domain – the garage where the washing machine and drier are, the kitchen.)

The local police were going to send down the FBI from Tampa until I persuaded the chief that it had been just a foolish old man's fancy. By then I had decided I didn't want the indignity of anyone discovering it was not a bomb and had opened the damned thing myself. Inside was shredded paper and no clues.

Rather than sit around making lists of those who might still want to kill me (my grandchildren), I went down to the local library and found the following on the microfiche of the *Biographical Dictionary of Genre Fiction*, ed. Pirie R./Rayner D.:

Household, Geoffrey, 1900–1982.
Author best known for classic manhunt thrillers, notably *Rogue Male* (1939) in which a sniper who has stalked, fired at and missed Hitler is hunted by a German adversary across a detailed landscape that is a fine example of the author's love of topography and romantic pantheism. Filmed by Fritz Lang as *Man Hunt* (1941), with Walter Pidgeon, *Rogue Male* was cited by the Warren Commission Report on the assassination of President John F. Kennedy in support of its 'lone gunman' theory. Household, although he never repeated the enormous success of *Rogue Male*, continued to publish into old age, alternating tight chase thrillers (*Watcher in the Shadows*) with picaresque adventure. His work forms part of a triangle with John Buchan and Frederick Forsyth.

Someone was playing a practical joke, I decided, another old retiree with too much time on his hands. (Nor is it out of the question that in my current preoccupied state I had ordered the book and forgotten about it.)

The rest of the day was spent making futile efforts to replace the broken jug, a quest met with general bafflement by local storekeepers who didn't stock my brand, Bosch. They wanted to know what was wrong with the machines they had. When I located a stockist late in the afternoon I had to drive nearly to Naples where I found that my jug belonged to an obsolete model and a whole new machine cost less than twenty dollars. I understood the confusion of the earlier retailers.

I brooded on the incident and decided what troubled me, apart from my own obtuseness, was that part of me can never be American or understand America. As in Mary's relationship with me, part of me has been withheld in my relationship with this country.

For the first time in as long as I can remember I thought of going back to Europe. One last time. If only to escape the ghost of Mary.

Mary is not here. There's nothing I care about. Nothing left to do.

The doctor's hands felt unpleasant, his touch soapy. Doing up the buttons of my shirt I recollected a similar moment of hopelessness seventy years ago, caused by what I no longer remember. I could, of course, use the sickness to ingratiate my way back into the children's favor, to excuse my poor behavior. In any case, I am probably exaggerating – always the hypochondriac. The doctor has referred me for further tests, which may be negative. It may, however, be the illness I always feared for myself: the defeat of the free radicals. Part of me feels skittishly alert at the thought, and prone to bad jokes. Nevertheless, staring at the squirming caterpillars, as I hosed them off the wall as part of my daily round, I did find myself asking how long was left, whether weeks and days, rather than the months and years I had always allowed myself.

When I got home there was a message on the answer-machine, an echo of my thought of returning to Europe. A voice I had known for sixty years, sounding the same, but a lot older and lot more slurred, as if it was in the middle of a long day's drinking. The message said: Hey Joe, old friend, this is Karl-Heinz in Frankfurt. How are things with you in the Florida sunshine? When are you coming over to grey old Germany? By the way, Kitty says thank you for your card.

Two things were odd about this. First, I hadn't heard from Karl-Heinz in years and would not expect to. Second, there never had been any card to Kitty. In the old days 'Kitty' had always meant: *We need to meet, something urgent has come up.*

I presumed this was Karl-Heinz's idea of a joke, like the book. We were men on the wrong side of eighty, after all.

Vaughan, Frankfurt

The end of the game, Turkey nil, Germany nil. It was raining hard German rain and everyone got wet leaving. The first sign of disturbance was an eddy in the crowd ahead. A low animal growl went up as the stampede began. Everyone ran or got pushed over. Spaces appeared as the charge broke up into skirmishes.

In the bar before the game, Siegfried, yuppie Neo: 'Riot is the voice of the unheard.'

Two skinheads attacked a man on the ground. Everything sounded far away and close at the same time. The feathery noise of boots digging into soft flesh carried above the din. They started on his head, the dull crunch of steel toecaps on bone, a dreamy look of concentration on their faces, like awkward boys dancing. Violence was the only thing that made sense. Everything else was just waiting.

'Many voices go unheard in Germany today. Real German voices.' Siegfried again, philosopher and expansionist. He said Germans have never felt comfortable with the constrictions of borders. He said Germans are never untroubled in their belief in themselves. He said nationhood is a matter of anxiety.

Siegfried and his muscle used mobiles to choreograph the violence. Word went out that the action was moving on.

There was an already sizeable crowd of hardcore support at the new location. The neighbourhood was a poor one, all sodium lamps and low box buildings. Siegfried seemed to have it in his power to keep the police away, and fire engines didn't turn up until long after the building was alight.

The place was an immigrant hostel. The skinheads made grunting noises as the inmates ran out, about thirty of them, including kids, who soon made themselves scarce. A skinhead shouted: 'Any Jews in there?'

The crowd applauded as the fire took hold. Someone pointed to the sky, then someone else, until there was a host of upraised arms doing the Nazi salute.

A woman in a headscarf was on the roof parapet, staring down, hand to her throat. The skinheads shouted at her to jump, expectation on their faces. This was the sort of grand finale they had been hoping for. Everyone shouted: 'Eins, zwei, drei!' Someone told the woman to jump because there was no other way down. Someone else shouted out that he was wasting his time; the bitch didn't speak German. The crowd took up a chant.

The woman ran along the parapet. For a moment she seemed to hang suspended, defying gravity, then fell, screamless, her outline blurring as she gathered velocity. The last noise she made was the crash of her body landing on metal. That shut the crowd up. Moments later we were gone, dispersed by the impact of her fall.

After the riot I was allowed to graduate to Siegfried, the yuppie Neo. Siegfried was bars and restaurants. Siegfried was cappuccino. Strong leadership was his special subject. He acknowledged the need for an understanding of new technologies, just as Goebbels had when he realised the possibilities of the microphone as a political tool. Siegfried's idea of a joke was to say that Hitler had been the first rock and roll star.

I told him I represented certain interests that were researching the possibilities of political investment. My backers were impressed by his profile and the way he packaged his politics. They wanted him to act as their technical consultant, for a negotiable fee. Siegfried looked pleased. I also said I wanted an introduction to Karl-Heinz Strasse. Siegfried nodded. Strasse was a big bad old Nazi, former SS. My request seemed to convince the Neo of my authenticity.

Thanks to my association with Siegfried, the skinheads became as polite as chauffeurs, and I wasn't made to sit in the middle any more.

One night we drank beer in a bar with two off-duty cops, crew-cut blonds, one with hair so pale it was almost white. The cops and skinheads fitted neatly, their camaraderie tight and narrow. The cops hinted that they did political work that made them important. They were told I was from England, looking at the scene. They seemed cool about that. They talked about the riot with relaxed familiarity. The woman who jumped off the roof had survived, the paler cop said. One of the skinheads mimicked her bicycling motion and they all laughed, and I watched her again, fall through the night.

At ten we left the cops and drove to a Chinese take-away where a load of food was waiting, enough to feed a small army. The skinheads laughed at my mystification. They bantered with the Chinese woman owner, imitating the way Japanese spoke German, and were all laughing away. The carry-outs filled the boot. Whatever the arrangement, it didn't involve paying over the counter.

We drove away from the city centre. The skinheads wanted to know other words for wank. Toss. Toss-off. Jerk-off. Jack-off. They recited the words obediently, polishing each one until it was as hard as a pebble.

Our destination was airport country, industrial zones full of anonymous big sheds. We turned down a side road, dotted with scabby litter and the first sign of a muddy green countryside. Railway lines ran alongside. We stopped in front of large security gates. The skinheads had a key. Inside was a big yard, stacked with house-high bales of pulped paper; at the far end a further set of gates and a Portakabin, with two cars parked outside, and beyond that a large windowless storage shed. The two men who came out of the Portakabin were from the Middle East or

Turkey. They looked incongruously smart in their slacks and soft dog-shit yellow leather jackets. Their cars were smart too, one a big 7-series BMW and a top-of-the-range Merc. The men looked like they could take care of themselves. The skinheads didn't do banter with them. Everything was carefully polite.

The food was for the people in the shed. We drove the car right in and unloaded it on trestle tables, behind which were racks of bunk beds. About a hundred people were milling around, not doing much, until they saw the car. The food produced a rush to the tables.

Apart from the chomp of eating, the only noise came from a couple of unwatched televisions in the background. The skinheads stood around drinking beer given them by the men from the Portakabin. No alcohol was served at the tables. Those eating looked like the united colours of Benetton. There were even some Chinese, sitting in a group.

The skinheads started kicking a football around. This developed into a game of five-a-side, in another smaller shed where two goals with nets were already set up, the skinheads making up one team, with me drafted in as the fifth, against the best of the rest. One of the men from the Portakabin refereed. Others stood around and cheered. The game felt like a regular fixture. The skinheads appeared concentrated, happy even. I found a substitute and wandered off in search of a toilet.

Outside, everything felt remote and mysterious. A plane cut through the sky on its way to landing. The sound of a goods train carried from the railway. The noise of the game sounded far away. A Chinese woman stepped out to bum a cigarette. She stood there, arms folded, staring at the moon, hugging herself, the pair of us wondering who on earth the other was and how the hell we had got there. She muttered what sounded like a prayer. I tried to talk to her. We had only scraps of language between us, and a lot of guesswork. She didn't seem to have any idea where she was, not even which country; nor did she know how long she had been there. She had left China with travelling companions who weren't with her now.

After a glance she was gone. One of the men from the Portakabin walked round the corner with an Alsatian straining at its leash. He spoke a language I didn't understand but his meaning was clear. No standing around outside.

Dog patrols – to stop the people inside from getting out or the other way round? I guessed the people were black-market labour, though how that fitted with the Neos' supremacy theories I could not see.

One of the skinheads mooned the crowd before we left and announced in English that they were all foreign-wanks. The other skinheads guffawed. Nobody else paid him any attention. It felt like this had happened before. On the drive back I asked who the people in the shed were and was told: 'Shit.'

Hoover, Florida to Frankfurt

Why is the professional smile considered an essential part of a cabin crew's repertoire? Perhaps it is offered as a positive alternative to the rictus grin, and as a distraction from the crew's other role as agents of death, ritualised in their bizarre performance called 'cabin safety exercises'. Now they don't even bother to do it themselves. They show a film.

The last and only time I had been to Frankfurt was in 1945, the day Hitler died. I wondered if I had given any thought then to what the future would hold. Probably not. Most of us were trying to remember what peace felt like. Now, nearly everyone I knew then is dead, and those that aren't dead are sick. Betty Monroe, who had recruited me in 1942, is in a Zürich clinic with Alzheimer's. I had written to say I was coming to Europe, and got a reply from her daughter. Karl-Heinz had sounded depressed on the phone. He insisted everything was all right, but his speech was still slurred and he took a while to recognise who I was and a lot longer to remember why he had contacted me. He was under the impression I was still his case officer and was going 'to sort things out'. He would not say what these things were except they referred to his 'immunity deal', and he expected me to liaise with Langley. I told him I was ancient history there, my contacts long gone.

'I had to blackmail that cocksucker Dulles for my deal!' he shouted. He didn't care that Allen Dulles had been dead over thirty years. Before he hung up he said, 'Joe, it's good to hear you again,' sounding half-hearted. It was a sad call: Karl-Heinz in a time warp when once he had been the sharpest. I had protected him for years, no questions asked. It was part of the deal. My silence and deference remained the cornerstones of our relationship.

As for that 'cocksucker' Allen Dulles, I had spent the war in awe of him. He had been in his forties then, a big shot already, running the US Office of Strategic Services in Switzerland, and a future head of the CIA, from 1953 until the Cuban mess forced his resignation, a couple of years before they shot the President in 1963. Dulles had the sort of self-confidence promoted in Hollywood movies, that uniquely American harmony of individual ruggedness combined with a general willingness to conform while refusing to kowtow. He came with the inherited fluency and confidence of privilege, not the exhausted mannerisms of European aristocracy – the energetic purpose of the elite of a nation big on achievement and short on memory. After his arrival in Bern in 1942 he did little to disguise his role as spymaster.

The first time we met he still dressed like a lawyer. Later he switched to well-tailored flannels and tweeds, worn with an old raincoat and a fedora, casually tilted back, reporter-style. He looked like a raffish academic, with his spectacles, moustache and pipe, but he was primarily a social creature, comfortable in smart hotels which he regarded as his prerogative. His espionage and social networks often over-lapped. I was never his protégé, as such, more an awkward necessity when it came to the trickier stuff no one was supposed to know about (myself included). Hence his request that I drive him to Frankfurt that spring of 1945.

He needed a driver because of his gout and requested me specifically. Earlier in the year he had been responsible for my transfer into uniform. Official title: Interpreter, Art Looting Investigation Unit, a division of the OSS. Freedom of movement was the key; we came and went as we pleased. Dulles the spymaster was able to incorporate many extracurricular activities under that title. During our drive to Frankfurt he told me it had taken a personal call to General George S. Patton to secure my release. Dulles enjoyed pulling strings and his summons was a sign that he was up to mischief. I would be witness to something beyond my understanding and be relied upon to keep my mouth shut. Pretty much my usual role.

We drove from Switzerland, a journey made slow by road blocks, footbound columns of refugees and convoys moving north. Dulles was uncharacteristically short-tempered. His gout was spoiling his enjoyment of the end of the war.

The first night we stayed in a Schloss outside Munich where he held meetings to which I wasn't privy. The place was some kind of headquarters, of what no one was saying. I ate in the kitchen and was given a billet in an outbuilding.

We arrived in Frankfurt on the evening of the second day as night fell. On a main road outside the city we stopped at a checkpoint and were given a map.

The map was little more than a set of compass directions. It looked like a blank puzzle. It's tempting to say that one flattened town looks much like another, but the ruins of Frankfurt felt very different from those of Munich or Berlin, as though the city had become a ghost of its previous incarnation. By moonlight its devastation took on the quality of a photographic negative and a heart-stopping beauty, for there is an enormous awe in mass destruction. Even Dulles was impressed.

Our only company that night was a distant rumble. Dulles, who had spent most of the war in Switzerland, seemed excited, and nervous. 'What's that noise?' he asked.

It was tanks. We soon came up behind a convoy of covered trucks with an unusually heavy guard of several half-tracks as well as the tanks. It was easy enough to guess its destination as there was nowhere else to go.

In a city rendered completely dark by the destruction of its electricity services we were confronted by a miracle of light, and the equally bizarre sight of an intact building, and an exceptionally large and official-looking one at that.

Its survival I assumed was due to carelessness or oversight. There was a checkpoint and a heavy guard. Barbed wire surrounded everything. Teams on scaffolds were mending windows while more shadowy figures on the roof carried out further repairs. The place looked like it had been a bank and from the tight security I guessed it was now a prison for top Nazis.

Dulles smoked up the car with his pipe and grunted at the sight of a line of rats crossing the road while we waited for the checkpoint to clear the convoy. With his permission, I opened the window a crack and could hear the sound of generators. When I got out to stretch my legs a guard ordered me back in the car. A checkpoint sign said it belonged to the 29th Infantry.

Regardless of Dulles's senior status our papers were checked and rechecked. We were escorted from our car to the building where we were questioned again by a major at a large desk in a marbled lobby. His uniform looked indecently new in such fusty, stiff-collar surroundings. Standing wooden crates, over six foot tall, were in the process of being loaded on flat-bed trolleys by teams of workers. The mood was quietly purposeful. The place wasn't a prison. It was still a bank: a working bank in the middle of the night, in the middle of a non-city. The US Army's recent appropriation was evident in dozens of stenciled signs. One warned that in case of fire, to use the field telephone in front of the main vault which connected to the civilian fire department, with an added footnote that no one spoke English.

When Dulles was ordered to hand over his briefcase he refused, saying it was a matter of national security. He won, after letting the case be examined a second time, and passing over the revolver that was in it. 'Do you think I am about to hold up your bank?' he asked, and gave the major his most charming smile.

Our escort was a tall colonel from St Louis, accompanied by two junior officers. The colonel asked if Dulles knew what he was looking for. Dulles produced a typed sheet of paper which he gave to the colonel, who studied it with a frown. 'This could be in one of several rooms,' he said. 'We've got a ton of stuff coming in every day, and nobody to catalogue it. We've got the Hungarian crown jewels if you want.' (I knew. I had helped put them there. Dulles winked at me.)

The colonel proudly informed us that the internal security system was based on the one used in the US Mint. Once we were locked inside the vaults he insisted on a tour of the spoils, including a sealed chamber stacked floor to ceiling with gold bars. 'Three deep, wall to wall,' said the colonel. 'Each bar weighs 25 pounds and is worth $15,000. How many of these are we going to earn in a lifetime?' In Dulles's case quite a few. He had been a successful Wall Street lawyer before the war and would return to his practice.

'Next door in one of those cages is the biggest gold nugget anyone has ever seen,' the colonel went on. 'Size of a grapefruit.'

'Any idea how much all this is worth?' Dulles asked casually.

'Upwards of five hundred million dollars.'

'Take a good look, Joe,' Dulles said. 'You are witness here to one of history's great failures.'

Vault after vault of stashed gold became overwhelming in its pointlessness, in contrast to the destruction outside. This was underlined by a room where even Dulles moved on quickly. It was filled with suitcases of gold pellets. Perhaps he knew their provenance too. There were forged English banknotes, stockrooms of gems, sculpture and art. A Van Gogh self-portrait had been left carelessly on the floor, his expression one of apparent disbelief. One vault was devoted entirely to alarm clocks in cardboard boxes, confiscated by the SS. Another contained nothing but fur coats.

The colonel said, 'We don't have the security to carry out the valuations. We have teams working round the clock securing the old air-raid shelters so they can be used for storage, and that takes up all our guards. We caught a labourer yesterday trying to walk out with a bag of gold crowns, worth over six thousand dollars.'

It was past midnight before Dulles got down to the purpose of his visit. He acted as though he had mislaid nothing more urgent than a term paper. When the colonel offered a team to help, Dulles declined, saying he couldn't describe what he was looking for but would recognise it when he found it.

He worked his way through several rooms of documents, mostly in filing cabinets, some lying unsorted on tables, while the rest of us stood around smoking. The colonel managed to order coffee from somewhere. One stack of memos was from I.G. Farben, the big German chemical company, manufacturer of the genocide gas used in concentration camps. According to the Colonel, the Farben headquarters was the only other large building in Frankfurt to survive the bombing. 'It makes you wonder. You would have thought the big bank and the big company headquarters would have been the first targets. Yet at the Farben place there was hardly a cracked pane of glass. What do you make of that?'

'Beats me,' I said, proud of this recently acquired Americanism.

'Maybe they didn't want to hit it. It's now being used as Occupation Headquarters.'

A couple of times the generators shut down and we had to use candles until they came back on. The soft light cast giant shadows. Whatever Dulles was looking for was proving elusive. I wondered what could be so important that he had to look for it himself. After several hours his tie was loose and his frustration showing. He said he found our presence disruptive and wanted to be left alone. The colonel stated that an escort had to remain in attendance. Later he relented and we adjourned to a nearby chamber where suites of furniture were stashed among the filing cabinets.

I dozed, slumped on a well-upholstered sofa, until woken by an officer who came in to announce that Hitler was dead, by his own hand. When I told Dulles he gave a sarcastic laugh and said, 'That spares us the expense of a trial.' Hitler was the least of his problems, he added. 'Why do the Germans commit every minor detail to paper? At this rate I'll be here a month.'

He produced a silver flask and took a pull. It was nearly empty but he insisted I finish it, saying he would send out for more, like we were in a hotel. 'There are dozens of crates of champagne in those rooms back there. Tell the colonel his news deserves celebration and that, one: it is entirely appropriate that the Führer's death is toasted with Third Reich champagne, and two: I will reimburse the Federal Exchange. It won't be chilled, but down here it won't be warm either.'

The colonel dithered before deciding not to be a party-pooper. I took Dulles a bottle. Of his search he said, 'Never has the expression "needle in a haystack" seemed more appropriate.' I offered to help and was told to go away and celebrate. 'You deserve it, Joe.'

We were all drunk by the time Dulles was done. 'Colonel, I thank you for your time,' he said, and handed him a wad of US dollars. 'That should cover the drinks.'

The colonel was so drunk he was barely able to count, but mumbled that it seemed too much even for vintage champagne.

'The price of victory,' said Dulles with a smirk. 'Let's go, Joe.'

Later he told me that the money he had used to pay for the champagne was cash he had found in the vaults. 'Reichsführer Himmler's counterfeits.' He laughed and I laughed too, thinking how from now on life would be about the road ahead.

The daylight hurt my eyes, but Dulles looked as refreshed as if he had just stepped out of a cold morning shower. 'Give me the keys,' he said. 'I'll drive. You get some shut-eye in the back.'

I dipped in and out of sleep, glimpsing crazily tilted ruins as we left the city, then sky racing past as the car hammered down the autobahn.

At one point Dulles pulled over and got out, on an empty country road untouched by war. There were trees in blossom. The shimmering foliage, lit bright by early morning sun, felt more unreal than the broken brick and dust and stench of Frankfurt.

I thought Dulles had stopped for a leak until I saw he had his briefcase with him. He took out a manila folder. So slim and insignificant-looking, I remember thinking, compared to the bulk of everything else we had seen that night. I wondered again what could be so important that it required his personal intervention. Dulles got out matches and put a flame to the file. He didn't see me watching.

Vaughan, Frankfurt

Siegfried was doing a late night at his regular evening hang-out, a middle-class joint avoided by the Neos, with a big window to show off its clientèle. Siegfried was with a couple of women who looked like models. The place smelled expensive.

Siegfried said he had arranged for me to have dinner the following evening with the old Nazi, Strasse. He first-named Strasse relentlessly, then, over several schnapps, practised his strong leadership riffs. The model-like girls sat in obedient silence. Lipstick, perfume, shampoo-smelling hair: it felt like an age since I had been anywhere near a woman. I missed Dora – complicated, impossible Dora.

I told Siegfried about the interesting trip to the yard. It looked like an unusual operation, I said. We played euphemism catch. It offered people a freedom of movement not normally available, he said. Reading between the lines, what he was suggesting was that the Neos were into people-smuggling as a growth industry. The Neos were into commodity and the black economy was an expanding market.

Siegfried showed a fan's enthusiasm for his subject. Hungary was the main road route into Austria. Budapest was good for Chinese because of a large local community. Chinese tourists – 'tourists' was what he called them – flew more now. I mentioned the woman who had lost her travelling companions. He was familiar with the problem. There were different transit points even when destinations were the same. The difficulty was supply in the final stages, by which I understood him to mean lorries.

One of the models had her jaw clamped in an effort not to yawn. Siegfried, oblivious, said that a problem in Rotterdam was causing a knock-back effect. Rotterdam was a major dispersal point in the final stage of the process but was temporarily closed because of 'technical difficulties'. This had resulted in congestion further down the line, hence the location I visited that evening.

The women looked bored enough to fuck.

I was slow to appreciate why the Neos should want to get into trafficking racial inferiors into Germany. Siegfried shot me a sneaky look. The tourist business was not only profitable, he said, it was directional. Thanks to their involvement, Germany was not a destination. Germany was transit only. They made sure everyone got shipped on – to England, mainly, he added with a joyless grin. The women were looking around for better company. Siegfried didn't care. He was saving his wad for the political orgasm. I rather regretted their going.

After that, Siegfried withdrew into a mysterious silence and left alone. I drank several black coffees. It was half one, half midnight in London. I left a message for Dora saying I would catch the first flight and be home for the day. She and I lived on recorded messages – cryptic blips from undercover, Morse code of the heart, SOS and Maydays combined, the last gasp of a relationship, or whatever it was that we had had, past tense. We would, of course, remain friends as we moved on, she to fuck my employer, Dominic Carswell.

I left a message for Carswell too. Charismatic Dominic Carswell, former television correspondent – Dominic Carswell, *News at Ten*, reporting from Beirut/Belfast/West Berlin/Afghanistan – fencing champion, a youthful fifty, trademark lock flopping across his brow, making him a little less earnest, a little more boyish. Carswell to me: 'I hear you're the best at what you do.' Sincere Carswell, so well-informed. He'd got the voice, the smooth delivery that could do one-to-one.

I did undercover well enough to have worked on a couple of TV series. Sometimes I got recognised in Safeway. Usually they thought I was a friend of a friend. I had the face of a friend of a friend. The website stuff I had showed the Neos was for a programme I researched but never filmed on UK football hooligans/the far right/website racism.

Carswell had been willing to pay an absurd fee for a couple of weeks' stealth in Germany. He would pay in cash, he said, which meant I wouldn't have to declare it to the Revenue. He told me he was rich and bored. His company produced what he called innocuous pap for the Middle East market, wildlife documentaries that earned him a pot of money, and left him hankering to return to hard news.

Target One: Siegfried, the yuppie Neo, considered by some a future national leader, the acceptable face of the far right, repackaging extremism for the mainstream. Target Two: the old Nazi who, according to Chinese whispers, was contemplating going public. My job was to persuade Strasse that I was his sympathetic ear. As for Siegfried, Carswell would turn up later, and together with our hidden cameras and tape recorders we would get him off-record, foaming at the mouth about dirty foreigners and Jews and all the rest.

'Sounds fun?' Carswell had asked at our first meeting. I had nodded. I didn't say that I was happiest when I wasn't having to be me. Carswell, by contrast, was one of the super-confident, fluent in all areas of exchange, especially those of the heart, followed closely by a proper dress sense. Carswell was the man other men wanted to be, and he went out of his way to make himself attractive to both sexes and, above all, to Dora. It wasn't hard to see why she had fallen.

Several coffees after Siegfried's departure I was not tired and could not face my hotel, which smelt of grime, saturated fat and industrial-strength cleaner. I decided to go to the airport early and got a taxi to take me back to the paper yard on the way. The driver was young, with a depressing taste for early Pink Floyd. He agreed to wait twenty minutes for an extra twenty marks, not bad for sitting and listening to 'Set the Controls for the Heart of the Sun'.

The gates to the yard were locked but the perimeter fence was easy to crawl under. (The reason for the dogs perhaps.) I heard the big diesel engines first, and had time to position myself behind a paper-stack. Two big container lorries left, followed by the Merc and the BMW. The Alsatian was sitting in the front passenger seat of the Merc, lit up by the lights of the BMW behind.

Everyone was gone. The big shed door was unlocked. Everything had been stripped out. It was as if no one had ever been there.

Frankfurt Airport was the polar opposite to the paper yard, a regulated and authorised world of arrival and departure, of sponsored consumption, corporate politeness and, above all, glass. Early morning and the first transatlantic flights were coming in.

Hoover, Frankfurt

Frankfurt, nearly six decades on: the airport was a city in itself. Its efficiency and the speed at which we were processed took me by surprise. The flight – apart from the distraction of the chicken or beef moment – had remained another metaphor for death, of which, as you grow old, there are too many. Passengers waited under the harsh light of the arrivals hall at the baggage carousel, a ritual that never failed to remind me of one last game at tired children's parties. Happy landings, time zones totally out of whack. Having had time to think, I decided I was running away from Mary's reproving silence, which was absolute now, and from the fear of medical diagnosis. Karl-Heinz was just a sideshow, a distraction, like Betty Monroe, once so beautiful and now everything forgotten in senility. The thrill of being old: visiting friends who are sicker than you.

The new Frankfurt was as big a shock as the bombed-out shell had been. It stood as a testament to the corporate urbanisation and suburbanisation of Europe; and, to think, one plan at the end of the war had been to turn the whole of Germany to pasture. Everything looked cosmetic and neatly fenced, as if to say that Germany had given up any designs on *Lebensraum*, and was content with its lot. Plenty of glass said that it had nothing to hide. In the city there was no sign of Speer's triumphalist vision, though in the swankily designed super-towers that dominated the centre you could see the aggressive braggadocio of international corporatism. This was the real union forged out of the ruins of war. The universal business logos of peacetime profit were everywhere.

I have never trusted what they – 'they' being the several overlapping interests that decide these things – had done to Germany but I have always admired the smooth switch from expansionist, genocidal policies into something so thoroughly acceptable and apparently house-trained. The irony was obvious. Like the Japanese, the Germans got the hang of peace quicker than their European conquerors.

It goes without saying that I recognised nothing of Frankfurt. I had been away so long it didn't even feel like coming back, more the case of the arriving stranger. My hotel was adequate in its steak-and-fries and patterned-carpet way, but a little desperate. The windows didn't open and a card on the TV offered me porno if I wished to pay.

The most noticeable thing about coming back was how nothing smelled any more. Everything had been assimilated and conditioned. Warmth and coolness had replaced smell. Where I had grown up in Liège, the smells had always been pungent – black tobacco, leaded gasoline, drains and that particular café mixture of liquor, baking and coffee. As a child I associated them with the adult life that awaited me. They were evocative of a whole world I wanted to be part of, and still miss. All Florida smelt of – apart from the baby talc odor of American old age – was warm tarmac and hot car-metal, and the level, semi-chilled smell of supermarkets.

1945 was the stink of bomb damage, sewage and drains, and, with the warmer weather, of bodies decomposing in the rubble. Being back it was impossible not to think of death, given the proximity of the present foundations to the charnel house. No doubt Norman Mailer would equate it all with buggery.

In the flesh, Hitler's master race had on the whole been unimpressive. Most looked more like their leader – short, plain and sallow – than the Aryan ideal. Americans, by comparison – black and white – were a different breed: taller, languid and with much better dentalwork. There was also an established commercial beauty program, a whole industry devoted to the improvement of people's looks, and a cult of hedonism, the insistence on having a good time, that gave Americans a quality of being in the moment that has always struck me as quite un-European.

For me, the abiding image of the Second World War was a smiling GI slouched in a jeep, cigarette in hand, behind him an old German town square. Memorable because it was like a snapshot of the shock collision of two cultures. The GI in the foreground made everything else redundant. In crude terms it struck me as an image that was marketable in a way that what Hitler and Goebbels had tried to peddle was not. With hindsight, I would say that what I identified was a shift away from ideology towards product. As for the GI slouched in his jeep, we saw his successor a decade later in the form of Elvis Presley (another marketable product), who duplicated on a universal level that sense of alien newness I had sensed, but not fully understood at the time, in that image of the GI.

Vaughan, London

Dora was Father's secret, one that had lasted until his funeral. Most of the mourners were unfamiliar, golf club members or Rotarians. I had seen Dora and wondered who she was. Tall, slim, younger than the rest, wearing a smart black coat with a hood. When I knew, I could see nothing of my father in her.

After the service she walked up with no hesitation, took off her glove to shake hands, and said, 'I'm your father's daughter, the one he didn't tell you about.' I liked the brisk way she said it, as though sharing a joke, which, given how we stood out from the rest, we already were.

The lilt to her voice came from her mother, Irish (too upset to attend). Her mother was the daughter of Father's housekeeper, Mrs Shannon, who had been responsible for raising me after my own mother had disappeared to Canada with a client of Father's. It was these overlaps Father had worked at so hard to keep separate. He too was a professional keeper of secrets, a bank manager, a man of security who became a victim of recession, dismissed two months short of the forty years that made him eligible for a full pension. Within a year he was dead of cancer. I had failed to see behind the fussy neatness, the silences and the discretion.

I had left his funeral with my newly acquired sister. We went back to her flat and got drunk. I thought we were flirting until we started kissing. An electric jolt of pleasure. Funerals and the shock of discovery. We carried on until we were breathless and told ourselves afterwards that we had just been fooling around. Desire and taboo, a piquant mix. Dora said, 'It would, I suppose, technically be incest.'

In the paper yard I hadn't been able to get Dora out of my head. It had nothing to do with jealousy. The correlation was an emotional smuggling in terms of what my father had done to her. I wondered if we weren't both inheritors by default of the deep assignments, and detachments, that had secretly conditioned his life. Undercover is a form of detachment too, of non-involvement, while also being narcotic and addictive.

Thanks to a combination of mortgage laziness and general domophobia, my flat was in a deteriorating block, a dumping ground for London's problem families and illegal immigrants. (Hello Siegfried!) On warm days when windows were open the smell of frying and spices hung in the air. Most families cooked campfire-style on Primus stoves.

The building was terrorised by feral children, particularly two preternaturally pale, shaven-headed brothers. They were dumb in a damaged kind of way and barely articulate, apart from basic swearing. Their wildness was evidence of a withering parental neglect and boredom but they made life unpleasant in so many little ways that it was impossible not to hate them.

I gave Dora until ten then phoned her mobile. She did her hello all surprised and glad, but there was a new coolness. It sounded like she was with Carswell who was the silent partner in a three-way conversation: 'You're in London,' she repeated. Only for the day, I said. She seemed surprised. She hadn't got my message, and had just swapped to the day-shift so could only see me before noon. 'Dominic wants a word,' she added and put him on the line. Carswell suggested meeting at his club for lunch.

Grays was a newish private members' club in Mayfair, run by well-bred young men, with attractive staff. Grays was exclusive to the point of being secret, and secret to the point of variable spelling: no card, no notepaper, no telephone listing.

Dora was waiting in the mews behind the club, smoking a cigarette. She looked different, dressed for work. It reinforced how much we were becoming strangers. I wanted to be intimate but not personal. My vocabulary had been corroded by the Neos. Word-blips ran interference through my head – Jew-wank, cunt-rag. 'You're looking great,' I said, and censored out that fucking Carswell agreed with her.

There was no point in discussing our semi-incestuous relationship. The ground had been gone over endlessly –

the dangerous novelty and the intense curiosity. It had stopped short of full knowledge, not out of deference to taboo but because we sensed that extricating ourselves would be even more painful. Fucking would have driven us even further into our father's world of secrecy and denial. It would have, in the end, only been a way of fucking Daddy, we had decided, tipsy at the time.

She had moved on quickly to Carswell. I had guessed before she told me.

Dora worked at the club to subsidise her art course. It was how they had met. Carswell apologised for the tactlessness of his choice and fixed it so Dora didn't wait on our table. I wondered what she had told him about us. He wore glasses to read the menu, the smart equivalent to school dinners. This was harder than Frankfurt. Dora and Carswell required a better level of acting. Dialogue with Carswell was notable for what was left unsaid; Dora the unspoken subject.

Carswell the fencing master drew me out and opened me up. I told him everything about Germany. He offered good audience in return, his attention holding, knife and fork poised, his food forgotten. Why, I wondered, should a man who had been on national television end up making crappy programmes for the Middle East?

The mask slipped once, maybe, when he said, 'My affairs never last. I'm too fickle and vain. Terrified of growing old.' He gave his best telegenic smile. There was bound to be a Mrs Carswell. Perhaps his unexpected display of conscience was a cover for a wider disingenuousness. I felt nostalgic for the skinheads.

When I left, Dora took a cigarette break and we stood in the alley. 'I didn't mean it to be awkward,' she said.

I shrugged and told her I was going back to have dinner with an old Nazi. I could imagine us never seeing each other again. We would disintegrate as fast and unexpectedly as we had started.

'I admire what you do. I haven't told you before,' she added. She was sounding remarkably sincere. 'You should come and work here for a while, undercover.'

We connected for the first time that day. Dora walked me to the end of the mews, head leaning into me, conspiratorial again. She was learning how the place worked, she said. The staff were there to be propositioned, discreetly. Not everyone came across, and those that didn't were told to refer guests on. The place was an upmarket dating agency. It even had its own hotel nearby, a knocking shop. I asked Dora if she participated.

'I'm tempted. I was offered enough to pay for two years' studying for going to bed with a rich Arab. A big Hollywood star pays one of the boys $100,000 to have sex with him whenever he's in London.'

I asked what Carswell thought.

'Take the money and run.'

'What do you know about Carswell?'

'Apart from being nice and charming? Not a lot. I'm waiting to see if there's a twist.'

'See what you can find out about him for me.'

'Why?'

'Because I can't work him out. Because he's spy-story stuff. Because men like him always have another agenda.' Because it gave me a degree of control. Using Dora was my revenge.

Hoover, Frankfurt

I slept badly because of the time-zone difference, having flown into the future with a head too full of the past. I lay awake and fretted about why I was there. The face in the bathroom mirror looked rough when I got up mid-afternoon.

At my age, the simple day-to-day tasks get harder to negotiate – the reception desk, ordering the meal, the shop counter – but downstairs everything turned out fine. The receptionist was friendly and efficient, but didn't hurry in spite of the queue building up; she told me where I could get a tour bus, marking a street-plan, treating me like I was only a tiny bit simple, for which I was grateful. The waitress in the café humored me by letting me try out my German. The afternoon was fine, very much like ones I remembered, the green of spring softer than back home, the sky more of a washed blue.

When I got back to the hotel there was a welcome message from Karl-Heinz suggesting dinner that evening, and apologising for not being able to meet before. There was also a letter for me. It was a copy of a fairly recent newspaper cutting, an obituary of a man named Jaretski. There was no note. The stamp was German.

According to his obituary, Jaretski had been a successful German financial businessman knocked down and killed by a tram in Strasbourg. It noted that he had served in the war, without specific reference to what he had done.

I had been in Strasbourg, briefly, during the war, but could not remember any Jaretski, although the name was vaguely familiar. There was no photograph. I felt the slow, familiar skin-crawl of fear. Someone knew where I was in Florida. Now someone knew where I was in Frankfurt. Both book and obituary seemed to be messages specific to events that had happened over fifty years ago. Why now – and who was behind it?

Sometimes I catch sight of myself unawares. Nothing prepares you for the shock of discovering you are old, none of the gradual advances of age – wattle, white hair, pouches and sagging – readies you for the moment when you look in the mirror and see nothing of the person you once were. I use an electric razor now as it avoids the need to look at myself. Pants I might once have worn with a sense of irony I now put on without thinking – ones with elasticised waists and comfortable pleats.

Where to begin, I find myself asking, not for the first time. And how to define what this might be about, given the prompts of book and obituary, without frightening anybody – because it will almost certainly turn out to be about human behavior at its worst. The old, having less to lose, can give the young a run for their money any day when it comes to bad behavior.

So here's me, back in Germany as a tourist. A cliché American, minus the wife most of them still have. Retired. Kids scattered, on Prozac, grandchildren on Ritalin.

Germany then, Year Zero, flattened. Germany now, the homogenisation of the economic miracle.

An old man with a bad stomach, in a cheap hotel. A fly on an upturned water glass. We are all old men now and whatever outrage we did was done so long ago that it is beyond the reach of apology. Maybe.

Vaughan, Frankfurt

Strasse's restaurant of choice was a bierkeller basement with rough whitewashed walls, Goldilocks furniture, the city's largest gingham reserve, and a staff of *zaftig* middle-aged waitresses in white peasant blouses with puffy sleeves. I got there early and waited at the bar. It was pure cartoon tourist board, all loud jollity, oom-pah muzak and foaming steins. Everyone looked like regulars, all elderly to old, no women apart from staff. I wondered if it was a haunt of geriatric gays.

When my man arrived there was no mistaking Siegfried's warning. Loosely translated, Strasse was a fat mess. With his restricted speed there was plenty of time to study him. Strasse was at least eighty and looked like he'd had a stroke, his movement reduced to a stick-shuffle. He appeared surprised when I introduced myself and I had to remind him who I was and why I was there. His delayed greeting involved a tremulous double-handshake, held too long, while he inspected me with pale eyes, confused still but angry and alert. He smelled of brandy and sickness.

Whatever medication he was on gave him the physique of a big baby, but his eyes were full of history. Among the ruined looks you could see traces of a handsome man. He still had a full head of iron-filings hair, incongruously dyed boot-polish black, and an imperious beak. Under a smart old hacking jacket he wore soft convalescent clothes.

The waitresses made a fuss of him, helping him to what he called his table, in an alcove away from other diners. We had just sat down when we were joined by another man, around Strasse's age, but rangier and fitter. He dressed like an American but spoke German, and looked like he had once been tough. Big reunion. They hadn't seen each other in a long while. The other man gave me a hostile glance and Strasse offered an embarrassed explanation that he had double-booked dinner. His forgetfulness pained him. I offered to leave. The American looked relieved but Strasse's sense of protocol won out. He told the other man in German I could just follow that they would land me with the bill. The American, introduced as Joe Hoover, remained uncharmed by my presence.

Strasse insisted on ordering pork knuckles and sauerkraut, and we drank heavily thanks to his indiscriminate ordering of steins of lager, punctuated with rounds of schnapps, and a metallic-tasting white wine served in green goblets which made it look even more acidic than it was.

Hoover sat there looking glum, making pellets of his bread. When I asked why he was in Frankfurt he gave me a sardonic look and said, 'I wish I knew.'

It turned out his wife had died not so long ago, which perhaps explained his distance.

For most of the evening Strasse acted as though I wasn't there. Siegfried's name did nothing to further conversation. He talked to Hoover in old friends' shorthand, their German too fast for me. In among all the compounds, I made out that they had a working relationship which went back to Egypt in the 1950s and Budapest in 1944 and 1956. They had also been together in Syria at some point. Strasse switched to English to complain that flying disagreed with his medication. Hoover said his own body clock was fucked from his flight. His daughter's recommendation against jet-lag had been to line his shoes with brown paper. He rolled his eyes. 'Karl-Heinz, what am I doing here?'

'We'll talk later,' said Strasse. 'First let's eat and drink and enjoy ourselves. Welcome back to Germany.'

Strasse's enjoyment consisted of pouring large quantities of alcohol down his throat to little apparent effect.

I couldn't work them out. Strasse was an old Nazi. Hoover was American, though he said he was originally from Belgium. I knew Belgium was occupied by the Nazis, and decided Hoover had been some kind of collaborator. Hoover said he had been working for the Red Cross in Budapest in 1944. 'Among others,' said Strasse. They toasted a whole list of names which meant nothing to me.

Hoover asked if Strasse remembered anyone named Jaretski, which he did, after some memory fumbles. 'He was DSK.'

The DSK, it was explained grudgingly, had been an SS currency division. A couple of drinks later, Hoover remembered coming across Jaretski in Brussels in 1942. 'He pulled me in and questioned me. But why would anyone send me his obituary?' Strasse was unaware that Jaretski was dead. He hadn't heard him mentioned in years. Hoover asked if Strasse had sent him a book in America. Strasse answered, 'Why should I send you a book?'

Hoover shrugged. Strasse held up his schnapps. 'Let me give you a name. To Willi Schmidt.'

Hoover appeared jolted. 'I saw a man who looked like Willi on television the other week.'

Strasse had seen the same item. Small world, I said. 'Not really,' said Hoover, eager to contradict. 'When you get to our age there's little to do except watch television.'

An argument followed over whether the man on TV had been Schmidt or not. Hoover was adamant. 'I tell you, Karl-Heinz, Willi's dead as doornails.'

'Did you ever see his body?' Strasse was starting to look choleric.

'I saw him fall in the river. Betty Monroe saw the body.'

'I know,' said Karl-Heinz. 'I fixed the death certificate, but that doesn't mean there *was* a body.'

Hoover: 'Willi's dead. Let's drink to the living, or the half-living. I'm seeing Betty tomorrow.'

We were all drunk by then. Strasse and Hoover turned to riffing about the war. They compared the British love of smut and secrecy to the Americans' combination of guile and gullibility.

'What about the Germans?' I asked.

Strasse turned to me with a hawkish gaze. Hoover said, 'Big meat-eaters, porkers to the last, drawn to the flame of genocide.' Strasse opened his hand in acknowledgement and knocked over his wine, which brought a waitress running. Hoover said, 'They should have strung you up years ago,' and Strasse did a big 'Who, me?' shrug, like he was the funny one in a double act, and that set them laughing.

'What exactly did you two do?' I asked. Hoover appeared droll. Strasse gave a shrug and took a big swallow of schnapps. He had his elbows on the table, being past the stage of trying to sit upright. Hoover said, without irony, 'We made it possible for the likes of you to sleep safely in your bed.'

'Witnesses to human behavior at its worst,' Strasse said heavily.

'Is he always so cryptic?' I asked.

'We were the cryptic boys,' said Hoover.

Strasse snorted and hauled himself off to the toilet.

Hoover refused to be drawn. 'It was a long time ago.' He asked who I worked for. I told him I was researching for a private source.

Hoover grunted. 'Sniffing around old Nazis, also known as scraping the barrel.'

'Who's Willi Schmidt?'

'Who *was* Willi Schmidt.'

I obliged by repeating the question in the past tense, but all he would say was that Willi had been a shoe salesman.

'A *shoe* salesman? How do a shoe salesman, an SS officer and an American from Belgium fit together?'

'Beats me,' said Hoover, refusing to budge. I said it sounded like Willi Schmidt had done the old Harry Lime trick of faking his death.

He looked at me wearily. 'It was a coincidence. The guy on TV was some owner of a chemical plant that got burned down. He had the right height for Willi, that's all.'

When Karl-Heinz returned, Hoover announced that he had bad jet-lag and wanted to go. Strasse dismissed the notion, ordered more schnapps, and washed down a handful of pills with a swill of wine. The mixture turned him bug-eyed. He stared at me for so long I thought he was about to have another stroke, then he banged on the table and announced, 'I was a black dossier man.'

I asked what that meant. After a long deliberation, Hoover said that Karl-Heinz had worked for Himmler. 'Didn't you, Karl-Heinz?'

Karl-Heinz looked irritated and smug at the same time.

'Top dog Nazi,' said Hoover. 'Karl-Heinz kissed the Reichsführer's ass on many occasions.'

'Worked for Himmler how?' I asked Strasse.

Again, Hoover answered. 'Horse-buyer for the SS. Wasn't that your official title?'

Strasse nodded. 'Eighty-seven years old and I still ride every day!'

'You old bullshitter, you haven't been in a saddle in years,' Hoover said with affection. He gave me a blank look. Perhaps the alcohol was doing its work. 'Karl-Heinz was in the business of selling Jews.'

I humoured him, saying I thought the Nazis had been in the business of getting rid of Jews.

Strasse shook his head. 'You shouldn't believe everything you read in history books.'

'Is he one of those guys who says nothing happened?' I asked Hoover.

Strasse gave an angry snort and grabbed my lapel. 'I was there.' We eyeballed each other as Hoover watched. Two old men who had been in tough situations. Finally Strasse let go and pinched my cheek. 'Ransoming Jews was an insurance plan for when the war was lost. "Look, we saved Jews!"' He shrugged. 'Cynical times, my young friend.'

'It saved *your* neck,' said Hoover.

I asked what Hoover's job had been.

'Just a runner. A go-between.'

'You were Willi's shadow,' said Strasse.

'Not really.'

'Willi was running you.'

'So were you.'

Strasse turned to me. 'Joe worked for everyone, didn't you, Joe?'

Hoover drew a line with his hand, as if to say enough.

'Cynical times?' I asked.

'Not as cynical as what happened afterwards,' said Strasse.

'He means we all ended up working on the same side,' said Hoover.

'Which one was that?' I asked.

Strasse gave a mock salute. 'US Intelligence.' He nudged me in the ribs and said, 'No questions asked!'

He wouldn't say what had earned him his black dossier. We all ended the meal too drunk to talk straight. But they still had the edge, and managed to stiff me with the bill.

Hoover, Frankfurt

It was way too late, but still early evening in Florida, and more than once that night I asked myself: 'What am I doing?' The time and distance between leaving Englewood and being back in Germany made me homesick in a way I could never have imagined. I was dismantled with tiredness by the time we left the restaurant and the boy but Karl-Heinz insisted I accompany him back to his place. During dinner I had watched the words slip away as he tried to reach for them, behind each hesitation a glimpse of the dark crevice that lay ahead. He seemed distracted and frail. The shock of the old.

Karl-Heinz lived in a smart white cube more reminiscent of a South American hideaway than suburban Germany. It came with the full panoply of paranoid security – a high wall, window grilles, alarms and cameras. The number of locks reminded me of my trip to the bank with Dulles.

Inside was furnished with Karl-Heinz's usual good taste, lots of blond wood and antique rugs. He showed off his stair chair-lift with childish enthusiasm and poured large drinks. We sat in an upstairs room with more wood and rugs. The surprise was it was a working room, full of marked-up maps of the Middle East. When I asked what they were about Karl-Heinz tapped his nose and changed the subject.

He crapped on about the old days. Betty Monroe's name came up again because I was going to see her.

'You know I never met Betty,'* Karl-Heinz said. 'There was always a go-between. You or Willi.'

I was surprised, given his connections. Betty Monroe had run Dulles's foreign operation throughout the war. She had recruited me in 1942, out of Lisbon. Betty was bright, in intelligence and personality, and unconventional. We all had big crushes on her. She was the older woman unbound by bourgeois strictures, who took lovers as she chose, including Dulles. There was a tame, dull husband in the background. Betty was artistic. Betty knew Carl Jung. Betty was brave. We were prepared to die for her. Betty sent agents in and out of Occupied Europe, myself included, while tirelessly working the diplomatic party scene, myself excluded. Willi Schmidt was always claiming that he 'made out' with her, but none of us believed him. Willi's grasp of American slang was always ahead of my own.

Nobody had questioned Willi's death at the time, least of all me. The river had been in full spate.

*In fact not true. According to Betty Monroe's diaries there were several crucial meetings at the end of the war.

Willi would have appreciated Karl-Heinz's insistence that he was still alive. It was very Willi. Willi had always worked like an optical trick. He had the knack of making himself appear marginal and in the middle of things at the same time. A man of memorable entrances and invisible exits; Willi was gone by the time you noticed. Half the time he hadn't been there when people had sworn he was.

Karl-Heinz recalling him was, I figured, old age's equivalent to the imaginary friends invented by children. Karl-Heinz was on heavy medication and got his wires crossed. He should not be drinking alcohol, not in the quantity we did at dinner. Once so elegant, Karl-Heinz now dressed like a large baby. I can still see him in Cairo 1956, in his white suit, hired by Nasser to teach his police interrogation techniques.

Karl-Heinz wanted to show me something he thought was in his bedroom wardrobe, but then he couldn't remember what he was looking for and we ended up inspecting his old shirts, all handmade and professionally neat in laundry cellophane wraps. He reminded me of Gatsby, and said that his collection of shirts had been inspired by him. *Gatsby* was a book he carried in his head throughout the war. 'It contains the word "holocaust", did you know?'

The house was being watched, he said, plucking at my sleeve. He was being followed, probably by Israelis except they weren't professional enough. (I looked outside. The street was quiet. It was an unremarkable night, quite forgettable. I knew I wouldn't sleep in spite of my tiredness.

Seeing Karl-Heinz had unsettled me. I saw my conscience: cold clinker at the bottom of the stove waiting for the rake.)

He kept telling me he had unfinished work, although he couldn't say yet what it was, and pointed to the maps strewn about. Hungary, Turkey, Syria, the Middle East, Germany, all were arrowed and circled – testament to some vast, final campaign. In his head; I doubted if it existed anywhere else. He showed me these maps proudly, saying that soon he would be able to explain. The old Karl-Heinz cliff-hanger.

Around one o'clock he stopped pretending.

He asked if I had held a Swiss bank account during the war. I shook my head. He looked surprised. 'I thought everyone did. It was like having a mistress!' He had got his on Willi Schmidt's recommendation, but had not used it to stash away loot like some others he could name. Once Karl-Heinz had lied better than anyone. Not any more. I doubted if he had used the account as little as he claimed. Even in uniform he had been a consummate businessman and deal-maker.

After the war he had 'forgotten about the account' and it had lain dormant, along with thousands of others. Most had belonged to Jews killed by the Nazis, and the subsequent refusal of the Swiss banks to turn them over to surviving relatives, citing the absence of death certificates as a reason, had taken more than fifty years and an international scandal to sort out. The banks – stubborn, proprietorial and ultra-conservative – finally owned up, only to find themselves involved in a further controversy.

The published list, meant as a late apology to the Jews, included the names of several Nazis, some of them war criminals. Relatives of those Nazis were entitled to claim the contents of the accounts regardless of their provenance. So stolen goods went to the relations of the stealer. Karl-Heinz had learned that much to his cost, he said: his name was on the list. A nephew he had no idea existed had made a claim and the story got followed up by a television company, who had come knocking on his door.

I asked about the Englishman who had been at dinner. Karl-Heinz shrugged him aside. 'He was recommended as someone who might be able to put my side of the story. I think it's more likely he is some sort of spy.'

He insisted 'they' were catching up with him. 'They' were building a case against him, despite his immunity deal. This, he believed, could still result in prosecution for war crimes. 'It's all bullshit, of course,' he added. 'Zionist cocksuckers.'

I suspect, like me, terror of medical diagnosis lies at the root of his fear, and the rest is embellishment. We both know without having to remind each other that there is no such thing as remission, only undiagnosed illness.

Karl-Heinz refused to accept that I wasn't in a position to help. He thought I had contacts and influence long gone. His paranoia did another flip. 'Of course!' he said. 'It's because everyone's dead that they are coming after me!'

I told him a good lawyer could probably delay the case until after he was dead, but Karl-Heinz's earlier good humor had deserted him.

I asked the next question with an old trepidation. 'Was Willi's name on the bank's list too?'

Strasse nodded. It had been printed just above his. He held up his fingers to indicate the tiny space that had separated them. 'Small world, like the Englishman said. Now it turns out Willi has a wife. I bet you didn't know *that*.'

'Willi wasn't the marrying kind.'

According to Karl-Heinz, the widow had written saying she had married Willi in 1944, and was looking for witnesses to vouch for her because all the relevant certificates and memorabilia had been destroyed. Her letter, he remembered, was what he had been trying to locate in his bedroom wardrobe.

'Tomorrow when you are in Zürich . . .' Karl-Heinz gave me a crafty look that said: I am not so forgetful as you may think, '. . . you will go and see Willi's wife. She lives there. I will give you the address.'

My job would be to check her out, he said. He tried again and failed to find the letter. He fussed around, helpless. I decided it was another of his delusions.

At the front door he gripped me with both hands, his eyes watery. He wept, a few stiff tears, and said that if it weren't for the work in hand he would kill himself rather than endure the half-life left to him. He still had his service Luger.

When the room phone rang in the night, I knew it was Karl-Heinz. 'I couldn't sleep either,' he said. 'I have found the letter. Do me a favor tomorrow, Joe, when you are in Zürich. Go visit Willi's widow.'

I was tired and in a sleepless funk thinking about my illness. 'Go see her yourself, Karl-Heinz. I'm not over here to meet new people.'

He sounded hurt. He had been counting on my help, he said. The journey to Zürich was far too exhausting for him to contemplate. He needed to conserve his energy. He rode my silence until I said, 'Give me the address.'

According to the letter, Frau Schmidt hadn't seen her husband since 1945. Me neither. What she didn't explain was how she had known how to contact Karl-Heinz.

Karl-Heinz had two answers to that. His favorite was that Frau Schmidt was a trap set by the people watching him. He feared kidnapping. He had given evidence in camera at Eichmann's trial in Jerusalem and believed that the Israelis had been after him ever since. His second answer was that Willi wanted to access his account but couldn't apply in person, being technically dead. The invented Frau Schmidt was his surrogate.

For the first time I seriously asked myself whether Willi were still alive. I remembered my earlier trepidation. It reminded me of the nerves I always got before making a run.

'Okay,' I said, and told Karl-Heinz what he wanted to hear. 'I'll go see the widow Schmidt. I'll run you one more trip.'

Karl-Heinz, rejuvenated, said, 'For old times' sake.'

Vaughan, Frankfurt

Lying hungover in my room when Dora called, early for her. She was keen to investigate her lover for me – a new form of our intimacy.

Curiously little on Carswell existed, and he himself was not forthcoming. It had taken her a lot of work to find out that before television he had been in radical journalism in the 1960s, after an initial spell at the BBC had earned him a 'Christmas Tree' file, meaning that he was marked down for subversive leanings. At the same time he had fenced to an Olympic standard, prevented from representing his country because of an obscure scandal. 'He gets moody if you ask.' He still fenced.

Dora sounded falsely cheerful. She had been offered silly money to go to a 'party' in Hampstead, fixed through a Grays member. She wanted me to say she should go. We ended up rowing. I told her she was getting out of her depth. I was distracted by the contradiction between Carswell's upper-class pursuits and radical leanings.

I called back to apologise, but the call lapsed into resentful silences and hostile questioning answered by more hostility. I hung up angrily, thinking: File under Impossible Relationships.

Beate von Heimendorf, Zürich

Dear Mr Hoover,

Thank you very much for your last letter with your schedule. We look forward to seeing you on the Sunday after your arrival. I will warn you in advance how distressing it can be to see Mother now. She was, as you have written, remarkable for her alertness and intelligence.

Since our correspondence began I have been thinking a lot about what Mother must have been like when you knew her. I have enjoyed writing in English again. Mother and I always spoke in English but I write it rarely, and find that the impression I have of her is different if I think in English not German.

On her good days, which sadly are few, she asks what she has done to be spared in such a terrible fashion, and, as she puts it, 'kept behind after everyone else has been called'.

You had the privilege of meeting her in the war, her

most extraordinary period in a life that was never ordinary. You will be well aware of her fortitude and charm.

In your letter you asked what she was really like, given that your own dealings with her were restricted. You know she was fiercely intelligent, and always determined. Her artistic side she attributed to Edith Wharton, a distant cousin. Mother was blue-blooded and bluestocking, and travelled to Europe to study at the Sorbonne. She then moved to Switzerland in 1936 to do her doctorate under Carl Jung, a study of taboo and 'cargo cults' in primitive societies. She was ahead of her time in her demand for equal treatment from men. Few were her equal in any respect.

She claimed she once partnered Nabokov at tennis. I believe that Nabokov taught tennis in Berlin but I have no idea if he was ever in Zürich. Mother could be fanciful on occasion. I remember Father once telling me when I was too young to understand, with a mixture of affection and something else I now see was exasperation, that Mother collected famous people.

Her marriage, to my father, has always been a source of mystery and some pain. It was the central enigma of her life and, for those of us that were the result, not an easy one to live with! If my father was hurt by her adventurousness he never showed it. He was a dedicated and private man, and careful in granting my mother her freedom, but saddened by what he thought of as his failure. He was in all respects decent and upright. I know it hurt him that she refused to take his name after they married.

But I risk being indiscreet. Perhaps I am writing this for myself, so please forgive me if it is not what you want.

When the war broke out in 1939 I know she considered moving back to the United States, in spite of being married. Her family put pressure on her because it was by no means certain whether Switzerland would succeed in remaining neutral. She has never told me what stopped her, but, given what follows, it is possible to make an educated guess.

You ask about Mother and Allen Dulles. Her account of their meeting is fresh in my mind because she spoke to me about it at the start of her illness. While her memory was still good she spoke a lot about the past. She said she was 'setting everything in order before putting it away'. It was only then that we began to become close.

I have never understood the assertion that America is a classless society. Mother and Mr Dulles came from that loose association known as the 'top drawer'. I have the impression they knew each other long before their first official meeting in 1942. Mother has never talked about this. She was well capable of playing the clam when it suited.

Their relationship is generally documented as starting with Mr Dulles's arrival in Switzerland in November 1942. According to Mother, he first came to see her on a clandestine visit in January 1942, just after the United States entered the war. She had been recommended to Mr Dulles by her uncle who was a senior partner in the same law firm.

Mother was struck by Mr Dulles's comical insistence on cloak-and-dagger secrecy, and spoiled his surprise by guessing that he had been asked to become a spy. His task was to start assembling an espionage network, which he would return to take charge of later in the year. That Mother was central to his plans was a surprise, she said, if only because she was used to speaking her mind rather than dealing in subterfuge. She was being disingenuous. She was quite capable of putting her life in separate compartments, and her recruitment was inevitable, given her nationality, her connections, her languages and her knowledge of Germany and Switzerland.

Mother said she measured the seriousness of Mr Dulles's intentions by the out-of-way restaurant of indifferent quality where he insisted they dine so no one would overhear, rather than somewhere more their style. Mr Dulles was nothing if not a social creature. Over dinner he explained that it would be their job to provide Washington with accurate information about relations between Switzerland and the Third Reich.

As a lawyer in peacetime he had represented many German and Swiss clients, and it would be his business to maintain contact with them while Mother monitored Switzerland's secret trade with the Germans and established clandestine links with occupied countries. Mother took that to mean that Mr Dulles would go to parties while she did the hard work.

We talked several times about that evening, and she

could still recite the menu (with a shudder) after so many years, as well as most of the conversation.

Mother suspected someone very smart was behind Mr Dulles's appointment. Mr Dulles was a very clever lawyer, with a keen eye for the loophole. He proved knowledgeable at explaining how Swiss banks and businesses were flouting the rules of neutrality and acting on behalf of German companies. He relished his involvement in the war, and insisted upon the widest possible reading. Did Mother understand, for example, the implications of Japan's recent entry into the war for China and Germany? (For all his willingness to treat her equally, she found he talked down to her in matters of business.) Mother could rattle off verbatim the answer to Mr Dulles's question: Germany relied on China for tungsten, essential to aircraft manufacture, but as of December 1941, and Japan's new alliance with Germany, trade between China and Germany ceased because the existing conflict between China and Japan, dating back to 1937, placed Germany and China indirectly at war.

Mother, who was capable of showing off with the best, said that Germany would have to get its tungsten from another neutral source such as Portugal, and had the satisfaction, as she put it, of watching Mr Dulles's 'jaw drop'.

In many ways Mr Dulles found his match in Mother. She was quick to understand his reading of the war, not in terms of politics or ideology, but in relation to essential raw materials. Tungsten, manganese, and chromium, as well as more common commodities like iron ore, oil and diamonds were what won wars. Trade, not troop movements, was what Mr Dulles called the bottom line, which is why the role of neutral countries like Switzerland would always be crucial.

In her way Mother was ahead of Mr Dulles. She told him that it was her understanding that the German war effort without Swiss help would last no more than two months, and she had the satisfaction of seeing Mr Dulles lost for words twice in one evening.

Her source was, ironically, a man she had met at a party, though the deduction was her own. The man in question was a German diplomat. He and Mother had become social friends, and, even before her meeting with Mr Dulles, he had intimated that he was against Hitler and for America, and interested in maintaining and developing personal relations in spite of their new status as enemies. I believe he went on to become one of Mother's most informative agents.

I would appreciate in return any memories you have of my mother. I find it a great source of consolation reading about her. It helps dull the awful sense of injustice at her incapacity. I am sure I can speak for Mother when I say that we both look forward to our meeting with you and we trust you have a safe and comfortable journey.

Yours sincerely,
Beate von Heimendorf.

Hoover, Zürich

Beate von Heimendorf spoke as she wrote, in perfect, formal English. She was waiting at the head of the platform, as she said she would be, a tall, supple-looking woman in her late fifties, wearing a Burberry raincoat. Her handshake was firm. I liked her immediately. She was somewhat distant, with a precise air that I suspect had been hard won and at the expense of trust. It could not have been easy growing up as Betty Monroe's daughter, and she looked as though she was only now emerging from the shadow. She said I was the first of her mother's agents she had met and left it at that. We drove to the clinic in a Mercedes estate, the last word in understated luxury.

Seeing Betty, shock as it was, didn't tell me anything I didn't know. We are all due out pretty soon, and time does the cruellest things to those who don't deserve it. Such a fine woman reduced to a husk. She was stick-like and frail. Even her cardigan sat on her like a topcoat, weighing her down. She gave no sign of recognising us, just as I had been warned. Betty had once been what life and intelligence were all about. The biggest shock was that she didn't look like she missed it. In contrast to her physical deterioration, the eyes were clear and serene.

How an old man's mind works: it works the way it always did, except it gets more selective and can operate on several levels at once, more than it used to. The here and now has become the least important aspect of any dimension.

It can get you pretty frisky, this long walk down the last corridor to that green door at the end (believe me, it's green) and I ended up wanting to bed the daughter and one of the nurses (squeak of rubber shoes on polished wooden floors). I knew this was a desperation measure, know too that I panic about all the things I won't do again. Who's to kid? Ejaculations reduced to a tearful flutter. When was the last time that Mary and I did it?

Betty was in what I could only describe as a Swiss room. The Swiss design fixtures and fittings for sickness better than anyone else. I'm sure you pay, but I kept thinking it would be a privilege to be ill in such surroundings.

For someone whose brain is still too active, and given to morbid thoughts, I almost envied Betty her serene blankness, and would be curious to know from her how it feels to find chunks going missing, whether it is scary or like watching snow fall. Better that way, than the full invasion my body might soon be undergoing. Memo: Go out leaving as many loose ends as possible. Resolve nothing!

Icebergs are among the most beautiful and mysterious things I have seen. Being with Betty reminded me. I can't describe it any better. Perhaps there is a poetic justice to her condition. We were in a business where memory was too often a curse.

I told Beate I was interested in anything Betty might still have on Willi Schmidt. (Why? I asked myself, when I had been telling everyone, myself included, that Willi was dead.) Beate was familiar with the name from her mother's papers. They had been sorting old documents and letters together before Betty's deterioration.

By then we were in a café drinking coffee and eating cake with sour cream. For the first time I fully appreciated that I was back in Switzerland, perhaps because everywhere so far had looked like it belonged to the same consumer state. Europe had become a landscape of convenience.

I asked if she thought Betty would object to my seeing any of her papers relating to Willi. Beate said she could think of no reason, it was all so long ago. She gave a brief smile of embarrassment, and apologised for her tactlessness. We arranged I would stop by after seeing Frau Schmidt, on my way back to the station.

Vaughan, Frankfurt

It is always a surprise finding out who's listed in the phone book. Idle curiosity prompted the search. There was a telephone directory by the bed in my hotel room. Still hungover, I talked my way into Strasse's place by claiming that he had agreed to the appointment at the end of dinner.

The old Nazi hung out with young men from the Middle East rather than the Nordic types you would expect – young men who looked like street toughs, although Strasse himself was a cultivated man, clear from his taste in furniture.

One of these acolytes answered the door. There was a shouted exchange with Strasse upstairs. I wondered why Nazis old and new seemed to cultivate Middle-Eastern connections.

There were another two men upstairs with Strasse talking a language I didn't recognise. He was worked up about what looked like an amateur tape on the TV. I recognised the football riot and the burning hostel. Siegfried featured in many of the shots, including infra-reds of him sitting in his BMW. The sight of Siegfried angered Strasse. To me: 'Tell your friend he is not as clever as he thinks.'

Strasse seemed to regard me as Siegfried's messenger. I wondered if they were enemies in spite of Siegfried's deference.

The men left suddenly. I asked who they were, but was ignored. I decided Strasse's problem was loneliness, so I played housemaid, fussed over him, made him tea, got his pills, acted the polite young fascist then hit him with the pitch. We wanted to make a film about his past that would be sympathetic, proper and respectful.

Strasse knew he was being courted and didn't want to make it easy. Each time I nudged him towards the past he returned to the present. He thought he was a player, with his maps of Syria, Turkey and Iraq, aerial photographs, and arrowed diagrams like in historical documentaries on the TV. 'What's this?' I asked. 'The next invasion of the Middle East?'

Strasse coldly informed me that the region's next big war would not be over its most obvious commodity, oil. 'But what?' he asked impatiently, snapping his fingers. It wasn't hard to guess, given several pictures on the wall of a huge hydro-electric project. Water.

'Precisely,' said Strasse. The pictures were of part of a huge dam project which would flood a massive area of south-east Turkey and turn the region into what he called the bread basket of Europe. 'A land of plenty,' he said, his mouth turning down. He made me fetch another VHS tape, and another pair of spectacles to read the label. He held the tape at arm's length, breathing through his mouth, sounding raspy. Close up, his skin was shiny and transparent, and looked even older than the rest of him. He wore Turkish slippers and no socks. The veins on his feet had come to the surface and looked like deltas.

The new tape showed a female TV reporter with a microphone, behind her a snowy landscape – more mountains, obviously European – and the remains of a burned-out commercial building. It was the news item Strasse had been talking about in the restaurant, the arson report. When the reporter tried to interview a very tall man with silver hair, dressed in a smart overcoat, he ignored her. Strasse froze the image with the remote and shuttled it back and forth. The chill of the man's gaze, invisible to the naked eye, was revealed in slow-motion. The reporter referred to him as Konrad Viessmann. Strasse shouted her down: 'It's Willi Schmidt, you stupid cow!' He bellowed Willi's name at the man on screen, adding, 'Listen, cocksucker, I know who you are!'

The man on screen looked too young to be a contemporary of Karl-Heinz's – he appeared sixty-five at most – but Strasse was in no mood to be contradicted. Here was a man he had walked beside many times, he said. The walk and the height went together.

Strasse: the factory had been attacked by a Kurdish rebel organisation – the PKK – because the company had been dumping inferior pharmaceuticals on Kurdish refugee camps in Turkey. As for Willi Schmidt, Strasse went on, his tone more hectoring, no one could appreciate how dangerous his reappearance was in relation to his own mission. Which was? Strasse ignored the question and ordered me to go to a drawer on the other side of the room. In it were several old photograph albums. He made me hold each one up until I found the one he wanted.

'Look,' he said, jabbing his finger at an old black and white photograph. It was very small with a crinkled border. It showed three young men standing in a field, one of them with a horse. 'See?' prompted Strasse. The photograph was tiny and faded. I peered closer. Strasse was the one in the riding jacket holding the horse. The man on his right was the American from the restaurant, Hoover. The third man, on Strasse's left, was a head taller and looked like a younger version of the man on television.

The photo album finally got Strasse on to the past, sort of. He talked me through his album – every picture a story, which he would allude to but refuse to elaborate upon. Strasse laughed, in a good mood all of a sudden, leading me a dance, playing the canny tease. Today he wasn't interested in the past, he told me, because big things were going on and about to happen. 'But tomorrow when we meet I will be able to tell you more because my agents will have reported in.'

Hoover, Zürich

Frau Schmidt is in every respect the opposite of Beate von Heimendorf. She is tiny and doll-like, slow-moving and apparently timid, except for eyes as sharp as knitting needles. She lives in an apartment block in one of those dreary residential quarters, mildly surreal in their banality, that cluster around European railway stations.

She had sounded breathless and surprised on the phone. We spoke in German, and an elementary grammatical error of mine prompted a nervous giggle. I told her I had been a friend of her husband and was calling on Karl-Heinz Strasse's behalf. 'Ja doch?' she said with an air of wonder. Frankly, she sounded soft in the head.

Conveniently for her story, she has spent much of her life abroad, first in Uruguay, then Peru, where her second husband, Friedrich (Fredi) Kranz, deceased, worked for Volkswagen. Strictly speaking the widow Schmidt is the widow Kranz. Kranz is the name on her bell. She is alone in the world, with no children and no living relatives.

I tried to imagine her with Willi Schmidt, tried to

picture them in the same room. She would have been attractive enough. Willi surrounded himself with good-looking people. It was almost a condition of entry into his circle.

We made small talk over coffee. The apartment was typical of a modest European standard, with a white linen cloth covering the dining table we sat at, the ubiquitous spider plant, and a generally dust-free environment that told of too many hours to fill. (I know this because my own empty hours since Mary died have been spent doing anything but housework.)

When I explained that Willi and I had knocked about together during the war, she responded with platitudes of her own: 'Willi was a fine man.' 'Willi always brought me proper chocolate from Switzerland.'

Frau Schmidt had worked for a German company which had become a subsidiary of Willi's firm – that was how they had met. She proudly showed me the only souvenirs of their time together, several boxes of children's party shoes. She opened one to reveal the shoes still wrapped in their original tissue paper. They were red and shiny patent leather. Her hands shook as she unwrapped them.

They had married in the late summer of 1944, but no record survived because the Rathaus had later been destroyed by shelling. Her copy of the marriage certificate was lost, along with all their photographs and Willi's letters, when American planes had bombed the wrong side of the Swiss border in error. She had returned to their lodgings from the canning factory where she worked to find her building reduced to a large crater. After the war, she said, the Swiss had extracted an enormous compensation from the Americans.

I still couldn't picture Willi married, but I believed her account of the empty years waiting for him to come home, her reluctant return to Germany, the hardship of the post-war years, her gradual acceptance of the fact that he would not come back, and the realisation that, rather than live in the shadow of his memory, she had to make a new life. This she did by remarrying and moving to Uruguay, then Peru – a period well documented by albums which showed her with a stout, round-faced man who resembled Al Capone. His name was Kranz, she reminded me. I apologised for calling her Frau Schmidt. It was all right, she said. It was good for the memory of Willi. She snuffled a few tears into a handkerchief which she produced from up her sleeve, and said that sometimes Willi felt like a dream. They had met only twelve times before they married, and were together eleven weeks. Sometimes it seemed better to leave the past alone, she said. Still, it would be nice to have a little money, because Switzerland was expensive and Fredi's policies didn't go very far.

When I asked how she had tracked down Karl-Heinz she said she had hired a private detective to find him. 'A private detective, at my age! As if I could afford one!'

Karl-Heinz's was one of the few names she remembered Willi mentioning. I thought Willi would have been more discreet. When I expressed my surprise she gave a sly smile. 'You are quite right. Willi kept secrets like the grave. To tell the truth, I was jealous. Jealous and suspicious! Willi could travel, Willi was handsome and there were plenty of lonely young women in Germany. He could have taken his pick. Willi had his little book. I'll fetch it.'

She came back with a pocket-sized book, with flimsy ruled pages. It was empty apart from a few scribbled names, or initials, and some timetables. On one page I read: *VH (Josef)[??]*, and on another what looked like a further reference to myself: *VH–Buda??* My full name was written on its own on one page. Karl-Heinz's appeared several times. The last page contained nothing but mathematical equations in pencil so faded they were impossible to read. I couldn't remember Willi's handwriting – wondered if I had ever seen it.

I asked why there was nobody who had known about their marriage. No one was left still alive, she said simply. What of Willi's family? I asked. There must have been some relatives who knew. Frau Schmidt shook her head. Willi had never informed them, because he wished to protect her from their disapproval.

I told her that hardly seemed a good enough reason. From what I remembered of Willi, he enjoyed flouting convention.

Frau Schmidt agreed, but then dropped her big surprise. 'They would have just about tolerated Willi marrying beneath himself – but never to a Jewess.'

'Jewish!' Frau Schmidt nodded. 'Working in Germany in

1944?' Germany's Jews had all been deported or killed by then, and the few left were in hiding.

Seeing my scepticism, Frau Schmidt said that she had believed herself sufficiently assimilated until warned by a friend who was a typist for the Gestapo that her case was on file, with an investigation pending. She had confided this to Willi, whom she happened to see the next day. He insisted she leave Germany immediately and drove her to a farm near the border where he said she would be safe until he arranged the paperwork. What she had not realised was that this would mean their getting married. Willi proposed only on the morning of the ceremony, and straight afterwards drove her across the border to Switzerland.

Willi had married her to get her out of Germany.

If the story is true, then Willi never ceases to surprise me. How to reconcile this unexpected humanitarian side to the party animal I remember? Willi to me in 1943, both of us drunk, pretty women all around, his jazz records on the turntable: 'Marriage is for the birds!'

Vaughan, Frankfurt

To	dcarswell@aol.com
From:	vaughan@freeserve.co.uk
Date:	Wed, 10 May, 18.06
Subject:	Top Nazi

I talked with Karl-Heinz Strasse and will see him again tomorrow at ten. He is nibbling, hasn't bitten. I am sure he will talk in full, but for the mo only to me as I come with the endorsement of Siegfried. Will try and film/tape him tomorrow and later, when he feels comfortable, you could come and take over.

Everything he told me sounded like a man rehearsing his story. He hinted there are already people prepared to pay a lot of money.

He remains vague about what exactly he was doing in 1942–3. This is what I have been able to work out in terms of rough chronology. He was in the SS and had cavalry connections. One of his main jobs involved buying horses, which required him to travel. He won the Iron Cross, which he showed me, on the Russian front. From what I can tell he was in Russia in 1941–2 and after that became a staff officer and possibly some sort of spy.

The point he is quite specific about is how he was recruited at the end of the war as an Intelligence Officer by the Americans, and later worked for the CIA, as did a lot of Nazis. On the Cold War his memory is date accurate. Anything before 1945, he'll fudge and change the subject while dropping enough hints to suggest he would go on record if a deal were done.

Strasse is also hanging around with the guy who recruited him into US Intelligence in 1945. I'm not sure what he is doing in Frankfurt. Says he's on holiday.

Strasse travelled to Switzerland a lot during the war. He showed me pictures taken there of him with the spook just mentioned. His name is Hoover and my guess is he too would have a tale to tell.

There's a third man in the Swiss photo, and Strasse is currently very exercised about him. Name of Willi Schmidt. Whatever they were all up to in the war, the three were pretty tight. Schmidt died in 1945 – Hoover says he was there when it happened – except now

Strasse is claiming Schmidt is alive and calling himself Konrad Viessmann. Interesting mystery.

Strasse's photo album is varied and includes a questionable range of contrasts. Peasants in some flat place (Byelorussia, who knows?). Strasse in SS uniform and death's head cap, possibly compromised by the train trucks in background. Lots of equestrian stuff which backs up the horse-buying story. Lederhosen: alpine R&R. After the war there are pictures of him in Cairo. The CIA guy Hoover is there too in a picture which Strasse says shouldn't have been taken. (They're out in the desert somewhere.) There are also photos of Strasse with a Muslim leader I'd never heard of, who was pro-Hitler during the war and living in Berlin, and afterwards went to Egypt. In Berlin this leader was looked after by the SS – hence pix of him with Strasse, I presume. What I didn't know was that the SS ran a Muslim division. (I knew they had Ukrainian volunteers.) I was confused by the racial implications until Strasse made the connections: Hitler didn't much like Arabs, but Himmler was an admirer of the Muslim warrior i.e. ganging up against the Jews and the British. There are also photos of Strasse with Roman Catholic Croatian churchmen. At some point during the war he was in Budapest because there are pictures of the city. He didn't say what he was doing there. Strasse is an infuriating mixture of the secretive and indiscreet. He seems to have been in contact with everyone.

Strasse is very excited about something that's happening. This may be an old man's fantasy but towards the end of the meeting he was hinting that he isn't a spent force and the foundations of an alliance put down in the war would soon pay off!

Oh yes, and the Willi Schmidt/Viessmann guy has something going with Kurds in Turkey because they burned down his chemical factory, to do with bad drugs being dumped in refugee camps.

Hoover, Zürich

The cab took me from Frau Schmidt's, in a district showing signs of aspirations to change, up into the hills behind the university where the old money lives. Grey stone gives way to red brick, greenery and high walls, and the dead Sunday silence of Swiss discretion. It was like being back in the centre of what Fitzgerald called 'the great Swiss watch'.

Betty Monroe's old house dates back to the early part of the last century and reveals little to the street. The house, with its quiet lawns, freshly mown in Betty's case, stands behind iron gates. A short sloping drive emphasises its grace and superiority – two qualities reflected in Beate von Heimendorf herself (milky skin, soft blue veins, blue blood pulsing through them).

Of a husband for Beate there is no sign. Just her Mercedes was parked outside. I was as tongue-tied as a teenager. I am attracted to Beate von Heimendorf, in spite of having about as much chance as any tongue-tied teenager. Less, because such impulses are considered unseemly, dirty even, in a man of my age. The attraction was intensified because she was a little breathless when she answered the door.

Her mother's papers weren't where she thought they were, in the garage, and didn't appear to be in the house either, she said. The house was absurdly large, she went on, and they could be anywhere. We were standing in the hall. There was an expensive wooden floor, good furniture and through the open door to the living rooms a view of cultured trees.

'I hate this house,' Beate announced unexpectedly. She doesn't live there and isn't sure what to do now her mother is ill. It would feel like a betrayal to sell it, she said, while Betty remained alive. She herself keeps a small apartment in town. I asked if a husband went with it. Not really, she said. It was hard to tell if the silence that followed was an invitation to further comment. She changed the subject back to her mother's missing papers, which she was sure had been in the garage. I suggested we take another look.

Garage was the technically correct term in that it had been designed partly for cars, but there was a whole small apartment above, once presumably the chauffeur's quarters. It was here that Beate thought the papers should have been. One wall was lined with shelves full of box files but none contained the relevant documents.

Beate does not look the forgetful type. A cleaner comes in twice a week, she said, and there are a couple of gardeners. Either the papers have been mislaid, like she said, or they have been taken, but I had no wish to alarm her. She thought it possible that the secretary, who comes in twice a month to deal with her mother's affairs, might know what had happened to them. She seemed relieved when I agreed. The explanation sounded plausible. Beate pressed her hands together. Her wrists, like her ankles, were slender and elegant. 'However, it's not all bad news.' In as much as she is capable of sounding skittish, she did. 'I have found one set of documents in Mother's desk relating to your friend Herr Schmidt.'

I followed her to her mother's study, continuing to admire her ankles as we went upstairs. The study was large and well-appointed, overlooking the garden. The shelves and paneling were beech. There was a daybed for afternoon naps, or daytime lovers, and lots of framed old photographs. Beate showed me the papers, typed on a translucent and waxy paper. They looked like carbon copies. I could smell her perfume, which was light and clean. We were standing close; I felt the ache of desire. It was pathetic, I told myself. The woman was showing me her mother's papers, that was all. Our eyes met briefly and gave out confused signals. 'Look,' she said, 'these papers are marked *secret.* We probably shouldn't be looking at them.' She laughed and said she thought her mother was probably very indiscreet. I read a lifetime of self-imposed inhibition into that remark.

She made me a gift of the papers, or at least a copy of them. We both seemed to be aware that they were a surrogate for a different sort of transaction. The encounter felt like a botched coda to a Truffaut movie, about thirty years too late.

There was a photocopier in a room downstairs. We stood in silence for a small age listening to the humming machine warm up. I watched the sweep of the green light under the cover as it copied each page, Beate's hands pressing on the lid. 'I suppose the fact that they are confidential papers doesn't matter now,' she said. 'I'll look again for the rest. There were boxes of them. I can't think where they have gone.' She looked at me and smiled and asked what I planned to do with the rest of my stay. I said I wasn't sure.

'Footloose and fancy free, as my mother used to say. That's the best way. If you come to Zürich again be sure to look us up.'

She phoned for a taxi and we spent the time it took to arrive standing outside. Beate showed me the garden and we made conversation about the house. For her it had always been for grown-ups and not somewhere she had been comfortable growing up. I had the strange feeling that if we went back indoors we would see the ghost of Beate as a child. 'Is something the matter?' she asked. The taxi arrived before I could answer. We shook hands, then she leaned forward and kissed me on the cheek. It was an impulsive gesture, rather than standard Continental politeness, of a sort that I suspect she is not often given to.

Betty Monroe, secret memo to Allen Dulles, Zürich, 1942

Memo: *M/420093/AD/01/31/42*
Yr eyes only: *read & destroy*
Subj: *requested assessment*

Intelligence source Gerontius: a consignment of leather is on offer for sale by the Vichy French to a Swiss shoe company, Brevecourt, who will pay a better price, in Swiss francs, than German firms restricted to payment in Reichsmarks.

While Brevecourt is not on the US Treasury's blacklist, it is suspected of German trade links.

Brevecourt is in discussion with our Consulate in Bern regarding export of a consignment of children's shoes to the US. There is a hitch as the product leather was purchased from a Swiss company which is on the Treasury blacklist. Brevecourt argues that the leather was acquired before the other company was blacklisted.

I have spoken to the Consulate and am being allowed to manage the Brevecourt case. In the role of a trade official, I have met two of Brevecourt's representatives. The elder, the overweight Herr R., is a windbag of no use to us, but Herr S. strikes me as promising, and refreshingly impudent for a Swiss. He pulls faces behind Herr R.'s back and supposes he is flirting. (I know you like a lively memo.) Herr S. seems to be there as an observer because Herr R. does the talking and plays an excruciatingly dull form of bureaucratic chess. The more boring the meeting, the greater the signs of collusion from Herr S.

Herr S. makes a point of arriving ahead of Herr R. As you are keen on my asides: Herr S. probably makes up in stamina what he lacks in finesse. He tells me he was in New York for six months in 1938 (his English is good) where he said he saw the future. After tasting America, he informs me, Europe seems unbearably stuffy. His flirting is somewhat stodgy. His passion is jazz, his tragedy that he is a shoe salesman. This is a somewhat misleading assertion as his family own the company. There must be more to life than selling shoes, he tells me meaningfully. I warn him never to underestimate shoes where a woman is concerned.

A fortunate breakthrough when Herr R. became suddenly indisposed after drinking a cup of the Consulate's coffee and had to excuse himself. (Ex-Lax. I nearly muddled the cups, which would have been unfortunate.)

In Herr R.'s absence, Herr S. proved himself an able negotiator. The export deal proceeded towards a smooth close, with previous objections less problematic. I have written formally to Brevecourt to inform them that, subject to final approval of the export papers, the consignment may go ahead, and to note Herr S.'s negotiating skills.

Herr S. is being encouraged socially and understands his position: were he to come and work for us it would (eventually) gain him an American permit. Herr S. regards his country's neutrality as a slur on his manhood, and entertains the idea of adventure. He has failed to spot that he is working for us already: from his gossip, we can gather that his uncle, who runs Brevecourt, has a German wife, and is staunchly pro-Nazi; also Brevecourt is buying extra storage space, thus confirming suspicions that the company is stockpiling leather. This ties in with Gerontius's intelligence. I have a feeling that Herr S.'s impatience (and greed) might be to our advantage.

Memo: *BM/420097/AD/02/10/42*
Yr eyes only: *read and destroy*
Subj: *Herr S.*

More positive developments. Sensing Herr S.'s desire to rebel, I have i) fed him Gerontius's information about the consignment of French leather on sale to Brevecourt ii) encouraged him to come up with a plan, quite a daring one, which would result in him earning lots of money.

We have surmised correctly that Herr S. likes money best. He has proved a quick and willing learner. A calculated recklessness appeals.

It is now possible to assess Brevecourt's illegal operations. In the years before the war, the company took advantage of the closure of many Jewish leather and shoe firms in Germany and bought cheap. Brevecourt has been stockpiling leather and, to avoid trade embargos, it maintains an illusion of independence from its German outlets. It uses an agent named Ruiz and a dummy company in Lisbon to provide false documentation to show any sale to Germany coming from Portugal. The leather is used by the German companies to make boots for the army. Brevecourt's foresight has led to huge profits.

Herr S.'s nerve is proving good. The other night I joined him in his office where he was working late and together we found the transportation timetable for the leather consignment. It will travel as part of one of the German trains for civilian goods allowed to pass through Switzerland. Its destination is a suburban station near St Gallen where the trucks are to be uncoupled and diverted into a siding to await unloading.

Since writing the above, the following postscript can be added. A reception party was waiting for Brevecourt's lorries. Once the wagons were unloaded, Brevecourt's drivers were detained and the lorries driven away.

Since then an anonymous caller has offered the stock back to Brevecourt at well above cost. Herr S., after his success in dealing with the US Consulate, has I believe successfully negotiated the repurchase, and I understand that Brevecourt is more than happy to get its leather back, in spite of having to pay twice over. The discrepancy will be reflected in its next bill to the Wermacht. Herr S.'s stock has further risen because of the export deal to the United States.

Hoover, Zürich to Frankfurt

The train speeds through the dark countryside. Given the seamless zone that modern Europe has become, it is hard to appreciate, now that access is so easy, the significance of borders in wartime. My grandchildren are being raised with almost no concept of boundaries – national, international, moral, religious, conceptual or otherwise. To them history is the past, a dead subject. Actually, it is a non-subject. It has nothing to do with the way they perceive their lives. They live in a literal world, flatly lit from above.

Thanks to Betty's documents I finally appreciate the significance of the death of the first man I was ordered to kill. Señor Ruiz's murder was the invisible footnote to Betty's memorandum. Another thing: even before I knew Willi Schmidt I find we were linked in advance, as though destiny not chance controlled the matter, and perhaps still does.

In keeping with that destiny, which in the case of myself and Willi was anything but straightforward, my passage to

Lisbon, via colonial French West Africa and Tangiers, prepared me for the life of detour that lay ahead.

I arrived in French West Africa after escaping in September 1940 on a boat from Brittany to Dakar, travelling on papers stolen from the Belgian fascist I had befriended. It was an open secret that Belgium's gold reserves were on the boat too, after being forwarded from Brussels and then Paris after the Nazi Occupation.

The template of French colonial civilisation was wearing thin by the time it reached Dakar, redeemed only by the luxury of a servant economy. A new pro-Nazi regime had been hastily installed but among its first tasks was fending off German requests for the return of the Belgian gold. I almost certainly saw this gold again when Dulles and I visited the Frankfurt vaults in May 1945, thus contributing to my theory that life's most important patterns are anything but sequential. My own modest role in the affair was restricted to interpreter for the local Dakar administration and a gang of recently arrived German civilians known by all to be Nazi agents.

So my first proper job in the war involved working for the Germans. There were endless meetings in stifling rooms whose fans failed to make any impression on the heat. The Germans sweated into their starched linens. They were quite humorless, dedicated solely to recovering the gold, and frustrated by the need to maintain diplomatic relations with their collaborators. The French, more ironic and casual in the ways of bureaucracy, and not looking to impress any Germans so far from home, were experts at deferral. The Germans agreed to provide the transportation. The French were finally persuaded to be responsible for the security and, after much wrangling, the fuel bill.

The Germans were suspicious of me at first but not inquisitive, being invasive by nature rather than colonial. The climate of French West Africa mocked their fiercely held beliefs. They yearned for the temperate zones of Northern Europe. Dakar sapped their wills. The untidiness of French colonialism, with its sexual laxity and riot of vegetation, torpor and maddening round of senseless ritual offended their sense of order. The only real punctuality, which you could set your watch by, was the first evening drink served at six on the dot. A hard liver was the price of collaboration.

By Christmas, only a small proportion of the 'consignment of goods', as the Germans comically persisted in calling the gold, had reached its initial destination in western Algeria because the Sahara had become vulnerable to Allied fighter attacks.

Uncertainty was the making of the Germans. It provoked them into a plan that rivaled the maddest visionary quest of the Conquistadors for El Dorado. Unlike the Spanish, the Germans had their gold, and all objections were overruled. Once they had succeeded in giving their quest a mythical dimension there was no stopping them. I was told to inform the French that the itinerary presented was non-negotiable.

Their journey was supposed to take two months. It took the next year of my life. I was kept on as interpreter and traveled with the first consignment. The plan was to ship the gold in several cargoes and stages, first by rail from Dakar to the terminus at Koulikoro, more than a thousand miles away, then nine hundred miles by boat along the Niger to Timbuktu. From there the river journey continued on smaller craft downstream to Gao where the shipment was transferred to trucks to be taken across the Sahara.

The voyage across the Sahara defined the madness of the enterprise, an epic transportation of a commodity that became increasingly meaningless in the context of such a vast emptiness.

The enormity of our task and the implacable terrain ate away at us, while turning us silently heroic. We inhabited a realm beyond language. Our minds became divorced from our bodies. Memory faded and with it desire. Distance, and time, ceased to have meaning. The burden of our journey and the unending harshness eroded identity, turning us into figments of our own imaginations, until we lost all sense of outside conflict and only the inner battle remained, for sanity and survival.

Progress, pitiful to begin with, was delayed by sandstorms. The trucks became useless. The advances of twentieth-century engineering were abandoned for donkeys and camels. We travelled as Bedouin. Everything was jettisoned apart from the gold. The Germans, so loyal and obedient to their ideals, ended up questioning the gold's worth and, by extension, their own. We stared at each other, scarcely able to remember our own names. From the southerly terminus of the West Algerian railroad it was a further thousand miles by train to the coast, the stations along the way serving little except punishment and labour camps.

Later I learned that by the end of 1941 only a third of the gold had crossed the Sahara and it would be nearly another six months before the full consignment reached Berlin.

By the time we arrived at Tangier I discovered that the desert had relieved me of any conscience. I worked as a thug for a local Mr Big until the end of November when I had enough to pay a fishing-boat captain to drop me near Algeciras. From there I traveled to Lisbon, arriving as news was breaking that the Japanese had bombed Pearl Harbor and the United States was at war.

Lisbon at the end of 1941 was much like any other neutral city port, wide open and dangerously tight at the same time. The regime was fascist and vindictive. The country's grand colonial dream had almost faded, along with its architecture, and the damp salt air and the proximity of the Atlantic, with its sense of uncertain departure, gave the city an air of fabulous melancholy.

I presented myself to the Americans and was dealt with by an official called Coburn whose cynicism seemed excessive for what was apparently a desk job and paper administration. My plan had been to reach the United States, but Coburn said my visa application would be delayed because of the war. Coburn was like a tough old cop in an American movie, his prejudices brought out by whisky. He thought I was a spy. His interviews were exhaustive and verged on interrogations.

Señor Ruiz ran an import-export company from a room above a shop, next to a café-bar. Most of his day was spent not working but sitting in the café-bar, drinking coffee and brandy, and reading newspapers. Ruiz was bored. He lived by himself and ate alone in local restaurants. His regular laundry was near the café. Most evenings he took home a parcel of clean clothes wrapped in waxed paper.

I had no idea why I was supposed to watch Señor Ruiz. I became familiar enough with him to know that he shaved only every other day and his teeth were stained from black tobacco. He was around fifty, had a moustache and was losing his hair, which he oiled with a strong pomade. Once I stood close enough on a busy tram to smell garlic on his breath. Liver cooked in the local manner was his regular dish.

Twice in the last week of his life he visited the same prostitute. Most nights he stayed and drank in the café-bar with other regulars, then stopped off alone at different bars for several nightcaps. By the time he got home he was staggering.

Lisbon, with its grand boulevards and labyrinthine alleys and side streets, was a city designed for surveillance. It could be said that to appreciate fully its street-plan and architecture you needed to follow someone for a week.

On 2 February, 1942 I killed Ruiz, on Coburn's orders; stuck a knife in him in an alley, after coshing him with a sock full of stones. It sounds very melodramatic now. At the time it had seemed the only way to convince Coburn to take me on trust. I was more anxious about bungling the job than taking Señor Ruiz's life. Besides, it was easy then to pretend that such acts were a proper test of manhood. The death merited one paragraph at the bottom of an inside page of the main newspaper. Someone had removed Señor Ruiz's wallet. That was my only mistake: I was supposed to have taken it, and could never decide afterwards if one of Coburn's men had been watching me stalking Señor Ruiz. That was Lisbon.

For a week no one could find me, and I have no recollection of that time. After that, Coburn told me he had a proposition. I would be sent not to the United States but to Switzerland.

The empty discipline of the desert made what followed more bearable. The world of subterfuge and espionage into which I was thrown was catholic and voluptuous by comparison – Shakespearean even in its capacity for embellishment and deception, for disguise and concealment.

Vaughan, Frankfurt

Siegfried drove. We were in his BMW, ultra-civilised classical music unspooling on the tape deck. We crossed over the river. Siegfried said nothing, concentrating on smooth gear changing. Traffic was light. We must have looked odd, us together at that time of night, lovers even, going back to his place in some rich outer suburb. Except we ended up in an anonymous industrial zone where my old friends the skinheads were waiting, less friendly now. They were in a VW camper with bench seats and a table in the middle, drinking cans of beer. They were drunk and belligerent.

They all shifted around and I was made to sit boxed in, with Siegfried opposite. With this rearrangement two skinheads were left crouching as best they could, trying to appear menacing. Siegfried looked at me. I stared back and found it hard to hold his eye. He seemed mildly expectant. The skinheads were chortling. Siegfried said, 'Are you going to tell us what is going on?'

I told him I had nothing to tell. We hedged around

until Siegfried nodded at the skinhead next to me who grabbed my hand and slapped it on the table while the skinhead next to Siegfried drove a hunting knife into the table between my splayed fingers. The skinhead holding my hand sniggered. It was only luck that the knife had missed. Siegfried was getting off on this. He was looking messianic. His time had come, he said. The old guard would soon be gone, by which I took him to mean Karl-Heinz.

Siegfried twanged the knife handle, making it shiver. Siegfried's beef: he had been told something by a little birdie. About me. I was a spy. They would be looking into that.

It went very quiet in the van. I could hear the man next to me breathing. I held Siegfried's eye and shook my head slowly, not trusting myself to say anything.

'What do you think about that?' he asked.

'It's not true. I'm going home tomorrow, to help my sister.'

The skinheads guffawed.

Siegfried said it was time to prove I wasn't what the little birdie said. He had a test. More fire. The building would be empty.

Or what? I asked. Siegfried said, 'We put you on a lorry to Turkey.' The skinheads laughed loud: best joke yet.

We drove in the camper to a poor part of the city, on the outskirts. The building they wanted to torch was an old shopfront with a plate-glass window painted over in white. Siegfried said it was a pirate satellite television station for Turkish Kurds.

We all went in except for Siegfried, who stayed in the van, and were there less than two minutes. Door kicked in, down a corridor and into a back room full of electronic equipment. Petrol thrown around. I wasn't asked to do anything, except be photographed, standing in the studio with a can of petrol in my hand. Flash photo, me stickily aware of my fingerprints all over the can, framed for a set-up.

We were away before the flames were evident, the skinheads hollering, heavy metal on the tape deck, me queasy and bursting to piss, in way too deep.

We got back to Siegfried's BMW. No lift home for me. I was left to walk through dead night-time streets, right out on the edge of the city. Siegfried said before he drove off, 'No more warnings. Go home and watch your step. We have friends in England too.'

Dear Dora. Dora's midnight call, waking me. Dora on a mobile from a party. Having fun, she said. Sounding high. 'Why are you telling me?' I asked. 'Because you weren't fun,' she said. I could hear music in the background. I asked where she was. In the toilet, she said. Dora coked, saying it was all very innocuous really. She jabbered on, the rush apparent. I told her I was thinking of coming back. She ignored me, did party gossip. She told me she was wearing suspenders. I felt her slipping away and thought of my fingerprints on the jerry can.

'Goodbye,' Dora said. I thought she meant for good until she said, 'Call me soon,' and after a long pause, 'I don't like this.' Before I could answer she was gone.

Hoover, Zürich/Brussels, 1942

It was Willi Schmidt, and not Betty Monroe, who turned up to greet my arrival in Switzerland, with Betty's apologies, and not for the last time. He collected me from the airport and took me to the commercial hotel where I would be staying. We drank a coffee and a beer together. I can't remember if he told me his name. He was very tall and smooth-skinned. His fair hair was worn flat in an effort to look older – he told me so. He kept a silver comb in his top pocket. With hindsight Willi reminds me of the rich young men who hung around and drove for the Red Cross in Budapest a couple of years later because it gave them a petrol allowance for their private cars.

Betty I finally met when she interviewed me, more or less formally, in an office above a Zürich florist (funerals a speciality). Betty was in her thirties then but she had the confidence of someone older. Men fought to be in her orbit. She made a great show of letting them know if they were in or out of favor. Betty's smile, when it came, was worth waiting for.

I did a couple of runs for her to Lyon, throwing up from nerves in the train toilet most of each way. I met Willi Schmidt again, in April 1942, on her recommendation. She vouched for us as a way of guaranteeing both sides. 'There's someone I want you to meet. Swiss but charming, and useful.' I was surprised when it turned out to be Willi. We laughed about it.

Willi was attractive company. He had the knack of making you want to be his friend, gave the impression that knowing him could prove useful, and amusing, as Betty had promised. Women were drawn by his thoroughbred ease, with its hint of something darker and more controlling. Willi had a temper which he kept on a tight rein, though he was susceptible to showing it in places with poor service. Willi insisted on the best restaurants.

He liked to speak English because he wanted to live in America, and boasted the best collection of jazz records in the country. Willi could dance, which made him popular.

Willi made out that I entertained him.

But Willi had his down days. He confided that he was frustrated. He derided Switzerland's neutrality. He hinted that he was involved in secret work. I dismissed him for a playboy, while envying his ability to loaf around, to drink and not feel the effects, and his easy manner. By comparison, I felt out of step and restless. The desert had stripped me of my ability to feel comfortable among people, never marked in the first place. So when he leaned forward and asked confidentially how I felt about making a trip back to Belgium, I shrugged and said, 'Why not?'

The job he had for me was working for the family firm. I took his offer at face value, until I saw that my papers would show me as a local representative of Brevecourt's Lisbon office. The irony was not lost on me: Betty Monroe's hand. There were itineraries, meetings and appointments, an official diary. There were tickets and permits showing travel between Lisbon and Brussels and Brussels and Zürich, and books of leather samples. I learned the basics of Willi's trade.

It was during this preparatory period that Willi invited me to join him for dinner. He was seeing someone he thought it would be interesting for me to meet.

Our dinner partner was German, dressed in an exquisitely tailored flannel suit. He was upper class in manner, aristocratic even, a little older than Willi. I assumed from his smooth manner he was a diplomat. I felt gauche and scruffy by comparison. In spite of my travels, I was not sophisticated. The worldly nonchalance I affected fooled no one. Karl-Heinz was civilized and ironic, and when, after too many glasses of wine, I learned he was an SS officer and asked if he was a devout Nazi he smiled and said that he was off-duty and in a neutral country. Willi added: 'Karl-Heinz is a gentleman, and gentlemen are never fanatics.'

I wondered if Betty Monroe knew of Willi's dining partner. I was distracted by Willi in the same way that I had been by Betty, by her imperiousness and her sharpness, and the way she patronised with her assumption that you knew as much as she did, while making it plain that she was indulging you, knowing perfectly well you didn't. Willi's only false note: the occasional use of the silver comb in smart public spaces.

My arrest in Brussels in July 1942 replayed itself for years afterwards in the form of a dream. Always the same dream: being taken from a dark space, escorted by an armed guard. The dark space was the cellar of a large public building, revealed to be a smart hotel. It was wartime but the hotel's guests seemed not to know. None paid us any attention as we marched up the central staircase with its faded expensive Persian carpet. As we made our way down a long empty corridor, an alarm bell rang and the corridor filled with people running the other way. Often in the dream I was aware of this detail being wrong: the actual hotel had been requisitioned and there were no civilian guests. The guard shoved me through a door into a linen-room and locked me in. Down in the courtyard the guests were shot as they ran out of the building, but the linen-room window was open.

The source of this dream was my third trip to Brussels for Willi. The previous two had been unremarkable, banal even, except for the state of my nerves. I learned with painful slowness that survival depended upon a lack of imagination. I learned to walk with my head down – I have little memory of the sky and weather in wartime, until the spring of 1945. The point was what you knew, it was what you didn't know. I learned to look for the warning detail – a counter-movement in a crowd, a sudden crossing of the street, a car reversing – anything that might signal the unexpected. On the first trip I handed an envelope under the table in a station café to a man wearing spectacles which had been repaired at the bridge with tape. The second trip, I left a small wrapped package in a waste-bin in a park. I assumed Willi was using me to make contact with the Belgian Resistance.

On the third occasion I was picked up at the station, just as I was about to depart. Two men in plain-clothes asked to see my papers. The second man was armed. Everyone avoided looking at us as I was led away.

My interrogator was an SS officer, who told me he was based in Paris, with a roaming brief. His favored method of questioning involved strip-searches and lit matches, a practise that he hoped he would not have to extend to me. He gestured towards the bathroom of his suite to indicate that it was in there that these sessions took place.

The tall curtains were always drawn. He smoked incessantly, black tobacco which clogged up the room. I let him see I was scared while trying to hide from myself how scared. I'd had no training to withstand questioning.

Over the next days he grew more familiar. He told me his name was Jaretski and he worked for the DSK, a department of the SS whose purpose was currency control. He was frank about how it worked. Local civilian agents set up illegal sales to entrap anyone attempting transfers of liquid assets. These agents worked to a 10 per cent commission. Jaretski gave me a worldly man-to-man look.

He wanted to know if I knew anything of such operations or whether I had been approached by anyone seeking to take advantage of my commercial position to move money around. He believed I was involved in transferring gold to Switzerland. Of course not, I said. My business was leather.

'Yes, I know,' said Jaretski. He had a habit of sitting back in his chair which made it hard to see his face in the deliberately underlit room. He turned out to be so well informed about me that I remember thinking: Who told him? I began to suspect that my arrest had not been coincidence. Jaretski was much exercised by the fact that a Jewish family, which had previously been in the leather business and traded with Brevecourt, was attempting to move money out of the country and escape to Switzerland. Jaretski wanted to know if I had ever met them.

I told myself that he was fishing. He was acting on partial information, didn't have names. But Jaretski's urbane manner was not reassuring. I suspected it wouldn't be long before we moved into the bathroom.

I escaped as in my dream – fire alarm, linen room – except I was taken by lift rather than the stairs, and there were no guests. The window was open and I clambered along the roof and down the back stairs of another building and walked out onto the rainswept street, minus papers, money or a hat. The only contingency plan was a memorized address in a suburb.

This turned out to be a big detached house in a prosperous district about an hour's walk away. It had a tradesman's side entrance, which I used. A nervous old woman answered then a man came. He was stocky, with a fine head of leonine hair, about fifty and careworn, with deep furrows down the side of his mouth. The old cardigan he had on must have been expensive in its day. He left me in the kitchen then went away and the woman returned and showed me a room in the servants' quarters, which hadn't been used for a long time. She was dressed in widow's black and behaved like a maid but I thought she and the man were related. At one point I heard their raised voices.

Nobody came to fetch me and the rest of the day passed into a strange convalescence. The lower windows were frosted. By standing on the chair it was possible to see a large walled garden with a green pond and a tall poplar beyond. The flowerbeds were untended and the lawn neglected. It stopped raining and two young boys in overcoats came out and stood by the pond and threw stones which separated the green surface scum, showing black water beneath.

Eventually the man came in and handed me an envelope, leaving again before I could open it. Inside was money and a name and a commercial address in central Brussels. I let myself out.

I decided that the man with the leonine hair was the Jewish man Jaretski had questioned me about.

The episode had been like a dream-play where you knew nobody else's lines. The impression was reinforced by several days' hiding in the attic above the commercial address, again in a more or less mute relationship with the middle-aged woman who appeared to be the only person in the office. When I was given a cardboard box I found it contained my papers and even my hat, but not my money.

Willi reacted to my escape with his usual panache. He threw a party. He had a gift for finding out-of-the-way places where noise wasn't a problem. Jazz records, free drink, plenty of women, and a liberal mix of Swiss, Germans and Americans, along with a few suspicious-looking Irishmen rumored to be IRA gun-runners. Willi set me up with a plump, easygoing brunette who performed expert fellatio in the room being used for guests' coats, which had the advantage of a lock. She was a bank teller and up for a good time. The American presence in Switzerland had helped promote pockets of hedonism and Marthe was a willing subscriber.

The surprise of the party was the reappearance of Karl-Heinz, mysteriously there and well-informed. He had been told of my arrest and knew of Jaretski; he described the DSK as a complete racket and a looting machine. The Germans were always strapped for cash and endlessly thinking up money-making schemes, he said, which was why they sucked up to the Swiss so much. The DSK gave the SS a bad name and he reckoned I was lucky to have got away. I should have read more into his look, but I was wondering at the wisdom of Willi telling an SS officer so much about what I was doing.

When I confronted Willi I was angry and drunk, and

for the second time that evening ended up in the coat room with the door locked. Willi told me to relax – my secrets were safer with Karl-Heinz than half the Americans or Swiss he could think to name. Karl-Heinz needed me, Willi said. The Obersturmbahnführer wanted me to run an errand for him.

'Karl-Heinz wants you to deliver a message to Allen Dulles.'

I had trouble making sense of what Willi was saying. I didn't know Dulles then and I couldn't see why Karl-Heinz should want to contact him. 'They are enemies,' I kept repeating. The darting moves made by everybody at the party, including Marthe, confused me. Jaretski's confinement had seemed straightforward by comparison.

In retrospect, I wonder what if the open linen-room window had *not* been an accident – the fire-alarm likewise? There had been no pursuit. Perhaps I had a guardian angel. Jaretski was SS. Karl-Heinz was SS. If Karl-Heinz had an interest in what I was doing he would have found it easy to trace me once it was known I was missing. What did he tell Jaretski? That I was a penetrative SS agent and must be allowed to escape without jeopardizing my cover? And there was Jaretski's line of questioning about the money transactions. Had he been trying to muscle in on connections of which he was aware and of which I was completely ignorant? Had he and Karl-Heinz done a deal over me? Did Jaretski manage to cut in on whatever Karl-Heinz and Willi had been up to?

Looking back, there definitely seems to have been some kind of progression to the sequence. Betty Monroe hired me and subcontracted me to Willi Schmidt, who introduced me to Karl-Heinz and made me the link between Karl-Heinz and Allen Dulles, which took us back to Betty Monroe, who was Dulles's confidante. The more I thought about it, the more I puzzled about Karl-Heinz's role, especially after remembering that my arrest was bookended by my first two meetings with him, both at the instigation of Willi Schmidt.

Nor could I get Frau Schmidt's reason for Willi marrying her out of my head. She was Jewish. Had I read Willi wrong all these years? Maybe even in Budapest when it was rumored he was working for the Nazis, had that been part of a greater deception? I was left wondering if something much more complicated was going on than I had realized.

The trace of patterns not seen before acquires the faintest outline.

Vaughan, Frankfurt

Strasse answered the door himself, very energised. A couple of dark young men came down from upstairs and Strasse kissed them on both cheeks. They glanced at me as they left. They looked like street boys.

Strasse wanted to sit downstairs in the dining room because he was expecting a delivery. The table was covered with stacks of papers and documents: the mess of a still busy man.

The signs were excellent, he said. He questioned me about my credentials and the people I represented. I mentioned Carswell, which earned a sharp look. Strasse knew the name. I said he made documentary films for the Middle-East market and Strasse nodded and said that was probably where he knew it from. 'It's a small world beyond Istanbul.'

I got out my tiny Sony video and asked if he minded my taping us talking. The camera's cute size and novelty value usually overcome most objections. Strasse inspected it, impressed, and commented favourably on the Zeiss lens. He had been something of a photographer himself. He made me go upstairs and film his room so he could see what it looked like on playback. 'If I like what you shoot . . .' he said.

I took some general views and close-ups. 'Make sure you get the rugs,' he called out. It was a pleasant room, bright and sunny. Strasse watched the playback with childish delight. He announced that I could make my recording, providing I made him a present of the camera. He grabbed my shoulder affectionately. I could smell the drink on him. My being there seemed rather pathetic.

But with the camera on he grew mistrustful. I asked how he wanted to be remembered and he said it didn't matter because history always got it wrong.

He made me fetch the phone when it rang and spent several minutes talking in German. The name Carswell was mentioned. Afterwards I asked him what he had said about Carswell and he shrugged for an answer and gave another ten minutes' non-interview. Any request for elaboration was dismissed until eventually he asked what I had been taught about the Second World War. That Germany had lost and the Allies won? That Hitler invaded Poland in September 1939, and killed a lot of Jews from 1942 on? I answered yes on both counts.

'What did they teach you about Jack Philby?' He had to explain that Jack was the father of the spy, Kim. He was starting to enjoy himself; you can see it on the tape. Quote: 'You need to ask yourself what Philby was up to with Allen Dulles in Saudi Arabia in the 1920s, remembering that Dulles became Head of American Intelligence in Switzerland during the war. You need to ask yourself what Dulles's *real* interests were, and those of his brother. You might ask yourself what precisely his brother John Foster knew, if, as we are reliably told, board members of I.G. Farben, the manufacturers of the gas that killed the Jews, were fully informed of all the company's activities. Because, you see, John Foster Dulles was a board member of none other than I.G. Farben, even *after* the start of the war in Europe.'

He sat back, weighing my silence, deciding whether to go on. 'If you want to hear an interesting story, remind Mr Hoover of our visit to the Hotel Maison Rouge in Strasbourg in 1944, and the time we met in Liechtenstein, and get him to tell you who our respective passengers were.' Strasse broke off. It sounded like he was coughing but it was laughter. I had to fetch him a glass of water.

'The Second World War,' he went on, 'was the first properly mechanised war. The first war of the corporate state. I.G. Farben. Krupps. Siemens. Mercedes. Volkswagen. Ford. Standard Oil. General Electric. IBM. Bell. Coca-Cola. The world was and remains a military-industrial complex. Bankers of all sides continued to meet in Switzerland throughout the war. Your computer is faster and cheaper than it was a year, even six months ago. Who do you have to thank for that research? The military. We live in a military world even when it is in civilian clothing. Your Prime Minister Thatcher understood that. Look at her arms deals. You are no doubt familiar with Saddam

Hussein's use of chemical weapons against the Kurds of Iraq. But have you asked yourself who was the first country to use chemical weapons against the Kurds? It was, I am sorry to report, the British. And who trained the Iraqi pilots and made the radio-sets the Iraqis used to bomb the Kurds? Not the Germans, although the gas they used was the gas first developed by I.G. Farben. You see, my friend, we have not even got to the invasion of Poland, and already the world has become a more complicated place.'

I asked him what his interest was in the Kurds. He gave a sly smile. 'This is off the record. Some might argue that the problem with Nazism was that it was destroyed by insufficient ideology – look who's the tough boy of the Middle East now. The Israelis would send the lot of us to hell in a handcart if they had a chance. I have heard it said that Muslim purity and zeal are the true inheritors of Nazism. The Kurds are a fierce and noble race, and there is a certain belief that the next great warrior leader will emerge from among their people.'

I wondered what to make of his ravings. Whatever his medication, it was giving him a big up. He went on to say that history lived was very different from history written. He told me to ask Hoover about the Cold War as a war of ideologies, and as the ultimate cul-de-sac of physics. We were now moving into the age of what Strasse called 'the new biology', a final Biblical phase in which all the old predictions would be realised. Quote: 'What if the Bible is right, and disease and pestilence will win in the end? That outbreak of foot and mouth disease in Europe, was it accidental or assisted? And what if it had been a virus that had killed people: who could say if it was natural or manufactured? Look at our friend Konrad Viessmann's pharmaceutical company – the irresponsible use of drugs and medicine in the treatment of illness in Kurdish refugee camps. They are using untested drugs to treat meningitis. Are you surprised someone burns down one of Herr Viessmann's factories?

'Nostradamus tells us that there is only one Pope left and he'll be the first non-white Holy Father – and get Mr Hoover to tell you about Mr Dulles and the Vatican while he is about it – and then it's all up. And it is shaping very nicely. What if the fundamentalists are right and the United States *is* Satan? Perhaps we will see that hot wind of retribution coming from the East. The son of Saladin and the spirit of the Waffen SS – riding shotgun – come to teach those Jewboys their final lesson, as some of our more extremist brethren might say. And why do I tell you this? Because I am ready to write history. Remember – I saw it from both sides. *And one side was as bad as the other.* I was Heinrich Himmler's envoy, but the CIA required me to do things that a man should not be asked to do. There's an irony. The Nazis never asked me to teach interrogation methods to anyone.'

Strasse's Nazi masterclass. I reckoned I had the measure of him. He could make equations all round his subject but when it came down to what the Nazis did he ducked and resurfaced somewhere else.

We were interrupted by the doorbell. I offered to go

but he insisted on going himself, struggling to stand then shuffling painfully to the door. He said it would be his delivery. It wasn't. It was Hoover.

There had apparently been a misunderstanding over when Hoover was supposed to turn up. Strasse said, 'I am just talking to my friend here.' Hoover looked pissed off, asked how long we were going to be, and was told fifteen, twenty minutes. Strasse suggested he join us. Hoover shook his head and said he was going to lie down. 'Take your time, Karl-Heinz, and tell it like it was. I'm going to be in your spare bedroom.' To me he said, 'I hope you haven't got me on that camera of yours.'

It took Strasse a while to get his rhythm back. He sounded both uncertain and boastful, saying that his story needed Murdoch rather than Springer. It needed a world market. He started to get muddled then, confusing me with a journalist from *The Times*. He asked me to get him a schnapps and his pills – half-a-dozen bottles on a tray. He took a stiff belt of liquor and a different coloured pill from each bottle, giving each a look of disgust before swallowing.

'We need the surprise of the English language. There are no surprises in German – no little bombs hidden in sentences. It is the language of premeditation, order and command. Look at General Stoop's reports for the destruction of the Warsaw ghetto. The language of genocide is no more emotional than the settling of any accounts.

'You see, I am in the end a fanatic, not a crackpot fanatic, but one who believes in inevitability and destiny, the weight of history. Everything I will tell you will come to pass. I won't be alive to see it, but I would like people to be able to point to what I said and know I was right. The auspices are good.'

Hoover's voice came down from upstairs. 'Are you bullshitting that boy, Karl-Heinz?'

Karl-Heinz threw up his hands in camp horror. 'Have your rest!'

'Tell him what you told me about the man he's working for,' shouted Hoover.

'Carswell? What about him?' I asked.

Strasse ignored the question and said, 'I can see you are both inquisitive and horrified, which is how it should be. This is not comfortable stuff we will be dealing with. The truth never is, as the old cliché goes. Is "old cliché" a tautology? There are areas where my English is not quite up to the job.'

Strasse moved into overdrive, speed-hopping between subjects. 'Willi was worried about what would happen when the leather ran out. He was doing a lot of research into synthetics. Imagine the money to be made from inventing a leather substitute in 1943!'

Strasse's voice suddenly began to slur and fade. I asked him to explain Willi Schmidt's name and career change into pharmaceuticals. Strasse did his familiar big shrug. 'We believed Willi was dead because the Amis said he was. Body identified by Betty Monroe. If Willi wasn't dead and the Amis said he was, it follows that they had something in mind for him.'

Strasse lost his thread and resurfaced after a silence to announce that since his stroke – 'Stroke! What kind of word is that? Stroke is what you do to a woman!' – he had suffered a debility that had messed up his immune system. He was on steroids and pills for diabetes, and he shouldn't drink but he did. 'And what do they ask me to do, these people who think they are running the show? They ask me to answer the phone. There's a consignment coming in on Tuesday, a shipment going out on Wednesday. Blah blah!'

When I asked what kind of shipments, he banged the table and said: 'People! The Party was in the people business sixty years ago. It practically invented mass tourism! What was a trip to Auschwitz in 1942 if not the ultimate package holiday? And the Party is still in the people business. I will spell it out to the backward boy. The Nazis never went away. They just took off their uniforms. The Third Reich judiciary became the civilian judiciary. Law courts stuffed full of hanging judges! The camp doctors got jobs in the universities. Does the name von Verscheur mean anything to you? No? He was the mentor of Dr Mengele, the Auschwitz doctor, and a leading exponent of racial hygiene. 1951, appointed Professor of Human Genetics at the University of Münster where he built one of the largest centres for genetic research in West Germany. The police force? The army? Where did they recruit from? And the ones for whom it got a little hot under the collar – why not a Mercedes posting? The Third Reich might have failed, but Mercedes conquered the world, like Japan and Sony. While the Amis crapped it away in Saigon, had the morale sucked out of them, who made the taxis that took them to and from their brothels and opium dens? Mercedes. Germany is as discreetly Nazi as it always was. Only Dr Goebbels has been removed from the equation. We have learned to do without publicity.'

He gave a hard laugh and I hit him with a switch of subject, asking about the people smuggling. Was it true that by controlling the distribution, you also controlled the flow?

'Of course! You make money from the process and you keep the streets clean at the same time! But I tell you, my friend, if it was as simple as that, it would be—'

The doorbell went again. 'Special delivery,' he said, relishing the phrase. He refused to let me help him up and slowly made his way across the shiny wooden floor and fumbled with the latch.

Some special delivery. There was a sudden movement towards Strasse's head, a blur of brown – the arm of a leather jacket, you realise on playback – followed by a dry noise, perhaps the driest sound I have ever heard. Then the back of Strasse's head exploded in a bouquet of blood and brain matter, one of the wettest sounds I have ever heard; it reminded me of watching a water melon being dropped from a window onto the street below. Strasse's shooting was like reality TV, my objectivity sustained by watching it on the little camera screen: Strasse's opening of the door matched by the upward swing of the gunman's arm, the blue-black of the gun in his fist, followed by an explosion where the back of Strasse's head was a second before. This was accompanied by a surprisingly sweet smell.

I was halfway up the stairs while the gunman – dark-haired, moustache, leather jacket, probably no more than five eight, but broad, and me trying to remember if I recognised him from the paper yard – was administering the *coup de grâce* with a bullet behind the ear, though Strasse looked like his lights were out already, and all the while gazing calmly at me.

I stumbled at the top of the stairs, like silly girls do in horror films. I could hear the gunman quietly close the door and his soft footsteps. By then my physical response to what I had just witnessed had become entirely predictable. My legs refused to work and my mind revved uselessly, trying to project my body into action that it would not achieve. I found myself crawling on all fours down the landing hoping to throw myself out of a window, praying that it would not be too far to the ground. I used the doorway to lever myself up. The only noise I could hear was the panic of my own body. The gunman swung round the top of the stairs, looking composed and remorseless, and devoid of any imagination while my own leaped all over the place, trying to realise that the sight of that corridor might be one of the last things I would see. The small part of my brain still functioning reckoned I had less than thirty seconds to come to terms with the meaning of eternity.

I made it through the doorway. Maybe I remembered

seeing them from the outside a split-second before they registered: the upstairs windows had grilles and were all locked up. Outside: greenery, sunshine and a light breeze ruffling the leaves. (In the last glimpse I'd had of him, Strasse's head had landed in a patch of slanting sunlight.) I wanted to hide under the bed until it all went away. When the man came through the door I had my arms out and was shaking like I was doing St Vitus's dance. I wanted to hit him with a barrage of words, stop him in his tracks, but not a sound came out. The camera was stuck to my hand, still filming, its red light on. My mind did all kinds of flips around the notion that it would carry on working and I would not. The gunman barely glanced at the camera. He stepped through the door, paused and raised his arm. His expression was flat, his eyes disinterested. (Still I couldn't decide if he was one of the men from the paper yard. I badly wanted to know, more than I had wanted to know anything ever before. Why kill Karl-Heinz? He was as good as dead anyway, and I wasn't ready to join him.) The man's indifference restored a modicum of dignity. My final reaction was one of anger at finding myself being dispatched by a bored mechanic. Fuck you, I wanted to tell him. So much for thoughts of eternity.

I must have shut my eyes because I missed what happened. The man grunted and when I looked he was falling down. My first thought was that by some extraordinary collision of events he'd had a heart attack at the very moment he was about to shoot me, that whatever prayer my brain had been trying to formulate had been answered.

In fact reality shifted again. In the space of less than a minute, since Strasse had fatally opened the door, events had tumbled through several unimaginable stages, perhaps most of all for the man with the gun, now lying on the floor having been hit over the back of the head with a brass lamp-stand by Hoover. He had been standing behind the door. The gunman's eyes were still rolling up and showing a lot of white when Hoover put a bullet in his head, around the same spot that the gunman had put one in Strasse's, while I tried to grasp that the bullet had been meant for me, and that my life had just been saved by an old man I had taken for a fool.

The gunman was doing death twitches and the camera recorded his final mortal seconds by chance. The camera shook – not surprisingly. Hoover sounded dry and ironic, like he had found himself in a situation he hadn't expected to be in again. 'Well, nephew, it looks like time to leave. Don't worry. Normal service has been resumed.'

He checked Karl-Heinz and pronounced him dead. He told me to wipe anything clean I might have touched. Then to look around upstairs and downstairs and take anything that looked like it might be useful – floppy disks, notebooks, Karl-Heinz's maps. He said there was no rush, we had plenty of time. 'Be systematic. Be thorough.' I obeyed like an automaton.

Hoover, Frankfurt

Several things I never got around to discussing with Karl-Heinz. I never got to talk to him about Frau Schmidt, which was one reason for calling round. He was telling the English boy his life-story. Which version? I wondered as I hauled myself upstairs. My insomnia had gotten worse. The European version was even more debilitating than the American kind. (English boy; he's in his thirties, so I should stop calling him that.)

I was dreaming when the doorbell went, but I was fully awake for the second shot – hand gun, silencer – and was up and waiting behind the door, a tight squeeze, with a bedside table in the way. The drawer was empty. I was hoping it was where Karl-Heinz kept his Luger. Vaughan crashed into the room like a cornered animal, in big contrast to the soft pad of the man following. They looked like they were acting out an experiment on speed and momentum in relation to life expectancy. The momentum was all with the second man, likewise the shots. The fluttery way Vaughan waved his hands: a moth hitting a light.

It's not often you get to play guardian angel. I kind of liked being able to surprise the man so soon after what he had done to Karl-Heinz, an exercise in poetic justice. The shooter obliged by folding up from the one hit – brass ornamental lamp-stand to the base of the skull. I silently thanked Karl-Heinz for his heavy taste. Had he bought plastic we would have been in trouble. Vaughan performed petrified's equivalent to several double-takes.

The gun was snug in my hand. Two head shootings in as many minutes was not what Vaughan had been thinking about over his breakfast, which I could hear him losing in the en suite. He emerged not so much white as fish-slab gray.

Do we trust each other? Do we understand each other? We have embarked on what Naomi would call a steep learning curve, and from the shaky expression on Vaughan's face it was one he would have given anything to get off. And at my age you don't expect to have to kill a man. It was such a surprise I felt nothing at all, except a vague déjà vu. As for Karl-Heinz, maybe he had a split second in which to feel relieved that he was being given a quick exit instead of the direction he was headed, which, by the time his body was done, would have been slow, nasty and stripped him of the last of his dignity.

We left carrying stuff. Vaughan sounded asthmatic. We went out by a side door in the garden wall. It was a beautiful day. The Englishman had gone very quiet. His first pertinent question came in a café where we went to reacquaint ourselves with normality. He wanted to know what

Karl-Heinz had said about Carswell. I told him there was a rumor he was an arms dealer. Vaughan nodded the hopeful nod of a man who didn't really understand the equation. Carswell plus x over y equals what? He looked desperate to hijack someone else's life. Two pretty women walked past the café's big window and Vaughan watched from the wrong side of the glass. I got that old 1942–3 feeling, the one where you tried too hard to make it look like you belonged.

The book I had been sent in Florida was about a man whose secret wartime work had resulted in him being identified later by his undercover role. He ended up being hunted because his pursuer thought he was the man he had been pretending to be. If there was a similar connection, it meant we were dealing with some obscure aspect of the past, some secret so deep that to uncover it would bring instant retribution. I had a bad feeling that Karl-Heinz had got himself killed because of something we both knew.

Vaughan, Frankfurt/Strasbourg

The second bad news of the day was finding Dominic Carswell in my hotel room. I said hello, assuming he was there as a friend, then 'Fuck' when I saw he was with one of the Neos, going through my things. Carswell smiled, which translated as: You have caught me out but I'll still have you for breakfast. We all froze then I ran fast-forward out of the hotel. Double fuck.

I lost them not through any skill – no chase through the streets, no pounding suspense. I simply ran until my lungs were raw, ducked left and right a couple of times, went in the front and out the back of a café, looked round and found no one following.

Hoover was in his hotel checking out. He made a crack about my condition, but didn't even register surprise. I had been supposed to be collecting my bag and had turned up breathless and empty-handed. Hoover seemed to have elevated himself to some plane of super-calm. His hand was steady as he signed his bill. He had decided we should leave town for a while, so I was to drive him to Zürich, he said. Frau Schmidt had sent him an old photograph from the war, he went on, showing him with Karl-Heinz and Willi. He was suspicious because he hadn't said where he was staying, plus she had told him she had no photos. 'I keep getting sent stuff I haven't asked for.

'You can drive,' he said, yawning. 'While I get some shuteye in the back.'

Hire car. Autobahn. No speed limit. I drove as fast as I could, to put distance between us and Karl-Heinz. And Carswell. And the Neos. Hoover slept while I pushed us into a zone where I no longer felt safe or in control, thinking: He should not have let me drive.

Hoover had an old man's hands, with liver spots and ancient purple veins. They had calmly picked up the gun that had just shot Strasse and used it on his assassin.

We made the third news bulletin on the car radio. Double shooting in Frankfurt: details to follow. On the evening TV news there were shots of Karl-Heinz's house marked off with police tape and a cautious statement from an officer who looked more like a university lecturer, describing Karl-Heinz as a businessman, which made Hoover snort. The dead gunman was named as a Turkish military officer. It was thought that the shootings had been carried out by what the newsreader coyly referred to as a Middle-East terrorist organisation.

The dead man's wallet, which Hoover had taken, told us little. Some money, a family photograph of a wife and two small children, a Turkish driving licence with an Ankara address.

In Strasbourg Hoover insisted we stayed at the Hotel Maison Rouge. I remembered Karl-Heinz mentioning the place just before he died. Small world, I remarked. Hoover grunted, his usual response. He stood looking for a long time at the old stained-glass medieval scenes on the stair windows and eventually said he remembered them from before. The view from my window showed the town much the same, an old city of steep roofs and sonorous bells.

Hoover wanted to eat at a restaurant he remembered from 1945. I thought the chances of it still being there were remote, but it was, down in the old quarter, on a bridge by the river. Like most of the buildings it had been standing for several hundred years and looked set to last another few centuries. The district was one of impassive and unfussy burgher prosperity. The restaurant was crowded with frighteningly normal people. We were shown to a table on a covered terrace with a view back up the river. Below was another dining platform at water level.

It reminded Hoover of Switzerland, he said. Like the Swiss, the natives of Strasbourg – stuck as they were between the Germans and the French, who both made claims on them – had realised the tactical advantage of burying any difference of opinion and reinvesting that energy into the solid returns of trade. Hoover suggested we should order pork knuckle in honour of Karl-Heinz's memory.

We pretended everything was normal, circling each other warily. I taped him secretly, not for any investigative purposes, more because the act of switching the tape recorder on and off made me feel less blank. Men his age didn't use guns. What the fuck had Carswell been doing in my room?

Of me Hoover said: 'You certainly subscribe to declining standards in the dress code, and I figure you're anti-corporate, anti-authority, anti-marriage. Maybe you find it hard to settle down, through a lack of application. You're straight, not gay, bi- maybe, but I doubt it. You have got some sort of a problem but I haven't figured out what yet. Perhaps you find it hard to commit?'

Six out of ten, I told him, and asked about him and Elvis Presley like Strasse had told me to. Both of us were happy to avoid any reference to the day's events.

Hoover, after a bottle and a half of wine, his voice holding steady, delivered his companion-piece to Karl-Heinz's rant. Quote: 'Whatever he said, Karl-Heinz was exaggerating. He usually did. And while we're on the subject, let me put the record straight. I did not recruit Karl-Heinz, merely lent the hand that enabled him to cross over.

'The thing with the Nazis was simple. We were in their country and when the war was over it was better they were with us than against us. It wasn't a moral choice. We needed them against the Russians. We also figured even after you had cut off the head there would be a lot of body left. So we recruited what was left of the head and bought everyone else off.

'We hit them with the one thing we had more of than

anyone else. Consumer culture. We colonised their subconscious and we did it very well. Money was no problem and there were plenty of unaccountable budgets. We hired from American families who maintained good social contacts and were well-connected to museums and galleries. We had worked out that the star system developed by Hollywood – the cult of the enhanced individual – would come to apply to other areas, even high culture. The argument was how far the system should extend. Wine and cheese parties with rich philanthropists who could be persuaded to endorse and buy a tacitly sponsored product, and realise a profit, was a very different proposition from the more volatile and unpredictable world of popular culture. Modern art was sniggered at, though accommodated as a necessary evil. Completely out of the question was any of that swivel-hipped nigger music.

'But there were rogue departments whose book-keeping flummoxed even internal auditing, and a clear phenomenon called rock and roll was waiting to be exploited. A few of the more enlightened spooks realised it was a more powerful weapon than all the rest put together, especially if it were broadcast directly into Soviet Russia.

'Rock and roll was pure American propaganda. It spoke of freedom, movement, opportunity and choice, however much it whined about "Since my baby left me". It was also an early collaboration between the spooks and the mob, which controlled the juke-boxes and radio airplay. So we gave them pop radio, jungle rhythms, and abroad the Voice of America – the emasculation and repackaging of black culture for a white mass market. Elvis Presley was its paradigm: the perfect image and the perfect double-bind, simultaneously empowered and impotent. We subsidised him, created him and promoted him. We knew Tom Parker didn't have a passport and was an illegal entrant, so we had him by the balls. When they got scared upstairs that we might have let the genie out of the bottle they sent Presley off to the army. It was rumoured but never proved that James Jesus Angleton, that high don of counter-intelligence and paranoia, and product of Malvern College, England, was responsible for the drafting of Private 53310761, having belatedly discovered that certain of his employees had been responsible for advancing the young man's career. At the same time, the propaganda value of putting Presley into the army and sending him to Germany was not lost on him. Presley the patriot was an endorsement of American values, and also a product of his country. So they took him out of the picture, channelled wildness into duty, and also had the boy perform one of the great ambassadorial trips of the Cold War.'

Hoover carried on in his semi-mysterious manner, getting drunker, letting me see that there was plenty of ironic space between the performance and the reality. I took this to mean that, given my failure to amuse him, he was going to amuse himself. I was left wondering how you got from Elvis Presley to the familiar use of handguns.

'Do you believe any of this stuff?' he asked.

I didn't. His response was, 'If it was there to control, we controlled it because if we didn't, someone else did.'

When we left the restaurant Hoover wanted to walk up to the next bridge. The cool night air sobered him and he grew silent. The river divided under the bridge, part of it forced into a tight, angry channel where it went into a mill-race. Hoover pointed at the surging foam and said, 'That's where I last saw Willi Schmidt. That's where Willi died.' He gestured back down the river to the lights of the restaurant. 'And where we ate was where Willi and I went before it happened.'

He stared at the churning water and suddenly looked tired and too old to bother. He repeated that he had been standing there and watched Willi being swept away, and for that reason was reluctant to entertain Karl-Heinz's theory of Schmidt's resurrection as Konrad Viessmann.

He shrugged when I asked what had happened and just said, 'He fell in the fucking river.'

He was being dragged back into Willi's past, he said, and therefore his own, whether he wanted it or not. It would only be when he fully understood Willi that he would understand the blanks in his own life. 'And I am sure they are gaps that will tell me things I would rather not know.'

'Why not leave it alone?'

'Because I'll be dead soon and it's about time I knew.' He looked up from the river and said, 'And I'd like to die in my own bed.' He didn't speak all the way back to the hotel.

Vaughan, Zürich

Frau Schmidt was not alone. She was with one of those little old guys who has ended up resembling a tortoise. He wore a white cap, even indoors, and large black-framed glasses with strong lenses which magnified his eyes. He had no colour or dress sense and was wearing polyester trousers, a clashing sports shirt and an orange jacket. The cap had an Aertex vent at the back.

Hoover seemed wrongfooted by the man's presence. His name was Sol and he made a point of not shaking hands. He also said hello to Hoover like he already knew and disliked him. Hoover gave him a who-the-fuck-are-you? look. Sol said, with a crackle of dislike, 'I've been waiting for you.'

When Frau Schmidt went off to make coffee, Sol asked if I knew Zürich. He spoke correct English with a strong accent which turned him into a joke that was probably calculated. Whatever was going on, Hoover said nothing as Sol and I made tea-party conversation.

Frau Schmidt came back and motioned us around her

dining table. It felt like playing bridge with no cards.

'Do we know each other?' Hoover asked Sol for openers and got a look that said that it was up to him to remember. Sol whipped his cap up like it was a lid and quickly passed his hand across his bald scalp.

I decided to kick-start proceedings.

'Just who the fuck was Willi Schmidt?'

According to Sol, Willi Schmidt had been running a wartime escape line for Jews, as early as 1942, with the knowledge and co-operation of Karl-Heinz and Hoover.

Hoover said, 'Not me. I was a go-between for Karl-Heinz and the Zionists in 1944, but 1942 was too early.'

Sol addressed himself to me. 'By 1944 it was expedient for the upper echelons of the SS to start laying down plans for postwar survival.'

Sol was keen to prove Hoover's involvement with Willi and Karl-Heinz's business from the start. He claimed that Hoover had been the link man in an escape line for Belgian Jews to Switzerland.

Hoover and Sol looked at each other. Hoover said, 'Did you send me the Jaretski obituary? And the photograph of me with Willi and Karl-Heinz?'

Sol ignored him and said to me, 'Offering this service in 1942 was extremely far-sighted, and dangerous, and these three righteous men deserved to be congratulated on their boldness.'

Hoover asked carefully, 'Does this have anything to do with Karl-Heinz getting killed?'

It took a while for that to sink in. 'Herr Strasse is dead?' Frau Schmidt asked slowly. 'When?'

Hoover reached round into the back of his jacket, took out the gunman's gun and put it on the table.

'Did Willi order Karl-Heinz to be shot?' he asked.

'Shot?' she echoed. 'Willi's dead.'

Hoover picked up the gun and levelled it at Frau Schmidt's head. 'Now tell me you were married to Willi.'

Frau Schmidt started shaking. Sol watched Hoover with a caustic expression and said, 'Put the gun down. It's true. Willi was never married.'

'And this is a scam to get his money, is it?' asked Hoover, replacing the gun on the table. Old man as thug.

Sol turned his palms up and shrugged. 'And of course you know nothing about any of it because you were just a courier.'

'I was the mailman. I never read the message.'

Sol gave him a beady stare. 'Messengers didn't normally enjoy such protection.'

Sol seemed to know Hoover's biography better than Hoover himself. Whether this was Hoover's selective memory or an old man's forgetfulness was hard to say, but occasionally his face betrayed signs of someone watching the lines being drawn between the dots of his life. Hoover claimed that the point of his job had been to connect other people without making connections himself; Sol was determined to show patterns that proved him wrong. He described how what he called 'the tight triangle of Willi, Karl-Heinz and Hoover' had developed an interesting offshoot when Hoover had become Karl-Heinz's messenger to Allen Dulles in Bern. Hoover shrugged and said that the war had made for strange bedfellows.

Sol's history lesson: different sides talked in wartime even when they were supposed not to – '*especially* when they were supposed not to,' Hoover corrected. But he refused to admit that it was through Dulles that he had got a job with the Red Cross in 1942.

Sol said, 'You were placed in the job by Dulles so he could use you to speak to the SS.' He looked at me and said, 'Grey men in grey areas.'

Hoover said he could no longer remember. 'You live with the fiction until the fiction becomes fact.'

'And who was your contact in the Red Cross?' asked Sol.

Hoover saw the question coming and deflated visibly. 'It was Willi Schmidt.'

'Willi got around, didn't he?'

'Willi had wangled himself an executive post with the Red Cross. He said it was for the perks.' Hoover sounded like a man who had suddenly ceased to believe a story he had learned by heart.

'What happened then?' asked Sol. Hoover was starting to sweat from the little man's sarcasm.

His first task, he said, had been to go house-hunting in Austria for the Red Cross, with instructions to find a small estate for use as a distribution centre. He couldn't remember much about it, apart from Willi and Karl-Heinz turning up at the inn where he had been staying.

'Coincidence?' asked Sol.

'I would have told Willi where I was. I think Karl-Heinz was on leave. He was in his best civilian clothes.'

Sol gave a sour smile. 'While you were enjoying your well-dressed freedom I was in concentration-camp stripes. It was where I first met Willi Schmidt and Obersturmbannführer Strasse.' Seeing my surprise, he explained. 'How else would a poor Jew meet a nice young Swiss boy in Austria in 1942, except through the SS?'

Sol had been one of the more 'privileged' prisoners, as a researcher in the science wing. 'I graduated top of my year, and they put me on the fast track, ha ha.' He looked at Hoover. 'You still don't recognise me?'

'Should I?'

Sol told Hoover to describe the place he had acquired. Hoover could remember a tower and some outbuildings. He had only made the one trip.

'There was another time,' said Sol. 'We spent the best part of a day in each other's company.'

'That doesn't mean I remember,' said Hoover.

Sol turned to me. 'He collected me and we drove to a barn near the Swiss border. At night we crossed the border on foot and he left me at a farm.'

Hoover got there at last. 'The crossing was upstream from a blown-up bridge, a hidden ford which we had to walk several miles to reach. You slipped as we were crossing and got one leg wet, and on the Swiss side you had to wring your trousers out. That's all I can recollect. That and the fact that you made so much noise I was sure we were going to get shot by a border patrol.' He shrugged and asked, 'What made you so indispensable?'

'Synthetics,' said Sol.

Willi Schmidt's leather substitute. Hoover wanted to know how Sol had got around Nazi laws preventing Jews from higher study. By going to Denmark in 1934: by the time the Nazis got there in 1940 his work was considered important enough for sponsorship by an eminent German academic. Ways were found for him to carry on in dusty rooms at the top of out-of-the-way stairs. Once finished, the thesis was appropriated, published under his sponsor's name, and Sol taken away. The academic had gone on to enjoy a distinguished postwar career in the United States, with the protection of the American government, developing space suits for NASA.

On Karl-Heinz's first summons, Sol had been so scared of being shot he had to be carried into the room by his guards, only to find Karl-Heinz and Willi in shirtsleeves, lounging around an overheated office drinking real coffee and smoking. They offered him his own research team under their protection.

But the job had brought little security. Neither Karl-Heinz nor Willi were around much, and rivalries among camp staff accounted for much spoiling of others' pet schemes. Sol had eventually reported his fears to Karl-Heinz, finding him more generous than Willi.

'Willi might have saved Jews,' Sol said, 'but business was business.'

Hoover added, managing a little irony of his own, 'The

combination of profit incentive and neutrality is always a dangerous one. You and your team were moved to the house I had found?'

Sol nodded. 'I was afraid to leave the camp. It seemed more secure than the unknown, and when they took away our uniforms and set us up in this place with fields all around we didn't know what to think. All we were told was that anyone trying to leave would be shot.'

Willi had turned up casually to announce that they would be working under something resembling regular conditions. But the peace of their surroundings only fed their anxiety. After one of Sol's team hanged himself, Willi and Karl-Heinz lost interest and the project was dismantled. When the others were taken off, Sol was made to wait behind. Then Hoover came. His arrival, Sol believed, was a sign he was about to be killed.

'But it wasn't,' said Hoover. 'My guess is Karl-Heinz wanted you alive, as a character witness, should the need arise.'

Sol said, 'Up to a point.' He looked at me and said, 'But why don't we show your friend what you and Willi were *really* up to in the war . . .'

Hoover, Zürich-Porrentruy

Sol had someone he wanted me to meet and somewhere he wanted to show us, a drive away. The little man enjoyed playing ringmaster and obviously derived pleasure from his grudges. It was equally plain that he had a nasty surprise in store.

Old habits kicked in: eyes open, mouth shut. I could see I was doing nothing to alleviate Vaughan's suspicions by exercising my right to remain silent.

Sol arranged for us to collect another man, introduced only as Jean-Pierre, from a downtown hotel. He was in his sixties, too young to have been in the war. He had curling grey hair, an imposing manner and wore an enviably smart cashmere overcoat. I thought of Willi and Karl-Heinz – both handsome, both dressers. They had the sharp air of men ahead of their time, men who dabbled with new and dangerous medicine, and made up the rules as they went along. I was different, much more the watcher.

Sol said our trip would take a couple of hours. Jean-

Pierre was keen to catch the late flight back to Brussels. He had been waiting for us, like Sol. In spite of his demeanor and firm handshake there was something missing in his eyes.

He was from Belgium, apparently, which made us fellow countrymen, in origin at any rate. I don't know why I spoke to him in French as he spoke good English and I have always had a problem with my first language. It reminded me of a petit bourgeois upbringing sooner forgotten, a deleted period, summarised by a single image of the crooked stairs of my childhood, with me standing at the bottom, one hand on the newel post, looking up into the dark.

Jean-Pierre talking about himself was like watching a slowly developing photograph. I don't know at what point I decided I had spent time in the house of his childhood, had in fact seen him: two boys in overcoats in a soggy garden throwing stones into a pond, a tall poplar in the background. The image was of course conditional. I had no idea if the boy I saw grew up to be the man in the car. But it was not impossible, in a world of assignation, that the owner of the house had been his father and the man Jaretski had questioned me about.

Part of me didn't want to know if he had been the son of the man in the house, because I could guess only too well what had happened. We avoided the word 'Jewish'. He talked about growing up in Brussels. He could not remember much about it. Most of his early memories had also been erased. In the first instance his had been a charmed and enviable upbringing compared to mine: the lash of the belt, the beating frenzy because I had wet myself. The terror of release; hence, perhaps, Dr Freud, the attraction of a life of secrecy.

Growing up in Liège there had been stories among us kids of a man who disemboweled children, and we all believed in him. From my convalescent bed – I was a sickly child – I could see into the back room of a house opposite in which a man lived and apparently never left. Mostly his curtains were drawn. The few times they stayed open he stood staring at me. I decided he was the murderer – even though I also suspected my father. After one particularly bad beating, I went down to the police station and denounced the man in the window over the way as the child murderer.

Since the murders were a myth, the police were bemused, and I was put down as a troublemaker.

When I was taken home, I expected the worst. There was the indignity of being collected by my mother, then the terror of anticipating my father's reaction. And yet. I am still not sure what lesson I learned from the incident – the value of deflection, perhaps, and of identifying another target. My father, I was sure, would be beside himself with rage. And yet. Perhaps he recognised something in me which conditioned him too: a profound deviousness. God only knew what dreams lurked in his head. He beat me, but perfunctorily, and we both knew it. He told me I had been right to be wary of the man in the window across the way because he was a Jew. I felt both vindicated and shamed. So, a confession of sorts: whatever Jean-Pierre's fate had been, I was complicit.

I had to ask Vaughan to stop the car. I said I was feeling sick from the road and needed air. His look at me in the driving mirror asked: guilty conscience?

A meadow sloped away from the side of the road, down to a thick belt of firs. The grass was dry and crackled underfoot. Vaughan stayed up on the crest by the car, leaning on its bonnet. Sol I couldn't see.

Jean-Pierre walked in the same direction, some distance away from me. We met at the end of the meadow. There was birdsong. High white clouds raced above us, yet on the ground there was barely a breeze. A cattle bell sounded off in the distance.

Jean-Pierre said we must be very close to the border. When he and his family had crossed into Switzerland from France in the summer of 1942 the boundary had been marked.

He had not been aware of what 'Jewish' meant until the Nazi invasion of 1940, then only vaguely. By the time of their escape he still had no proper understanding of the reasons for their flight, apart from what it was costing his father. He knew about this because his mother, for want of anyone else to confide in, had told him. She had called him her little man. He had offered to remain behind to save money.

They had crossed France traveling on local transport, which had taken days. I had made the same sort of journey myself, trying to look like a man of limited horizons, used to traveling only small distances. In spite of their parents' tension, Jean-Pierre and his brother had managed to turn the journey into an adventure.

Their border crossing had been at a spot much like the one where we were standing, with a slope and trees like those below. By then Jean-Pierre and his brother were flagging and scared of the dark. He had clear memories of the final hike and luggage being abandoned. His father had taken them by the hand for the last stage, repeating all the while that they were climbing to freedom. Their guide had handed them over to another on the Swiss side who had taken them to an empty house in nearby woods where they had stayed several days. There his father had announced they were safe at last. The Swiss, he said, were a good people, tolerant and not warlike.

At this point Jean-Pierre broke down and was inconsolable. He waved me away and I left, hoping to save him embarrassment.

We returned to the car separately. Vaughan was standing with his hands in his pockets. Sol was in the car, unreadable as ever.

We drove in silence to a small, typical Swiss town, solid, prosperous and unchanging. It seemed to have a special significance for Jean-Pierre, who grew more restless and anxious.

Sol directed Vaughan to a street at the top of a hill in the old town. Where two roads joined stood a tiny square, little more than a widening in the road with a chestnut tree and parking for a few cars. We stopped and got out. Jean-Pierre stood silently for a long time.

Finally he said, 'It was the Feast of the Assumption. From the window I could see the procession in the street. The nun had told us when my brother asked.'

Sol pointed at an elegant grey building in Early Baroque, more secular than religious, surrounded by a high wall, and asked, 'Is that the convent?'

Jean-Pierre nodded. I looked at Sol, figuring it was time for an explanation, but Sol was still riding the mystery.

The convent was not locked. Big wooden doors with heavy handles opened to reveal a long, cool hallway. Nobody was around. A smell of lavender polish hung in the air. Vaughan seemed uncomfortable in religious surroundings. Sol gave me a nasty smile.

Eventually Jean-Pierre found a caretaker, an old woman bent from arthritis, who kept her eyes averted as she muttered that the nuns were in retreat and unavailable. Jean-Pierre, previously polite, turned cold. 'Isn't God's mansion always open to His humble sinners, madame?'

She mumbled something incomprehensible. Jean-Pierre started banging open the doors lining the corridor. Shafts of evening sunlight spilled onto the dark floor. The caretaker flapped her arms and told him to stop, then scuttled off.

I was trying not to guess what this might be about, afraid that my own understanding would be brought into question. I was sure now that what Jean-Pierre was looking for in those rooms implicated me, as Sol well knew.

The nuns were sitting in the refectory in silence, about twenty of them, white-habited, at three tables positioned at right angles, as in portraits of the Last Supper. They were staring at Jean-Pierre. He told them his name and said, 'I have come to speak to someone who was here in 1942.'

For all their reaction, he might as well have not existed. They appeared quite intractable.

'I am staying here until someone speaks to me,' he said, louder. 'I will shame you into talking.'

He moved into the space between the tables, directly asking the older nuns if they remembered him from 1942. None answered. Sol watched with grim intensity. Vaughan gave me a shrug to say he didn't know what was going on. The nun in charge finally spoke and told us we must leave as nothing could interfere with their retreat.

'And if we don't,' said Jean-Pierre, 'will the police come, like the last time? A Jewish boy in a Catholic convent, now there's a fine thing. And what a welcome you bitches gave!'

There was a collective intake of breath. Jean-Pierre said if anyone spoke up he would make a large donation to a charity of their choice. When that drew no response he picked on the senior nuns at the top table, asking if any had a conscience. Finally an old sister stood up and shouted, 'Enough!' This drew a flurry of whispers and the Mother Superior banged a bell on the table, like a judge bringing a court to order. She called for silence and ordered the sister to sit down. In a clear act of willed disobedience, the old nun refused and walked out.

She led us to one of the rooms off the corridor and locked the door. 'Do you remember me?' Jean-Pierre asked and, eyes cast down, she admitted she did. She was about my age but her face remained unlined. All the nuns at table had been round-faced, well-fed and complacent. A life of contemplation clearly did wonders for the complexion.

Loud bangings on the door were followed by different voices ordering the sister out, one telling her, ridiculously, that it was against regulations to be in a locked room with men. Jean-Pierre opened the door and swore. His language appeared to electrify the nuns.

On relocking the door, Jean-Pierre said to the sister, 'I don't have long. Let me remind you. My family and I came to Switzerland from Belgium in 1942, seeking asylum, but when my father tried to register with the local authorities, we were detained. My mother, brother and I were taken here where we spent some days locked up in the roof, next door to your bells, which rang every quarter and made sleep impossible. Such was the consideration shown us by the Holy Sisters.'

The sister nodded and said she had brought their meals. Jean-Pierre told her to tell us what had happened. She would not speak until he squeezed her arm hard. Her hands shook. She whispered, 'You were sent back.'

Turning to us, he said, 'Let me give you an example of Swiss diligence. The Gestapo were waiting for us, which means someone must have phoned to say we were coming.'

The sister fell to her knees, a picture of remorse and pity, saying there was nothing she could have done. A banging started outside again. Jean-Pierre told the sister that we lived in an age of meaningless apology, and offered a sneering one of his own for interrupting their meal.

A man's voice outside the door announced that he was from the police. At this, Jean-Pierre looked around, like someone whose nightmare was catching up. He gabbled his frantic account of their deportation. There had been a police escort. Their father had been waiting outside the convent and passers-by began remonstrating with the police. There had even been pushing and shoving after the boy's mother had pleaded not to be sent back to a certain death.

The sister was still on her knees, weeping, hands joined in supplication. Jean-Pierre told her he would not be mocked by her prayers. He shouted for everyone to go away and to leave him in peace. Vaughan looked embarrassed. The gleam in Sol's eye remained.

Jean-Pierre leaned down towards the nun, ordering her to listen. He said his mother had been wailing like a scene from the Bible. The fight had already been punched out of his father. Until that moment, Jean-Pierre had believed in his parents' ability to keep them safe. 'We were taken away in a big old Citroën taxi, and at the border my father was made to settle the fare. Soon after we were separated and I never saw them again. My brother died six months later from an illness I never learned the name of.'

The banging kept up. Sol prompted Jean-Pierre, 'Tell us what you remember about this man.' He was showing him another copy of the old photograph of Willi Schmidt, Karl-Heinz and me. Jean-Pierre said, '*He* was standing in the square watching as we were taken away.'

'How can you be sure?' asked Sol.

'Because he was the man who arranged the escape.'

I shook my head in denial. 'Who are you talking about?'

'Willi Schmidt,' he said.

I asked how Jean-Pierre could remember a fleeting glance after all these years. He pointed at the picture of Willi. 'He was standing outside. My father, when he was being pushed into the car by the police, staggered like he had been hit. The blow was caused by something he had seen. I looked and saw this man standing in the street watching, smoking a cigarette, away from the rest. He had organised our escape. My father told me in those last minutes.'

I experienced what I can only describe as a gallows-lurch, followed by a sensation of falling, as if every foundation I had known had been kicked from under me. The banging on the door became the banging of my heart. I knew what I was accused of. Sol had his case all worked out.

'It was a whole fucking operation,' Sol said. 'They weren't the only ones.' He looked at me with hatred. 'You and your friend Willi sold them all out. You let the poor bastards buy their way out for a fortune, then pocketed their money.'

It wasn't true, I protested. Even the sister was looking at me queerly. Absurdly, I wondered how we were going to get back to Zürich. The idea of us traveling in the same car was unthinkable. It crossed my mind again that Sol had been involved in Karl-Heinz's death. He had the motive and he probably wanted me gone too.

Jean-Pierre stared at the sister, the surviving witness to his family's fate, then slipped from the room. This caused an immediate hubbub outside, marked by a voice of ponderous authority.

Half-a-dozen nuns flapped around two uniformed policemen. The older one looked resentful and under-promoted, a slow-moving ruddy-faced man with a large head. The other one was barely eighteen. The incident was typical of the Swiss: a minor infraction followed by a full recital of the rule book. The Mother Superior chipped in, the voice of righteousness. Jean-Pierre ignored her. The officials who had sent the family back to the Gestapo were probably not so different.

Jean-Pierre walked away without a word. The difference this time was that he could, however strong the tug of the past. The police called after him. They were so ponderous that even the Mother Superior's patience was tested. Jean-Pierre's disregard of their authority had unsettled them and they conferred uneasily.

A sense of throwback cloaked everything: nothing had changed in sixty years, since Jean-Pierre had last been there.

Which was when I realised what he intended. I had

been so dumbfounded by Sol's accusation that I had failed to read Jean-Pierre. I asked the Mother Superior which way he would have gone. I had to ask twice. I told her to keep the policemen there, unless she wanted another death on her hands.

The stairs were steep. I was breathless well before the top. Sol, following, kept having to stop. I doubted my power to reverse destiny.

Jean-Pierre was sitting in the open window, the last of the evening sun behind him. It was hard to make his features out. He seemed calm as he surveyed the room which he had last seen as an eight year old. My arrival barely registered. He was talking to the dead as if they were there with him. If I could get close enough, I decided, he would let me lead him away.

Sun in a dusty room, no furniture, the feeling of a space that had been empty a long time, the distance between us only a few feet and narrowing. I grew confident. There was a serenity to him. He looked at me now with recognition. He appeared reconciled, with none of his earlier agitation.

The room fell into shadow. It was like throwing a switch. The space between us became insurmountable again; the trample of boots on the stairs, the Mother Superior having failed or refused to exercise her authority. Bad timing. The convent clock chimed the hour, its vibration shaking the room. Jean-Pierre looked at me with resignation and irony. In the echo of the last chime he whispered, 'Goodbye,' and leaned back like he was tilting a chair. His image seemed to remain in the window afterwards, and the air was full of the near silent rush of falling matter, followed by the sound of his impact. Jean-Pierre died without a shout or a scream: his exit a silent accusation to the authorities who came stumbling into the room. The Mother Superior crossed herself, another anachronism in a day of too many.

Vaughan, Porrentruy

I felt rather than saw Jean-Pierre's death. I had gone outside and turned too late, thinking at first that it was Hoover, falling under the weight of accusation.

The bureaucratic aftermath took hours. We were questioned at the convent, then at the police station. The police were boringly thorough. They seemed to regard us as accessories to an enormous inconvenience and it was their job to inconvenience us in return.

Much time was spent on who was responsible for the body, given the absence of next-of-kin. Hoover suggested that the town should pay for the funeral as it had been indirectly responsible for Jean-Pierre's death. At that point we ran up against Swiss law. The police endorsed the position of his predecessors. The family had entered the country illegally in 1942 and what happened consequently was nothing to do with the citizens of Porrentruy.

We drove away in silence, apart from Hoover saying, to Sol, 'I hope you're pleased with what you did.'

I wondered whether Jean-Pierre had lived his entire life in anticipation of its ending. The clarity of his death left everything else feeling approximate and muddled, like running blindfold. I didn't want to live with Hoover's guilt. I told him I would drop him off wherever he wanted and then I was going back to London.

He asked if I believed him. Sol strained for my answer. I told him he was maybe a better liar than the ones I was used to dealing with.

Hoover said, 'I know my innocence. I'm less sure about Karl-Heinz's. Sol believes Karl-Heinz was in on Willi's scheme. Say Willi was transferring these people's assets into Switzerland, maybe Jaretski and the DSK currency-control mob were in on it too. But that doesn't sound like Karl-Heinz to me. Karl-Heinz was a businessman, a negotiator, he worked the system. I would be very surprised if he was a conman. Money was easily available to men like him in the war, and on top of that he was a realist. It doesn't make sense to go to all that trouble – and risk – only to have them sent back.'

Sol confirmed that Jaretski had been taking a cut and turning a blind eye to the smuggling operation in exchange for his 10 per cent.

Hoover said, 'What interests me is where Sol fits into all this. Sol knew Willi. Sol was obligated to him. So what did Sol do after Willi brought him to Switzerland?'

Sol was sweating hard in spite of the cool night. I could smell the funk coming off him.

I was aware of the empty seat. Hoover caught my eye

in the mirror. 'Going back there killed him,' he said. 'The past reached out and took him. He had a ticket home.'

Sol finally spoke up, saying it was the last thing he had expected. They had talked a lot about a return to Porrentruy, he said. Jean-Pierre himself had referred to it as 'an exorcism'.

Hoover asked Sol bluntly, 'And where were you the day Willi stood under the chestnut tree and watched Jean-Pierre's family being taken away?'

The car was filled by Sol's embarrassed and almost intolerable silence. Then, in a halting voice, he told us instead about how he had worked for Willi Schmidt after his delivery to Switzerland. He had found himself increasingly beholden. Willi fixed his papers. Freedom went to Sol's head and he started gambling heavily. Willi paid his losses. Sol became bound and trapped by his gratitude to Willi for liberating him. Willi, playing on Sol's obligation, burdened him with his own knowledge. He transferred his conscience onto Sol. In time Sol became the trusty (and trusted) Jew, the friendly face that welcomed the escapees, helping them settle in, sorting out financial matters that needed bringing up to date, *prior to betrayal.*

Hoover asked Sol how he had felt being party to that. Sol said that the situation was easier to live with than it sounded. One of the psychological points about any persecution was that it put the emphasis on survival, and that became the single rule of existence. 'I learned to think of myself as a unit in the plus rather than the deficit column. No more, no less.'

He had made his own devil's pact in persuading Willi Schmidt to let some escaping Jews go free, on the grounds that it was good politics. Willi had agreed to a figure of 30 per cent – based on Judas's thirty pieces of silver – so long as Sol decided who should live or die. It was the same tactic the Nazis had used, using Jews to police Jews. Diligent Sol had stuck to his word and kept to Willi's percentages. And now he faced his post-existential crisis: the guilt he felt at not feeling more guilt.

Hoover asked, 'Did you send the book and the package I was supposed to think was a bomb?'

Sol nodded. Hoover asked him why. Sol said, 'I wanted you to share the punishment.'

'Not Guilty,' said Hoover.

'That's not what Willi said.'

'That's bullshit,' said Hoover, but he sounded unsure.

'Willi talked about you a lot,' said Sol.

'You have the advantage there. He never mentioned you to me.'

They sank back into their own thoughts. Hoover slept, or pretended to, and Sol stared at the road. I asked Sol about the book he had sent Hoover, and the obituary. He had wanted to prick Hoover and Karl-Heinz's consciences, he said. He held them accountable. He was hoping to shame Karl-Heinz into endorsing Frau Schmidt's claim, so they could access Willi's account and share whatever was in it with the surviving relatives of Willi's victims. As for finding out Hoover's whereabouts, he had his son Abe to thank. Abe was a computer whizz. Hoover's CIA file had been cross-referenced from his original name; his credit-card transactions had alerted them to his trip to Europe, and his travel agent's files had contained dates of travel, destination and hotel.

'Him turning up is a bonus,' said Sol. 'Now he can authenticate Frau Schmidt's claim and do a little to clear his conscience.'

He asked to be dropped at a taxi rank we passed in the outskirts of Zürich. We parted without a word.

It was too early to call anyone so Hoover and I ended up killing time in an all-night workman's café. We had nothing to say. I checked the times of the flights to London from a pay phone, then waited for Hoover to make his call, and drove him up to an address in an expensive residential area. The house belonged to Betty Monroe, he said, and he would be staying there a while. I helped him with his bags. Hoover stumbled from tiredness. A tall woman was waiting. Hoover introduced her as Beate von Heimendorf, Betty Monroe's daughter. We shook hands. She granted me an appraising stare. Hoover and I barely said goodbye. I didn't turn back as I walked away. I didn't expect to see him again.

Beate von Heimendorf, Zürich

My life has always been bourgeois, Swiss and uneventful – circumspect in a word. My work is in art restoration, heading a distinguished team of professional restorers. My focus and attention go into the job. In the formal world in which I move it is easy to keep people at a distance. Now I do less physical restoration than committee work, negotiating with museums and fitting their requirements to our busy schedule. I have come to regard restoration in a metaphysical, even spiritual light.

I live ordered days and dress well, and tend to my sick mother as much as possible. I have learned not to think of myself as either unhappy or in hiding. I have led a life of minimum risk. Strange then, to my mind, to be drawn to Hoover, a man so much older than me, whom I decided upon first seeing had been another of Mother's lovers.

His arrival also caused some anxiety as it reminded me that I had not been organising Mother's papers as promised. Such tardiness was uncharacteristic of me. Her files were messy and disorganised and their jumble offended, yet I had done nothing to put them in order.

Hoover's return brings with it a double edge. He seems a broken man and it is the least I can do to look after him, for Mother's sake, if nothing else. But I fear that my initial deception will return to haunt me. After his request at our first meeting for material on Willi Schmidt, politeness demanded I give him something to take away, so I passed on Mother's account of his recruitment. It made it easier for me to lie about the rest of her papers being missing.

Hoover, Zürich

I work in Betty Monroe's old study on the first floor of the house. If I stand at the window I can see the lake. Karl-Heinz's papers are spread all around like a snowfall on the old landscape of Betty's life. There are framed black and white photographs everywhere, including one of Betty Monroe and Dulles, taken in Dulles's garden in Herrengasse. Others, similar (always the same frame-maker) show her in smart social evening groupings, surrounded by extra-attentive men, who look as though they might be famous, or at least highly regarded. The men appear aware only of Betty while her gaze serves the camera, willing it to make her photogenic, which it always does. Betty was one of those fortunate women who was well-nailed by time's shutter and appeared absolutely sure of the moment. Dulles, by contrast, looks shifty next to her. A portrait of two consciences – one as clear as a bell, the other muddied – yet in person Dulles gave no sign of a troubled interior.

I spend days making lists. Every meeting I can remember with Willi, Dulles and Karl-Heinz, and Betty too, although we met less than half-a-dozen times, and only twice in this house. I am aware of these lists serving two purposes. They act as a reminder and a distraction, a form of surface order only. Being in the house, right in Betty's room, I feel as if I am haunting a place where I don't belong. I feel like an interloper. I suspect there are traces of Betty's past still in this house which would throw light on my own life.

Her bookshelves testify to a well-read woman. Signed copies of Jung, even one by Freud, and personally inscribed dedications from Rosamond Lehmann, Max Frisch and Elizabeth Bowen, as well as an early Nabokov that Beate didn't know about, which adds credence to their tennis partnership. I draw solace from the presence of these books, from their order and their finished state, compared to my own messy work-in-progress which refuses to obey the rules of narrative organisation. There is a copy of Scott Fitzgerald's *The Crack-Up* (first edition, uninscribed). I am aware of its relevance, know too that I have undergone an acute, if shortlived breakdown in the aftermath of the events at Porrentruy. They have thrown me back into the past – a past I have no wish to confront – as surely as they pitched Jean-Pierre to his death. As he fell, part of me thought that it should have been me, and more than once I have found myself ambushed by the idea of ending it too. Fitzgerald's lists were a symptom of his crack-up, and so are mine, no doubt. Part of my depression relates to negligence of my current illness, whatever that is. Advanced hypochondria becomes another form of paranoia.

In the furrow of my depression I am aware of how I lagged behind men like Willi and Karl-Heinz, whose ruthless aspiration I could never match, however hard I tried. Karl-Heinz with his shirts taken from Gatsby's wardrobe, Willi the more oblique with his calibrated manners and American sense of timing, born of his love of jazz.

Equations in death. Gatsby dead in his pool after being shot; Karl-Heinz's death by shooting, a gangster's death for the gangster he really was; and Willi's death by water – symbolic or real? *We shall see*, I write, knowing that I have no wish to see. I wish to think of Willi only as belonging to a dark past.

I must be aware too of misreading my mental symptoms, just as when Fitzgerald thought he was recuperating, he cracked. I cautiously admit that I have started to feel better. I feel more cheerful in this house than I did in Naomi's, where I was also a houseguest rooting around in the past – a dry run, I suspect, for the real thing. Looking forward to Beate's evening arrival gives me energy for the struggle. Days feel as though they are starting to knit. At the risk of sounding corny, Beate's feminine presence gives me reason to live. By that I mean both her general womanhood and what is specific to her. I draw reassurance from her simplest gestures. Her evident self-control has, with years of practice, translated into an effortless poise. A different kind of ambush: the heart-stopping beauty of the everyday, the pleasure of watching someone perform mundane tasks well; her insistence on opening the wine and her grimace as she pulls the cork, followed by a small smile of pleasure as it comes free. There is a frisson between us. I nurse that feeling during the day when I plunge back into the icy waters of the past. I use this crass metaphor deliberately. The effort of will that it takes to go back reminds me every time of the churning river that swept Willi away. As for Beate, if one subscribes to Fitzgerald's theory that life has a variable offensive – and it is difficult not to – then I read into my pleasure in her an ebbing of my grief for Mary; just as everything else falls apart.

Beate's coming each evening affords me a lifeline out of the past, she the light towards which I move. At worst I feel literally as though I might drown. I tell Beate some of this. I sense compassion beneath her formal reserve, a passion also, inherited from her mother, but controlled.

She willingly and cheerfully cooks my supper and stays chatting long into the night. I often tell her I am surprised that she has nothing better to do, meaning that she should not feel obliged to me. Sometimes the remark produces a fleeting sadness, as though this were true and she has shut herself away too long. Other times it seems as though she is waiting for me to ask her to stay, not yet with me but in this house where she appears so ill-at-ease. Most evenings I light a fire to ward off the summer chill, with memories of Dulles doing the same, on hands and knees, carefully arranging the kindling. Beate and I eat in Betty's study and stay there afterwards, as if leaving the room would break some kind of spell.

Outside, the soft greens of June and one rainy day after

another keep me indoors, hard at work on my writing. The weather front is similar to the one that famously kept Byron and the Shelleys confined during that summer of *Frankenstein.* Given such a prompt, I am bound to ask: what monster might I be creating?

I am bound too to examine Willi as I knew him then. I find myself snapping at his heels for signs of what I know now, and still I want to give him the benefit of the doubt. Frau Schmidt's act was a deception, so why not Sol's – and to what extent could an eight-year-old boy be taken for a reliable witness? I test Willi in my memory, a kaleidoscope of images revisited for signs of the hairline crack of betrayal, and I find none. I had always believed that Budapest and the terrible events of 1944 were what turned him. Now, if Sol's version is true, he was deep into his seam of corruption two years earlier. Was I?

Chronology is not my strong point. Besides, with age, linear progression becomes somewhat elastic, and its recollection prone to fancy. What's more, I kept no diary and worked to short-term deadlines, which encouraged an edited sense of memory. In our line of work one preferred to forget.

Dulles's garden was in full summer bloom that velvet evening we first met. I remember that detail but little of the meeting that followed, apart from us standing on the terrace, Dulles's pipe-smoke repelling the midges, which then gathered around me. Sol attributed my Red Cross appointment to deep scheming, when what I recall was Dulles nudging me in its direction, apparently without ulterior motive, saying that it was useful work and full-time. My impression was that I was being given the brush-off. Jaretski's arrest had compromised me for Willi's runs. Betty Monroe appeared to have dropped me. With Dulles I sensed that I was tainted by Karl-Heinz's insistence that I deliver his message personally. Whatever I had been doing since arriving in Switzerland I thought of in terms of failure. So when the Red Cross approached me I persuaded myself it was coincidence. This was, I see now, part of a necessary process: in the controlled biography of the double life it was the shadow that got forgotten. I packed my bag and left for Geneva. Willi said that he hoped I appreciated scenery because there wasn't anything else.

Geneva in wartime, empty and dreary as a succession of Sundays. The slow rhythm of diligence. There was plenty of work but the town was always Sunday-dull and the Swiss, fearful of German invasion, were more than usually well-behaved. Willi Schmidt avoided Geneva where there was little carousing to be had.

The Swiss made up for lack of wartime involvement by forming committees. The Red Cross administration was well-intended but cautious, and much given to in-fighting. Co-ordinating committees were created for committees that would not otherwise talk to each other, and behind their founding lay a history of exhausting meetings. I was appointed Liaison Officer, which involved driving bureaucrats between the Central Prisoner-of-War Agency, the International Committee of the Red Cross and a new committee intended to improve relations between the Red Cross and the League of Nations. This new committee was responsible for organising relief to occupied countries, particularly civilians.

One flurry of activity had me requisitioned (in writing) to yet another co-ordinating committee responsible for 60,000 pairs of spectacles collected by the Swiss Women's Civilian Service – which was very precise about the amount – to be forwarded to prisoners-of-war who were complaining of worsening eyesight as a result of a poor diet. In warehouses I saw the results of these charity drives: dozens of table-tennis tables, rooms full of musical instruments – banjos and flutes, mostly – and a stack of Polish Bibles. Three years later their equivalent was stockpiled in the vaults of the Frankfurt Reichsbank. Both left me wondering at the point of human activity.

Nothing was black and white. Nothing separated out the way they said it did later. I used to watch in wonder whenever my wife Mary separated the white from the yolk of an egg. It reminded me of men like Karl-Heinz, Dulles and Willi who seemed to be able to do the same with real events.

I suspect that the job I was doing was not dissimilar to what went on in large office departments all over Germany with the confiscation and redistribution of Jewish assets, which would have amounted to equally routine office and committee work, with everything ratified in triplicate. Paperwork in Geneva, and the carbons required, was a business in itself – sometimes the only one, it seemed. Whole sections were needed to organise its clerical production, distribution and filing. The Swiss were minute-mad. An abiding memory, the sound of multiple typewriters at work, room upon room of female secretaries.

I remember a considerable lapse of time between meeting Dulles and moving to Geneva for the Red Cross, yet it must have happened faster, because by the time Jean-Pierre's family was taken away I was traveling between Geneva and Zürich, and can date that by Willi's birthday party, which was two days after the Feast of the Assumption, the day of Jean-Pierre's deportation. On that memorable night of 17 August, 1942 Willi showed no signs of being anything other than a man out for a good time, kissing all the girls.

Beate von Heimendorf, Zürich

By any conservative estimate there were at least six of Mother's lovers at Willi Schmidt's birthday party. This was something I could hardly tell Hoover about when he began to refer to it.

During Hoover's recovery there is a growing recognition that both our lives have been governed by blanks and secrets kept from us. I wish nothing more than to be his guide yet am forced to keep my own counsel to protect Mother's reputation – particularly with regard to Willi Schmidt, and how that relates to Hoover.

Many of the connections Hoover seeks to make in his own life I know about. What to him is coincidence is to me a matter of affiliation. With his return, the past took on an extra and unwelcome significance and I became increasingly compromised. Yet the attraction between us persists, however much in one respect I rue the day we first met. It was only because of him that I went through Mother's papers for the first time. Otherwise I suspect my tardiness, which I see now was a form of self-protection, would have continued.

However much I already knew, I was still shocked to the roots by the casual confessions of so much promiscuity. Mother, usually so correct in her language if not her morals, writes of 'fucking' Allen Dulles. I was upset by this unloosening, and frustrated too because she avoided the real subject, which for me was Father.

Family seems to have meant very little to Mother, compared to her other world of intrigue, adventure, control and assignation. I read on with a sense of terrible discovery that left me with a dirty sexual itch, which frightened and compelled. When Hoover came back that first afternoon I was surprised to identify my feelings towards him as close to lust. Sex with Hoover would be a negation of my mother, I decided in the dark corner of my mind. It was hard not to make a fool of myself with him since my life has been lived on emotional ice. My first husband's accusations of frigidity still cut deep. My second marriage aped my mother's, without her infidelities. My second husband and I live apart, an arrangement disguised by his constant travelling.

My subsequent reticence towards Hoover has been governed by duty. Power of attorney over Mother's affairs takes precedence over my emotions. Before she became too ill, Mother gave me a sealed letter to post if any element from the past announced itself. This, I presume, extends to Hoover.

Mother's papers are what she in that refined but racy

East Coast voice of hers would have called dynamite. Her private correspondence with Allen Dulles reads like one long breach of security. There are dozens of letters and diaries and notebooks too, some pornographic descriptions of lovers, and undated jottings on the headed writing paper of different hotels. Also included are many secret government papers which should have been destroyed or returned and not left to lie around in the garage. Many deal with what I can only describe as boring spy stuff, a kind of intrigue that holds no interest for me, or so I tell myself. But the sense of personal danger I get from reading them persists. I now see them as a form of time-bomb, which was perhaps Mother's intention.

Hoover, Zürich, 1942

Willi Schmidt's birthday party was attended by several hundred guests and held in the gardens of the German Embassy of all places. Willi was proud of having fixed that. He had called in a lot of favors. Even God had complied by providing a balmy evening, if not the Chinese lanterns, which made for a miraculous sense of intimacy not at all Germanic. For Willi the beauty of the place was that its diplomatic status meant that the Swiss couldn't complain about the noise. Later there would be an informal party, he told me, in a cellar club where they could play American jazz. German tolerance did not extend to that.

Willi introduced me to three other guests, including a comical-looking little man with carroty hair and gap-teeth – Bandi Grosz, the Smuggler King of Budapest. Bandi looked pleased with the description, more so than the others who were described by Willi as, 'Herr Kleer, a German spy, and his friend Herr Busse.'

Bandi pointed at Busse and added, '*Big* German spy.'

Kleer said, in the tones of a man already very drunk

though it was barely seven, that it was as well they were in Switzerland otherwise they would have Bandi shot. Bandi looked at me and mouthed the word 'Jude'.

He was being outrageous, I presumed.

Bandi was content to play the knockabout drunk, though not as drunk as Herren Busse and Kleer on that first evening. His patchwork of languages included English which remained incomprehensible. A Jew at the same party as Nazis, even if it were in a neutral country, was by 1942 the unlikeliest sight, and I assumed that he and his companions were playing a joke at the expense of their hosts for the evening, the German Diplomatic Corps.

How on earth did Willi manage to avoid the taint of compromise? I wonder now. By making sure that everyone got drunk and had an excellent time, I guess. Dulles – should he have even been there? – and I bumped into each other in the gentlemen's lavatory and studiously ignored each other as we flanked a reeling man with a Nazi armband who stood pissing in drunken circles. Betty Monroe was at the heart of the party, working the ambassadorial set. I saw Karl-Heinz behind a haze of smoke, in what looked like erotic conversation with a feral woman in a pink silk shift. Given the array of dignitaries on show, I wondered if the party really was Willi's and if he hadn't managed to insert his own guests, somehow, into a larger diplomatic affair.

Bandi loudly informed me that he had agreed to work for the Nazis in exchange for his freedom. He had done this to avoid arrest by Hungarian customs after being caught supplying Austrian Jews with Hungarian papers and running gold in and out of Switzerland. What he called his survival kit included an impressively embossed document stamped by the Vatican (he said) and a letter from the director of Actio Catholica announcing his indispensable work for the Roman Catholic Church, to which he had converted. But his real hope of safety lay in the services he believed he could provide to all parties. Bandi's motto was that everyone ended up talking in the end. Even the Nazis and the Jews would talk in the end, impossible as that might seem.

Bandi Grosz went on to earn a few mentions in history books, which referred to him as a sleazy courier in Eichmann's and the Nazis' 'trucks-for-Jews' ransom negotiations in the summer of 1944. This footnote has gained him a tiny, dubious immortality.

Kleer and Busse remained oblivious to Bandi's indiscretions the night of Willi's party. Kleer was on a drinking marathon and Busse's priority was finding a woman. Busse had travelled down from Stuttgart, where he ran the bureau controlling espionage in Switzerland and Spain, Willi told me afterwards. When in Willi's jazz cellar Busse got what he wanted I was surprised to note Willi's disapproval. I mistook it for Swiss Puritanism, and only properly understood later when he told me that he regarded money for sex as an unnecessary transaction. Women were not to be paid for. It occurs to me now to ask if Willi's moral blind spot was rooted in money, in spite of his generosity, and whether his emotions remained controlled by a Calvinist thrift.

Willi remained ambivalent towards Bandi because Bandi was a sentimentalist and Willi was cool, and he didn't like being with people who weren't physically attractive. There was something else about Willi. For all his assurance and social front, he was keen to go out of his way to prove to me that he was serious and an operator. He flattered me, told me that he couldn't do what I had done. 'It takes a special kind of nerve to go undercover,' he said more than once. I had given the matter little thought. I had never thought of myself as going or being undercover because I had no idea of what I was under the cover of. I simply thought of my excursions as more or less dangerous journeys.

Willi's importuning was evident the day after his party when he dragged me out of my hangover bed to watch him operating with Bandi Grosz. Bandi's ostensible task was arranging the purchase and delivery of food for Germany. Rice, cocoa and chocolate were on his list. He was also trying to find out the names of Swiss transport firms dealing with the British, and the names of companies selling bomb fuses to the Allies. But his real purpose was to create tight relations with Willi. Bandi had smuggled platinum as a sweetener for Willi who traded it on to an associate of Karl-Heinz at a good profit. Karl-Heinz's papers make a reference to the sale.

Bandi needed Willi for the Swiss end of his business. Swiss corruption was so institutionalised that an inside contact like Willi was essential. Bandi joked that in Switzerland his kind of work was done by bankers, also the

Swiss had fewer illusions than the Hungarians. Hungary was run by a man calling himself an Admiral in a country that was as sealess as Switzerland.

I was about to make my first trip to Croatia in search of supplies for the Red Cross. My trip to Zürich for Willi's birthday parties – Willi: 'Why have one party when you can have two?' – had been passed off as work. I had told Geneva I needed to attend another session with the Croatian legation whose travel requirements were subject to constant revision.

Bandi warned me Croatia would be a waste of time and advised me 'to get my ass' over to Budapest, where he could help me locate produce and transportation. He implied that the Germans had a vested interest in Red Cross channels too, so there would be no interference. He made the universal gesture for money, rubbing thumb against forefinger.

Hoover, Croatia, 1942

Claude Buvier was a businessman. I once told Jackie Kennedy I had travelled to Croatia with a man called Buvier, a slightly different spelling to her maiden name. She hadn't been amused and that was the full extent of my social contact with Jackie K (or Jackie O for that matter). Buvier was what Dulles had in mind for me. It was Willi who had made the actual introduction some time before his birthday. Buvier needed a driver.

Buvier had had a long career as a wholesale buyer and shipper of provisions, and was recruited out of retirement on the recommendation of Willi whose family were friends of the Buviers. Buvier's task was to acquire food and provisions for Red Cross relief. As the Red Cross ranked low in the list of wartime priorities, aid had to be scrounged. Transportation was poor, fuel hard to come by, communication unreliable. A rumor of a warehouse of maize would turn out to be several tons of bonemeal.

It wasn't until later, when Willi and Bandi Grosz became involved in Budapest, that any significant results were achieved, just as Bandi had predicted. Bandi and Willi knew who to buy off and who to bribe. There was a difference, I learned. They knew what would later become known as the Catch-22 of any given situation. Buvier was dead by then. He died, unnoticed by me, somewhere on a road in Slovenia, his polite expiry masked by the rattle and thump of the car. Guards at the Austrian border were curious to know why I was transporting a corpse, and when I told them I was unaware that I had been, they fell about laughing, held me for forty-eight hours while they did the paperwork and knocked me about a bit as a matter of course.

That first trip with Buvier in late August 1942 involved an unreliable old Citroën which overheated. In spite of the summer weather he travelled in Homburg and overcoat. He wore pince-nez glasses, had a politician's moustache, and grey skin that looked like it had never seen outdoors. He was old and fussy, and dressed like a diplomat. His mild manner was, on acquaintance, unpromising.

Once past the Swiss border the white Citroën with its large red crosses attracted plenty of stares. We clipped the top of Italy and passed into Slovenia where for long stretches we had the road to ourselves, apart from the occasional horse and cart. Once we were buzzed by a fighter plane, which forced us to pull over for the convoy it was escorting. As we travelled on we found ourselves in an old Ruritania, a summery landscape of heat haze and ripened crops, with few signs of military order apart from the occasional nineteenth-century barracks. Buvier regarded it all with equanimity: flat tires, the overheating engine, slow to non-existent service in cafés, the ubiquitous tomato and cucumber salad (often all there was), and the way we were looked at as though we had stepped out of a novel by Jules Verne.

It wasn't until we reached a small town near Rijeka that he addressed his first personal remarks to me. There were many refugee camps in Hungary, he said, and in winter the temperature would drop into the minus thirties and refugees would be without warm clothing. Most of his own business had been in Spain where we could easily have found what was necessary to prepare the camps for the coming winter. Yet here we were, because of bureaucratic in-fighting, hunting chickpeas in Croatia. I barely knew what a chickpea was. Chickpeas were Muslim, Buvier informed me. The potato was Christian, and that's what we should have been looking for.

Buvier was a strict Roman Catholic and he attended early morning Mass. Sometimes I went with him, if only for the familiarity of the universal ritual and the bright feeling of stepping out of the gloom into sunshine. Buvier would stand on the steps and converse in Latin with the priests. Our promissory note for the chickpeas was to be guaranteed by the Church and to this end Buvier carried an important-looking letter of introduction to Dr Stepinac, Cardinal of Zagreb, stamped with the Vatican seal (shades of Bandi Grosz).

In Zagreb, Buvier was entertained variously by the Church, the local fascist puppet government, the Ustashi, and Nazi diplomats. The priests were everywhere, better dressed for the most part, focused by celibacy and unencumbered by meaningless familial and matrimonial duties, their sense of politics silky and insinuating. The power of the Holy Mass fed directly into that of the state. The doltish Ustashi was their blunt instrument.

The Nazis cultivated blandness and were friendliest towards me. Herr Veesenmayer, German plenipotentiary, with his gracious incline of the head, was a good listener, expert at small talk. 'Aren't we having marvelous weather? Let me introduce you to my friend Wisliceny.' 'Till we all meet again,' he had toasted on our first departure. And we would, with the exception of Buvier (RIP), in Budapest in the summer of 1944. Wisliceny, big-boned and amiable, spoke of what he was doing in Zagreb: technical adviser. He showed his teeth when he laughed. He and Veesenmayer regretted being stuck in a provincial backwater and were happy to entertain visitors. 'Chickpeas?' I remember Veesenmayer repeating with a raise of the eyebrows. They were men of clear-eyed ideology, at ease with the implications of what they were doing, who would resent the guilt imposed on them later.

We were also separately introduced to Fr Draganovic, who talked airily of a policy of rapid conversion of Orthodox Serbs to Catholicism. I am ashamed to say I yawned at all these backyard politics, ignorant of the implications. I sympathised with Veesenmayer and the others' boredom.

We first met Draganovic at an evening recital of local

music and poetry. There was a children's choir and a lot of native doggerel, presided over by a room full of badly uniformed men who laughed and smiled and pinched the children's cheeks and clinked glasses.

Draganovic's kingdom might have been of the next world but he was thoroughly adept at negotiating his way through this one. In private he touched one's arm to make a point, the point being that he was there 'for all to talk to'. I was twenty-three at the time. Through men like him I came to see that the ways of the world were unfathomable. He was forced to spell things out for me, in so far as a man of his circumspection was willing to. The Church would act as intermediary for people otherwise unable to talk, he told me. He hinted that the Allies and the Nazis should find ways of opening a dialogue about everyone's next problem, Communism, which was the real enemy. Placed where it was, Croatia was especially vulnerable and the Catholic Church had been in the front line of the fight against the heathen for centuries. I told him I would pass on his thoughts.

'To Mr Dulles only,' he warned me. Dulles's name came as a surprise. I realised I had a lot to learn.

That afternoon I was arrested by the Ustashi. A lieutenant interviewed me in atrocious French about currency irregularities. The man was drunk enough to be dangerous. At one point he opened his desk drawer and threw something on the table. It wasn't until he tugged my ear and pointed to the bayonet in his belt that I realised what it was, at which point we were interrupted by an SS officer who marched in and shouted the lieutenant out of the room. Then I decided I really *was* in trouble.

Only when he took off his cap, after milking his dramatic entrance, and its effect on me, did I recognise him. I had not seen Karl-Heinz in uniform before. He made fun of my surprise as he sat down and casually put his immaculate boots on the table. He offered me a Balkan Sobranie cigarette. They were a present from Fr Draganovic, he said. Of my obvious confusion over how much he was supposed to know he remarked, 'You wouldn't be in Zagreb if it weren't for me!'

Karl-Heinz was all knowing smiles. 'I think you may find that Fr Draganovic will turn out to be a friend to all of us yet.' And he was right: at the end of the war Draganovic was active in the Vatican in assisting the safe passage of many of Karl-Heinz's colleagues out of Europe.

Karl-Heinz also proved well-acquainted with my chickpeas. Unfortunately, they had been reassigned, he said. When pressed he sounded tetchy. 'Anti-guerrilla Muslim forces, if you must know.' I told him what M. Buvier had said about chickpeas.

He assured me that my trip would not be wasted. Produce would be made available to us and the matter was being given priority. Fr Draganovic had issued a statement saying that charitable donations to the needy would lead to considerable dispensations in the next world. Herr Veesenmayer, an economist as well as a diplomat, was studying the problem.

Thus I got my first inkling that co-operation over aid was one way of facilitating this other secret alliance Fr Draganovic was servicing.

Our meeting lasted as long as it took to chainsmoke three Balkan Sobranies. Karl-Heinz stubbed out the third, looked at his watch, stood, clicked his heels ironically, gave me a lackadaisical 'Heil Hitler', and was gone, leaving me to work out that my arrest had been for the sole purpose of allowing us to speak in private. Again I realised I had a lot to learn.

Herr Buvier was doing some spying of his own, and being less than discreet about it, as I learned when I went through his belongings – after telling myself that such precautions were necessary. His copy of the *International Christian Press*, published that March in Geneva, contained a report, which Buvier had underscored in ink, noting the extent of persecution of Orthodox Serbs in Croatia. As Fr Draganovic had indicated, his aim was to turn the country into a full Catholic state by 1952, and to that end Orthodox churches had been seized and their priests assassinated. Several hundred thousand Serbs had already been killed. The persecution was endorsed by the Archbishop of Sarajevo, whose sermons asserted that the struggle against evil should not be carried on 'in a noble manner and with gloves'. Cardinal Stepinac personally approved the efforts of the Ustashi whose policies were succinctly summarised by its leader's remark that 'Blood will be shed and heads will roll'. The Germans, still finessing their own policies, watched with interest.

It was hard telling Buvier that I had been snooping among his possessions. My excuse was that I had been detained by the Ustashi and, as I was responsible for his safety, it was my business to make sure he was not carrying anything that might compromise him. I could see he thought less of me, but he agreed to destroy the article. 'I no longer understand the world,' he said.

Dry old Buvier. There were few I misread more than him. He was one of only a handful of men I have met who possessed real courage.

We made several trips to Zagreb over the next months as the aid supply line was set up. Veesenmayer, who was, as he put it, 'always popping in and out of Zagreb', was helpful when it came to scrounging rolling stock and train schedules from the Croatian railways. Veesenmayer was a schedule fanatic. He was making a scientific study of train timetables, he told me. Like Draganovic, Veesenmayer developed the habit of taking me solicitously by the arm when we talked, which I came to interpret as a sign of my necessary compromise. I was not altogether naive, though it wasn't until Budapest that the exact nature of his work became apparent.

In Zagreb, Veesenmayer used Red Cross wagons for the transportation of crates of his own, marked *Fragile.* We reached an agreement that they would be unloaded en route. Later, in Budapest, Karl-Heinz told me they had contained paintings. Veesenmayer was acting as intermediary between Hitler himself and his art adviser who lived in Zagreb of all places. The crates were always accompanied by three armed Germans dressed as civilians who reminded me of those in Dakar, poorly disguised spies.

When I reported back to Willi, he quizzed me most about Buvier. I stuck up for Buvier and it was only after his death that Willi showed me one of Buvier's secret accounts of Ustashi atrocities. How it had come to be in his possession Willi never said. He wanted to know if I had ever met Pavelic, the Ustashi leader, who was in the habit of displaying baskets of plucked eyes to diplomatic guests. Even Willi, who liked to make a point of being worldly if not cynical, wondered at that.

In fact, the Nazis were not as unflustered as they made out. Karl-Heinz's papers contained the following undated note: 'Germans prefer their atrocity cool. It should be more systematic, with steps taken to disguise each stage, especially from the victims. German anti-partisan activities, as they are called, are fine for summer sport, but the psychological toll is incalculable. The process needs to be more technical – more of a business – especially now that the Reichsführer has been a (shaky) witness to the more direct method. Always sensitive to the pressure it puts on the men, he is determined to find a more orderly way, controlled by regulation and office, and suited to the talents of administrators.'

I kept the existence of Veesenmayer's crates secret from Buvier. It was hard for him to accept that the help and aid we were being offered was rigged. It saddened him even more when we returned to Geneva with a potential supply line and were hailed in triumph. After a particularly fulsome set of congratulations, Buvier's eyes watered and everyone looked away, thinking he had been overcome by embarrassment, a quality not usually attributed to him.

Karl-Heinz Strasse, Zagreb, 1943

The Reichsführer has approved the establishment of a Croatian Muslim division. This has led to a few expressions of surprise in the name of racial purity, but the Reichsführer is steadfast in his admiration of the Muslim warrior. He views them akin to the British Gurkha. It also keeps His Eminence The Grand Mufti of Jerusalem happy. The Mufti, currently resident in Berlin where he is regarded by the Führer as something of a joke, is tolerated for his propaganda value. His trips to Zagreb to exhort the Muslim troops seem to fire them up sufficiently.

The region seethes with age-old feuds and hatreds. The Croatians seem predisposed to private melancholy and savagery. Zagreb is full of German technical advisers who express private doubts. The government is a ramshackle affair, run by a bunch of bloodthirsty puppets with large wives who wear frightening floral prints and hair-dos which suggest that Zagreb is in need of a decent salon. Church sermons on good and evil are taken literally, crude Catholicism dished out by clever men who understand the power of superstition. Fanatical priests drive their congregations with an enthusiasm not seen since the Spanish Inquisition. They certainly do the job. Their followers indulge in Red Indian savageries. Croatian bloodlust amounts to a crude approximation of the Church's cannibalistic practices. My God! All that throat-cutting and skull-crunching! It was too much even for Veesenmayer, and he had been responsible for it in the first place!

Veesenmayer, with his slide rule and graph paper, wishes to turn death into a science. Before the war he worked in communications. He hints to me that he has use of an American collating machine, a prototype donated by the Yankees, which has revolutionised his work.* His dream is to create an assembly line, a process

*Elsewhere in Karl-Heinz's papers there appears the following margin note, an apparent reference to Veesenmayer: 'The genocide hot-shot fooled everyone afterwards into thinking he had been a diplomatic cipher. He worked before the war for German subsidiaries of US companies, including ITT and Standard Oil. The speed and efficiency with which he did his wartime round-ups was aided immeasurably by the secret weapon of the extermination programme, the equivalent in many respects of the Allies' decoding machine. He was at the forefront of the technological revolution, with his punch-card system provided by American IBM. For all his smooth cocktail-party talk in Zagreb, he was there for two reasons: to get the Jews out of Croatia and to ensure that the Croatian fascist militia stayed in power. The point about men like him is that they were having the time of their lives. They all knew what was going on, and also knew on which side their bread was buttered.'

of distribution and dispatch that functions in a clean and modern way, at no inconvenience to the German citizen.

I am thankful that my trips to Zagreb are intermittent. The Hotel Milan is insufficient compensation and the town's third-rate architecture looks like a job-lot bought only with military parades and troop movements in mind. The main square is too big for anything other than public executions. Those here on long postings complain that there are too many priests at social functions and the women are as unpredictable as the men.

A year ago the Reichsführer asked me to make certain enquiries as he sought to extend what he calls 'his channels of communication'. I understood him to mean that he thought the usual Vatican lines had become too clogged, or compromised by Canaris and the Abwehr, the German foreign service, which the Reichsführer detests and mistrusts. The Vatican had become, he said, like a bazaar with priests auctioning meetings between diplomats and the usual international riff-raff.

I can say we have succeeded beyond expectation. New friends have been made and Draganovic, whose influence is considerable, is being used only by us. Although the Croatians are not discreet it seems that their churchmen are and the large cupboard-like confessionals in the city's ghastly cathedral are as good a way as any of conversing in privacy. My confessions are so long that anyone observing would be left wondering at the extent of my transgressions. The Reichsführer is pleased, he tells me. It is vital he has access to what he calls 'wider opinion'. But he frets about security and already wishes me to find another means, having decided that the Croatians are too easily compromised. He recommends Budapest. He thinks we shall be there before too long.

It transpires that M. Buvier was not only resistant, he was active in gathering reports on civilian killings – this according to Willi Schmidt. I wonder if it was he who told Veesenmayer, which raises the question of whether Willi is selling information to Veesenmayer when he is supposed to be working for me.

It has been decided that van Hover will go to Budapest. I have taken pains to reassure him that he remains an important link in an invisible chain, and that my patronage could be important to the success of his Red Cross work, which will require a more flexible approach than the one adopted by the late M. Buvier.*

*Karl-Heinz makes no specific reference to the death of M. Buvier, apart from a single note in faded pencil: 'B. died, which saves us the bother. V. not happy at all with what he had been told about B., who was not quite the dry old stick he looked. V. rather cast down by the news. He was keen to try out the gas used in the euthanasia programme for what he called "a personal experiment". He talks too of a gas truck being delivered, now they are no longer required in Poland.'

Hoover, Budapest/Istanbul, 1943–4

Budapest was an outpost city, pleasured and pleasurable before the Germans came in 1944. Its edge was reminiscent of Lisbon. Willi always said Budapest should have been a port – it was like a sailors' town without the sailors. Being one of the few capitals in Central Europe not enemy occupied in 1943 contributed to its air of licence and exemption. Hungary's position as an increasingly uneasy ally to the Nazis, its proximity to Balkan intrigue, its own taste for theatrical politicking, acted as a siren lure to the flotsam and jetsam of wartime Europe. Where Zürich was smug in its neutrality, Budapest was given over to illusion, ritual and plotting. It was a tragedy waiting to happen.

Willi Schmidt, drawn to the hedonism of Budapest, wangled a transfer on family business and declared himself up for a good time. Those early Budapest days saw Willi at his lightest. I could see almost nothing of the calculation described by Sol and Jean-Pierre. Willi played the entrepreneur, promising local jazz bands Swiss contracts (which never materialised) and enjoying the free drinks and impressionable young women that went with it. The darker side was there, but well in the background. Willi's family firm had outlets in Budapest, run by a Jewish concern that saw no contradiction in belonging to a parent company which had bought Jewish firms off the Nazis at knock-down prices.

For another of his innocent rackets Willi had me copying and distributing bootleg prints of the latest Hollywood movies, brought into Switzerland by American couriers and transferred to Hungary on Red Cross transport. After local use they were sold on by Bandi, to the Germans. As an example of how things came to work, the new Cary Grant movie, first seen by me at a private screening in Budapest organised by Willi, was sold two weeks later to a high-ranking German diplomat. 'He knows you,' said Bandi. It was Veesenmayer, the plenipotentiary from Zagreb, temporarily resident in Budapest. Veesenmayer, according to Willi, went on to sell the print to Dr Goebbels for twice what he had paid for it.

This invisible chain struck me as significant without being able to say why. It was Bandi who pointed out that these channels would later serve for clandestine diplomatic negotiations. They were the first signs of people wanting to talk.

Willi's arrival in Budapest coincided with a complex jigsaw of political favors snapping into place, which enabled Red Cross supply lines to operate with increasing efficiency. Perhaps Willi's coming had been responsible for the change. Aid and relief quickly became a form of laundry, and with Bandi and Willi a lot got rinsed. Their contraband travelled in Red Cross crates, indistinguishable apart from a discreet red spot on the corner of the lid, to make identification easier for Willi's men when unloading. What was in them hardly mattered. They were just part of the racket.

Bandi taught Willi his basic philosophy, which was to play all ends against the middle. Whoever taught Willi to keep his mouth shut it wasn't Bandi, who was, by his own reckoning, 'as unreliable as an old queen'. He gossiped about all his dealings, especially those with the German foreign service, the Abwehr, which was considered cosmopolitan and indulgent by Nazi standards. 'They employ a Jew like me, for Christ's sake!' Bandi said, convulsed. Since his conversion to Roman Catholicism he constantly invoked the name of the Son of God.

Bandi also represented emerging Jewish groups in Budapest keen to establish contact with similar organisations in neutral Istanbul. As for his business with the Abwehr, it was the contradiction that proved the rule. 'Everywhere there are Jews going up in smoke, and the Abwehr pays me because it wants to find Jews it can talk to! It's a crazy world!'

Bandi's indiscretion, I came to realise, was a form of insurance. The more he broadcast his dealings, the more compromised everyone became and the more immune he felt. It was not a view shared by Willi, who said, 'Why doesn't someone just shoot you?'

'They all need me too much,' said Bandi, with too much bluster.

Willi bet Bandi a substantial sum that the SS would be running Budapest within a year. He was quite adamant. As he said it I had a clear memory of Wisliceny smiling at me in Zagreb when describing himself as a technical adviser.

It was Willi who first mentioned Eichmann's name that same night as one of the main organisers of the Jewish deportations. Eichmann, according to Willi, was the German officer who had refused further offers from Hungarian fascists to take more Jews, citing transportation difficulties. Eichmann's was not a name anyone knew at the time, which meant that Willi was remarkably well-informed. Teasing, he once said to me: 'You and Eichmann are in the same business, more or less. You have both been given the train set to play with.' It was one of Willi's favorite quotes, from Orson Welles. Willi was a big film fan, *Citizen Kane* his favorite movie. His reference was to my recent promotion to Co-ordinator of Transport for Relief Goods, Budapest.

That summer we were Eichmann's social precursors, staying in the Astoria, which would become a Nazi head-quarters. Budapest would prove the undoing of the incorruptible Eichmann, who took its hospitality at face value. Like him, Willi – to a much lesser extent myself, and Bandi not at all – went hunting and riding with the local aristocracy. Those I met were keen for Swiss contacts, to discuss the possibility of charitable work in exchange for Red Cross identity cards, which would give them the chance of a safe exit if the Russians or the Germans came, as many were now sure they would.

Bandi's bet with Willi was based on his belief that the empire-minded Hungarians – 'We're nearly fucking Austrians!' – were too afraid of Communism to stand by its German alliance with the Russians on the advance. 'We tried it once,' said Bandi, 'and it was a disaster, for Christ's sake! I tell you, the Amis will be in Budapest before the Nazis.' The wager was somewhat unfair, given that Bandi was probably already in secret discussion with Hungarian Intelligence about the matter.

Willi made one of the few overt references I can remember him making to the subject when he said, 'It's about more than that.' He argued that the Nazis were bound to come because Hungary retained one large plum, a large portion of Europe's remaining Jewry.

'As well as its gypsies and pederasts,' added Bandi, gloomy and in his cups. Budapest was one of the few places in Europe where gypsy musicians still played. Then he rallied briefly and thumped the table. 'No. The Krauts have bigger fish to fry than Hungary's Jews.'

'Not with men like Veesenmayer in town. They are only here for one reason,' said Willi.

I realised I was in the process of learning one of Betty Monroe's main lessons, that most intelligence work is social and 'not to do with hanging around in ditches, dear'.

Just as Bandi predicted, Budapest became a city of go-betweens and the different sides showed signs of wanting to talk, even as the civilian slaughter reached its peak. The more prescient Nazis were looking ahead to their alibis.

Jewish and Zionist organisations set up in Istanbul and Bandi shuttled between there and Budapest, servicing the emerging local Jewish resistance, while trafficking in the overlapping channels of black market and exchange of intelligence. Both cities became familiar with men like Bandi, Jewish or half-Jewish, criminal or semi-criminal, who counted German Intelligence among their clients. It was whispered in back rooms that Canaris, the head of the Abwehr, ran his own Jewish spy ring, which he had transferred to Budapest to keep it safe from the SS. Canaris was known to have cultivated Allied contacts through the Vatican, and there were stories that he was doing nothing to discourage plots to kill Hitler. Karl-Heinz became wary of sharing the Catholic Church as a secure line of communication.

Summer drizzle in Budapest; bright morning sun on the Bosphorus. The two cities, Budapest and Istanbul, became part of the same mental zone, indistinguishable under the surface. Bandi and Willi and I traveled between the two often enough to keep separate wardrobes. Willi, suave in sharkskin suits, Bandi with what looked like half the night before's dinner spilled down his. According to Bandi, the real reason Willi did the Istanbul run was morphine. Hungarian supplies were running low, as were the Germans', and he planned to sell to the highest bidder, after running it back to Budapest through Bandi's contacts in the Hungarian Diplomatic Service. But Bandi put about so many unreliable stories to obscure his own dealings, and

friend who likes jazz.' She kept asking if I was trustworthy and she eventually committed herself by telling me that two of her Abwehr friends wished to defect. Would I help?

I asked Bandi. He contacted Palestinian Jews for whom he couriered and they organised the defection through Syria to Cairo.

Nelly wanted to get out too and persuaded me to leave with her. By then I was staying a week at a time in Istanbul, and in wartime intimacy was quickly achieved. I remember Nelly's brightness in an otherwise gray life of subterfuge: Nelly in colorful print dresses buying food in the market, splashes of dappled sunlight through the stall awnings, like the patterns of her dress. Nelly strolling. Strolling was an activity unknown to me. Strolling equaled peacetime, equaled a woman, equaled the casual purchase, all those things I had never had.

The defections started early in February, 1944. The couple went first, followed by other Abwehr employees happy to leave and with intelligence to sell. News of the defections was slow to reach Budapest. Bandi had misgivings. He was sure that the resulting scandal would harm the Abwehr's standing and he had good relations with them. 'The last thing we want is to have to deal with the fucking SS!'

Little did he know. Karl-Heinz's diary contained the laconic note: '10.02.44. The Abwehr defections are having the desired effect. The Reichsführer informs me that the Abwehr will be disbanded. *All duties will be handed over to the SS* [*Karl-Heinz's emphasis*]. The final transfer of power will take several months in order to preserve what some wit has called "the delicate lines of communication". Things really could not be turning out better!' A further note makes the object even clearer: '11.02.44. Canaris fired! The thought of him shafted is almost too much for the Reichsführer. As our armies retreat the Reichsführer expands. Departmental Lebensraum! *Now we shall have Budapest to ourselves!*'

I happened to bump into Willi straight after Bandi. When I told him I was thinking of getting out with Nelly, he bought me a drink and wished me luck. 'See you after the war,' he said, making out we were both men of the world, with an ironic, casual half-salute by way of farewell.

The night before I was due to return to Istanbul I was arrested by the Hungarian secret police and questioned about my association with Bandi Grosz and others, including Willi. I was held over the seventh and eighth of February. Nelly was due to leave on the eighth. I heard later she delayed until the ninth. I didn't get there until the fourteenth, still feeling lucky at being released. I had put my arrest down to chance. Random pick-ups by the Hungarian police were frequent, especially of those they suspected of Intelligence connections. What I refused to accept was that it might have been Willi's doing, with my connivance, given what I had let slip. I had not told Nelly of my own double role. I was also ten years younger than her. (The casual streak of misogyny, mistaken for adventurousness.)

*

Beate surprises me not at all by possessing the same sharp mind as her mother. She understands the difference between running and being run, understands the nature of collusion, and of collaboration in its different forms, comfortable and uncomfortable. She appreciates my denial of, and identification with, Willi Schmidt, and my misgivings because – perhaps as with Willi too – my deeper involvement began earlier than I had thought or had been led to believe.

Beate asked, quite reasonably, what I thought I had been doing and accepted my answer that I was not sure, beyond being involved in the tentative opening approaches by various enemy parties, ultimately answering to Reichsführer Himmler or Allen Dulles, with Willi the wild card.

That Reichsführer Himmler would want to communicate with Dulles, Beate took as a given. She also understood that Himmler needed to find someone who was not a representative of official Allied policy. 'I can see,' she said, 'how the straightforward motive must be the hardest to read.'

She found inconsistencies intriguing. She thought they were largely deliberate as they gave everyone the leeway to lie, perhaps even to themselves. When I told her that she had a very clear understanding of how self-deception was necessary to the process, she looked as though she was about to say something but left it at a wry smile.

She was also capable of remarkable foresight. 'Of course,' she remarked, 'the obvious way to have kept Dulles in line would have been blackmail.'

From certain angles she resembled her mother, the sense of throwback uncanny. A wormy part of me thought, If not the mother at least the daughter. I took this uncharitable nugget as a sign of my recovery.

She asked, 'How much can these moves be predicted and how much are they chance?'

I wanted to ask her the same question, only with reference to us. If conspiracy is an affiliation of silences, then she and I must be conspirators. I want to reach out, want to brush against her accidentally, want one of us to drop our reserve, but I am out of moves for the moment.

Beate von Heimendorf, Zürich

I have offered Mother's postcard from Istanbul as the sole piece of evidence of her trip. Not so. She noted approvingly in her diary that Nelly Kapp's heart was broken swiftly but effectively by Willi Schmidt in an intense, two-week affair during which he posed as a German trade official whose sudden disappearance Nelly was led to believe was the result of defection. That Hoover's role had been to encourage the seed of defection already planted by Willi. That the Abwehr defections were planned as part of larger strategy whose purpose Mother does not reveal. Of her own stay in Istanbul, she remarked (of Hoover?): *Each night I sucked him dry.*

Of Bandi Grosz she wrote, *Everyone has plans for Mr Grosz!*

I remind Hoover of my mother, which is not what I want for the basis of our alliance. With Mother today I saw nothing of the woman Hoover sat with in Istanbul on a terrace overlooking the Bosphorus.

I try to avoid the subject of my mother with Hoover. The irony is that the more he reaches for the truth, the more I am obliged to lie, to protect her. I hate her legacy and my obligations to it, hate my circumspection which prevents me from being honest.

I understand completely how it would be possible to live life in wartime in the conditional. I recognise the world Hoover talks about, with its emotional checks and balances, and deceptions. These are things familiar to me in a different context: a world of doubt and deferral, where, in a sense, the present does not count, where hope and fear discount any sense of now. Each evening we sit in Mother's study, trying to catch the moment, Hoover exhausted from each day's immersion (the word he uses) while I think of the tangled briars around my heart, and everything I want to and cannot give. I move with a sense of physical trepidation when I am near him. He is old as well as older, and I cannot tell if I would succumb or flinch were he to become intimate.

Each night before going to sleep I wonder if I should not stay. Instead I drive home, a model of bourgeois propriety, and read Mother's papers for half an hour, making my own reluctant excursions into her past, realising that I am putting myself in her position, of being several moves ahead of him. Better that he never knows. I tell myself that I am shielding him rather than Mother. Sometimes the truth is better left unsaid.

The weather continues to be miserable, the city a grey wash. Everything feels as though it is in the wrong time.

Even the leaves look as though they should not be out in such a beastly climate.

I followed Mother's instructions and sent the letter as she asked while she was still well. The respondent's name is Mr Ballard. Mr Ballard came to the museum and we talked.

Very occasionally Hoover mentions his wife. Tonight he told me a story about how they had gone to see a film on his daughter's recommendation and they had to leave almost straight away because he was feeling sick. He said it had taken him a long time to identify its correct cause as one of revulsion. The film had contained a severed ear, found in the grass, and brought back memories of the Ustashi lieutenant in Zagreb. He had never returned to see the film, but discovered after his wife had died that she had gone back the following day with a man who may or may not have been her lover.

I am not sure what to make of the story or of what he meant when he wrote (I had not meant to look): *I entertain the fantasy, given whose daughter she is, that she might be my interrogator and, despite the softness of our surroundings and her manner, that this is my final debriefing.*

Karl-Heinz Strasse, Budapest, 1944

19.03.44 We arrived quietly this Sunday morning before church bells in a dark column a mile long and met with no resistance. The Hungarians, so uppity until now, have capitulated without a murmur.

21.03.44 Let's all gang up on Fatty Goering! The secret negotiations I am here to conduct for the takeover of the Manfred-Weiss steelworks will give the SS its own industrial power base. In exchange the owning family – which is, unfortunately for it, Jewish – will be allowed to emigrate, after agreement over its various donations, leases and agency fees. Until the dotted line is signed, neither the Hungarians nor Goering are to know.

22.03.44 Loose ends to tidy. The Hungarian Intelligence Officer Hatz will be recalled to Budapest, arrested and questioned (by me). Likewise Bandi Grosz. Both to be released once they understand what their roles are. Hatz to be allowed to resume duties as a staff officer on the condition that he volunteers for service on the Russian front (!). Grosz is on standby.*

24.03.44 The Jews are finding a voice. They are sniffing around Wisliceny, having heard that he takes a bribe – unlike Eichmann. Up to a point. He tends to pocket the money and go back on his word. Fifty thousand dollars he walked away with in Slovakia and still the trains rolled. They have offered him two million dollars for a guarantee of no ghetto or deportations, with a down payment of $200,000, based on the Slovak precedent. Once my current negotiations with the Weiss family are over, I shall leapfrog Wisliceny and present myself as the best person for the Jews to talk to. By then I will be able to show them that I am a man of my word.

29.03.44 The Weiss family is very understanding, grateful even for its unique position of being allowed to barter its future. It has loaned me two large townhouses side by side on Andrassy Street to make my job easier. Of course the family suspects a trap. They all fear they will be taken away and shot once they have handed everything over. It takes all my considerable powers of persuasion to convince them that we are, as the English would say, 'playing with a straight bat'.

*Elsewhere Karl-Heinz hints that Hatz was run jointly by Dulles and the SS to discredit both the Istanbul OSS and the Abwehr. A visit by Hatz to Canaris, head of the Abwehr, was used by the SS to implicate Canaris in the Hungarian plot to break the German alliance. Of Bandi and Hatz's release, Willi remarked to Hoover, 'This is highly unusual in itself.' Arrest by the SS was more usually on a permanent basis.

Eichmann, that dull fanatic to the last, calls me behind my back 'the officer in kid gloves'. Absolutely. Those of us who can see far enough ahead have always remained gentlemen, anticipating a time when we can lounge about in hotel lobbies with a clear conscience.

Eichmann is the other 'negotiator', the public face to my private deals. He is the most blinkered man I know. As long as things at his end are in order and he believes that he has done everything to facilitate his clients – I have heard him call them clients! – then the process is, so he manages to convince himself, a civilised one. My God! They will go to their deaths crammed into cattle cars while he argues niceties with the Jewish Council who are as bad as the rest at pulling the wool over their own eyes and everyone else's. The Hungarians can't wait to get on with the job of shovelling the Jews onto their trains.

03.04.44 The first big air raid and of course the Jews are blamed, with talk of reprisals already – so many lives for each Christian one lost.

08.04.44 Wisliceny, over cocktails at the Astoria: deported Jews will be made to write a postcard from a destination called Waldsee where they will report everything to be fine. The postmark, to which a lot of thought has been given, is to suggest an image of a lakeside holiday camp! The cards will be sent by SS courier to the Jewish Council for distribution to relatives and friends: *wish you were here.*

Drunk, Wisliceny calls Eichmann a 'ponderous bureaucrat' and 'an arselicker', who is forever moaning on about his transportation headaches. Wisliceny does a good impersonation of the crooked smile and insistence on the stock phrase 'You and I are as chalk and cheese,' which is *just* how Eichmann would put it.

Eichmann honestly thinks of his work as helpful exercises in scheduling. His other skill is table tennis. He talks of organising a league! The light and airy – and modern – quarters in which his department is based up in the hills of Buda appear so harmlessly suburban that it is impossible to believe that anything too awful could issue from them.

Wisliceny tells me that at the first meeting, half the unsuspecting Jews turned up with their bags ready to be deported. The bribable Wisliceny boasts that he is being heavily courted. The Jews prefer him to Eichmann who indulges in a rather unctuous pretence of identification with his victims, of wishing to understand their problems. Wisliceny is the master of the soft-pedal. His simple request for blankets and mattresses soon led to a free auction of mirrors, typewriters and paintings, many of which now adorn his apartment on the river. A request for a piano resulted in eight.

The Jews rely on hope in what is a hopeless situation.

12.04.44 Identify and isolate, the same old story. The Jewish Council is happy to provide lists of everyone to the Ministry of Supply in the misguided belief that its request is about the fair allocation of food. Yellow Stars of David are now worn by Jews. There has been much finicky insistence on the correct size of the star. A washable armband version is apparently in preparation. Hope is a strange creature.

29.04.44 Eichmann's mind is entirely one-tracked, all the way to Auschwitz (the first departure was yesterday). He detests my being in Budapest because it interferes with what he thinks of as the clarity of his orders. 'We are not here to barter,' he told me. But, Adolf, we are. It's the only way we are going to get out of this war alive.

He alternates between the chipperness of a man who is having the time of his life – good posting, comfortable surroundings, the satisfaction of working with a team that knows how to do its job, an air of social confidence that wasn't there before – and the sad-clown smile of someone who suspects the writing might be on the wall, if only he could read it. (It's in Hebrew, Adolf.) Eichmann's fate – and I suspect even he is starting to realise it – is bound up with that of his victims. In theirs lies his own. When all the Jews are gone he's out of a job. He feels unappreciated and undervalued. He suspects that everyone regards him – the most vital cog in the entire machine – as small fry. He knows that behind his back he is called 'the travel agent'.

Ransoms, deals, negotiations . . . all are anathema to Eichmann. He fails to understand that it's time for a new trick and not the same old one. It's getting a bit late for that. He fails too to see that the new trick will be the far harder one of how we made the Jew *not* disappear. How we saved the Jew, how a few master conjurors managed that.

03.05.44 Anti-Semitism seems to affect the Jews as much as anyone. Hungarian Jews are quite happy to see alien refugee Jews removed. There are rumors all over the city that the deportations will soon begin in the countryside. As we sit around the polished mahogany negotiating table with the refined and extremely well-bred members of what is a charming family, you can see the question in their eyes: *Where will they draw the line?* My appeal is that of one gentleman to another. They have my word. This is probably as good as given, seeing that both the Führer and Reichsführer are in agreement about the negotiations. The Hungarians will be hopping mad when they discover that the business has been lifted from under their noses. In the past we have always been generous with local Jewish assets, which (by and large) have gone to the country in question.

05.05.44 Today we viewed the Weiss family's art collection. It contains a particularly fine El Greco, an indifferent Tiepolo, and a Gauguin that would no doubt be viewed as too decadent for today's taste: I have to confess, I have my eye on it. We move into tricky areas here. The museums are after the said works on the grounds that they should remain in Hungary. But already

I think that the family feel these masterpieces would be better appreciated elsewhere. The word 'family' has become like a talisman. What we are talking about is an industrial complex employing over 40,000 workers, as well as there being other enterprises.

15.05.44 Our negotiations reach their delicate conclusion. In the case of the Weiss family we are also talking about the rescue of Jews, which these days is a radical notion as Eichmann and his crew race ahead. Eichmann: 'We are getting into the swing of things.' Meanwhile, we are discussing a twenty-five-year lease of all assets with the family Weiss. This is how we shall get around the matter of the paintings. With the expiry of the agreement everything reverts back to the family. We have conceded their foreign currency to them. I am bending over backwards thinking of my own references. We reach a generous private arrangement as to what money they can take with them and our cut as trustees is only 5 per cent of the gross income of the concern.

17.05.44 The family has signed! The Hungarians will protest that their sovereignty has been overridden. My lawyers are studying the problem. The Hungarians will use the National Bank to try to block the takeover as it must approve any foreign purchase of Hungarian securities. Some smarty-pants has decided that the answer is for me, and selected others, to declare ourselves legal residents, to which end papers are being drawn up. My slight worry is that when this is all over the Hungarians might use that as an excuse to extradite me to stand trial in Budapest. The Hungarians are vindictive, and as lovers of theatre and opera, are fond of their trials.

For the moment they are as keen as mustard to co-operate. Even Eichmann is impressed by the speed and relish with which the Hungarians have gone about their business. The local Colonel in charge has set himself up in the hills, to be closer to Eichmann's team, and his town office calls itself International Storage and Transportation Inc. This is the kind of thing the Hungarians fall over laughing about in their drink.

18.05.44 Dinner last night with Willi S. He seems to be in his element, showing an almost clinical curiosity for these strange days. He told me he started out wanting to be a doctor, which I can believe. He seems interestingly modern and ahead of his time, an amoral moral diagnostician, much like our friend in Bern from whom I suspect he has learned a lot.*

19.05.44 Bombs again. The British this time. We have soon learned to tell the difference between their

*Elsewhere Karl-Heinz remarked, presumably also a reference to Dulles: 'The Reichsführer still cannot believe that someone as senior as "our man O" has been so adventurous in his dealings with us at a time when everyone else is bending over for Uncle Joe and the Ivans. The Reichsführer, eyes agleam, has asked more than once, "Are you sure he is someone we can work with? It's not a trick." I assured him it was not. I have identified "our man O's" driving force. Greed.' The reference to Dulles as 'our man O' was apparently a joking one to the letter O being the only thing standing between the SS and Dulles's OSS.

Lancasters and the American Flying Fortresses. Another reason to remove the Gauguin from Budapest to safety elsewhere. The family is now quite in agreement, and is already thinking in terms of the future. They get everything back in 1969. You can see them calculating, thinking that isn't so long. Let's hope the Führer doesn't change his mind and decide to put them on the train after all.

Hoover, Budapest/Zürich, 1944

I didn't know it then but Karl-Heinz used Willi for my contact. We met down by the river, the day after Willi and Karl-Heinz had dinner (to which no reference was made). Willi seemed out of sorts and I saw for the first time how much of a nocturnal and indoors man he had become. Daylight and fresh air seemed to disagree with him. He had a hacking cough as he told me there was an urgent and highly confidential message to deliver to Dulles.

Although nothing had been mentioned, relations between us had cooled since my brief arrest by Hungarian Intelligence after my confession to him about Nelly. When I asked why he couldn't deliver the message himself, he sounded snappish. 'Because I'm Betty's boy, and Betty is out of favor since this Abwehr business.'

He was referring to her having had several lovers and Intelligence sources in the Abwehr. According to Beate, Betty had complained once to her of losing Dulles's confidence towards the end of the war.

Willi also said, 'This meeting never took place.'

I travelled to Switzerland the next day on a special emergency pass issued by the SS. Willi had given me a sealed envelope whose contents I was to commit to memory and then destroy. I have no idea if Willi knew what was written in the message. He claimed he didn't, saying, 'This is nothing to do with me. I'm only doing it as a favor.'

Dulles was shaking by the time I had finished reciting the message. He asked, 'What do these people want?'

I said that I had been told to warn him that his cables to and from the United States were being intercepted. If he wanted proof of that he should refer to the recent one from Washington criticising the quality of his intelligence, which was considered 'ill-informed, inaccurate and substantially wrong in its details'.

According to a snippet of Betty's, dug up by Beate, Dulles had received a tip-off at the end of the previous year that the Abwehr was feeding damaging information about him – 'all damned lies' according to Dulles – to US Treasury agents. In the light of what has been subsequently learned, the information was remarkably accurate, and provided an extra reason for Dulles wanting to discredit the Abwehr. Of course, this information became available to Karl-Heinz once the SS takeover of the Abwehr was complete.

Dulles didn't say much in the way of a response to my message apart from 'Christ Almighty!' several times to himself, then: 'And what the fuck am I supposed to do about it?'

I said it was recommended he reroute any money transactions through Brussels for the time being and not through Switzerland.

We then entered the stage of what might be called reckless secrecy, when men like Karl-Heinz and Dulles were prepared to risk everything, and use anyone. I had an uncomfortable image of them dining together openly after the war, grinning survivors, while I lay dead and done in some ditch.

Karl-Heinz was playing opera on his gramophone when we next met in his lavish private quarters on one of the city's smartest boulevards. He later told me he was worried about microphone bugs. Karl-Heinz in shiny jackboots, braces and a silk shirt, 'on top of his game' as the sports people say.

'Strictly between us, it's getting too late to fuck about,' he told me almost inaudibly. 'I have a mole in the Swiss banking system. We are moving into a difficult period where nothing should be recorded, only memorised and erased.'

He asked what I was thinking. I said I wondered if he was working to orders or playing the entrepreneur. The diva hit the high note. Karl-Heinz turned the question around and asked, 'What do you think?'

I told him the one thing I had learned was that everyone had a deal on the side.

'And how does that make you feel?'

'Very exposed.'

'Your problem is you're too honest.'

The scratch of the needle at the end of the record; sitting in such sumptuous surroundings (requisitioned) I had a clear flash-forward to life among the ruins.

I was given a time and an address in an unremarkable part of Zürich for meeting Karl-Heinz's banker.

The first appointment I had to pass up because I thought someone was tailing me. It was during an unseasonably late snowstorm, big dry flakes that showed up the silhouettes of the two men. They didn't seem good enough to be on Dulles's payroll.

When I told Dulles about being followed he was concerned they were Treasury Department agents. I didn't think they were, but I was picked up later by the Treasury and grilled. It wasn't out of the question that Dulles had made the tip-off himself, to see if I could find out what the Treasury had on him. Nothing that they were telling me, it turned out.

The Swiss banker was, as he put it, prepared to deal with the devil. He was urbane and ironic and had the same upper-class mannerism as Betty Monroe and Dulles of starting his conversations in the middle. 'The price of oil is about to take a leap,' he began by saying moments after we had met. 'Why do you think that should be?'

I said I was flattered that he thought I might know the answer.

The oil companies, he pointed out, were perfectly aware that the Allied armies were about to embark on an invasion of Europe. He said this equably and left me to draw my own conclusion.

'Who provides the oil in the Middle East?' he asked.

'The Arabs.'

'Who then would the American oil companies be keenest not to upset?'

'The Arabs.'

'And who do the Arabs dislike most?'

'The Jews.'

The man nodded. 'The Jews are short of friends at the moment. Would you describe your friend Mr Allen Dulles as a friend to the Jews?'

I said it would be presumptuous of me to call Mr Dulles a friend, or to answer for him.

The banker smiled patiently. 'A man of diplomatic skills. What is Mr Dulles by profession?'

'A lawyer.'

'And if Standard Oil of New Jersey were one of Mr Dulles's main clients, who would that make him a friend to?' He didn't wait for an answer. 'Let us stop playing games. Mr Dulles is a committed anti-Zionist on account of longstanding legal, banking and business interests, dating back to his early Istanbul posting. I am quite open about my antagonism. There is acceptable greed and unacceptable greed, and Mr Dulles falls into the latter category. Furthermore, Mr Dulles has large financial interests in the Third Reich, involving many American clients whose German investments he brokered before the war. Does any of this surprise you?'

It did and it didn't. The allegations were enough to astound, but by then the hidden motive was an inevitable feature of the world through which I moved. I asked how I could be sure he was telling me the truth.

The banker said, 'You can choose to believe me or you can believe Mr Dulles. Of course, bear in mind that Mr Dulles is a thoroughly respected, respectable and believable character. The likes of Allen Dulles will always get away with things. But Mr Dulles, for all his bonhomie and civilised manners, hates "Yids", but will go to enormous lengths to disguise it. We are dealing with a far more sophisticated and dangerous enemy than rabble-rousers like Goebbels.'

We were in a stuffy Zürich apartment. The place felt as if it hadn't been lived in for a long time. The brief snowfall had been followed by several days of heavy rain. We were in a room at the back, overlooking a courtyard. In spite of feeling unoccupied, the heating was on and the place was too warm.

The banker said: 'Mr Dulles has been instrumental in building Saudi oil interests on behalf of his American clients, particularly Standard Oil; another oil company, Socony Vacuum, employs many agents from Mr Dulles's organisation. His interests have long caused him to oppose any policy within the United States government for a Jewish homeland. These interests resulted in an interlocking financial network created by Mr Dulles on behalf of American oil companies, Saudi Arabia and Nazi business corporations. Many of these interests continue to do cloaked business despite the war. It should not be too difficult for your contact to work out which these companies are. He could start with I.G. Farben.'

It was the breadth of Dulles's ambition that astonished me most. I knew him well enough by then to know that he would have acted in the belief that he would get away with it, and regarded himself as sufficiently protected to avoid disgrace or exposure. I had the small consolation of relishing the memory of making him shake from the shock of my news.

The banker said, 'Since the start of the war, Mr Dulles's client, Standard Oil, has been able to overcharge on the price of oil, against the threat of withholding supply, and has been behind the payment of large bribes to Saudi Arabia. And you thought the war was about armies fighting.'

I asked if he believed Mr Dulles could be exposed. The banker gave a weary smile. 'If I thought that he could be brought down by any other means, I would not be giving you this information to pass on to an enemy I detest even more than Mr Dulles. Mr Dulles is a lawyer. He is an expert at laying down false trails. He has the advantage of being in Switzerland where under the cloak of neutrality he can consort with many of his former colleagues. Mr Dulles still has many contacts with the German Schroeder Bank, for which he has acted as an adviser in the past. Through them he is in a position to shield his American investors. Once President Roosevelt had frozen all Swiss bank accounts in the United States, on the grounds that they contained disguised Nazi assets, Mr Dulles was bound to come to Switzerland, and here he remains.'

We met twice more. On the third occasion he didn't turn up and I failed to spot my followers who bundled me in a car and stuck a gun in my side. They didn't seem like German agents or Americans. Given the banker's abrupt no-show I sensed they were probably working for him.

David and his gang were the last players to slot into place.

Our immediate destination was a deserted mechanic's garage under a railway arch where we went through the shameful process of extracting information and confession. They couldn't decide if I was an agent for the Nazis, in which case they wanted to kill me, or the Americans, in which case they wanted to turn and run me, or both.

The torture was of symbolic rather than actual importance, in part a result of their own frustration at fighting a war without enemy contact. They were not experts in the way I am sure Jaretski would have been. What I had always dreaded was made endurable by the belief that I was instrumental to their plans and they would therefore not kill me.

I told them what I knew, which I did not regard as much, more out of a sense of accumulated isolation than anything else. It was a salutary lesson to discover that any illusions of loyalty I might have had were meaningless. If there was anything shameful about the process it had to do with our complicit awareness of how little our small drama counted for in the face of so much death and suffering. We were playing self-conscious games, way off in the margins where forbidden alliances were forged. We were already shamed by the compromises of survival.

David wore glasses and had a high forehead. His dark hair was already receding. He was wiry and intense. David, echoing Dulles, to me: 'Information is either priceless or very dangerous, so use it well.' He reminded me that I worked for the Red Cross as well as for Mr Dulles, and it was time both of us did something to help the Jews.

The meeting between Dulles and David took place at Betty Monroe's house, with myself as the agreed intermediary. Betty let us in and out, saving an ironic aside for me – 'Well, look who's here' – but otherwise remained absent. She made a point of not offering tea or coffee. We used her upstairs study, the room in which I now sit.

Dulles was uncomfortable dealing with someone as young as David, and tried to condescend. 'Well, boys,' he said. 'What can we do for you?'

David's emerging message was clear: help us, or we dish the dirt on you. He was well-informed on Dulles's hidden activities and knew that the older man's security had been penetrated on several fronts, including ones Dulles didn't know about. Swiss Intelligence was also feeding the US Treasury information on Dulles's irregular financial dealings. What's more, David had the name of Dulles's mole in the German Foreign Office, which gave Dulles pause to consider: the mole was a German diplomat named Kolbe.

The bottom line was, Dulles was being blackmailed and he knew it. He afforded himself a pained chuckle as he said, 'You boys really are serious, aren't you?'

Other than that he covered his surprise well, kept up his pipe-fiddling act and conducted the meeting as though it were an academic discussion on nothing more threatening than Spenser's *Faerie Queen*, his mild discomfort a result of overindulging at lunch. But I could read his mind by then, calculating the odds, figuring out how best to accommodate David while using him. I could picture him saying to Betty afterwards: 'I'm going to fuck that boy every which way.'

Dulles's only betrayal of interest was an almost imperceptible leaning forward, until David told him about his line into the Kremlin, which made his eyes bulge and gave him the look of a man who had just been offered something he wanted very badly.

'Are we talking about the same Kremlin, son? As in Kremlin Moscow?'

David ran the exclusive ring of Jewish agents protected by Canaris, who had allocated them on paper to the Hungarian secret service. The rumor we had heard was correct.

The attraction of David's network was that it offered a faster and more secure service than the old Vatican routes, as well as having access to something no one else had. David had spies in Moscow Intelligence and knew what secrets lay at the heart of the Soviet empire. Years later it emerged that he had been the Kremlin's agent all along and had fed crucial disinformation on Soviet military strategy to the German High Command.

Karl-Heinz makes no mention of David in his papers, which doesn't mean that he was ignorant or not involved. A passing remark suggested he knew perfectly well what was going on. Karl-Heinz contended that Dulles deliberately sacrificed his agent Hatz. Hatz had volunteered for the Russian front, as ordered, then defected to the Russians at the end of 1944, with the intention of operating as Dulles and Karl-Heinz's agent behind enemy lines.

It is left to me to suggest that David was given Hatz's name by Dulles in order to prove his Moscow contacts. David duly passed Hatz's name on, resulting in Hatz's arrest, which gave Dulles his answer. (Hatz spent ten years in a Soviet labour camp, after which he was allowed to return to Hungary, which was then Communist, where he became coach of the national fencing team. Poor Hatz! He was one of those historical connectors, like Bandi, who ended up unaware of the extent to which others had used them.)

Dulles gave an awkward laugh. Helping what remained of Europe's Jews moved swiftly up the agenda.

Beate von Heimendorf, Zürich

Like Mr Dulles, Mother didn't like Jews, not in so many words though her manners forbade any direct expression of the sentiment. Besides, she professed to be forward-thinking, emancipated and of liberal persuasion, and was clever enough to know that her prejudices were best kept to herself.

When Hoover told me of his meeting with Mr Dulles in Mother's study I experienced a shock of recognition. It took me a while to identify its cause, perhaps because I had suppressed it. Was Mother referring to the same day as the meeting with Hoover when she wrote, undated: 'Allen turned up this morning ten minutes early for his meeting in a state of agitation. He needed a fuck, he said, to clear his head. He spat into his hand to lubricate me and kept his raincoat on but deigned to take his hat off. He told me not to bother to lock the study door even though the cleaner was in the house. He took no time at all and afterwards he said, "Thanks. That's just what the doctor ordered." He looked smug and bashful. It is not often that

I allow myself to be used by a man and I shall not co-operate again in "clearing Allen's head" however important his meeting.'

Hoover and I have now entered what might be called the meaningful phase. We are both perfectly aware of our own and the other's desire, yet do nothing for fear of spoiling everything. Sometimes I wonder if I should not take the initiative, and treat him like Dulles treated Mother, spitting into his hand so he can wet me.

I feel infected by Mother's crudeness. What for me is a subject of reticence, and fear of exposure, was for her a simple matter of appetite. To appropriate her forthrightness for a moment: *a fuck had is better than one not had.* She wrote that somewhere. Elsewhere she noted, *I shall learn to take sex like a man with no thought for the consequences.*

I showed Hoover Mother's note, hoping that it would release something in us, but it had the opposite effect and we ended up giggling nervously. Hoover seemed depressed. He said, 'Ironic, isn't it? Excuse my language, but Dulles got a fuck before we fucked him in the meeting.'

Hoover, Budapest/Switzerland/ Liechtenstein, 1944

History, Don DeLillo once wrote, comes down to people talking in rooms.

And the great battles, an eighteenth century French General used to say, are nearly always fought in the points of intersection on staff maps: what happens in the joins.

We move into areas so deniable and undocumented, and so far into the interstices, there is now only my word to say it happened, and I have never spoken of it before. There was no record. There were no witnesses apart from the four of us and I am the last one. Karl-Heinz's papers make no reference to the meeting, nor do history books even hint at it, though Dulles's Nazi involvements have been noted, if not widely broadcast. But given what was at stake, the meeting was both logical and inevitable.

Karl-Heinz sent word that we had to speak urgently. Our private communication was not through the local Red Cross office but a solitary tailor, the shabbiness of whose shop was misleading. He ran a large concession to provide the SS with uniforms.

Karl-Heinz's suite at the Astoria was what he called his 'afternoon lodgings'. There was a mistress in jodhpurs with a Wallis Simpson hair-do, and a small furry dog ignored by Karl-Heinz. 'Magda is just off riding,' he said. Apart from the irksome prospect of being arraigned for war crimes, it wasn't a bad life.

We left Budapest that night in a Red Cross car. Karl-Heinz traveled on German Red Cross papers. There were no delays at the borders, which suggested that the guards knew who they were waving through, even though Karl-Heinz traveled in civilian clothes.

He asked me what I was going to do after the war. I had no idea. I had no real understanding of what life in peacetime involved. He said he was thinking of emigrating. The opportunity to indulge his passion for horses would be more easily realised somewhere like Argentina.

The darkness, the isolation and the empty road allowed me to ask the impossible question. 'What about the Jews?'

He didn't miss a beat. The answer came out sounding easy and well-rehearsed. 'That was Heydrich, and he's dead. There are others who will be held accountable. It was complete madness, but on the other hand you didn't hear anyone protest too much. The Allies did fuck-all to stop it. That Jew-lover Churchill, for instance.'

Karl-Heinz was not an evil man, yet I have no doubt that he had seen and done evil. His deviancy was a matter of record. There had been an investigation of him by the

SS judicial authorities in Warsaw for corruption and sexual co-habitation with a non-German. Karl-Heinz's survival skills were demonstrated by the fact that he escaped indictment after the war when his immediate superior was hanged for his Warsaw activities. As for his time in Russia, he once told me, much later, he had served with the cavalry brigade of the Kommandostab Reichsführer SS. It was as close to a confession as he ever got. The brigade was one of three divisions created in 1941 under Himmler's personal command, and therefore an elite among the elite, which carried out many of the early mass killings.

We are talking about a period of what? Six weeks, perhaps only four, which Karl-Heinz deleted from his life. According to the record, his brigade, under the command of Hitler's future brother-in-law, had cleared the large marsh areas south of Byelorussia which were accessible only to cavalry. The invasion was in June and at the end of the first week in August Karl-Heinz was transferred to an administrative post.

His record is exemplary for its elisions, given how easily he could have tripped up. Iron Cross, first and second class, received 1941. No signatures on compromising documents. A dose of the clap in the summer of 1941, and a transfer back to Berlin to an economic department of the SS where again his signature did not appear on any of the wrong documents. Karl-Heinz on paper: all the marks of an ambitious and red-blooded junior officer.

*

We drove to Vienna and flew on a Swiss plane to Zürich where our papers were scrutinised more thoroughly. We parted at the main station, where I would arrive again so many years later on my way to see Betty Monroe. I think I had guessed by then who his passenger would be.

Dulles and I drove through the following afternoon in an ambulance across Switzerland to Liechtenstein, on the Swiss-Austrian border. The back had been adapted into a travelling saloon with comfortable seats and a toilet. I saw nothing of Dulles even when we stopped to fill up.

The ambulance was a brute of a Mercedes. Each gear change, and there were many on the winding mountain roads, involved a double declutch.

'Nothing you see in the next twenty-four hours will have taken place,' Dulles had said to me before the journey. He looked conspiratorial. He knew I would report back to David in Budapest. It would be useful to him for me to be able to tell of a secret conference with top Nazis. No doubt I would be fed some line about the proposed rescue of Jews too to assuage David's fear that Dulles was stalling on the issue.

In fact, I never mentioned the meeting to anyone, sensing that even knowledge of it was enough to get me killed, and the more people who knew, the more likely that was to happen.

I suspect that David did learn of it, but through Karl-Heinz who had a very clear line by then, which was to be seen to be aiding the Jews as much as possible, both as Himmler's secret envoy and as part of his own private efforts to save his neck.

Our initial destination was an isolated private house by the border, timed for arrival after dark. We swapped to a private car. The crossing involved no checkpoint, just a forest track whose directions were explained by the man who organised the vehicle swap. He didn't seem like the owner of the house, more like a groundsman or gamekeeper.

On the track through the forest, a deer got caught in the headlights. Dulles said, 'Look at that,' and otherwise said nothing until we arrived at the inn. In the rearview mirror he looked preoccupied and nervous, his earlier cheerfulness gone. A man way out on a limb. I wish I could have said three words to him then: *Bay of Pigs*. He would have nearly another twenty years to wait until his nemesis. By then he would be head of the CIA. His night in Liechtenstein would amount to one of his greater triumphs, albeit one omitted by the official record.

The inn was all lit up and busy, which surprised me, until I realised that it would provide perfect cover. A working inn was the last place anyone would expect an off-the-record conference to take place. The downstairs bar and restaurant were crowded and noisy. The place was unusual for there being no uniforms: Leichtenstein was another European pocket noted for its shady neutrality. I checked the inn out while Dulles waited in the car. There was nothing suspicious.

Their meeting took place upstairs. Access was by an exterior staircase. It was still cold at nights even though it was early summer. The air was fresh after rain. A dozy Alsatian patrolled the courtyard.

Men who shouldn't be in rooms together: Allen Dulles and Heinrich Himmler.

Categorically two men who never met. I was there to deny it. History would fail to record such a meeting taking place, partly because it made a mockery of history, which, in the end, is just someone's official account. Putting Dulles and Himmler together was an historical impossibility. Both men were aware of the fact and much of their enjoyment stemmed from making it happen, and extended to maintaining the pretence of their travelling names as they introduced themselves: Mr Davis to Herr Kott.

Dulles in tweed suit, Himmler in a sports coat and flannels, both wearing fanatically shined shoes. I rather fancied that Dulles had cleaned his own, Himmler not. (Dulles had a fondness for simple tasks like fire-building. He had a housekeeper but complained to me that the man didn't clean his shoes properly.)

There were English-style sandwiches and bottled beer. Himmler looked like he'd had a haircut that morning, severely razored up the back. He was a mild-looking man, with a receding chin, deferential almost, with cautious rather than good manners. He was several stages short of the Aryan ideal and resembled nothing more than an off-duty scout-master talking to his old professor.

Improvisation makes for strange bedfellows.

Karl-Heinz and I waited in another room, perhaps for half an hour. I had trained myself to be blinkered in such circumstances, but I do remember the flat, unreal quality to the introductions, how both Himmler and Dulles for all their knowingness seemed diminished by the furtiveness of the encounter. Even Karl-Heinz, usually so imperturbable, was betraying nerves.

What was at stake that night? The future as we have come to know it? Possibly. Karl-Heinz, as an economist, was in no doubt. Perhaps because of his nerves he talked. Perhaps because I was less nervous, having the least to lose, I asked what was going on. He mimed deaf, dumb and blind.

I said, 'We're way beyond anything treasonable here.'

Karl-Heinz eventually said, 'Success in chess is about how many moves the player can see ahead. In historical terms, what is being discussed next door is about as far ahead as it is possible to think. They are talking in terms of moves that the rest might get around to seeing in five years' time, if that.'

Karl-Heinz was privy to the future. Karl-Heinz had the Reichsführer's ear. Karl-Heinz never said as much but he hinted that what was being discussed next door was based partly on his own proposals. Like the criminal who needs to share his crime, Karl-Heinz spilled the beans, in a low, urgent monotone. Our age was one where religious and moral absolutes no longer applied. For the moment the vacuum was filled by the principle of will, the totalitarian state. The upheaval we were witness to – the wholesale destruction of civilian populations – would become the norm. It was the corollary of mass production. It was his belief that totalitarianism would be followed by a modification of that system: the military-industrial state, which already had wide support in the United States.

Karl-Heinz knew about such things. The SS had whole economic offices devoted to future predictions.

Karl-Heinz, ironic, starting to look pleased with himself. 'Off the record, Hitler's problem is that he has no economic policy other than one that is defined in terms of blood and territory – which is fine for the average German dolt but of little use in the long term.'

He smirked and said that an economic policy based on looting was not the best foundation for a thousand-year Reich. 'Capital is the big issue. That much is clear to the gentlemen next door because they know that the next conflict will be between capitalism and its adversary, Communism – and unless precautionary measures are taken, Germany will become the battleground. There, I have said it.'

Karl-Heinz, confidence restored, a man with an investment in the future. His final prediction was, 'There is no such thing as unconditional surrender. There are always conditions.'

To my surprise we were summoned. It was Dulles who fetched us. 'Boys,' he said, 'we need some help with translation.'

I suspect there was an element of hubris involved and they were keen to have their visionary plan witnessed.

Both men had an instinctive understanding of what was involved and how events would play out. Himmler was fostering a vision of his own role in its unfolding, as a power player in a quasi-democratic form of New Germany. The war was already lost. The immediate task was to preserve German assets. The second was some form of Russian containment. The third would be to reinvest German assets in the new German state, once containment had been achieved. That night, in essence, the postwar German miracle was hammered out.

Dulles would take care of the first: German assets would be moved out of Germany and its territories. Dulles had the wherewithal to do that, through a combination of German and Swiss contacts. He looked smug. He said he had already negotiated transactions for German businessmen, through Schroeder's Bank, where he had kept connections, and the Bank of International Settlements. The money was now safely in Argentina where he had good contacts, right up to the top. Himmler looked even more like a scout-master who had, to his delight, found himself entertained by a pirate. Dulles warned that these routes would be under increasing scrutiny as the war went on, but that would not necessarily prove a deterrent. Swiss banks would come under investigation but he was well placed to use the Vatican as an alternative. The Vatican was ideologically pliable as it was anti-Communist. Himmler nodded and added that he too had his Vatican connections.

Regarding the containment of the Russians, Himmler suggested that if events were to play out correctly in the near future, he would be able to make a formal proposal involving Germany's surrender to the Western Allies. Dulles was more pragmatic. 'If you're talking about a coup d'état it might be feasible,' he said, 'but it would have to be something swift and decisive to budge Churchill and Roosevelt into abandoning Stalin.'

Himmler must have known how unacceptable he would be to the Allies, and realised that Dulles would know it too. Nevertheless, he obviously planned to be around for a long time. Appearance would count for him: unmartial, unwarlike, unbloodthirsty. Could this be the architect of so much – thanks to the factory methods you could hardly call it bloodshed – *elimination*? He looked at me with clear, under-educated eyes: no trace of doubt, no trace of conscience, only the certainty of destiny.

Dulles and Himmler were on the money. Get the loot out, stash it, and reinvest it back into Germany when the time was right. Don't let those Commie bastards get their hands on it, and make sure none was around for reparation to the Jews.

The Jews came under Any Other Business. Himmler discussed them politely, didn't call them Yids or Kikes. The Führer had approved a policy of exchange, Himmler said, which they were pursuing. Himmler called Karl-Heinz by his rank and full name, and he said he had already made successful negotiations towards an adoption of this new policy and was in discussion with the vice-president of the Zionist Organisation in Budapest which was trying to raise money for sixteen hundred Jews to buy their train tickets out of Hungary. Himmler asked Karl-Heinz what the

German cut for the deal was, and was told 10 per cent. (When I asked Karl-Heinz afterwards if the train was for real rather than another way of extorting money, he looked hurt. 'If it was just the money there's nothing to stop us from taking it.') In addition, Himmler said, an agent for the Zionist Relief and Rescue Committee had already been sent to Istanbul to offer one million Jewish lives in exchange for supplies and ten thousand trucks, to be used 'only on the Eastern Front'.

Dulles nodded politely. He didn't use the word 'ransom', just said that he thought this was a judicious move under the circumstances. He considered it would be advantageous to involve Jews as much as possible in these new discussions. Dulles offered a secure courier service, run by Jews. He added that, given what was at stake, Jews proved the best messengers. Dulles didn't call them Yids or Kikes either, but there was a ghost of a smile between them.

The meeting lasted no more than a couple of hours. Dulles drank, Himmler didn't. His open bottle of beer remained untouched. Both men were clear-sighted and precise. I left believing they were right about how things would play out, and they would get away with it. Himmler clicked his heels on departing, but refrained from saluting. Karl-Heinz winked at me behind his back while Himmler and Dulles shook hands. 'A pleasure to do business,' mumbled Himmler in English. 'Likewise,' said Dulles.

After they had gone, Dulles sat down and loosened his tie. He looked at me like he was figuring to what extent I was trustworthy. This must have been a calculation that went through his head quite often. We were supposed to return to the house near the border for the night, but Dulles had other plans. He wanted to stay in the inn and told me to fix rooms. He also wanted to eat downstairs in the restaurant. I questioned the wisdom of this. 'Fuck it, Joe. Just fix it,' he said. 'I'm in so deep, what does it matter? I just want to sit with ordinary folk tonight.' This was rich coming from Dulles, not known to have ever given a thought to them before.

We ate downstairs. The restaurant was emptying but the bar was still full. The kitchen was closed but we were offered what was left: a large hunk of pork with a sweet cabbage. Dulles asked me to sit with him and then proceeded to ignore me. The restaurant was dark wood and candlelit and looked like it had been standing for hundreds of years. Dulles ate greedily and drank two bottles of wine to my one, followed by several schnapps. He ate with his napkin tucked into his shirt collar and gnawed on the knuckle, eating with his hands. After he was done he belched, said, 'Pardon me, and not a word to Mother, Joe.'

Hoover, Budapest, 1944

By the time of the Liechtenstein conference, I knew pretty much all there was to know about Dulles's financial activities. Thanks to Karl-Heinz's banker mole I had embarked on what Naomi would call a steep learning curve.

Dulles worshipped at the masonic and occult altar of money and was intimate with all its transubstantiations. In the banker's words, it was both a sacred and a profane process. 'The miracle of money laundering is like anything else,' he said. 'It depends on who you know, and Mr Dulles knows a lot of people.'

There was his brother, for a start. As early as 1923 John Foster Dulles had been involved in working out a complicated system by which Germany borrowed from US banks to pay off its war loans. Dulles worked in his brother's law firm from 1926 and went on to make huge profits from investments in Nazi Germany.

I watched Karl-Heinz using an expensive Mont Blanc fountain pen to write down what I told him, a fragment of which survives: '. . . deals include arrangements between

IGF [I.G. Farben] & Standard O[il] of N.J. Farben = 2nd largest shareholder in Standard Oil after J.D. Rockefeller . . . Rockefeller controls United Fruit, a Dulles client, which continues to trade with the Third Reich, as does Standard Oil.'

Even Karl-Heinz, who did not surprise easily, was astonished by the volume of Dulles's investment in the Third Reich, in excess of a billion dollars on behalf of clients, most of them tax-shelter deals from the 1930s. Karl-Heinz translated this into a year's budget for the German war effort. 'Imagine,' he said, 'a billion dollars invested in the Third Reich during the American Depression. Think of the legal fees!'

Karl-Heinz's mistress, Magda, wandered in and out of the room, comfortable with whatever compromises she lived with. Her life consisted of riding, having her hair done and organising Karl-Heinz's social life. 'What tricks are you up to now?' she would ask affectionately.

Further scraps among Karl-Heinz's papers include a list of US firms – including International Harvester, du Pont, Ford and General Motors – that bought directly into German ones and used the profits for investment in requisitioned Jewish firms or German arms production. Karl-Heinz, peering over the top of the spectacles he very occasionally wore, said, 'So, who paid for the arms that are killing all those young American boys, mmm? It's not a black and white world.'

What Dulles invested with one hand he hid with the other. Dulles was the paper-trail king. The banker in the stuffy Zürich apartment had explained how in 1940 Dulles's firm made the Swedish Enskilda Bank the dummy owner of the US subsidiary of Bosch, the German engineering company, and now makers of coffee-machines (including mine in Florida). This act of deception was specifically designed to allow the German parent company to continue dealing with its American subsidiary.

The main inconvenience of the war was that it created borders. Dulles's Swiss operations were largely about undoing those borders, and were for the most part extra-curricular. The wherewithal for these clandestine activities was in place long before 1939. The war was almost a sideshow to what was really going on.

It was a world that Beate understood very well from her mother: one of leather-bound address books, a loose association of international contacts with mutual interests – money mainly – and strategic marriages, all compounded by an understanding of how to work the law.

There was a beauty to many of the moves, and Karl-Heinz taught me to view them with a connoisseur's appreciation. Everything was already in place to facilitate the transfer of money out of Germany. Himmler and Dulles were going to make it disappear from under everyone's noses.

'Just imagine,' said Karl-Heinz. 'And no one will be any the wiser.' I suspected that Karl-Heinz's indiscretion was a way of loading me, should he need me as a future character witness. By being involved in the theft of the Third

Reich's funds – for that is effectively what it was – he could be seen to be conspiring against the state.

Dulles held several aces. There was Perón, an old client, in charge of Argentina, happy to stockpile Nazi assets and welcome whomever necessary. Another Dulles client, Rockefeller, had South America sewn up after his appointment as Co-ordinator of Inter-American Affairs. This dull-sounding title allowed him to develop his own corporate interests at the expense of the British. The British were overcharged, bullied and blackmailed so that Rockefeller could increase his market monopoly by using local shell companies which were set up to trade with the Nazis. Co-ordinating committees were run by executives from Standard Oil, United Fruit and General Electric, all pro-Nazi.

Beate, also with a connoisseur's appreciation of the clandestine, asks, 'At what point does vested interest become a conspiracy?'

'When those interests are sustained through illegal means,' I tell her. She is quick to grasp that conspiracy is always read as exceptional, supernatural almost, when in reality it is an extension of everyday business. It is how things operate.

Between us we come up with a definition, which Beate writes down, using an old fountain pen of her mother's. *Conspiracy is when those affiliations that make up any vested interest become concentrated, usually for short periods of intense effort, to achieve a particular end through underhand or illegal means.*

'Yes,' she says, when she has finished, pleased with our effort.

For Dulles, money was the real action. Killing or rescuing Jews was a useful distraction, behind which he could get on with the real work of shifting the money around so no one would notice. His profession was the profession of the twentieth century (oil its lifeblood). A legal background would be the preferred qualification of several future heads of the CIA. Lawyers of similar persuasion to the Dulles brothers went on from Wall Street to work for the government where they continued to serve their clients' interests. Prescott Bush, grandfather and great-grandfather to future presidents, hired Dulles to conceal assets he had invested in Germany.

As members of a segregated society, these men had no problem with the Germans doing the same to theirs. Germany's internal affairs were not their concern.

During a summer of intense negotiations, mainly over the fate of Hungary's Jews and then, after the rural clearings, Budapest's, which, in Karl-Heinz's words, 'kept everyone busy', I retain several mental snapshots of Willi Schmidt, each a little more etched with a sharpness not previously evident. The Occupation had hardened him.

Willi to me, in one of his smart café-bars, mirrors on the wall reflecting our murmured conversation: 'I hear you are moving in interesting circles. Nobody is sure who you are working for.'

The remark hung in the air. I could not tell if this was a threat. Until then I had assumed we were still friends.

Rumors clung to Willi too. One was that he was working for the Nazi security forces, another that he was helping Jews, yet another that he was involved in the redistribution of their confiscated assets. (Willi said the Jews were making it too easy for the Germans.) He had recently moved into an apartment with one of the best addresses in the city, and said he was renting it from a family which had just moved out.

Willi told me that Budapest was going to be treated as an open city for Jews. Later David told me that this story had been created by the SS to allay fears, which raised the question: how close was Willi to the source?

While Budapest waited at the top of the slide, Willi hung out more often in the Astoria, happy to be seen sitting with all sides, cultivating his notoriety. Willi knew the secrets before they became gossip. He told me that Auschwitz had complained that it could not process the numbers Eichmann was sending and transportations were being kept in sidings until they could be dealt with. Meanwhile those Jews who had tried to buy their way to freedom were stalled in their own siding in Bergen-Belsen, he said, waiting to see if Himmler would change his mind. Willi laughed about how everybody had been made to get off the train and panic set in when they all were invited to take a shower. 'German sense of humor,' Karl-Heinz said later, sourly. 'They were just showers.'

Between Willi and Karl-Heinz there developed a rift,

which first showed itself as an impatience at any mention of the other's name. Karl-Heinz accused Willi of using Nazi connections to run local fascist gangs and take over Bandi's black-market operations while Bandi was 'off somewhere'. Willi denied it and said that Karl-Heinz was out of sorts because Bandi being 'off somewhere' was a peace-seeking mission that was not going to plan because 'no one wanted to be friends with the SS'.

Their falling-out was over an 'ideological matter', Willi confessed with an arched eyebrow, well aware that such concerns were usually beyond his consideration. Karl-Heinz had hi-jacked the Jewish ransom train negotiations off Wisliceny and had tried to up the price to two thousand dollars a ticket; he later settled for a thousand.

Several 'actor and actress friends' of Willi's had been promised places first by Wisliceny then Karl-Heinz, who went back on his word in spite of Willi already having paid Wisliceny. 'On top of that he was charging a fee for the direct requests, then adding them to the official list and charging again.'

Karl-Heinz remained ironic. 'I was only obeying orders. Anyway, Willi's full of shit. You want to watch him.'

The day we met, Budapest was getting its first news of a failed plot to kill Hitler – censored by all the usual outlets. Karl-Heinz said, 'Warn your friends that the deportations will start again.'

Were the two connected? I asked. Much later in his papers Karl-Heinz wrote of the July plot: 'What no one seems to have guessed, even now, was the significance of Bandi Grosz's role. Bandi was the Reichsführer's secret ambassador, through me, and his purpose was to use the Jews-for-trucks business being conducted by the agent for the Zionist Relief and Rescue Committee in Istanbul as a screen for peace-seeking with the British (rejected). The great unanswered question was, How much did the Reichsführer know of the plot to kill the Führer? Was Bandi put in place in the anticipation that the Reichsführer would, in the event of the Führer's death, be in a position to negotiate a swift and alternative settlement? Coincidentally, or not, the Hungarian deportations were halted some ten days before the assassination attempt.'

At the time Karl-Heinz dismissed my question, and the one after when I asked if he thought that the assassination attempt was what Herr Kott – as we continued to call Himmler between us – had been referring to when he and Mr Davis had talked about a coup.

Karl-Heinz looked at me. 'This should not even be thought, let alone mentioned, even between us.'

As he showed me out, he said, 'They are saying that plotters will be hanged with piano wire and their deaths filmed on Agfa-Gevaert's new colour stock.'

I met Dulles the week after the Hitler plot failed. He made no mention of it and didn't seem unduly concerned to hear Karl-Heinz's news about the deportations beginning again. I was in Switzerland, on behalf of Karl-Heinz who was involved by then in unofficial talks with independent and neutral agencies about extending diplomatic immunity to Hungary's remaining Jews, who were by then concentrated in Budapest.

Dulles said he wanted me in Strasbourg on 10 August. The stated purpose was a conference with the German Red Cross about the reallocation of prisoners-of-war in the face of the Russian advance. I would be contacted.

Dulles in his Herrengasse apartment: I fancied I could smell the trace of Willi's aftershave in his room, grew sure that Dulles was running us in close tandem. Too many people were using me on deniable operations. I was more and more fearful of Hungarian counter-Intelligence which, piqued by the Germans, was quite capable of taking me off to the Hadik Barracks. I once asked Willi if he was worried. 'About what?' he said, mystified. 'I'm Swiss. What do I care?'

Hoover, Strasbourg/Transylvania 1944

I made two more excursions before the final crisis in Budapest, which showed how strangely the Nazis were redefining themselves, as men who could be reasoned with, while ostensible bystanders like Willi committed themselves to a deeper ambiguity. Both journeys remain memorable for their sense of isolation compared to the tangled politics they served, and their contrast to the centrifugal force building up in Budapest.

The train for Strasbourg left Zürich with clockwork Swiss efficiency. After the border I traveled with three uniformed German officers, a mother and two whining children, and an imperious, well-dressed elderly woman with brandy in a jar which she offered to the soldiers. Life in wartime. The three officers smoked too much and looked demoralised beyond weariness. We were delayed a long time, waiting for a troop train to pass. Conversation remained confined to careful pleasantries, while I wondered if they knew about the cattle trucks. It was absurd: what master race?

There was an inspection of papers. Mine attracted curiosity and afterwards the old woman asked where I was from. 'He is a neutral,' she observed, so nobody was left in any doubt. What was more, one with a window seat. I offered round my chocolate. '*Ach, die Schokolade*,' said the tired young mother, with an air of ecstasy. She told me it was the children's holidays. I was surprised there still were such things.

The chocolate had been taken along on the advice of Betty Monroe, who had given me my papers and ticket. 'You're getting around quite a bit these days, ' she commented, and asked if I was enjoying myself. From her blithe tone she might have been talking about summer camp. Practical Betty: 'You look like you could do with feeding up.' She told me to take lots of chocolate because the Germans were suffering from food shortages.

We had met at her house rather than downtown. There was a lawn party. I had been asked to use the back entrance. We did the transaction in the kitchen. It was the last time I visited the house until Beate.

Strasbourg smelled of summer, its ancient buildings a declaration of its immunity. French was heard as much as German, its influence most apparent in the bars. A man was painting a front door. This small domestic scene seemed all wrong. I was sure all the paint would have been requisitioned for the war effort. Several limousines – expensive prewar Mercedes – went by. Their destination became obvious. Outside the Hotel Maison Rouge a line of rich men's cars was parked, watched over by their chauffeurs, men too old for active service. Important people hung around the lobby, mainly civilian businessmen. Standing out for being much younger than the rest was Karl-Heinz in a dark suit.

'We meet again,' he said archly. I presumed he was why I was there. He ordered tea, giving the waitress some English Earl Grey he had brought with him; Karl-Heinz as usual was able to produce the impossible. He said, 'Give me Strasbourg any day over Budapest.'

Karl-Heinz's papers give some insight into the real state of his mind that day. 'Desperate days,' he writes. 'We walk the high wire of treason. The Reichsführer's softening on the Jewish question is done with the Führer's knowledge. What the Führer does not know is that this is a blind for more urgent dealings which will leave the Fatherland with some honour, especially should the worst befall us in the form of those bloodthirsty rapists, the Ivans. Since 20 July I am informed that the Führer is both fearful and rabid, and the most frequent sound to be heard is the scuttle of rats leaving the sinking ship, apart from the fanatic core. Unfortunately, the policies of divide and rule fostered by both Führer and Reichsführer now have dangerous consequences. That jumped-up puppet-master Eichmann has worked himself into a frenzy over the end to the deportations. Even after they had been officially stopped he ordered Wisliceny to sneak in one more trainload. This had been turned back by the Hungarian government. Eichmann's response was to summon the Jewish Council for a huge dressing-down:

rat-a-tat gangster-like screamings, spit flying. He has heard that the Führer shouts, too. He kept the Council waiting the best part of a day while the SS carried out the job using its own men and lorries. He was still sniggering at his deception when I next saw him, and amused because the Hungarians were going to be reprimanded by the International Red Cross for breaking their word about the deportations.'

That day in Strasbourg Karl-Heinz was saying very little, and I wondered if his coolness was to do with his falling out with Willi and continued association. He told me, much later, that he and Dulles had met privately in Bern to discuss the events at the Maison Rouge and he had overruled Dulles sending Willi to Strasbourg. When Karl-Heinz had insisted on me, Dulles said, 'Don't you think the boy knows too much already?' Dulles tried to persuade him that I was unreliable and 'an agent for the Jews', to which Karl-Heinz answered that his own pet Jewish agent was exactly what a man like him needed under the circumstances.

Karl-Heinz told me to lose myself and come back later. He would offer no explanation about what was going on. When I asked him what the matter was all he would say was, 'Too many cooks.'

A desultory, flat day with nothing to do, a day with no edge, left me restless and nervous. I tried and failed to sleep, tried and failed to read, failed even to make much of a walk round the park. Eventually I dined alone at the restaurant where I would eat with Willi Schmidt the next spring and, nearly sixty years on, with Vaughan.

As I was walking back through a small square I heard a sound familiar from Budapest: the thin pop of air-defence guns and the growing drone of aero-engines. Passers-by looked confused. The noise was new to them. Strasbourg was about to have an air raid. Dulles had told me I would at least be spared that because everyone agreed it was too pretty to bomb. He was wrong.

There were no signs to any shelters. I was in a small square. A gang of young boys dared each other to stay and watch. I hid in the deepest doorway I could find. The boys hopped up and down as the planes grew louder and squealed as the first bombs fell, as excited as if they were watching a firework display. The ground shook from the impact. The noise threatened to suck everything in. The boys staggered around like drunks, hands clapped to their ears. They didn't look so excited now. Above, the nervous tracery of searchlights patterned the reddening sky.

The last bomb left behind an image of the square shrouded in smoke and empty apart from the legs of one boy still running after his torso had been sliced off. A column of blood gushed from the trunk. A white dray bolted across the square in the other direction, hooves clattering on the cobbles.

I made my way back to the Maison Rouge, shocked but shaky with the exhilaration of survival. Shards of glass lay everywhere, like jewels in the moonlight. I remembered Bandi Grosz laughing as he pointed out how most of the bombs that had destroyed London had been made by the British themselves. The hotel lobby was very crowded. The immediate effect of the raid was wearing off and everyone was jabbering as panic turned to anger. Like the Jews of Budapest, these people had thought they were exempt and were full of growing indignation that the town had been bombed – the British were barbarians. A woman had fainted and was being revived. I found Karl-Heinz in a state of silent rage. My head was still ringing. Two distinguished elderly men walked by looking inconvenienced. One wore a monocle, the other a Prussian moustache.

Karl-Heinz half-dragged me into a servants' corridor, pushed me against the wall and, gripping my lapels, asked if I had told anyone about my trip to Strasbourg. Of course not, I said. He was sure his security had been penetrated. An enemy agent was thought to be in the hotel ready to receive a report of the conference.

'What conference?' I asked. It took some convincing to persuade him I had no idea why I was there. 'I didn't even know it was you I was supposed to be meeting.'

I think he explained not because he believed me – it had occurred to him that I was that enemy agent (I no longer know whom to trust) – but out of a sense of moral and physical exhaustion. That day a clandestine, and treasonable, meeting of German industrialists had taken place to implement the secret removal of their assets to safety via a pre-existing set-up of carefully disguised foreign subsidiaries, many of them US companies.

'I dream that my life comes down to a choice between

the Allied hangman's rope and Hitler's piano wire. I have seen the films of what they did to them, *pour encourager les autres*, and believe me, you would rather take any other way out, including full disemboweling,' he told me. 'I have the only set of notes of the conference for you to pass on to Mr Davis. *That* is why you're in Strasbourg.'

Under the circumstances, Karl-Heinz thought it too risky to entrust my return to public transport, so we drove. The car came courtesy of one of the industrialist millionaires, with a driver. It was a huge Mercedes, not the sort of car anyone would stop without extremely good reason.

We sped across the Rhine plain while Karl-Heinz and I dozed in the back. He dropped me at the border. As we parted he said, 'I have no idea when we will see each other again. I think my luck is close to running out. A final word of warning: Hitler wants Budapest's Jews. Tell that to your friends, but don't tell Willi Schmidt, and say to them it may be too late for me to do anything to help them.'

Immediately after my return to Budapest Willi sent me off on a trip to acquire a stockpile of tuna in a warehouse in Transylvania. The tuna turned out to be two hundred and eighty cans of sardines, four years past their eat-by date. The labeling was in French and the tins had come from Dakar, of all places, with various customs stamps still on the boxes.

Willi seemed scarely bothered when I told him that the trip had been a waste of time, and dangerous. The contact referred to by him had taken me to an industrial zone of a deserted small town where most of the buildings had been daubed with the Star of David. While there we were ambushed by three young men with very old rifles. They had shot my guide out of hand up against the wall of the warehouse and taken me into the forest where their leader, an older man with a pistol on each hip, accused me in crude German of being a black-market collaborator profiting from the Jewish clear-out. Apparently someone posing as a Red Cross agent had been doing a tidy business.

Only a chance mention of David's name saved my life. Word had reached them, even in the forest, that there was a man in Budapest organising resistance. These men were among the few survivors of the Jewish conscripts who had been sent to the Russian front to work in the labor battalions. All were gaunt and aged well beyond their years, weathered to a leathery brown. Two shorter and darker ones were Bosnian Muslims who had been recruited into the Hungarian army and deserted. Their leader had been a dentist before the war, a circumcised Christian who had been consigned to a labor battalion. I thought of the Strasbourg big-shots laundering their money, their immunity so rudely interrupted by the air raid, compared to the desperate, scavenging nature of this trip.

Willi had heard the same story about the bogus Red Cross agent, but only after he had sent me off to Transylvania. 'I had no idea,' he insisted, but I wonder now if he had been taking an idle gamble on my life because the fancy took him.

'They're saying this man was really a German agent who tricked deportees into thinking they would be safe,' he said. '"Quite soon you will go east to help with the harvest," is what he told them, and they went off in trucks marked "German worker-resettlers". He traveled around showing them an educational film of a camp like the one where everyone was going, a neat community full of grinning children. Is that what you heard?'

'Yes, except afterwards he went back to organise the redistribution of their possessions.'

'I didn't know about that part,' said Willi with the casualness of a man telling the truth. 'And I suppose you were told he was very tall?'

'That's the point of the story,' I said.

Willi shrugged and laughed. 'There's no crime in being tall.'

It was typical of him at that time that he appropriated the story and, while denying it by claiming that the incident had been made up by Karl-Heinz to slander him, he nevertheless related it in a way that was tantamount to an admission. He even changed the punchline to: 'People are saying he looked just like me.'

Karl-Heinz Strasse, Budapest, 1944

15.08.44 Magda, devout and carnal little Catholic that she is, attends Sunday High Mass at the cathedral. She reports that the priests seem to be praying harder than usual. The same goes for the congregation. Good turnouts are guaranteed. She witnessed a strange sight among the worshippers last Sunday: the atheist Eichmann in civilian clothes, supercilious in the company of Hungarian society.*

Life goes on! Eichmann at summer parties, Veesenmayer and Wisliceny in attendance, a few discreet murmurs about the state of negotiations. I have a photograph of him at an outdoor reception, grinning his cocked smile after organising a group of himself and pretty office secretaries. Eichmann is jealous of my

*Karl-Heinz remarks elsewhere: 'For years I wondered if Magda had not imagined this image of Eichmann at High Mass, but perhaps not. Writing about the Danube, Claude Magris has a note on him: "The technocrat of massacre loved meditation, inner absorption, the peace of the woods, maybe even prayer."'

camera, a Leica, a present from the Weiss family. He wants one too.

14.08.44 Sunbathers in the parks at weekends and at the Hajos pool. Imagine! Working on your tan this summer.

Expense account lunches are still being held to discuss something as frivolous as the financing of entertainment. 'Our man O's' contacts include a Budapest film producer keen to explore the 'possibilities of Hungarian co-production with Swiss companies'. The producer has made a donation to the Red Cross – almost certainly Jewish assets given him by Willi S. He and [van] H[over] have met several times – for lunches of pork stuffed with goose liver brought in from the country and paid for by the producer. [Van] H[over] reports that 'several film companies are now ready to commence production'.*

'Our man O' continues to be investigated by rival departments and may well end up in the dock with everyone else. The Maison Rouge affair testifies to the shakiness of the edifice. Spies in corridors. Reports suggest that the bomb-happy Mr Churchill ordered the air raid because he knew exactly what was going on and he had a full report of the conference within twenty-four hours. Fortunately for us, we have moles in the English

*Hoover notes: this enterprise would lead to an investigation of Dulles's (and my) activities, thwarted by Allen's flat denial of any irregularity when, in fact, we were using the film companies to launder Nazi money taken from the Bank of Hungary.

banking system with close contacts to the ruling classes. Windsor Castle remains a monument of indiscretion!

18.08.44 I continue to bend the Reichsführer's ear about the necessity to be seen to be doing what one can for Europe's remaining Jews, otherwise our report cards shall result in our not being asked back. Yet the Reichsführer vacillates, however much he understands that the Jewish negotiations are there to serve as a bridge to peace talks with those Allies who wish to stop short of complete annihilation. But the Allies are proving obtuse on the matter and I am jumped around all over the place. Honestly, it's enough to make one think of throwing in one's hand with the Russians!

18.08.44 According to Veesenmayer, the round-ups will recommence on 25 August. Thanks to our bureaucracy and its passion for duplication, the details seem easy enough for everyone to come by. The first six trains are scheduled to leave two days later with a transportation of 20,000. Thereafter daily trains will take away 3000 each.

The Red Cross and others are setting up Jewish safe houses in the diplomatic quarter, including one elegant modernist building not far from here. Dufy of the Red Cross and the energetic new Swedish diplomat Wallenberg are the ones with the reputations for getting things done, according to van H[over]. Wallenberg is embroiled in negotiations with Eichmann about the proposed emigration of eighty-seven Jews to Sweden. His tireless efforts to raise the number are matched by

Eichmann's stubbornness. I suggested to Eichmann that he play Wallenberg table tennis for them.

19.08.44 Magda has suddenly packed up and left – another little rat – which saddens me more than I expected. I rattle around this big house on my own. Fine wines and crystal glasses bring only so much consolation.

To Switzerland for what one has to tell oneself will be the breakthrough. But history will judge us badly, I fear.

Hoover, Budapest, 1944

I met Eichmann for the first time, summoned to a private meeting set up by Willi who told me that he 'wasn't such a bad fellow if a bit dull'. Eichmann was looking for a third party, such as the Red Cross, to act as a referee in Jewish negotiations. At first I wondered about the accuracy of Willi's information as he seemed unaware that the deportations were about to start again. Then I wondered about his sincerity. Acting as Eichmann's broker suggested his role was not straightforward. Willi had opted for Eichmann over Karl-Heinz. But his motives beyond that remained clouded.

Willi's eyes were starting to deaden and he was popping American Benzedrine courtesy of his Istanbul contacts. 'Much better than the local stuff. Try some. We're all going to need it before too long.'

Eichmann's downtown office was in an arts faculty building on the university compound, a strange, round affair with a rustic appearance more appropriate to woodland than a centre of learning. The location was significantly close to the headquarters of the Jewish

Council. The place retained its tatty institutional air despite the presence of several fine pieces, presumably 'gifts' or confiscations.

'You know who I am,' Eichmann liked to say. He enjoyed his notoriety. 'There isn't much else for him to enjoy,' was Karl-Heinz's tart verdict. Eichmann talked of the worthwhile work being done by the Red Cross, up to a point. He was annoyed by the establishment of safe houses for Jews at a time when there was a need for 'more team effort between respective organisations', with 'everyone pulling together'. 'No ambiguity,' he said on several occasions, giving me a measured look.

Sometimes he seemed surprised by his authority and then he looked like the travelling salesman he had started out as. He was keen to discuss his transportation problems, which he thought gave us a shared interest. He complained how few people could appreciate the difficulties of his job, and treated me to a cameo of his rage regarding the inefficiency of everyone else. 'I have made my position quite clear throughout – on behalf of my superiors – yet nobody takes me seriously. How stupid are these Jews? We sat at the same table. Normally they are the first to drive a bargain. And now they are all bleating.' He put on an effeminate voice. '"Please, mister, don't start the trains again."'

But the real point of the meeting was to frighten me.

'Obersturmbannführer Strasse is off somewhere,' he said, 'and unless you tell me what he is doing I shall have you on the first train out.' He grinned at the prospect.

I told him I had no idea where Karl-Heinz was.

'You must know. You are his spy!' He looked pleased with himself as he fiddled with his cigarettes. 'Are you familiar with Kafka's fable of the cat and the mouse? No? It's very short and this is how it goes. "Alas," said the mouse, "the world is growing smaller every day."' He put on a high falsetto for the mouse's voice. '"At the beginning it was so big that I was afraid. I kept running and running, and I was glad when at last I saw walls far away to the right and the left, but these long walls have narrowed so quickly that I am in the last chamber already, and there in the corner stands the trap I must run into."'

He looked at me, relishing his performance, knowing I had his full attention and was uncomfortably aware that the story was of personal significance and had been told by him many times before. 'Now can you guess the punch-line?' I shook my head. '"You only need to change direction," said the cat, and ate the mouse up.'

Eichmann gave one of his practised thin smiles and insisted we drink a glass of schnapps together. 'That story always goes down very well with the Jewish Council,' he said. 'They seem to appreciate its allegorical significance, its sense of what we might call historic destiny.'

He gave me my schnapps and insisted on touching glasses. Karl-Heinz had always dismissed Eichmann as a lackey and a jobsworth, but that day he seemed like the man with the cards. 'Cheers! You will be reporting directly to me now. You will inform me of all Obersturmbannführer Strasse's moves. But the choice remains yours – historical destiny or some maverick who, my spies tell me, can't find a Jew to talk to. Think of the mouse, think of all the one-way tickets waiting to be issued in this town. So, now you have a personal stake in my delaying the deportations, you and a lot of Jews. Spy well, my friend.'

Karl-Heinz didn't respond for three days to the message I left with the tailor. In the meantime, I kept thinking I would be lucky to survive the week. I threw myself into my work and at night wandered around town in a funk, drinking too much, looking in vain for Willi. I was angry with Willi. I was sure he was using me against Karl-Heinz, knowing very well what purpose Eichmann had in mind for me, and even discussing it with him (clinking glasses).

Everyone was saying, 'The war will be over soon. What's the point of killing all those Jews now?' An unspoken belief grew up that a collective drunkenness would ward off disaster, that hedonism would subvert totalitarianism. In smart hotels the bar pianists' requests from customers grew more bittersweet.

My dilemma was how much to confide in Karl-Heinz, how much to trust to him having the upper hand. I only had his word that he had the Reichsführer's favor. It was possible that he was just another go-between, like me. At last I got word from him to meet him at the Rudas baths where he had bribed an attendant for us to have a room to ourselves, and there in the clammy heat I told him about my summons from Eichmann.

'All right,' he said. 'Tell him what he wants to hear.'

I found his coolness infuriating. 'Is that it?'

'Did he start quoting Kafka at you?'

'What's that got to do with it?'

'Trust me. It's the best way. Whatever you do, do not for one second think of throwing in your lot with him. The man's days are numbered. Do not be afraid of him. Feel sorry for him, if anything. Eichmann is one of the ones who will end up taking the blame. Eichmann is what James Cagney would call the fall-guy.'

The next time it was sweet liqueurs in Eichmann's office. Wisliceny put his head round the door to say hello. Eichmann, pleasantly surprised, asked, 'Do you two know each other?' He took it for a good sign. 'You will feel quite at home here.'

I was still not sure whether Karl-Heinz's diagnosis was correct. It didn't seem like a good time to bet on either of them.

A city heatwave made Eichmann's offices uncomfortably sticky. Eichmann removed his jacket, with my permission. He said, 'I think it is better if ours is an informal relationship. So, have you news for me on what that Jew-fucker Strasse is up to?'

I reported that Karl-Heinz had been in Switzerland pursuing Jewish negotiations through Swiss contacts. He was trying to arrange a lump-sum payment in exchange for Jewish lives. The earlier negotiations in Istanbul had come to nothing after details had been leaked to the London *Times.*

Mention of the newspaper article threw Eichmann into a tantrum. 'The article was written by a Jew! It was all lies and inaccuracies. A hundred thousand Jews exterminated? Where do they get their figures? Do they have so little faith in our efficiency? We are talking *millions*! And I resent this little worm calling me a blackmailer because of my demands, and not even having the professional competence to name me. I am not ashamed. I am an official of the Third Reich undertaking state policies. I am underwritten by the law, and they make me sound like a cheap gangster.'

I told him Karl-Heinz seemed privately gloomy because the Jews were incapable of getting organised.

Eichmann snorted. 'He doesn't need to go to Switzerland to find that out. He can come here any day of the week and I will tell him to his face. The Jews have a death wish, it's as simple as that. The sooner everyone stops beating around the bush pretending to deny it the better it will be for us all. What else?'

'He said there might be a delay of two weeks to the deportations while the negotiations exhaust themselves.'

Eichmann grumbled. 'Here I am, having to rely on you to know my own timetable.'

Karl-Heinz described his trip as a 'fucking farce'. He had found himself standing in the middle of a border bridge in the rain because the Jewish representative he had been meeting had failed to get him a temporary visa. Swiss customs had refused to let them use their building, and the

Jewish representative had declined his offer of the German customs shed, so they had stood out in the open and got wet. The Jewish representative had proceeded to give Karl-Heinz a humanitarian lecture and denied all knowledge of German demands.

'Standing in the rain, being made a fool of. One, this arsehole was supposed to be negotiating the release of his fellow people. Two, he was meant to bring an American with him so we could start trying to get this war to an end before those megalomaniacs running it bring the whole thing crashing down. And there I am with two other officers – a humiliation you cannot imagine – and three hundred people from the ransom train as a gesture of our good intentions, and this standing-in-the-middle-of-the-bridge arsehole admits he is in no position to negotiate, so I yell, "Then what the fuck are we all doing standing here getting rained on?" And I could see him thinking: Big nasty Nazi. He was this little guy from Switzerland who did not have even half a clue, so I had to be nice and explain that many, many lives were in the balance, which we were trying to do something about. I gave him a week to go away and come up with some solid proposals. I told him I couldn't negotiate if he didn't bring anything to the table, and do you know what the little cocksucker said? "Not to the table, to the bridge," and I realised he had meant for us to meet there all along! The little fucker was there just to score a point. So I lost my temper again and said if he didn't come up with something fast he would have the fate of the Jews of Budapest on his conscience for the rest of his life, which left him with something to think about.'

Karl-Heinz recorded in one of his elegant notebooks: 'The Rescue Committee was given three months to prepare for these negotiations and has done absolutely fuck-all. Unbelievable! It is not a difficult transaction. I did not tell the Reichsführer what a balls-up it was in the hope that he will still stop the deportations.'

Eichmann, greedy for scraps, kept summoning me to his downtown office. One time there was a big panic going on, with secretaries rushing in and out, and Eichmann taking several calls during which I had to leave the room. Eichmann under pressure; secretaries whispering in the outer office. I gathered there was a military flap and the Hungarians were being difficult about restarting the deportations. Eichmann was enraged. He came out of his office shouting that if no immediate action was going to be taken, then they might as well all pack up and go home. Seeing me, he screamed: 'Out! And count yourself lucky!' Then to the secretary: 'Get me Veesenmayer. Get me Wisliceny.' Then, as I was leaving: 'Your friend Strasse won't be having his way for much longer if I have anything to do with it!'

The military development became clear. The Soviets had broken through German-Roumanian lines and the Roumanian government had declared an armistice and kicked the Germans out. As a result, the Hungarians were refusing to authorise the deportations. Eichmann could not act without their approval. Karl-Heinz filled in the gaps. Eichmann, emboldened, had dispatched Wisliceny to Berlin with an ultimatum to Himmler saying he should be recalled if no immediate action was to be taken.

On the day the deportations were due to recommence, a message reached me from Karl-Heinz saying the order had been rescinded. Himmler had finally acted.

Through September the mood lightened. On the streets people clung to the semblance of normality. Food had got scarcer, but most people had country relations. Geese, eggs, cheese and vegetables made their way into the city. The black market was a source of everything from forged papers to apartments. Pistols (Lugers) could be bought at the eastern railway station from soldiers back from the Front. Hungarian pessimism, a form of double-bluff – expecting the worst while enjoying the best – became both more complex and straightforward. The general gloom was countered by people drinking in private to peace in the hope that civilisation would prevail. An architect explained his theory to me in a bar. The city was conditioned by the feminine curve of the river that ran through it: Budapest was ironic and civilised; Budapest got on with life regardless of government.

When Eichmann's department was disbanded there was a real feeling that the Germans had been seen off and the city would be safe. It became fashionable to be pro-Jewish.

Karl-Heinz, that astute reader of character, recommended Eichmann for an Iron Cross, to distract him from his sulk. Meanwhile, Karl-Heinz's Swiss negotiations dragged.

Elsewhere, warning signs were there for those who wished to take note. Despite the recall of Eichmann's department, Wisliceny and the Gestapo had remained, and Eichmann hovered close to the Hungarian border as house-guest in a friend's castle. The petty bureaucrat grown used to high living, awaiting recall.

I am aware now of searching for evidence of some grand design, of, perhaps, evidence of Dulles in the ruins of history. Himmler and Dulles, it seemed, had vaulted ahead, abandoned the immediate unfolding for the endgame. Perhaps only Eichmann had the figures in his head and was keeping score. Himmler was playing for something else by then, with Karl-Heinz the adventurer still operating in the belief, just, that at some stage he could turn the situation to his advantage.

And Willi. I grew to see Willi as a projection of my own darkest imaginings. Of all of us, he seemed most suited to those times. Willi fraternised with everyone, a man of many performances, who had stolen something from all our souls. Black-marketeer. Emissary, for whom and what, nobody was sure. Leather-company representative. Ladies' man in his slim-waisted double-breasted suits, drinking cocktails. (Willi in Budapest: Magritte's portrait of a young man looking in the mirror, seeing not his face but the back of his head.) Rogue. Spy. Double-agent. *Bon viveur.* Jazz fan. A symbol, to me at any rate, of the sophistication of duplicity, my own efforts gauche by comparison. Willi always the better company. Willi's moves more glamorous than mine. Willi had a Hungarian countess for a lover. Willi rising to the challenge. I granted him a sense of purpose lacking in myself. Willi understood the text of which I was only the messenger.

The biggest shock was seeing him one day leaving David's hideaway, hat set back on his head, Dulles style. He didn't see me, or gave no sign if he did. My first thought was that his presence there had something to do with a betrayal of David by Dulles.

David refused to take my warning seriously. He bought Willi absolutely and stifled my objections. He knew Willi was almost certainly a double-agent but believed he would not betray him. I was also aware of no good reason why David should trust me any more than Willi. Word was going round that I was Eichmann's spy.

Willi was providing David with ready-stamped residence forms, which by-passed the law of registering any change of address with the police. He was also offering copies of something called The Order of Heroes, which precluded Jewish membership, and therefore granted any holder obvious exemption from the round-ups. But these turned out to be poor forgeries, so it was possible that my misgivings had been correct and that Willi was handing them out knowing their holders would be detained. Willi Schmidt was emerging as a bad puzzle with lots of bits that didn't fit.

On the morning of 15 October the radio gave out repeated announcements that the Hungarian government would be seeking an armistice with the Allies and the Germans would leave.

The streets were full of people. You could see where the Jews had torn off their yellow stars. It was the most beautiful of days, crystal clear, the likes of which happen only a few times a year. People's faces had a radiance. Everyone remarked on the weather as the quickest way to show the joy they felt. 'What if it had been raining?' a woman remarked.

I went round to David's place. It was already full, an open house with any pretense of security abandoned. As a man grown too used to false hope David grinned with caution while all around him others got drunk and kissed and, in the case of one impulsive couple, fucked on the floor. I wondered what Dulles would make of such spontaneous exuberance. Dulles and his shadowy moves, Dulles behind closed doors, working his paper trail; Dulles dry and untactile. Even Willi was there in spirit. Some of his jazz records had found their way to David's apartment. 'Black Bottom Stomp' on the turntable, played over and over. A young woman danced a crazy Charleston, and I imagined Karl-Heinz packing impeccably laundered shirts, prior to a quiet departure. We celebrated while history made its moves.

Nobody wanted to believe that evening's first broadcasts, not when they were so drunk and disinclined to let anything spoil their fun. Maybe fifty people were crammed into the apartment. Someone came in with a special edition of the paper with the news that there had been a coup d'état. Hungarian fascists had taken over. The Nazis would stay.

Everyone stood around in shock, drunk, hungover and crying all at once. Five minutes later they were all gone. David said to me, 'Eichmann will return. Save as many lives as you can.'

Outside, the streets were deserted, in forlorn contrast to that morning. I avoided main thoroughfares except to cross them. Each provided an illustration of the day's brutal change: on one a German convoy of tanks, with trucks of troops massed down side streets; on another two straw-haired teenagers with rifles and bandoliers, representatives of the new order, clubbing passers-by. One stopped me, wanting to know where I was going. I could smell the drink on him.

This was how it would end, I thought: some last act of absurdity at the hands of a near-child. I wanted to kill those boys more than anyone. I fired off a stream of German invective at one of them, which knocked the cockiness out of him, and cuffed his ear, a measure of my recklessness. The boy burst into tears while his friend gripped his rifle tighter. Any other day I believe he would have shot me.

The encounter was made even more unreal for happening in a busy street. Until then Budapest's terror had been largely invisible and orchestrated to take place off-stage. This new reign, administered by conscienceless, misfit children was a sign of things to come. They were representatives of a hitherto unimaginable level of infestation.

Embarrassment was the underlying mood of the next few days, each of us privately shamed for having dared hope. The weather reflected the turn of events by becoming bitterly cold. The new regime dispensed its thuggery. Corpses floated in the Danube outside the Ritz. Any sense of Nazi protocol – of the masked brutality at which they were so adept – was abandoned.

At the Red Cross office Dufy was in charge of organising the Jewish safe houses and had us working twelve- and fifteen-hour shifts preparing for the worst. Most of the rich young men who had signed on for the petrol ration could still be found in the city's smarter cafés with their cars parked outside. Dufy said, 'The rats are out from under the floorboards.'

Dufy, bald and sweating and previously mild-mannered to the point of invisibility, lacked Wallenberg's presence. Nonetheless he had been turned by Budapest's tragedy into a tenacious and committed figure. The Red Cross safe houses were full to capacity: David's false passes had seen to that. Dufy knew he would have to beg every favor going and each dubious contact I had could make all the difference, so he and I formed an uneasy alliance. Once he asked me straight out if I was a Nazi agent. I had a growing sense of how few liked me.

Dufy and Wallenberg held meetings with government appointees who were happy to be seen in their new authority and smart surroundings. Dufy, in his effort to save lives, was shameless in flaunting the possibility of full diplomatic status to the new regime. Karl-Heinz, still lacking a Swiss visa, wanted me to get a message to Dulles, warning him that unless his negotiations with the Americans took a different turn, the Russians would be in Berlin. I told him it was too late for messages to Dulles. I had to stay in Budapest. Karl-Heinz was dismissive: 'I should have you shot.'

'Join the queue,' I said and left thinking, Let him hang.

They were like ants scurrying through the streets, it was said afterwards. Less than a week after the coup the Jews were rounded up in heavy rain. Even those issued with protection papers weren't safe. The Hungarian police dug out any fit Jewish male, regardless of permits, to work on the eastern wall ordered by Hitler to hold back the Russians. ('More madness,' grumbled Karl-Heinz.)

Dufy wanted a film camera and stock to record some of what was going on and get it back to Switzerland. I spent an evening with my Hungarian producer who was reluctant until threatened with counter-Intelligence, who would be keen to discuss his illegal services to the Third Reich. All he managed to come up with was a little home-movie camera and a stack of three-minute spools of film. It was inconspicuous, if nothing else.

Dufy drove me around in a marked Red Cross car and we filmed the round-ups through the window as the gendarmes went about their business with zealous officiousness, under light supervision from the SS. I learned to film in two- to three-second bursts to save stock. Once we were stopped by an SS patrol and an officer asked what we were doing. Dufy said we were members of the Red Cross and the officer replied: 'I can see that. I asked what you were doing.'

'Filming this street theatre.' Dufy sounded in no mood for nonsense.

When the officer asked for the camera I thought he was going to confiscate or smash it, but he just inspected it and handed it back, with a shrug, as though to say nothing we did could make any difference.

Karl-Heinz Strasse, Budapest, 1944

To Switzerland – with a visa at last! – to meet an American representative at the Hotel Baur in Zürich. With hat, overcoat and briefcase, a civilised man undertaking civilised discussion. Not all the news is good. I have cabled the Reichsführer to stop the marches and heard nothing back. It is possible that he isn't the final authority in the matter as they are technically a work deportation.

The Arrow Cross is aware of its unpopularity and probably limited tenure of government and makes life unpleasant all round. Apart from Eichmann, everyone treads carefully. On a good day my own backpeddling high-wire act is the most adroit in the Nazi Budapest circus, with Eichmann's close behind as death's humourless clown.

Willi Schmidt, a surprise visitor to Zürich, quite the rich man these days, is booked into a suite in the Baur. He tells me how a whole gang of Arrow Cross men barged into the Red Cross offices after discovering the secret presses that had been producing forged protection papers.

We made ironic discussion, our earlier differences, whatever they were, quite forgotten. Former friends, enemies for a while, now friends again, it would seem. Our peace-broker was Magda, who has fetched up with Willi. 'She still pines for you,' he told me, with a trace of smugness.

'The Arrow Cross are not delegators,' said Willi, ruminative over a good wine, 'unlike you Germans. They want to see the effects of their work, close-up. They made Dufy inspect all the papers and decide which were false. There was a quota he had to meet otherwise everyone got taken off.' Willi grew speculative. 'How do you select? It would be possible to overlook some false papers, but not many. The more attractive would stand a better chance, I suppose. A displacement must take over, a willed concentration on the irrelevant detail that makes it possible to get through the job – angles of light, the cautious negotiation between bodies, the double-knots in a child's shoelaces. What do you think?'

It was, I remarked, almost as though Willi had been there.

'Not at all,' he said. 'I am interested in the psychological pressure involved in these decisions. How did you select?' he asked, mischievously. 'Or did you just, um, not select and mow them all down?'

Willi laughed. I left it at a smile. Willi said he had heard the raid had been carried out because the Arrow

Cross was annoyed that Dufy had managed to set up a Red Cross office in the Jewish ghetto. The ghetto, right to the centre, would be sealed off 'Warsaw-style', according to Eichmann, Willi said.

What he didn't know was that it was Eichmann who had ordered those with false papers to be pulled from Dufy's protection. Eichmann was finally displaying the fruits of his labor: no sealed trucks to obscure destinations but a forced march down the country's main road, four abreast, two thousand a go because his precious train-set was fucked. Eichmann's grand gesture towards nihilism.

Eichmann, who has invested all of himself for his masters, realises that the one job at which he excels will soon be taken away. Eichmann is running out of future. Eichmann, in so far as he is able, is in spiritual crisis.

These are not days to be proud of. I am told that many of those left in the safe houses were grateful for Dufy's expulsion of the false-paper holders as they believed it bettered their own chances. Even before the raid a delegation from the safe houses had protested about the number of inmates with forged papers. What is the point when the imperative to survive undermines all chance of collective action? Eichmann and his stooges, myself included, have succeeded in reducing crowds to numbers, individuals to ciphers. The process of dehumanisation is complete long before the technicality of death.

Hoover, Budapest, 1944

My narrow-gauge camera recorded what it could as everyone set off into the gray dawn, followed by a small convoy of relief trucks. Many valid exemption papers had been torn up by the Arrow Cross. People had turned up lugging suitcases too heavy to carry. Everyone was expected to keep up, women in high heels, children as well as the old. The hardest thing to reconcile was that many of the marchers would have once driven along that road on business or family outings. They still wore their own clothes. Their anguish was witnessed. We marched through villages and towns where shops and bars were open and people went about their business, stopping only to point and stare. (One mother, to frighten a disobedient child, threatened to have him put on the march.)

Dufy said little. He smoked. We kept spare packets in the car because the cigarettes we carried were soon handed out.

Some marchers tried to establish good relations with the older guards. 'They can't shoot us all,' one woman said, though it was clear that she herself couldn't last much longer, having abandoned her shoes. All but the most stubborn discarded their luggage. Any cases still being carried were seized by guards looking for valuables. Ransacked cases lay disemboweled by the road. A good coat turned into the price of death. One Arrow Cross boy took to wearing a stuffed pink silk brassière over his jacket.

My little camera recorded a body jolted sideways by the force of a bullet, its impact doubled by the surprise of the image being in colour. The film producer had given me the new Agfa colour stock: the Arrow Cross boy parading up and down in the flesh-coloured brassière; the bright shock of such intimate pink. I shot 4000 meters of narrow-gauge stock.

At first the human crocodile looked like nothing more than a bizarre outing. The camera generalized and depersonalized. It couldn't cope with detail and those that it did record looked like inserts from something else – gutted suitcases; a close-up of a dead man's face, swollen from beating; a hand floating in the river. Then the line again, its more or less orderly fashion in stark contrast to the previous images. Sometimes it was possible to prevent violence by letting a guard see he was being filmed; not always. One gendarme looked straight at the camera before clubbing a weak old man and driving him into the river. He laughed about it afterwards as I continued to film him.

Then Willi Schmidt turned up.

When I asked why he was there he had no answer. But Willi always had a reason. He could have been spying for the Germans even as he handed out charity, or just come to sniff death and add to his wartime scrapbook.

Deprive a person of basic human requirements, multiply that by two thousand, and you have a sobering lesson on the thinness of civilization. Shit in your pants, the marchers were told. At some of the nightly stopovers elaborate loudspeaker systems were set up so warnings could be broadcast that the guards would machine-gun the crowd if anyone tried to escape.

While the marchers starved, their guards ate: an Arrow-Cross man obscenely waggling a wiener at a woman, offering her a place on a truck back to Budapest if she 'sucked his sausage' in front of everyone. Another, his mouth so full of bread and beer he could hardly speak, being made to laugh by another guard, and spitting out a half-chewed wodge which people later fought over.

Where Dufy and Wallenberg used a mixture of cajoling and threat in their dealings with the gendarmes and Arrow Cross, Willi became inspired by a newfound relish for confrontation. He took to pulling guards aside and telling them it was his duty to report cases of brutality to the SS, who would make sure that offenders joined the marchers on arrival at Hegyeshalom. Willi also put word around that the guards wouldn't be making the trip back and were going to be set to work alongside the rest.

At Göynű everyone was crammed into barges for the night. The guards forced marchers to run along rickety gangplanks slippery with ice. Fog and freezing drizzle made conditions all the more treacherous. Those who fell in the river froze and drowned. Two guards in particular were making the most of their sport, a big sadist and his protégé, who looked about twelve. The boy laughed as he smoked and watched, contemptuously flicking his butt at a drowning man.

Willi waited until they took a break on a jetty, then begged a light off the older guard, leaning in to catch the cupped flame. The guard gave a high-pitched squeal of surprise as he realised that Willi had shot him, in the groin.

The report made no difference in a night full of gunfire. The guard stared in disbelief at the blood staining his overcoat while Willi studied the man's face, teetering on the edge of eternity, and registered the terror of his last mortal moments, which ended as Willi delicately prodded his chest enough for the man to lose balance and topple back in the river. All the while the man's cigarette remained stuck to his lower lip, even as he screamed: a comic detail, a memory for life. Willi's honed curiosity left me in no doubt that he had wanted to do this for some time.

Meanwhile, I had told the boy not to move. He started sniveling. Willi to him: 'The shoe's on the other foot now, son.'

The boy's fear liquefied. He tried calling Willi 'mister'. He took on a shrunken appearance. His fingernails were chewed. Under normal circumstances he would have been whey-faced and pretty in a diluted sort of way. He tried to barter with his age. The whiff of shit was strong on the freezing air. Willi shot him in the jelly of the eye. The other popped in surprise. The spray of blood from the exit wound looked black in the dark. Willi was breathing hard as though after running a long race. Where the boy had been, a void between us. Willi blooded.

After that Willi became tireless in his efforts to pull people from the march. He seemed to have acquired an immunity through contamination. Willi ambiguous to the last, operating in the thinnest of margins on both sides of the fence.

Karl-Heinz Strasse, Budapest, 1944

11.11.44 An SS general tells me how he came across one of the marches while in his staff car. He considers it too late in the war for such non-humanitarian behaviour (correct) and that the Hungarians are exceeding their brief (correct). Three years earlier, the same man was much less circumspect. Many others like the general are busy revising their CVs. Matters previously boasted about are downplayed. A calculated moral ambiguity is the latest thing. What is called the getaway suit is becoming fashionable – a country bumpkin's outfit suggestive of a wartime spent in a rural backwater, mowing lawns in an asylum for the insane; or perhaps not, given what went on in those asylums. Getting one's story right is taxing even the sharpest brain. Russia? Never went there. Channel Isles posting, Entertainment Division.

14.11.44 Every day the marches get worse because those who follow are made to camp in the refuse left by those who went before. A particularly virulent form of dysentery has broken out.

I have nothing to offer the Reichsführer except bluff. No one is interested in negotiating with the SS. Eichmann has made a point of telling him that his will has prevailed. The marches continue.

Last night he was celebrating the deportations with mare's-milk alcohol, exclaiming that it was the first time he'd drunk it. (Fancy!) Veesenmayer and others were on hand for one of a series of intimate soirées, intimate because most have grown wise enough to refuse the invitation. Everyone was toasting each other and congratulating themselves on the lack of local resistance. Eichmann was sad too that his job was nearly done. He declared 1944 his *annus mirabilis*, the year he had come out of his shell. He was congratulated on 'an elegant performance' by Veesenmayer at his most smoothly diplomatic. Eichmann, with false modesty, replied that he could not have done it without the order from the Chief of Security Police and the SD. To me Veesenmayer tut-tutted about Hungarian brutality and agreed the marches were lunacy.

Eichmann on being asked by me if he didn't think that the Hungarians had used excessive violence: 'That is their problem.'

Hoover, Budapest, 1944

No one knew why the marches suddenly stopped. Some said it was because Dufy had threatened the Arrow Cross with Allied reprisals. I believed that Karl-Heinz had persuaded Himmler that his peace negotiations would stand a better chance if they were ended. At any rate, the day after, he had a message for Dulles, which was that all gas chambers were to be destroyed on Himmler's orders.

But Dulles seemed preoccupied with his own moves. History was a private affair for him, a series of deals of more or less his own making. His overriding concern was to move Germany's money. The rest was secondary. The peace negotiations were to keep Himmler sweet. Himmler was almost certainly no part of Dulles's postwar plans. Dulles had to keep the Jewish rescue negotiations going because David had threatened to expose him – while protecting his own position with his Moscow intelligence. Being seen to be making the moves was something Dulles excelled at, the appearance of getting things done. Formality and cheer, the pipe-smoker's tricks. Give any man a pipe and he will appear smart and a good listener.

Dulles's money convoys went about their business. Trucks from Budapest via Vienna into Switzerland; Red Cross markings. Trucks from Berlin. The same routes, the same border crossings; no hold-ups, no technical hitches. Always a night crossing into Switzerland and from there to a castle over the Italian border in the Brenner Pass. Turn round, go back, do it again. Dulles's reward for my loyalty: US citizenship and the prospect of a job in the United States when the war was done – doing Allen's mon(k)ey business.

In Budapest Eichmann had one move left, done to spite Karl-Heinz and all those who had worked so tirelessly at their rescue work. He had the Arrow Cross round up seventeen hundred men, who had protection papers and were employed in the city clearing bomb damage, and put them on trains to Germany. Eichmann: a man with an itch who couldn't stop scratching.

German newsreels were still laboring under the illusion of a glorious victory. Budapest grew full of importuning. A prostitute complained that the number of bourgeois women willing to sell themselves was causing a glut, and where were the men anyway?

Through the chaos walked Willi Schmidt, a handsome man come into his own. What was Willi doing besides getting rich and bringing relief to the ghetto? I still find it impossible to make up my mind. However, Willi was consistent in certain respects. He always had the most attractive female staff, and in the ghetto was no different.

The Arrow Cross were afraid of him because of his SS connections. I had to wait until Saigon to encounter Willi's equivalent again: men who thrived as everything fell apart, who were born to exist at those historical junctures where the general collapse is exploited by the few who operate outside of any moral laws.

I bought the notion of Willi as life-saver and his line that it was no longer possible to stand by and do nothing. Swiss Willi converted from a lifetime of neutrality. On the one hand, Willi was a series of shifting moral refractions, capable perhaps of redeeming himself while also cultivating a profound ambiguity in the face of a moral absolute: *Thou shalt not kill.* Experience had taught me that there was always more to men like Willi and Karl-Heinz. So what was in the ghetto for Willi – and for Willi and nobody else?

The ghetto was the opposite to the dance of death of the marches. Stagnation prevailed. Cold ate at the marrow and the soul. You stepped over people, even in dark cellars. For most there would be no coming back, even for the survivors. They would remain eviscerated by the experience.

Willi used his position to barter for medical supplies and borrowed a German nurse. The place was an epidemic waiting to happen, he said. He insisted I took injections. We did them in his apartment, in a luxurious block with a carpeted entrance and a lift. Willi was living in ever greater opulence; the previous owner was an Arrow Cross official who had taken early retirement and decided to leave the city. Willi was sharing with several actresses and Karl-Heinz's former mistress. He had his own bathroom, which he kept padlocked. Inside, it was like a dispensary. Willi did the injections himself. He said: 'I should have been a doctor.' Then: 'We will all be gone by Christmas.'

By the time Christmas approached, everyone in the ghetto was suffering from malnutrition, and there were outbreaks of typhus and diphtheria. No food was delivered for five days and there were frequent power-cuts. When Russian bombing left casualties in the ghetto Willi did what he could to get them to hospital. A particularly virulent form of diarrhoea broke out, which was as psychologically undermining as it was physically, and many died. At 32 Kalona Jozsef Street five lunatics were living in the building; Willi said: 'Perhaps madness is the only answer.' His own sanity seemed in the balance. He became feverish and for the first time I wondered if he would survive the war. His eyes acquired the burning, dangerous clarity that could be seen in those in the ghetto who were about to die.

By then the Danube was full of tortured corpses. People were hanged from lamp-posts. Willi, cackling, said: 'They are known as Christmas decorations.' He told me that he had found abandoned Jewish orphans, previously under Dufy's protection, roaming the streets, skeletal two year olds hopelessly lost and screaming in fright from the bombs. 'It's the children I feel sorriest for,' said Willi. 'Nobody does anything for them.'

Was Willi a hitherto unsuspected sentimentalist when it came to children? His perhaps greatest humanitarian act went almost unremarked, except for a drunken commentary from Bandi Grosz on the last occasion we saw each other: 'Willi would sell his mother for profit, and he arranged for Dufy to move a whole lot of children out of orphanages to the monastery at Panonalma, with no fee involved. Even Dufy is surprised by that. Willi must be saving up in holy dispensations for the next world!'

Karl-Heinz suggested I move to the Astoria where it was still possible to get something resembling a meal. He was sure I could negotiate a good rate under the circumstances. There are few more delightful absurdities than a smart hotel trying to maintain standards in the face of catastrophe. We sat in an empty dining room, waited on by a couple of octogenarians, Hungarian fascists of the old school, who still clicked their heels. Karl-Heinz: 'Budapest is fucked. Budapest can look forward to a thousand years of Communist rule, and that won't be any fun since they backed the wrong horse in 1941.'

We ate poached eggs on toast, with a bottle of French red wine from the hotel cellar, followed by cheese. Karl-Heinz said that if the Germans had run their war effort as efficiently as they had redistributed their assets it would all have been over by 1943. Most of the money had been taken out of Berlin, he said, and no one was any the wiser.

For once I knew more than he did. I knew where the money was, a small sign of the shifting balance of power.

Karl-Heinz was keen to know more. He'd heard that the money route doubled as a German escape line. He offered to pay me to find out more. I thought about the end of the war, and wondered whether aiding and abetting men like Karl-Heinz was the wisest course.

Willi Schmidt was right. We were gone from Budapest by Christmas. One last cameo remained to be played. On Christmas Eve the radio announced a program of summary executions for, among other things, anyone hiding Jews. On that day Eichmann, I read somewhere, slipped like a gray ghost out of Budapest. More or less.

I still can't explain why I took Willi with me, what bond obliged me to find him in the ghetto and tell him it was time for us to leave. Willi was near delirious, shitting himself with sickness. He had some final things to do, he said, and told me to come and fetch him that night.

When I went back he wasn't alone. He was with a man dressed in civilian clothes, inspecting the last of his work, stepping through the diseased and the dying, a ghoul at the feast of the dead. Willi, stinking of death, said, 'We have another passenger.'

'No,' I said. 'He can make his own way.'

Eichmann gave me his familiar mirthless grin. Willi said to me in a whisper: 'Men like us are no longer in a position to make moral judgements. Take him and you can take one Jew too, any Jew you want. Some are still pretty.'

Four of us left in a Red Cross car. Willi, swathed in a huge nappy of blankets, vomited out of the window and shat himself; a semi-conscious child who passed the journey in a state of delirium; Eichmann, incognito, sat in the back of the car, inscrutable, dull again after his notoriety. He feared flying, he said. He feared enemy aircraft strafing his staff car. It had left with his possessions, he said, before adding unnecessarily that he wasn't in it.

Eichmann permitted himself a smile as we sped along the ancient Weiner Landstrasse down which, less than a month before, sixty thousand Jews had marched to his orders. Their suitcases still littered the verges. At Hegyeshalom the border post had been abandoned and we passed into Austria unnoticed.

Beate von Heimendorf, Zürich

Hoover and I spend our evenings talking about the end of the war, inching nearer to the point where I will have to lie. We sit in Mother's upstairs study, sipping whisky, and the room is full of our unmade moves. Perhaps we have grown too addicted to anticipation and tension. A ritual has grown up neither of us is willing to spoil. I suspect Hoover is afraid that his masculine pride will be hurt. I am not sure what my role is supposed to be. Part confessor, part confidante. He wants to be free of his memories. He has grown obsessed with the notion that Willi Schmidt is in some way his darker, unlicensed self. He came out from the ghetto feeling as though Willi had infected him with a moral sickness. Willi had made him select, and in his derangement had enjoyed forcing Hoover to make his choice.

Where Hoover remains haunted by his suppressed past I wish instead he would see me, us. I wish I could reach out, but a lifetime of caution forbids it. I wish only to preserve our idyll.

Vaughan phoned threatening to spoil that. He wanted to speak to Hoover – urgently, he said – and without thinking I lied, saying that he was no longer here.

Maybe he sensed I was blocking him because he asked in an unpleasant tone, 'Did you tell him about you and Dominic Carswell?'

I shook as I put down the phone.

When Hoover wanted to know who had called I told him it was no one of consequence, then, without preamble, I asked if he had been one of Mother's lovers.

He looked startled. 'What on earth makes you think that?'

Mother used the same trick, I remember: denial in the form of a question. I was disappointed. He was lying. I told him I was certain he had been, and wondered why I was trying to drive a wedge between us. Hoover qualified himself. He had *almost* been one of Mother's lovers, he conceded – still lying. I am more jealous than I care to admit.

Hoover finished the war in uniform. He must have looked good in one, I think. He was in Berlin by June 1945 as a 'cultural attaché'. Before that he had continued to do his 'private work' for Mr Dulles, who had arranged a job for him as interpreter for the commission responsible for the retrieval and safeguarding of looted treasures. This, he freely admitted, was a cover for doing Dulles's business. His last task as go-between for Dulles and Strasse had been the planned disappearance of a trainload of stolen Hungarian goods.

What Hoover doesn't know is that I have this from Mother's account: 'A[llen] full of boasts about his pirate exploits. He is quite right that the United States is not being far-sighted in terms of future security, hence his own efforts to redistribute large amounts of money for what he calls insurance purposes. A[llen] tells me his efforts are so successful that he can afford to sacrifice the contents of a Hungarian train carrying German loot. He is tickled by the fact that it was his personal call to General Patton which identified the train's whereabouts and the General complimented him on his excellent intelligence.'

I know from Hoover that the Hungarian crown jewels were on the train and they were later shown to him and Dulles in Frankfurt 'on the day Hitler died'.

But I am getting ahead of myself. Mother and Hoover.

In late May Mother summoned Hoover to the Hotel Maison Rouge in Strasbourg, which already held some significance for him. According to Hoover, she had made it plain that she wished to become better acquainted. Loyal service was to be rewarded with one of Mother's dalliances.

Hoover claims Mother showed up a day late. Instead he had been met by Willi Schmidt who was there with a message explaining Mother's delay.

Hoover had spent the evening with Willi who was still thin from his illness but seemed returned to his normal spirits. They deliberately avoided talking about Budapest and discussed only the future. Willi was looking forward to going to the United States, he said. They dined and walked afterwards through the deserted city. Then, on a narrow gantry over a millrace, Willi, without any warning, tried to kill Hoover. But the gun had jammed and Willi was still weak; after a very brief struggle he had slipped and fallen into the river.

Hoover told me this story with a flatness that almost amounted to a denial of its happening. His voice was empty but his hands fidgeted, betraying his discomfort. He said, 'I will never understand why Willi wanted to kill me.'

'I know why.'

'You do?' He looked reluctant and afraid. I could understand that, after my own lifetime of finding it easier not to live with the truth. 'And?' He spoke listlessly, like a man in shock.

'Strasse arranged for Willi to kill you because it was thought you knew too much.'

Hoover looked at me, and said: 'I see.' I wondered if he did see, and why he had never guessed what was staring him in the face. 'How do you know?'

'Mother's papers. I remember reading her account before they disappeared. I never thought we would ever meet.'

'Did she say if she was the person who identified Willi?'

I said I could not remember and watched him putting together what he thought were the final pieces.

'Once Karl-Heinz was safe under Dulles's protection then getting rid of me was no longer a priority,' he said. 'Did Betty say whether Dulles was in on it too? Dulles always worried about how much I knew.'

I shook my head.

'Dulles appointed me Karl-Heinz's controlling officer and sent us both off to Berlin. That was typical of the man. Expendable one week, indispensable the next.'

I offered to take him to my bed. He declined, saying that it wasn't a good night for him. Tomorrow.

And so we move on, stepping politely around each other, neither forward nor backwards, in our blind *pas de deux*.

Vaughan, London

London was supposed to have been about finding Dora, but turned into a zig-zag of paranoia. People I wanted to speak to avoided me while men I had no interest in were keen to talk.

From the start I was followed – fact or imagination? On the tube. In the streets. Even when I doubled back or jumped a bus I couldn't rid myself of the thought (or them). They could have been Kurds. They could have been Turks. Or someone else.

Fact: Carswell's office has been closed since my return, his mobile dead. Dora's got clogged with my unanswered voice messages.

Fact: No Dora. No Carswell. Find one, you find the other – fact or speculation? A search fuelled by worry and resentment (fact).

Fact: I experienced a strong wish to discuss my growing

isolation with Hoover and ask whether it was how he used to feel.

Paranoia is fast-spreading. The mundane assembly of previous existence disappears. Everything regroups in hostile form, a world only of bad connections, seen through a tight funnel. Paranoia is a state of pressurised ego, and the wild surmise of endless self-reference leaves you hopelessly trying to connect it all up, which you never can.

You become followed because you believe you are being followed. Extreme caution becomes a form of carelessness.

Paranoia as virus.

Fact: the women street-sellers on the Holloway Road, dealing in black-market cigarettes, are Turkish Kurds, as are their minders. Illegal liquor stores in the neighbourhood are fund-raising fronts for Kurdish terrorists.

Fact: one of the main drug wars in North London is between the Kurds and the Turks, an extension of the domestic war between an oppressed militant minority and the state. It is also the bottom line of a liberal asylum policy which aids the seeding of criminal enterprise. It is not out of the question that this war connects back to the people who killed Karl-Heinz: drugs, illegal migration, criminal activity as fund-raising for terrorism, nationalism, statewatch.

Step in past the walk-through blinds into the back rooms of the illegal liquor stores in Green Lanes or the Seven Sisters Road: London, Frankfurt and Ankara become interchangeable. The men lolling around at the back of the shop are tough and self-contained in a way that reminds me of Karl-Heinz's assassin.

I offered them my story in an effort to assuage a bad conscience left by the Neos. No one was interested beyond my eventual referral to a Hornsey Road men's social club where I waited until I was told to go to another, then another, to no emerging purpose. These places were always on depressed streets full of closed-down shops, nearly always empty inside, with frosted windows, a concrete floor, an old pool table, posters, and bottled beer in crates.

Half-a-dozen moves later I emerged in middle-class Haverstock Hill where I was told to wait at a pavement café. Three men turned up, smoothly cosmopolitan in a Mediterranean way. Two looked like they could be doctors at the Royal Free Hospital. The third was older, more academic and poker-faced. I could not tell what he was thinking.

Fact: he said that Mr Carswell, just mentioned by me, interested him very much. He told me he would be in touch.

Joining up the connections: paranoia realised.

Fact: Dominic Carswell's sexual preference is for heterosexual buggery. Quote: 'Dominic liked to put his thingy up women's bums, whether they liked it or not.'

Fact: Dominic Carswell was married to Beate von Heimendorf.

The cold sweat of pre-recognition as I was being told that Carswell had once been married to 'a Swiss woman': *I know who.* The near sexual pleasure of paranoia justified. Of all the unexpected facts, none causes more astonishment than this. It seems symptomatic of the associations clustered around the events of the last weeks – another connection no one could have guessed.

For all his elusiveness, Carswell belongs to a loosely affiliated world where old associates, and old girlfriends, of whom there are many, are only a call or two away. Purpose: to investigate contacts for possible leads on Carswell's whereabouts, and Dora's.

Source: a self-confessed 'dolly bird' turned parody of upper-class, middle-aged do-gooding, running a Clapham charity shop with colonial efficiency. Three gins down, old girlfriend (unmarried) grew indiscreet.

Fact: Dominic's sexual predilection was shared by Graham Greene. Old girlfriend's quote: 'Terribly overrated writer. All that tatty Catholicism, and a spook, of course, just like Dominic. I blame the public schools. The only things they come out understanding are secrecy and buggery.'

Rush of anxiety, frisson of discovery. *Spook.* It was the first time anyone had said it out loud.

Three night-time gentlemen callers, something out of a bad dream, kick down my door – white men in plain clothes: muscle in boxy suits, both with buzz cuts, and a well-spoken gent, actor handsome, with hair handed out only a few times each generation – a luxuriant Bryan Ferry hi-jack. One goon did something very fast and nasty that made me thrash on the floor. The handsome man informed me that how far we went depended on me.

He produced surveillance photographs of me in Germany with the Neos. Quote from the handsome man: 'Stop everything you are doing.'

As well as my German activities he knows of my Kurdish contacts. However, he seems to know nothing of Carswell or of Karl-Heinz's death.

Promise from me: 'I will.'

Fact: the next morning a phone call from a woman I had never heard of. She worked in television and she asked me out to lunch. She had a cancellation, she said. We went to Orso's and she offered me a job; afterwards I half-fucked her, having spent lunch trying to remember her name. Such social embarrassments were voluptuous compared to the memory of what the handsome man's goons could do. Coffee followed lunch at a café where she could smoke.

She had a great walk. She impulse-bought a load of videos (fuckably good taste, I thought). I was on vacation from the rest of my life. We ended up in a hotel room watching one of her videos. When she took a bath I was no longer sure what the signals were. A casual conversation through an open bathroom door, in that suspended state of afternoon hotels all over the world. I reminded myself of rule one – don't fuck the office – but decided I wouldn't really be, it would be one against Dora. I hated Dora for going off. That was what I had decided.

Post-bath, pre-coital in a big towel wrap. We drank mini-bar champagne. She provided the rubber. 'What a good little scout,' she said, and rolled the condom on to my effortful erection.

I realised – while fucking her in that summer afternoon hotel – what the underlay was. I was being bought off. We were in the handsome man's domain. We were there because of him. It was how these people worked. Eliminate opposition by absorbing it. The job on offer would be real, up to a point. On the pretence of making sympathetic programmes, we would infiltrate protest groups and activist circles to gain counter-intelligence. I would become a spook, by default. No programme would get made. The commission would never materialise. The plug would get pulled.

Paranoia and detumescence. I told her I was withdrawing, from her and from the job, pleased with the pun. File under strange fucks.

I met the Haverstock Hill Kurds again and told them about the Neos.

That night I arrived back to find my building on fire.

The heat was so intense that the windows across the street had blown out. Alarms were going off everywhere. Everything glowed orange. A large crowd had gathered to watch. More fire engines came. I wondered if I was supposed to have been in the fire and who had started it.

Minicab to Paddington, grave-like bed in a cheap hotel. I took an early train to Heathrow where I bought a ticket to Zürich. Nowhere else to go. In moments of unparanoid concern I worry about Hoover. Frau von Heimendorf, formerly Carswell, is lying when she says she doesn't know where he is. She wanted to know how I got the number. I don't tell her, to piss her off. The answer is easy: Betty Monroe is still listed in the book.

At the check-in the woman asked for my passport. I panicked until I realised I had been carrying it since my return, perhaps knowing all along I would be going back.

Hoover, Zürich

Just who is Bob Ballard? He claims to be 'a friend of the family' i.e. of the Monroes, but Ballard is a company man, I'd bet my bottom dollar. The cliché is appropriate as Mr Ballard is something of a cliché himself: the spook posing as suit, the elite pretending to be ordinary. He's pretty good at it.

My guess is Mr Ballard is playing the coincidence card, while he checks out what is going on. Beate knows him, or pretends to, but their behavior is not that of old friends. Her explanation – that he was a protégé of her mother's who has taken to calling round – sounds lame. Ballard is here to sniff.

Bob Ballard is thirty going on fifty, his act a rehearsal for the *gravitas* of middle-age. He is portly, with Clark Kent hair and black horn-rims. Bob Ballard and his X-ray eyes. His gaze rarely settles on anything or anyone for more than a second, like he is tracking an invisible fly. (Maybe he is. He looks like a man whose head is buzzing.)

Bob has the caution of someone who knows too much.

His job title suggests a dreary desk-bound attaché whose actual brief is operating at the outer reaches of national enterprise. Bob comes over as steady and boring, despite his darting eyes – he dulls the other person into talking so effectively that it is difficult not to tell him everything that has happened since coming to Europe, if only to pep up the conversation.

Meeting two: I decided to get leaky with Bob. This was not a matter of trust, more that I am too old for his conservative tactics. I put him in the picture, with regard to Karl-Heinz, and Willi, plus the hypothesis that Willi equals Konrad Viessmann. Bob nodded, offered nothing back, issued a standard denial about his own capacities while calculating who he needed to call.

Meeting three: By then I could remember how many sugars Mr B. takes. He confessed to a likeness for an English-style brew. Bob threw a curve ball. Up till now we had been content with gentle lobbing.

'Viessmann is Viessmann,' he said, 'going all the way back.'

'Meaning that Karl-Heinz's resurrection theory is bullshit?'

Bob nodded. The sceptic in me wondered if he was trying to mislead. I asked straight out: 'Are you here as a wrinkle?' Bob's eyes alighted on mine a fraction longer than usual. He was enjoying himself, playing dude to the old hand, patronising me ever so slightly. I told him the seat of his pants would be shinier if he was as desk-bound as he made out, which made him laugh. Bob was not a practised laugher. It was a wrong laugh, the gulping motion of a man sucking in air before going back underwater. His awkwardness made me warm to him. Something had become clear: we both knew what our subject was.

Next day, next meeting: Ballard used the proximity of his office – ten minutes down the hill, he said – to justify calling by. He says he walks when I know he comes by car. I liked him more for the lie. This time he came with an offering. A report by British Military Intelligence dated February, 1945. It was a facsimile of a document typed on semi-transparent paper. The print was faint, as though the typewriter ribbon had needed renewing, and had a misaligned letter 'a'.

The report noted the establishing of a Tropical Institute in Basel, with an affiliated office in the winter resort of Davos. The report's author, an English army brigadier with a double-barreled name, was as dry as a biscuit. He questioned Switzerland's need for such an institute, given its landlocked insularity and lack of channels through which such diseases might enter the country, compared to, say, Germany, with its colonies and international ports. The brigadier concluded that the Institute was a front for the disbanding Nazi medical profession and a forward base for its realignment. The Institute's journal, a review of tropical science and medicine, included several Nazi medical authorities among its contributors. The brigadier concluded: 'Is anything more probable than that German tropical scientists, backed by big chemical industries in Germany, are already planning ahead so as to lose no time in re-establishing their dominant position in the control of chemotherapy of tropical diseases?'

The board of directors made for interesting reading. It included former members of I.G. Farben, who had conveniently relocated to Switzerland just before the war, a leading researcher in pesticides and, among those attached to the Davos Institute, one Konrad Viessmann.

In print the name acquired an occult quality.

Ballard looked pleased with himself and wanted good-dog congratulations for his powers of retrieval. In fact, the rest of his news was not that hopeful. In company terms Viessmann was not even a file. Ballard had been able to find nothing except Viessmann's civilian biography, which indicated a full and complete life in the pharmaceutical industry.

Ballard grinned. 'Apart from?' I asked. Apart from one company reference, discovered by chance while accessing old Turkish files. He produced his second offering from inside his jacket. Bob was sweating on a cool day.

He handed me an old US assessment of Turkey's Cold War defensive capabilities dating from the 1950s. Its emphasis was on the depth of anti-Communist feeling in the military. Strong racial and fascist tendencies were noted, so was the fact that its elite troops were being trained by ex-Nazis employed by US military advisers to act as a stay-behind guerrilla force in the event of Soviet invasion.

Bob Ballard commented as I read: 'Looks like they had themselves an ass-tight, buddy-love situation.' He appeared mildly shocked by his observation, less, I suspect, for its expletive nature than for his momentary break in character.

Cold War Turkey – certainly Karl-Heinz had ghosted his way through that set-up, prior to Cairo. He had lectured junior Turkish officers on propaganda and psychological warfare, a euphemism for the extraction of information by physical means. This was a skill Karl-Heinz had learned after coming to work for us, as he never missed the chance to point out.

The report contained information on sponsored American lectures, among them an Ankara conference in May 1955, hosted by an American institute which was a front for the CIA. It included an address to an audience of invited Turkish military and academics on the subject of *Disease and Warfare* by the Director of the Tropical Institute of Davos. Speaker: Konrad Viessmann.

Ballard put his fingers to his lips which he tried to disguise as a pensive gesture. He inhaled. I finally understood the reason for his nervous eye-movements – it was down to his effort to quit smoking. He admitted that his body was patched together with nicotine pads which did nothing for his craving.

He made a joke: 'Perhaps the Turks were in the habit

of dispatching their political prisoners to Viessmann's tropical diseases clinic.'

Neither of us laughed. The penny dropped, all the way down. We stayed silent a long time, listening to the day wind down.

I told him to go out and buy cigarettes and a bottle of whisky. I gave him the money, so that his conscience would feel less bad. Waiting for him to come back, I thought again of Willi's baptism by death in the icy waters of 1945, of Willi's gift for exits.

Ballard sucked on his cigarette. His head disappeared in a wreath of smoke. We drank whisky steadily. I told him the CIA was getting old, like everything else. Organisational deceleration occurred at a faster rate than human ageing. The CIA was suffering from memory loss. Data corrupted. There were no longer the people to remember. I said: 'There's nobody left who knows what Viessmann was there for, and you've been ordered to find out.' Ballard studied his cuticles, looking almost coy.

We ran with speculations. Was the Viessmann file missing, deleted, removed or reallocated? What if? What if institutes and private empires traded in information just as the Medellin cartel did in drugs. Ballard drew comparisons with the old Texas cattle barons, capable through their wealth of running their own fiefdoms. We agreed on the essential lawlessness of the frontier. We agreed on the notion of oil barons as successors to the cattlemen, as men who had developed foreign interests, aided by friends and relatives in government, all of them with deep interests to preserve: the stuff of conspiracy theories.

We disagreed when Ballard argued that conspiracy theories always fell down because the last link couldn't be proved or made. I told him it didn't work like that. Conspiracies weren't linear and parallel, they worked in clusters, in successions of cause and effect. There was no mastermind. Dulles, for all his influence and big ways, was working a narrow channel. Big subjects – oil and money – narrow application; all Dulles's moves could be read as oil or money.

We agreed again. A secret organisation like the CIA fractured and its secrets extended to its own internal workings. Few, if any, knew or saw the whole picture. Operations got lost or superseded or hung out to dry. The ones funded by non-existent, non-provable budgets, could go into twilight in perpetuity, like those Japanese soldiers who stayed on in the jungle years after the war was over.

Ballard looped back to conspiracy, saying that in real life there was no such thing as tying up all the loose ends. He said: 'Even if you know all the moves in the JFK shooting down to the last calibration, it's still not enough.' I agreed. The truth is usually disappointing. Ballard asked about Dulles. I told him that Dulles was a combination of the carpet-bagging spirit of the Wild West and an East Coast education, a perfect fusion of lawlessness and the law, with a career devoted to breaking the rules and providing the necessary paperwork to prove that you hadn't.

We moved ahead, swimming in waters blacker than Chappaquiddick. We ended up speaking in whispers, the whisky oiling leaky brains. We asked ourselves if Viessmann was still covered by some ancient CIA umbrella and whether he was running a legacy of Dulles's wartime operations, which had blurred and mutated into a descendant of the Nazi genocide program with the same overlap of business and government interests.

There. We have said it. Ballard has nodded out. I have scared myself too much. The room is dark apart from a desk lamp. Heavy drapes, which I don't remember drawing, extend to the floor. I have no impression of a world outside of this room and what we have been talking about.

Vaughan, Zürich

When I door-stopped Beate von Heimendorf she denied again that Hoover was there but was too flustered to carry it off. It turned out he wasn't there but should have been.

'I don't know where he is,' she said, upset by my return. The last thing she wanted was me spoiling her fun with Hoover.

The phone in the hall rang and she ran to answer. She shielded the receiver and asked in a disappointed voice, 'Does that mean you're moving out?' She wrote down a number, taking care not to let me see. I asked to speak to him but she hung up first.

'Mr Vaughan,' she told me, 'Mr Hoover is not a well man. He should avoid excitement.' I said it was news to me that he was sick. She said he put on a brave face.

We traded. I said it would be a shame to have to tell Hoover about her marriage to Dominic Carswell. She gave me Hoover's number in exchange for my silence.

When I called he sounded pleased. 'Well, hello, nephew,' he said. 'Why don't you come on down?' He was at Sol's downtown office, he said. Beate stood in the hall, watching with a stricken expression.

I was shocked by Hoover's physical deterioration. Beate was right. He looked sick. He was smoking too. I asked if he should be and he responded with a cough he turned into a laugh, and said it didn't matter. Sick or not, he was enjoying himself. 'Come upstairs and meet the gang.'

The room he led me into was a huge space given over to untidy storage and vast amounts of junk. The building was an old factory, and Sol had the whole of the upper floor.

Hoover made a big show of introducing everyone like we were at a party. There was Sol. Whatever animosity had existed was forgotten. Sol's magnified lenses made him look more than ever like a cartoon grasshopper. There was Manny, a sardonic-looking man apparently beyond surprise. Hoover said: 'Manny and I think we were holed up in the same castle together in the Brenner Pass at the end of the war, but neither of us is sure.'

Manny had been working for the SS, Hoover explained. They enjoyed my mystification. Manny did the laundry, added Hoover.

'Forging German banknotes for Heine Himmler,' said Manny. Manny chainsmoked. He rated smoking as the last subversive activity, a willed act of self-pollution. He smoked Celtique, a fat cigarette of black tobacco which reminded Hoover of Belgium. Manny associated it with adventure, gypsies and Apaches, and slick knife-fights and absinthe, unlike American tobacco, which tasted only of the chemical process.

'And there's Abe,' said Hoover, 'somewhere out the back. Abe is Sol's son.'

Abe tracked information. Each transaction created a spoor and Abe traced people's movements just like American-Indian scouts used to, said Hoover. He saw a record of passage where the less experienced eye would see nothing. 'You, nephew, are an open book to a man like Abe.'

Abe's software programmes had been given state honours in Tokyo and there was a photograph to prove it. Abe looked like Oliver Hardy as computer wizard. With Sol standing next to him at all of five foot six, Abe had to be at least six five. He hadn't dressed up for his award – jeans from Switzerland's Mr High and Mighty and a black hat. They looked like a sad comic act.

Sol looked proud as Hoover described how Abe had a mind way out on its own. 'No small talk, but when it comes to keyboard skills he's a genius.'

I looked at Hoover and Sol and said, 'So, everyone's made up, then?'

'All buddies as of now,' replied Hoover. 'I strong-armed Sol into believing I had nothing to do with Willi's con.'

Sol said, 'He has kindly agreed to verify Frau Schmidt so that we can access Willi's account.'

'And if I get caught I'll be dead by the time it gets to trial.'

We laughed uneasily. Abe emerged from the other end

of the room where he had been hidden behind a stack of shelves. He was quiet and courteous, in contrast to his initial alarming hugeness in all directions. He still wore the hat from the photograph and the hair that poked out of it was long and plaited. His handshake was gentle. His calling was a solitary one, made lonelier by his intelligence.

The space we were standing in was being used to store a mess of junk, an accumulation of decades of debris. Sol called it a warehouse of memory. I picked up a Zürich tram ticket stub from 1943. There were papers, old clothes, books, documents, forgotten bank statements dating back forty years, a couple of old 78s, which had belonged to Willi Schmidt. The place was like a deconstructed Schwitters collage.

Sol was pro-dirt, unlike the Swiss. What the Swiss did best was laundry. They rinsed money like they rinsed everything else. Sol was anti-laundry. Pro-mess, pro-life was his motto.

Hoover said, 'Can you imagine, nephew, I saw Willi playing those records, and here we are all these years later. It makes you think. Willi should be here.' He sounded sad, like everything had gotten too old.

But then he grinned. I was pleased to see him. He said: 'This is my swan song. Let's go eat.'

On the street we made the oddest quintet. Sol announced that he had declared himself at war with Switzerland, dropping litter wherever he could. He wanted Zürich to look as messy as Greece or England. In the restaurant, an ersatz kitchen with Bohemian pretensions in a nearby warehouse, Manny resorted to playing the exaggerated Jew. Any difference embarrassed the Swiss, said Sol. I wasn't sure. The crowd was young and too concerned with being cool (Willi Schmidt's successors).

Talk turned to Carswell. Hoover thought I had been used by him to test the security of some aspect of his operation. I had been put in to see how far I got and to report back. Manny frowned and said, 'It's obvious.' Manny's response to being in public was to look even more sardonic. 'There was a split in the organisation. Carswell suspected and when this was confirmed, Strasse was dealt with.'

Stuff started to dovetail. We resumed. We pooled. Back at Sol's place Hoover got Abe to show me his party tricks, starting with all the details they had on Hoover – home address, travel arrangements, hotel bookings, medical insurance details. Abe had even hacked into Hoover's CIA file, including an internal report by Dulles from the mid-1950s which made for double-edged reading, sidelining him after a breakdown in Egypt. Hoover seemed unperturbed. 'I asked for a transfer, and they called it a breakdown.'

Abe did me. Address, credit-card payments outstanding, aerial photograph of my street before the fire. He even located a computer copy of the story on the fire due to run in the local weekly paper. It listed two fatalities and blamed risky cooking practices. Residents complained that many of the rooms weren't equipped with proper kitchens. More to the point, there were photographs. One was of the blaze itself, another of the watching crowd, with me out of frame, and a vaguely familiar face caught on the edge.

It came in a double tap. At the time I had been so preoccupied with Karl-Heinz's killer as Nemesis I couldn't connect him back to the Neos, and anyway had been more struck by their smart cars. His sidekick was the man in the picture. Hoover agreed that two dog-shit yellow jackets was too much coincidence.

Hoover said, 'The shooter was Turkish army till five years ago, then a blank. Which means that he was either outside of any system or so far in that he went off-record.'

'Meaning?'

'Secret military police, some covert anti-terrorist outfit.'

We did Carswell. We did Viessmann. There was almost nothing on them. It was as though they understood and mistrusted normal channels of communication for what they could give away.

Hoover said, 'I want to see Willi's face one more time before I die.'

Hoover, Zürich

The muddled and fretful ghosts of the past return to haunt me. Betty Monroe's capacity for subterfuge lives on. I imagine her permitting herself a sly smile, in the unblank moments allowed by her disintegrating mind, as she continues from afar to oversee our frantic lives. How she would laugh out loud – the familiar high peal, the head thrown back, teeth bared, her gutsy laugh – to be told of what I have just learned. It is her legacy as much as anyone's.

Abe, while rooting around in the great yonder, making idle internet investigations into the Monroes and von Heimendorfs – those connected and well-listed families – came across a tiny detonation in parenthesis: *(m. Dominic Carswell 1967; dissolved 1968).*

Cold rage and a silent taxi-ride up the hill to Betty's house where Vaughan witnesses the row between me and Beate and watches with growing alarm the angry pulse popping in my neck.

First I discover Vaughan already knew about her and

Carswell when she accused him of telling me, after promising her not to. Perhaps to avoid his guilty conscience, he turns on her. Then, on the question of how she and Carswell met, he stumbles across the great, unsuspected connection.

Beate says that their families were friends. 'Or it might have been Uncle Konny who introduced us.'

Uncle Konny: Vaughan and I look at each other.

Konrad Viessmann, present whereabouts unknown, has in spirit been looking over our shoulders all the time. Willi Schmidt was familiar with the house we were standing in; so, it transpires, was Konrad Viessmann.

An interesting point that has not occurred to me before. Among all Betty Monroe's souvenirs and memorabilia there are no photographs of Willi and none of Konrad Viessmann, family friend. After all, Beate knew Viessmann – Uncle Konny – since she was a child. Konrad Viessmann, the adopted uncle, friend to her father. Childhood summer holidays, apparently camera-less, were spent at his summer villa on Lake Locarno.

Beate denies all knowledge of Viessmann's possible previous incarnation and won't budge when challenged, two red spots of anger high on her cheeks. If she is aware of the connection then her lies are even better than her mother's.

To embarrass her I say in front of Vaughan, 'And I'm the dope for getting goofy about you.'

Beate has a singular beauty when trying to keep her temper. It offers a rare glimpse into a private self. Once her control is regained she is quick to point out that no one had brought up Carswell's name, let alone Viessmann's. She was hiding nothing.

We end up shamed by our argument. I suspect we are using it as a surrogate for personal frustrations.

Vaughan plainly thinks Beate is still hiding something and I am too caught up with her to see it. I watch ripples of animosity pass between them.

Vaughan reminds me of my younger self. Perhaps Beate can read this identification and it makes her jealous. It's like Vaughan and I are family, while her reticence has resulted in her exclusion. In Vaughan I recognise the same clumsiness, the same wariness, combined with an ability to trust the wrong person. The same willingness to run and be run (Carswell his Willi Schmidt). My boys used to buy airplane models. *Read instructions carefully before assembly* it always said inside the box. The sentence was not one that could be applied to my own life. Vaughan appears similarly prepared to act on the minimum information. In fact, he looks as though he doesn't even know there is a set of instructions.

It occurs to me that Beate hasn't properly identified her mother as the source of the anger she fights so hard to control. Much of my own anger toward her is not personal and more to do with being in the wrong time, of my not being ten or fifteen years younger. There is nothing more pathetic, or tragic, than falling in love too late. Beate and I were meant for Budapest, sixty years ago, before she was born.

*

Beate made a peace offering in the form of the phone number of Dominic's mother on the grounds that Mrs Carswell might know where he was. In the end she was more or less bullied into placing the call too. The only phone in the house was inconveniently situated in the hall, leaving the three of us awkwardly posed. It was not a straightforward call. Carswell's mother had promised not to pass on his mobile number to anyone and Beate was trying to wheedle it out of her and was already flustered when the doorbell went. Vaughan looked instantly nervous, bad memories of earlier intrusions stamped on his face. I looked through the spy-hole. It was Bob Ballard on one of his spontaneous house calls. He grinned as he stepped inside.

We stood around listening to Beate, like we were extras on a film set, watching her resolve ebb until, in a moment of inspiration, she invoked Viessmann's name: 'Konrad said it would be all right for you to give it to me.'

After she was done she handed me the number. Her hand shook slightly. She was still mad at me and clearly resented Vaughan and Ballard. She walked out with no more than a brusque good night. I went after her, tried to talk to her, took her arm, which she snatched away. She said, sounding cold, giving me the brush-off, 'You have his number now. Do whatever you have to do but don't involve me.'

The excitement of Carswell being a handful of digits away was too much for Vaughan. He wanted to know what I thought. I was thinking at my age why should I care what a woman thought, while knowing that the surface anxiety hid a deeper one: fear of the inevitable deferred, final meeting between Willi and me; fear that the assignment between us still had some way to run. In truth, the real worry that lay beyond that was far more stark. Soon I would be lying in that last hospital bed and Willi would have nothing to do with it. Willi was just one more distraction, whether he still existed or not.

'Call Carswell,' I heard myself say.

Carswell was switched off, so we sat around and what emerged was the added curiosity of Bob Ballard's role in all this. He knew about Carswell for a start, even though we had never discussed him. 'Now there's a surprise,' I said and he gave me one of his coded looks. He told us there was leverage on Carswell, who could be investigated for illegal trading to Iraq and other sanctioned states. Again showing his cleverness, he said, 'It sounds like the old wartime Brevecourt scam. Trading with the enemy. Isn't that where you came in?'

'Whose files have you been reading?' I asked.

In my mind's eye I saw a direct correlation between the visible junk at Sol's place – accumulated, unsorted clutter, all forgotten about – and the near invisible traces left by Ballard's and my superiors down the years, of aborted operations; forgotten operations; operations supported by some hideaway fund long past their date of usefulness; unrecorded operations, reported only on a mouth-to-mouth basis, where one of the mouths had gone silent;

whole castles of intelligence abandoned like medieval ruins.

As I get older I grow more afraid of the dark. On some trashy TV program the grandchildren had been watching I heard it said: 'There is no such thing as *total* darkness,' with the emphasis on the penultimate word. I can't imagine it but I know it is there and waiting, and Mary with it, acrimony in eternity.

I was woken by Vaughan, a man with things on his mind, needing to talk, even though it wasn't yet six-thirty.

He told me about his half-sister, and their blocked relationship. Uncle Joe had no advice, painfully aware of Dominic Carswell's intrusion into our respective lives. Dora was missing, he said, and he felt lost.

All he could see was muddle, concealed motives and fragments. He told me about a Chinesewoman in the Frankfurt smuggling yard who had no idea where she was or how long she had been there.

I said it always felt like this, for the longest amount of time. You made moves, you repeated moves, made wrong moves and in the end they added up to an approximation of sense, though not all of the moves turned out to have counted. If you were lucky, you walked away with a clearer idea of what had happened.

He felt like that about his Kurdish contacts. Real names were missing, communication uncertain, explanations were garbled. At the familiarity of these casual and fractured arrangements, I felt almost nostalgic. Vaughan had spoken to them for an hour in the middle of the night. From what he was saying it sounded like they were wanting to stir things up. They wanted to meet. They were muscling in – as they had every right to do – but they were an unknown and potentially volatile factor, because where they went, Turks followed. The Kurd Vaughan had talked to wouldn't give his name. He told him to call him Maurice. Maurice!

It occurs to me to wonder whether Vaughan is part of my story or am I part of his?

We met in a street café specified by Maurice, who made us wait. To be reminded of ordinary life was a surprise. See the mother with the baby buggy. See the man going to work. See the driver cutting up the cyclist. Vaughan talked of how nothing had felt like it fitted in London. The same applied here. Real life was looking strange. People, streets, weather had all receded. My sightseeing these days was in my head.

Maurice wore a beige suit and suede shoes and walked and talked like a respectable middle-class businessman. He smelled of Old Spice. His companions were two well-dressed young toughs alert to any potential hostile movement. Both wore shoulder holsters, and one looked like he was carrying extra on his leg.

Maurice was suspicious about who I was. I said I represented certain interests concerning the past. He looked like he hadn't considered anyone else might be involved.

Maurice was clearly important. He was educated and

ideologically tooled-up. The plight of his people was his only consideration and he would do whatever it took to alleviate their suffering. When he asked me if I wasn't too old to be involved I answered: 'It's a lifetime's cause.' Said with a straight face, it prompted a glimmer of a smile. Maurice with his guarded manner, smart clothes and taste for up-market cafés was a case of terrorist as aspiring diplomat, a negotiator-in-making. Our eyes gave out clear signals that we didn't trust each other, but we weren't enemies as such. It was the old Middle East game of my enemy's enemy is my friend.

Vaughan let me do the talking. Maurice wanted Carswell. I offered Carswell for Viessmann. I watched Maurice carefully. He knew who I meant. I said we wanted to know where Viessmann was. Maurice said Viessmann had a house in Budapest. He also volunteered that Budapest was where Kurds attempting to escape from Turkey got picked up and turned around (shades of the old Istanbul-Budapest shuttle). I asked why they were allowed to get that far.

'To encourage the illusion of escape,' he said. From there they were taken back and ended up in gaols where they disappeared.

He believed that the Turkish army had American support in its war against his people, and therefore British backing, which was where Carswell fitted. He told us to keep him informed of our meeting with Carswell, and in return he would find out more about Viessmann. It felt like old times – the uneasy alliances, the trade of information, the general untrustworthiness. There was a phone number to memorise for getting in touch. Any message would reach Maurice within an hour.

'And Viessmann, why do you want him?' he asked.

I said that Viessmann and I had unfinished business from before he was born. Maurice said he had no quarrel with Viessmann. It was he who had told them that escaping Kurds were being abducted.

'Excuse me?' I said, thinking I must have misheard. Maurice repeated himself. My heart banged like it had done earlier over Beate's revelations.

What Maurice was saying made no sense, seen one way. But looked at from a more acute angle the move was pure Willi Schmidt, with all the old qualities of Willi working both sides of the fence.

'What was the trade-off?' I asked. There was always a trade-off.

Maurice appeared caught out by the question. 'That we leave his factories alone.'

'Is that a fair trade?'

'No, but it gives us access to Herr Viessmann who might yet prove a useful ally.'

Willi again.

Vaughan, Zürich

Down at the station I saw Hoover, Sol and Frau Schmidt on to the Bern train, off to sort out Willi Schmidt's estate. Instead of going to Abe's like Hoover had told me to, I hung around trying Carswell. After twenty minutes he picked up.

He said straight off that I sounded tired. Carswell had that trick of deflecting everything with some personal remark. He did it again when he said, 'I expect you want to talk about Dora.'

He offered to meet. I could choose where. Sensing my mistrust, he said, 'Make it somewhere busy if you want.'

He sounded relaxed and normal. I asked if he was in Zürich and he said, near enough. A radio was playing in the background at his end. It sounded like he was eating. I pictured him in some sunny room with a plate of toast and had the strongest feeling Dora was with him.

The sentimental notion that Dora gave us something in common was a dangerous one, but, because of some perverse aspiration, it was Carswell I wanted to talk to most.

I still felt like Carswell's man, dupe or not, because I had gone in for him in the first place. He had the good grace to say, 'I probably owe you an explanation.'

Many people unconsciously equate good looks with moral worth. Carswell's voice – sincere and practised after years of reporting the world's disasters – had the same effect. He sounded like a man who could be trusted. I believed he had the answers and he would share them. I took him to be saying, 'Forget about the others. We'll sort this out between us. I'll get you Dora back.'

We agreed to meet at one. I suggested the street outside Frau Schmidt's, opposite the Opel dealership. Only when I got there did I realise how exposed it was. Nobody was buying Opels that day. Every car that went past looked like it was slowing down. I gave him twenty minutes and left in a cold sweat. I tried his number, got no answer.

He picked up an hour later, sounding angry. He said: 'I told you to come alone.' My protests must have sounded convincing because he then said: 'In that case you were followed,' and hung up.

I hadn't seen anyone. I went to Abe's. The way Bob Ballard came calling five minutes later, giving me funny looks, made me wonder if it hadn't been him.

Hoover, Bern

Bern's green stone reminded Sol of mausoleums, as did the potted geraniums everywhere. I remembered geraniums on the balcony of the house in Budapest where Eichmann had lodged. I told Sol. He said: 'My point exactly.'

Bern looked and felt exactly the same as when I had last been there in the war, entirely to order and reasonable, its history displayed with a pride that told of uninterrupted upkeep rather than renovation, as elsewhere in Europe, or wholesale replacement as in the United States. Bern was life as museum. The town was full of clocks that struck every quarter hour.

The lawyer's office was up in the old town, close to where Allen Dulles had lived in Herrengasse. It was in a tall, old building full of dark wood whose age and permanency lent weight and continuity to the practice of the law and its interpretation, reducing any transient human presence to insignificance.

The lawyer was a no-nonsense young woman who refused to be impressed by Frau Schmidt's performance of a lifetime. She remained brisk and sceptical of the law's ability to accommodate a case as vague and unsupported as ours. She hit us with technicalities, evasions and that excruciating Swiss slowness that grinds you down every time. Swiss legal time runs at a speed quite unrelated to the rest of human experience.

I hit the desk hard with the flat of my hand. The room probably hadn't heard a noise like it. The woman jumped and I told her I was glad because I hadn't been sure till then if I was dealing with a human being or a legal parrot.

How *dare* she doubt my word, I said, when I had been an official of the government of the United States, and had witnessed Frau Schmidt's wedding, as a result of my friendship with her husband, as well as being responsible for her safe passage to Switzerland. Willi Schmidt should be a national hero, I said. He was one of the few Swiss who had chosen *not* to sit on the fence!

Sol and I revised Willi's history. Willi had lived dangerously spying for the Allies. He had saved many Jews, including Sol. Sol showed the woman the number on his arm and asked: 'Do you think I had that put on to fool you?'

The woman flushed. Sol said: 'Willi Schmidt risked his life for other people, and you sit there and don't even offer us coffee. You desecrate the man's memory in your refusal to acknowledge his wife.'

'Bravo,' I said, but should have reserved my applause for Frau Schmidt. She sat with a trembling lip, radiating an enormous hurt. Outside, the clocks struck. Frau Schmidt opened her handbag and withdrew a child's patent-leather shoe and placed it on the desk. It was one of the pair she had shown me when we had first met. There were tears in her eyes.

'This is the last souvenir I have of my husband. He sold shoes, but you know that. Everything else is gone. The photographs, our possessions, the certificates. Sometimes it feels that even the memories have gone and I really have to remind myself that we met and married. Are you married?' The woman shook her head. 'Willi marrying me was a small miracle, and because of him I survived instead of being put in an oven. He wasn't in love but he did it to save me. Then we did fall in love, which was another miracle and I wanted only to spend the rest of my life with him. The last thing he said to me was, "I'll see you later." And part of me still waits, every day.'

Even Sol was getting misty-eyed. The lawyer stared hard at the shoe. Frau Schmidt wiped her eyes with a clean handkerchief. The lawyer shifted in her seat. Eventually she asked: 'What did your husband look like?'

'Very tall. Handsome, like an eagle. I was so proud of him.'

Another long silence, then the lawyer said in a small voice, 'I cannot accept your claim.'

I said, 'Surely Frau Schmidt deserves an explanation?'

'She does. But I cannot give it. There are complications.'

Frau Schmidt, still drying her eyes, asked, 'What sort of complications?'

The lawyer shook her head and looked miserable. Sol leered and said, 'Get a load off your chest.' Frau Schmidt was pushed not to snigger. Sol lit up a cigar without asking, playing the rest of the meeting as Groucho Marx. He added, 'It's not often you see a lawyer squirming, so we might as well sit back and enjoy it.'

Frau Schmidt said she wasn't budging. The explanation was slow in coming. Sol and I understood at more or less the same moment, but it was Frau Schmidt who said it out loud.

'Willi is alive!'

Willi Schmidt was indeed alive. Not only that, he had been in to claim his account, with documentation.

Wanting to see what sort of reaction it got, I said, 'I was with Herr Schmidt when he died in 1945. The body was identified by a colleague.'

The lawyer, confidence restored, said, 'You must be mistaken. There is no doubting the veracity of Herr Schmidt's claim.'

Willi Schmidt in that very office, turning up after Frau Schmidt's initial enquiry, had raised the question of her authenticity. Willi had denied ever having been married. He had been adamant. No Frau Schmidt, not ever.

Frau Schmidt asked, 'Does that mean you do not believe me?'

The lawyer looked uncomfortable. 'No. I believe you. And I shall tell that to the police. They asked me to take further meetings to see if there was a case for criminal proceedings. That will not be necessary.'

It was the emotional angle she was finding hardest. Frau Schmidt had no legal recourse yet this lawyer, to her own surprise, had ended up feeling sorry for her. Willi had lied to deny his wife's existence. Frau Schmidt's worst fantasy had been confirmed: Willi was a rat who had dumped her.

We were about to go when the lawyer volunteered one last piece of information.

'If it is of any consolation, I can tell you there was nothing of value in the account. It was empty, apart from a few francs.'

Sol blurted out, 'That's not possible!'

'He must have known it was empty,' I said. 'Why did he bother?'

'For the deposit box,' said the laywer.

'And what was in that?'

'Only Herr Schmidt knows. You'll have to ask him.' But she wouldn't tell us where he was; client confidentiality, a Swiss last laugh.

We sat in a café opposite Allen Dulles's old house, all of us in a state of shock. Sol, because he had proof that Willi was still alive; me, because Willi had broken cover; and Frau Schmidt because she said she had grown so comfortable with her fabrication that she had started to believe it. The tears she had cried had been real, for her lost husband.

Hey, Willi, I thought, sitting in the café. We're getting close enough to smell each other.

I went for a walk, leaving Sol and Frau Schmidt (it had grown impossible to think of her by any other name) drinking pear liqueurs. Even by full daylight I could feel the ghost of Dulles hovering. After the slow tick of legal time in the lawyer's office, everything felt telescoped and the years fell away. I could feel Willi and Dulles and Betty and Karl-Heinz crowding me, their scene-shifter.

Dulles's house appeared the same as it ever was, naturally. It was a fine and solid bourgeois building, with his old apartment on the ground floor, fronting right on the street, with heavy security grilles on the windows. I remembered the bars, and the chestnut tree, and the suspended street lamps which had gone off at ten at night during wartime, giving the city an eerie, abandoned feel.

Except for the cars, there was nothing to say that I wasn't back in 1942. The road sloped away from Dulles's house. To the right, in a hole in the wall, a familiar set of boxed-in steps went down to the wooded river bank. They were exactly as I remembered, different only for being covered with spray-painted graffiti. I thought of Sol's pro-mess motto, but sadly the Swiss turned out to be boring and pseudo-American even in their subversion. *Darryl Sucks* had been amended to *Darryl Sucks What?*.

Dulles had liked the steps because with one smart move you could disappear from the street and materialise on a lower level without being seen, and the treads being wooden made it hard for anyone to follow.

The space was now the resort of junkies. Halfway down, a couple loitered, making it hard to pass. 'Hey,

Dad,' one said in English. He had mouth scabs. There was a hypodermic on the steps. I trod on it and said: 'Whoops, boys.' Foolhardiness, perhaps, but I wasn't in any mind to put up with their trouble. The other one wanted to make something of it.

There is a tremendous cheap thrill for someone of my age being able to take out a gun and show it around. Why was I carrying it? I figured Maurice and his pals would be, so it seemed stupid not to. It had the desired effect. The boys held up their hands in a 'just kidding' gesture and swallowed hard.

The steps emerged onto a dog-leg path, hidden by trees. The noise of the fast river cut out any other sounds. The back entrance to Dulles's place was still there, a door recessed into a tall, gray garden wall way too high to climb. It was locked. Dulles used to leave it open when he was expecting visitors. I had forgotten how secluded and sinister the place was.

The path climbed and turned below Dulles's house, by the buttress of the big suspension bridge running high over the river. In the dirt by the pillar were the remains of a bonfire, more needles and a bunch of used condoms. The sound of the river merged with the slap of tyres on the bridge above. Metal service steps ran up the buttress to a platform, with a gap to stop the public from climbing on the sub-structure, a complicated mesh of steel struts. A man dressed in faded denims sat on the platform, legs dangling, and made a point of ignoring me.

I was certain I was treading in Willi's footsteps. He too

would have come this way after meeting the lawyer, for old time's sake. I could picture him, enjoying a rare day off from being Konrad Viessmann, being Willi again, signing Willi's name on the release form.

Hoover, Zürich

Vaughan is in the dog-house after his escapade. I had told Bob Ballard to keep an eye on him because Vaughan was unpredictable and a possible liability; I also wanted to see how good Ballard was, which is pretty good in that Vaughan didn't spot him – but not that good, because Carswell did.

But it doesn't answer my real worry, which is that Bob, and maybe even Beate, are Carswell stooges.

Abe's desk space looked like a small crowd of football spectators had passed through, leaving discarded Styrofoam cups and half-eaten hamburgers. Shallow tin-lids served for ash trays, full of the remains of Manny's heroic smoking efforts.

Sol asked, 'What have you got for us?'

'We've got a mole in Verco, Viessmann's pharmaceutical business,' said Abe.

Manny was more cautious. '*Might* have a mole.'

Abe was in contact with the prospective mole via e-mail through a series of carefully created blinds that bounced their messages through several untraceable stages. 'We hope,' said Abe. 'He knows of drugs being tested on people without their consent. And has evidence of bad drugs being dumped on to impoverished markets.'

Manny explained. Several drugs companies had secret links to specific relief and aid organisations. In some instances these organisations amounted to hidden subsidiaries of those companies.

'It's the perfect method of control and distribution,' said Sol, impressed by the neatness of the conceit.

Vaughan asked, 'What about the World Health Organisation? Don't they monitor stuff?'

'Like traffic cops monitor speeding,' said Manny. 'But that doesn't stop anyone.' He shrugged, lit another cigarette.

The mole had come via a regular contact of Abe's, a previous whistleblower who had fingered the banks over their bad handling of Jewish wartime accounts and afterwards had gone underground to offer his services as an information broker and systems spy. His present name was Riese, meaning Giant. The new mole was being offered under the name of Krebs. Cancer. Manny looked ironic. 'Star sign, not illness. I get my lungs checked every six months.'

'He's scared,' said Abe. 'Last year a journalist working to expose Verco was killed.'

'In a routine traffic accident, ha ha,' Manny put in. 'According to Krebs, a backpacker who died in Turkey in a mountain fall was an undercover journalist working on a story about aid relief and drugs company connections – particularly the role of an organisation called Faraid.'

Manny flicked ash. 'Faraid has a reputation as a troubleshooter. It gets in where others don't.'

'Or can't,' added Abe. 'It functions a lot in cesspool countries. It's the Foreign Legion of aid relief organisations. Mobile, compact and tough.'

Abe had chased Faraid down a maze of false company set-ups and offshore locations, and had come up with the slenderest of connections, which he nevertheless believed was the first strand in a thread that would prove Faraid was run by Verco.

The connection was a name. Van Boogaert.

'A tale of two Dutchmen,' said Manny.

Abe said, 'The other's called van der Valden.' He had a print-out on van Boogaert. It showed a Dutch military background, specialising in hostage negotiations and counter-terrorism, a subject on which he had become a leading expert.

Abe said, 'Van Boogaert went solo and made a lot of money selling terrorist scenarios to governments before working out there was more money in the private sector.'

'He became head of security at, guess where?' asked Manny. Verco. Van Boogaert was a board member of Verco and a founder of Faraid.

The Dutchman was also listed as being a member of a quasi-religious body with a Latin name that translated as Arms of Christ. I remembered it well. It was an extreme-right organisation with occasional CIA funding, a direct successor to the anti-Communist arm of the Church which had accommodated the fascist riff-raff during the Second World War.

Manny asked if we remembered the terrorist siege on a Dutch train which had made headlines in the 1970s. He turned to Abe, who said, 'I'm pretty pleased with this nugget. Van Boogaert was one of the hostage negotiators. He was the guy delegated to deal with the media. The next bit was pure hunch.'

He called up an item on the screen. It was a program shot list pulled from the ITN archive, which translated into a terse shorthand log of the news item filmed and coverage involved.

> WS HOSTAGE TRAIN, plus GVs of vicinity, incl. WS negotiators' command post. INTERVIEW with COL VAN BOOGAERT: states optimism at the way negotiations going. *[Dur: 00.45 secs. Interviewer: DOMINIC CARSWELL.]*

'Where do you dig up this stuff?' I asked.

Abe said it was just gumshoe work. Where once he would have had to make a lot of house calls, and several trips abroad, now he could sit and do it from home. 'Provided you know where to look.'

'On the matter of Verco's security,' Manny said, 'Carswell is the main supplier of its surveillance systems. Our friend Dominic is a non-executive board member of Faraid. He has a TV company office in Ankara on the same floor as Faraid and an electronic security company called Systemsinc. Systemsinc has further offices in Budapest and London. Company director?'

Abe said, 'DC himself. Systemsinc in Budapest shares an office floor with a wholly owned subsidiary of Faraid called – and this stretches the imagination – *Fair*aid, and some registered charity organisation we can't identify, named the Kalona Institute.'

Manny said, 'We checked it against Verco because everything else connects up. Nothing yet.'

Abe brought up several images sent by Krebs, showing tough-looking men entering or leaving buildings, and getting in and out of cars. The pictures were not well-defined and looked hastily grabbed, but their point was clear. These men were there to protect the privacy of the company.

Vaughan asked, 'Just where is Verco based?'

Manny said everywhere and nowhere. The company produced several high-street brand products that were ubiquitous, including a shampoo range. But these had been recently sub-contracted to another concern, and Verco seemed to be in the process of relocating in the Third World and the Far East. 'Cheap labor,' Manny shrugged.

'And a less regulated market,' finished Abe. 'But if Verco is anywhere it's in Turkey. Turkey's the key. Carswell, Viessmann and van Boogaert all connect through Turkey.'

'Faraid is well dug in there, though it doesn't publicise itself there or anywhere else.'

The question was whether Krebs would break cover

and meet. Abe wasn't sure. Manny looked doubtful. There was another side to the story, according to Abe's original mole, which made Krebs a tricky prospect. He had been fired by Verco for stealing drugs. Abe said he knew this sounded like standard disinformation but unfortunately it was true. Krebs was a doper, eager to sell information for cash.

So, we had a flaky mole. I asked if Krebs had given them anything by way of a sweetener. That was the standard method. Some juice, payola, and maximum garbage once the money was down.

'Two things,' Manny told me. 'The other Dutchman, van der Valden, is also based in Budapest, but spends time in Turkey. The guy has a background in drugs research and is now some kind of sales broker. According to Krebs, Valden will talk. At a price.'

'Talk about what?' I asked.

'We pay, we find out,' said Abe.

Krebs also had a line on Viessmann. Apparently he was now just the titular head of the company and no longer knew the score. Manny said that Viessmann seemed to have moved into a realm of his own. 'I guess you'd call it saintly disassociation. He spends most of his time doing good works and running some model refugee camp. I checked it against the Kalona Institute and got nothing. Anyway, the word is, Viessmann's got God on the line. A faction at Verco is annoyed by having to underwrite some cranky utopian dream, plus putting up with a man way past retirement age. But everyone agrees on one thing:

Viessmann looks terrific and has the energy of someone half his age.'

Sol caught my eye. 'I wish he were dead already, so I could have a few days to myself not having to think about him. You can't punish a man who has repented.'

I asked Abe again if he thought Krebs would meet. Face to face there would be a chance of evaluating the quality of his information. We can ask, Abe said. Krebs came back with a demand for a heap of money, which we didn't have, even after we had beaten him down five thousand. Manny told Abe to ask if US dollars would be acceptable and the answer came back affirmative. Sol was grinning by then, Abe too. I repeated that we didn't have the money. When Manny went and fetched a pile of dollars from out the back, we were all laughing. I hadn't realised he was still active. Manny lit another cigarette, with hands that had forged for Himmler.

Vaughan, Zürich

Krebs agreed to a preliminary one-on-one to see the colour of our money, in a car park on the shore of a small lakeside town, after dark. I got delegated once it had been established that he spoke English. Everything was going undercover again, and I didn't like it.

It was squally over the lake. I had done my best to see I wasn't followed, but I was no expert. Krebs turned out to be not the wired skinny guy I had been expecting but a bulky man who looked more like he belonged in the Verco security programme.

We stayed in our cars and talked with the windows down. First he wanted to make sure I had the money, then he proceeded to lecture me on pharmaceuticals. Krebs had a bore's voice. 'Billions of profit,' he said and lit a Pall Mall.

He explained that Verco's trick was to control everything. Through carefully screened outlets it offloaded surplus requirements while guaranteeing maximum tax write-offs, including dumping old drugs into the charity market. 'Example,' said Krebs. 'Verco wanted to donate a large supply of an influenza vaccine to the Philippines, but was told it was the wrong strain for the local population. It ended up there anyway, via another route and a different set of charities. Verco had known it would be useless, but got its tax write-off.'

He moved on to generic drugs, explaining that he wasn't talking about copies of market drugs produced legally after a patent had lapsed. He meant those being produced illegally in violation of the patent. These, and the large sales of substandard and counterfeit drugs packaged to look like the real thing, accounted for a tenth of the world market, maybe more. The big companies spent fortunes hiring people to chase and close them down, but Verco took the line, If you can't beat them, join them.

'Are you saying Verco operates its own black market?' I asked.

Krebs chain-lit another Pall Mall. 'Oral contraceptives. There's a repackaging exercise. Nearly a million lookalike sachets produced for a test run. The pills inside are useless. What happens? They "get stolen", before they can be destroyed, and end up on the black market in South America and, hey, lots of unexpected babies. That was one of van Boogaert's operations. Go to Tijuana and you will find Verco Méjico, except it doesn't call itself that. It's a handful of people in a tin hut repackaging drugs past their expiry date, pushing the date on a couple of years. It's all profit, man.' Krebs looked at his watch. 'Time for the money.'

'Tell me about Viessmann.'

'Ask van der Valden.'

'How do I get to speak to van der Valden?'

'Go to Budapest. He'll only do face to face.' Krebs grunted out a laugh. 'Missionary position. If he's in town he's at the Astoria. If he's not there he's out of town, but usually he is a couple of days a week.'

I handed him the money and said others wanted to talk to him. Krebs counted the notes carefully before folding them away. 'Okay. Saturday. Hotel Baur. Book a conference room for eight o'clock PM. We meet in the lobby. I want to see who I am talking to. If I don't like them I turn around and walk out. Tell Kiss to e-mail details of everyone who will be there, no more than three, and bring the rest of the money.'

It took me a while to work out that Kiss must be Abe's tag.

It was late when I got to Betty Monroe's because I had stopped off at a bar for whisky relief and not called Hoover as promised. He answered the door as angry as an anxious parent, wanting to know where I had been. I told him he had an attitude problem. We were joined by Beate, dressed but sleepy. Propriety led her to explain that she had fallen asleep upstairs in her mother's study.

'Not giving the old man a poke?' I asked, sourly.

Hoover hit me. Hit me hard enough to knock me over when I had been expecting a hero's welcome.

Hoover nursed his knuckles. I should have apologised. (I could hear Dora's voice telling me not to.) Tension ripped through the room. I knew I ought to back down. Instead I accused Beate of holding back information on just about everybody and Hoover of being too besotted to see.

Hoover warned, 'Watch your mouth, nephew.'

Beate looked disdainful. 'Are you accusing me of being involved in all of this?'

'The opposite.'

'Meaning?' snapped Hoover, coming to her defence.

'Meaning neutral and complicit. Isn't that the Swiss way?'

She went very quiet so I asked, 'Hey, did we hit the target?'

She wept with as much restraint as she did everything else; elegant, snot-free crying. She made a pretty picture. I was being a heel, but saw a growing ambiguity in Hoover who perhaps privately relished seeing Beate humiliated. This made neither of us nice people. I had watched him do the same to Frau Schmidt; the sorcerer's apprentice.

We blew Bob Ballard out of the water first. Bob Ballard was the guy that had turned up. Bob Ballard was a safety switch. I didn't get it until Hoover explained that Betty would have had a contact procedure, even though everything was closed down, in case any unfinished business made a late appearance. 'Me turning up, I suspect,' he said. 'What happened? Betty left you a set of instructions? What to do if one or any of the following happens? Contact this number?'

'Post a letter,' said Beate. 'I never saw what was in it.'

'And, hey, Bob Ballard turns up. Do a little checking, do a little fire-fighting, run through the records and make sure everything is tucked up.'

'I'm sorry,' said Beate. 'I wanted to trust you.'

'Well,' said Hoover. 'It's a long time since I placed a whole bunch of hope in *that* direction.'

Beate stalled on Carswell, saying she had not had any contact for years. 'We live in different worlds,' she said.

I continued to give her a hard time. Hoover shared my suspicion, I could see, but he was a perverse old bird because he started sticking up for her. 'Leave her out of this,' he said. 'The equation is complicated enough already.'

'But I want to help,' she said.

I replied, with more sarcasm than intended, that this was indeed an historical moment and Hoover told me to stop being a pain in the arse.

Beate looked at me with a clear calm gaze. Turning to Hoover she said, 'There is a website on the internet about the camp for refugee children where Konrad works.'

I told her we'd know about it already through Abe.

'Why should you?' she wanted to know. 'It's a private charity. Konrad's name is not connected with it but that's where he is.'

It took all she had to say that. When she had finished

she was trembling. Hoover took her by the shoulders. She flinched then relaxed. 'Thank you,' he said. Hoover, knight errant, consoler of damsels, gave me a look that said I wasn't worth shit on a shoe.

Beate von Heimendorf, Zürich

Where there should have been humiliation there was, to my surprise, clarity, even gratitude to Vaughan. My life has been spent avoiding confrontation, or the nightmare of being singled out – except in the case of professional excellence. I was ridiculed by Vaughan. He detests what I stand for. I suspect in the end we are alike. We both lead lives of subterfuge and he is drawn to disorder where I take refuge in its opposite.

A hanged man is not a sight that is easily accommodated. (See? My preference is always for understatement.) The irony is Mother was one of Dr Jung's groupies – as she would be called today – and it has taken dozens of his disciples to try and mend the broken pieces of my life. I am promiscuous when it comes to analysts. My fees are paid not so that I may seek understanding. I move on as soon as there is any sign of analytical penetration. Yes, I am aware of the implications. I use analysis as a substitute for intimacy, just as I use masturbation. For fear of knowing others, I have chosen to know myself.

I have gone out of my way to avoid my mother's élan and recklessness. I should detest her for what she did to Father, but he remains the ostensible object of my hatred, for his silent endurance of her rampant indiscretions, and for the way he let me find him. I suspect he had intended Mother to discover him, but I came home from school after complaining of feeling ill, drawn to him by what felt like telepathy. Many psychiatrists have since wanted me to confront the idea that I might have wished him dead all along, but I am too clever to go down that route.

Nobody talked about it afterwards, especially Mother who would talk about everything else. Revenge on her took the form of obedience and duty, of being my father's daughter, uncomplaining and risk-free. I was like one of Mother's spies, except I was spying on nobody and for no one. My marriage to Dominic was based on her approval rather than any conviction of mine, other than knowing he would make me unhappy. I was in rebellion against the insulation I wrapped around myself for protection. I wanted to be exposed raw.

What I sought through Dominic was an introduction into Mother's world. I understood the attraction of action and irresponsibility over passivity and virtue. I had read my De Sade (courtesy of Dominic). Mother had, in her own crude phrase, road-tested him to her satisfaction. Even this, when Dominic told me, failed to dent my admiration for her, which is indicative of a strong level of repression and low self-esteem – hidden by patrician good manners and my imposing height.

*

I drove to the clinic and sat with Mother. She appears frailer and in the process of slipping away. Faraway eyes. I wondered what they were seeing, and whether she has any sense of where she is going. She made me think of men being shot into space; such a long journey.

I have always preferred departure to arrival. Rooms are for leaving. One of the rare times I have laughed out loud recently was when I found myself intently studying a magazine article on euthanasia.

This is Mother's last room. Her mind has already gone. Has her brain been damaged from the strain of keeping so many secrets? Have the complexities of all the different strands in her life caused it to short-circuit?

In her great beauty Mother had a feline quality, a predatory grace, and she still moves through my dreams like that. Somewhere in the outer reaches of my psyche an unbridled liberty runs counter to a life of respectable increment and percentage.

In my own looks I see only Mother's missing beauty, which allowed her the life denied to me. 'It is my turn for adventure now,' I told her. At that her eyes seemed to focus, followed by what looked like a smile of approval, or was it a more knowing grin to say she didn't believe I had it in me? What she didn't know was that after today she will not see me again. One last time that afternoon, to say goodbye, then abandonment. Duty done.

I phoned Dominic from the clinic to tell him about Mother. I have his number, of course. Whatever our differences, there still exists a complicity. This is a matter of background and association, of common social attitudes, and, dare I say, breeding. We possess sufficient reserves to have overcome our difficulties. Where others see Dominic as English, I understand the Swiss in him. We also shared a disastrous wedding night, which I have perhaps over-dramatised, seeing it in terms of his aggression rather than our sexual incompatibility. I was not at all my mother's daughter in the bedroom.

Dominic has always remained devoted to her and has visited whenever he can. He detects in her an affection never displayed by his own mother, one which was of course withheld from me by mine. Dominic and I have become more like brother and sister, he the son Mother never had. My tolerance is that of one who understands. Our public lives intersect in the institutional, diplomatic and social receptions of the upper end of Swiss society. We move in the same orbit, and through some of the same rooms.

Recently we met again, introduced by my errant husband, Adam, of all people. Adam wished to draw to my attention the fact that Dominic was involved in the latest developments in security systems adapted for what Adam pretentiously described as curated spaces, and he wanted me to introduce my contacts in the museum world to Dominic.

Adam, about whom no one thinks to ask, is a banker. I would never dream of asking him if he manages Dominic's Swiss affairs, but it would make perfect sense if he did. I know Adam takes care of Uncle Konny because it was how we met, just as it was through Uncle Konny that Dominic met me.

I am trying to make something clear that Hoover does not fully understand because he is not one of us, which is that most things can be traced back to an introduction and worked out from there. In the end it all comes down to meetings, and doorways and the rooms in which those meetings take place.

Adam and I no longer live together. Our separation is cloaked by his constant travel. For years now he has been on free air miles. My marriage is both a carbon and a reversal of my parents'. I have taken on the role of my father – one of hurt, reserve and withdrawal – while Adam, like Mother, and Dominic, is expansive and predatory.

Dominic arrived at the clinic with flowers, an exquisite bunch that must have cost him an absurd amount. Dominic is careless with money, not Swiss at all. I needn't add what my own habits are.

Mother's condition makes him sad, nearly tearful. Like many cruel men, he is sentimental. When Mother starts to drool he tenderly dries her mouth.

We sat lost in our own thoughts, Mother most of all. When I made my deal with him, he seemed surprised. I am pleased. It takes a lot to surprise Dominic. My side is that I will ensure he gets the museums contract for his security system. He asked me what I will get in return and I answered, 'My freedom.' He kissed me, more than his usual fraternal peck, and said it's what I deserve.

'I'll call him, and sort it out,' he said as he walked out of the room.

Hoover came to say goodbye to Mother in the afternoon.

I am determined to be honest. So we embarked on that awkward conversation I have been running away from since reading Mother's papers. (Not entirely honest; I had removed Dominic's flowers before Hoover's arrival.) There are many things I have not been able to tell him, I began, because of my loyalty to Mother. With my feelings for him, I now want that to change. We have talked enough about his and my lives. What I wish most is for us to go away, to leave immediately and drive south to Italy. There is a villa where we could stay. I know there isn't long left (I know about his condition), and I want us – how strange and unused the word sounded coming off my tongue – to spend as much time as we can learning about each other.

Hoover looked surprised and, I think, gratified. 'Are you sure?' he asked. I told him yes, even though the superstitious in me was fearful of breaking silence. Mother sat between us mute, silent judge or dumb witness, maintaining her right to silence.

'It's time we shared your secrets, Mutti,' I said. She always hated being called that. I told her how her legacy had forced me to lie to Hoover, a gentleman with whom I wished only to have an honest relationship. I was tired of years of circumspection and the polite sham of my marriage. (That I am taking on a man of limited lease is not lost on me. I might be jumping in feet first but it will not be for long. Afterwards I might be inconsolable, but better that than more years of polite swallowing.)

Jealousy has played its part. Among Mother's scribbling in her private diaries I read that she had sampled Hoover and pronounced him 'highly-sexed'. After a lifetime of avoiding the subject, it was not easy to mention this to Hoover. Given this overcoming of reserve, I expected my honesty to be matched by his. Why I thought it would be so straightforward, after so much prevarication on my part, I don't know.

Hoover issued a flat denial, declared that there had been nothing between them. We looked at Mother. She wasn't saying anything; Mother the Sphinx.

We wore ourselves down arguing. Mother's written testimony versus Hoover's verbal denial. Why should Mother lie over such a thing? He had no reason to either, he said. Unless it complicated his feelings towards me, I ventured. He answered that he was too old to want to hide anything.

'This is how it was,' he said. He and Mother had always had a flirtatious relationship. Mother was like that with most men. It was her currency. She had indicated to Hoover that she wished to take things further. 'It never happened,' said Hoover. 'So I can only conclude there was a level of sexual fantasy to her diary.'

'Why?' I asked.

'Your mother was a very sensual woman,' he said. The sentence hung between us like a reproach. Mother's inert presence mocked him, and my desires. The taste of dust, even in that clinical environment: Mother's past turning into the graveyard of hope and expectation.

I was jealous of the current that had existed between them and knew my jealousy would not go away unless I destroyed his illusion. 'It nearly happened, didn't it?'

He looked at me carefully. 'What do you mean?' He was slowly realising I knew more than he did.

'Strasbourg, the Hotel Maison Rouge in March, 1945. Mother summoned you.'

Hoover shrugged. 'We already talked about it.'

Mother's throat rattled in apparent protest and her eyes flicked from side to side. Hoover said, 'I think she understands.'

'Let her,' I said. 'It's time someone else had their say. The Maison Rouge where you were to meet Mother, I was there last week.'

He looked surprised. 'Why?'

'I was doing some detective work. Mother was always a progressive woman, weren't you?' My mother's eyes continued their frantic dance. 'Even after her marriage she retained her original name. The Maison Rouge is an exemplary keeper of records.'

'What are you saying?' His voice was hoarse.

'Mother was at the Maison Rouge that night, registered under her married name.'

Hoover thought, then said, in a whisper, 'It was her and Willi all along.'

His surprise was mine. I believed she had been writing about Hoover in Istanbul when it had been Willi. Willi had boasted of being Mother's lover but Hoover had chosen not to believe him. What he never could have guessed was the extent of their complicity.

He addressed Mother with something like admiration. 'I never got even close to working it out, even the next morning when I ran into you in the lobby and you made out you had just arrived. I never made the connection, even when you had used Willi as your messenger.' He looked at me as though the discovery were too much. 'What did they decide between them – that Willi should survive the war with a change of identity, and they had the bright idea that my body would serve for his? RIP. But there was no corpse. It was just Betty's word Willi was dead, and mine. I didn't think anyone could have survived that. Oh Betty, you really had me fooled for a lifetime.'

Vaughan, Zürich

Today's first prize, an air ticket to London, courtesy of our sponsor Dominic Carswell. Carswell at his most sincere called my mobile, offering to pay my way home.

Hoover was out somewhere with Beate. Carswell told me to look out of the window and check the blue Mercedes down the hill. He got out to show he was alone. He looked untouched and above it all. A man on a Saturday afternoon, like the days of the week still meant something to him.

What the hell, I thought. I went down. Carswell looked a touch rueful. It was imperative I left Zürich, he said. Things were getting too dangerous. I thanked him, sarcastically, for his concern.

He took the line that everything I had heard about him was lies. He was involved in work he had been unable to talk about and had been for a long time. Infiltration, for the government, monitoring the Turkish conflict with the Kurds as it moved to London, bringing with it a drugs war. The Kurds had no diplomatic voice, he said. They had to resort to terrorism to broadcast their message and illegal enterprise to finance operations. The Turks were just as ruthless at counter-insurgency and were using Neo-nazis to police Kurdish escape lines.

Carswell was good. There should have been TV cameras there. It was what he had done for years, offering a plausible précis. Carswell the spook, Carswell the undercover man. He pointed out that his role was the same as mine, an investigative one. Carswell knew it backwards. He seemed completely relaxed.

'Who burned down the flat?' I asked.

We looked at each other. Carswell pursed his lips, deciding. 'His name is Makal. He is a major in Turkish counter-Intelligence.'

'I saw him in Frankfurt too, and an associate of his nearly shot me.'

Carswell ironic: 'You have been drawing attention to yourself.'

'Why did you have me target Strasse? Did you fix to have him killed?'

'I didn't arrange anything. He got on the wrong side of somebody. He probably didn't even know who.'

'Now you're going to tell me you have no idea what you were doing in my hotel room.'

'Proving my credentials. Friend Siegfried was convinced you were an agent.'

I looked at him for signs of guile. I was tired enough to want to believe him.

Carswell mopped up. Hoover was an old spook who

should be in a retirement home, a rogue element. 'Tell him to go home too,' he advised, 'before he gets hurt.'

Carswell the fixer gave me the name of a man to talk to about the absence of personal insurance for possessions lost in the fire. A policy would be created and backdated. I would receive £35,000 in compensation. I stared at my shoes. If that was the cost of a buy-out, it was better than Major Makal's alternative. I wondered at the ease with which Carswell and his like could fuck around with bureaucracy and conjure sums of money out of nowhere. I had the impression he was sorry for me. I felt pretty stupid and washed-up. I asked that dumb question, 'Why me?'

Carswell knew when to parry and when to thrust. When he hit he hit true. Because I had a verifiable history. Because I had no background, by which he meant I was a virgin in his world. And because Dora had wanted me out of the way. Dora said I was too intense.

'Same old story,' said Carswell, very flip and man-to-man. I had a flash of Hoover hitting me for insulting Beate. Carswell the fuck everybody had in common. I was past anger.

I asked if he knew where Dora was. Not exactly, he said. I then asked if he had known about the parties. Not exactly, he replied. What *did* he know? I asked, sarcasm rekindled. That Dora had been going through some kind of crisis, he said, which she wouldn't talk about, except to say she wanted to go away and sort out her head. What kind of crisis? Carswell thought it wasn't the usual kind to do with money, or work, or a man. Spiritual crisis was the only other kind that come to mind. Carswell nodded a maybe. 'Your father.'

I had no answer to that. 'Give me the ticket,' I said.

Carswell, handing it over: 'Think of it as a way out of an impossible situation.' No handshake, just a half-nod of apology and he was gone.

Hoover, Zürich

Vaughan called Abe's and said he wanted to come and say goodbye, but for me not to tell the others. I was still in shock because of Beate's unexpected lifeline. Consummation was not a word I had expected to apply again. I felt abashed and obscurely privileged while apprehensive at the thought of betraying Mary's memory. Fidelity to the dead is far harder to break with than the routine physical kind.

Vaughan arrived and said he wanted to talk. I suggested a café. Then they all wanted to come. Ballard was hanging around too, and insisted on tagging along.

Vaughan drank three straight espressos. Abe said, 'Herr Viessmann's website is a tad disappointing.' It had been. A couple of photographs showed grinning children, neatly dressed, and the equivalent to a parish newsletter related the steps being taken to care for the children and to reunite them with their parents. Of Viessmann there had been no sign in photographs or text, only ingratiating notes on new volunteer arrivals, most of whom were travelers who had heard about the place and ended up staying to help.

Vaughan and I loitered on the way back long enough for him to tell me he had heard from Dora and wanted to go home.

Bob Ballard walked in front of us, head cocked. We ran into a big crowd of people going the other way. Ballard called out, 'It's the festival.' Sol said that there was a big community get-together downtown that evening. 'See the Swiss enjoying themselves,' to which Abe added, 'If that's not a contradiction in terms,' and Manny had capped that with, 'The Swiss are the one nation it is still possible to make racist jokes about.'

Vaughan wanted to leave before the Krebs meeting. I told him he was needed, otherwise Krebs would walk. Ballard slowed down, trying to eavesdrop. Vaughan said, 'Fuck off, we're having a private conversation here.'

'No such thing,' said Ballard amiably.

I told Vaughan I was leaving too, but after the meeting with Krebs because I owed it to Sol. 'Do the meeting,' I said, 'and we'll drive you to the airport.'

He gave me a crafty look. 'You and Beate? Okay. To the airport.'

So long, Willi, I thought. We don't need to meet again. We're renouncing the quest, and by the sound of it you have turned into a sanctified old bore, all atoned for. Who knows what would happen with Beate. We would probably have a bust-up before the border. But trying to release her from her past struck me as more worthwhile than hunting down an old Nemesis. Willi getting out of the river was nothing to do with me.

Beate von Heimendorf, Zürich

I have often been told I work too hard and take insufficient holidays. I lied slightly as I made the necessary telephone calls to set up my sabbatical, saying I had been ordered to rest by my doctor. I was disappointed to be treated with only polite concern that probably masked indifference. A professional lifetime of what? Duty, service and reputation, none of which would last a week of my being gone. Such diligence for nothing.

The apartment strikes me as sterile, with its careful selection and its unchanging good taste. Not many pass through its doors, certainly not into my bedroom. Adam slept in the spare room on the few occasions he was here. It was an unspoken arrangement neither of us questioned. He would plead jetlag and insomnia, I nocturnal restlessness.

The afternoon had resulted in a brief elation, the giddy joy of a disobedience too rarely indulged. We had kissed like teenagers in my car, in full sight of passers-by. He kissed well, not that I can claim to be a judge of such things. He kissed like he was enjoying it, and I hope I didn't betray my nervousness, thinking how much more this was Mother's territory. He said, 'I never expected to do that again.'

After we parted, after arranging for him to collect me around nine-thirty, deflation set in. With him I can cope. Alone I am not sure. The past dominates my life. Everything has been conditioned by it. A future seems frighteningly alien.

Our plan is to drive through the night until Italy. No stopover, no embarrassment of a hotel check-in. Hoover seems to understand my qualms.

My last night in Switzerland feels anything but real. The town is rowdy from the street festival. Stalls have been set up below my window and thousands mill around buying beer and Wurst. Annoying loud music from different sources competes with the start of fireworks which will later turn into a huge display, with synchronised music. A celebration of my departure.

I have packed, including items of silk lingerie never worn before. I have tried, and failed, to introduce a feeling of anticipation into my preparations, wondering under what circumstances I will next take off my clothes. All I experienced was a vague anxiety at the prospect of driving in the dark. Then Hoover called to say we would be going via the airport on our way, to drop off Vaughan. So much for a romantic escape, I thought, hiding my disappointment. 'I'll make it up to you,' he said. 'It wasn't in my plans either.'

I play Patience, as I often do when I have a problem, except this time nothing is wrong, I tell myself, so it doesn't matter whether the cards come out.

The festival is on the television, with a camera crew in my street. Everyone tries too hard for a good time. The television commentators are young and too enthusiastic, with a point to prove that fun is being had. The commentator below my window is a foolish young woman in a yellow coat who says in a sing-song voice, 'Not everyone is on the street yet, but we're expecting plenty before the night is over.' The broadcast is live but with a short delay because I can see myself on television still standing at my window after I have moved away.

A burst of Chinese crackers echoes on the set. I get up to turn the sound down, just as something happens to make the young woman commentator stare in panic, her horrible enthusiasm quite gone. Her hand is pressed against the side of her head as she tries to decipher what someone is saying into her earpiece. Her face isn't coping and her mouth is dragging down. I think, meanly, it is like watching the opposite of someone winning a prize.

A bass drum thumps like a migraine. Through the window I watch the crowd barging around, many of them aggressive and drunk already. People behind the commentator make inane faces at the camera as they have done all evening. I want to run downstairs to hear directly what she has to say, rather than watch her make a fool of herself on television. But I don't and I leave the sound down.

The crowd remains oblivious to anything being wrong.

The commentator's bright coat looks inadequate for whatever is happening. Some of the crowd are drunk enough to start laughing at her distress, which makes her cry. Sirens bleed into the drumming but people ignore them or can't hear. Why am I so calm? I wonder. Because I have known all along it is too good to be true. (Silk lingerie I have never worn, tempting fate by packing it. It crossed my mind at the time and now fate is answering back.)

A controlled-looking man comes on the television. He is in a studio and wears a sober suit. Along the bottom of the screen appears the running text of a newsflash – SHOOTING AT DOWNTOWN ZÜRICH HOTEL – NO DETAILS YET – CHAOS ON FESTIVAL STREETS – IMPOSSIBLE FOR EMERGENCY SERVICES AND FILM CREWS TO GET THROUGH. I turn up the sound just as the man says, 'There are fatalities but we don't know how many.'

I switch him off and sit down to wait for Hoover, telling myself he will come. I have a glass of wine and then another as it doesn't matter because we will be leaving in the morning now. I return to my game of Patience. The cards come out.

Vaughan, Zürich

We had been in the lobby, hanging around like bad actors, waiting for Krebs. All I could think about was whether Dora had ditched me quite as ruthlessly as Carswell said.

Manny wore a smart cashmere coat, though the weather didn't demand it. Sol was in the suit he had worn to the lawyer in Bern. Among the casually dressed crowd they had looked like old hitmen on the way to a Mafia funeral. Abe wore something tent-like and black, with his hat. Sol had performed the opposite of his usual role, berating anyone he saw dropping litter. An old hippie in a rainbow tee-shirt had said, 'Hey, man, it's a party,' to which Hoover replied, 'Fuck off, son.'

Sol had been upset when Hoover told him he wouldn't be staying on. My loss he could cope with, but Hoover's news had cast a damper. Even getting rid of Bob Ballard hadn't been as enjoyable as it should have been. Ballard had been promised a Carswell meeting outside Frau Schmidt's.

The hotel was super-smart in an executive-magazine way, and hushed after the street. Abe was at the desk checking about the room. Sol was unwrapping a cheap cigar and dropping the cellophane. Manny had sat down and was watching proceedings with humourous detachment as he reached for another cigarette. Hoover was inspecting a big luggage trolley used for guests' cases, which was standing in the hall. The staff were wearing party hats. There was a casual, off-duty air. Bunches of people hung around, including some people in evening clothes discussing taxis.

I was thinking about Dora and Viessmann's shitty little website. Had it been her in one of the pictures, half turned away? Could she have ended up there? It wasn't impossible, given the connections.

Abe and Sol were walking over to me when several men came through the door, moving faster than everyone else. Suddenly the place was full of smoke and noise. I was thinking it was fireworks, and the festival had moved indoors. Sol seemed to trip and fall over, and a woman over the other side of the lobby collapsed. For a crazy second none of it made sense. I registered only incoherent details until I saw guns pointing at me out of the smoke and felt myself being jerked backwards as though my body was anticipating the hail of bullets. It was Hoover yanking me behind the baggage trolley. He pushed me in the direction of a corridor off the back of the lobby and we ran down it, away from the gunfire. A man rushed past going the other way. He was carrying a machine-pistol but paid us no attention. He looked like one of Maurice's henchmen. The adrenalin flood made me light-headed.

We got out of the back of the building. Hoover said to keep walking and not look back. We moved away from the lakeside, down empty side streets, before rejoining the crowd. The mood was more drunken and abandoned than before. People were starting to spew. Hoover and I were breathing hard. Fireworks crackled in the sky like an echo of the gun battle. Hoover said, 'I always hated fireworks.' He looked old and panicked. He had seen nothing of what had happened. Me neither, apart from Maurice's man. I wasn't sure if Sol had been hit or diving for cover.

We used a pay phone to try Ballard's mobile. He sounded pissed off. No show from Carswell. Hoover said to meet us at Abe's and it was urgent.

It took forty minutes to push through the crowds to Abe's. There was no such thing as a taxi and we wasted time waiting for a tram that never came. Hoover looked angry enough to have a heart attack, and kept repeating that he had walked us right into it. We had been set up. He said: 'I was suckered by the mother. Why should her daughter be any different?'

Abe's key was in its place above the lintel. Upstairs everything was normal. Abe's computer was still on. There was no sign of Ballard. Hoover tried Beate. They spoke for a long time, sounding like they were on the brink of quarrelling.

I kept expecting to see Abe and Sol and Manny coming in the door. The TV wasn't saying much. TV was normal, I thought. It normalised everything, even tragedy. It became someone else's story, even if you had been there.

I decided to take a piss. That was normal, I told myself. The bathroom was down a corridor lit with a red bulb. It gave the passage a dark-room feel. I noted every simple action, like switching on the light, to remind myself that everything was deeply unreal for the moment. I opened the bathroom door. The handle was slippery in my hand, which gave me a moment of warning but not enough.

Bob Ballard was sprawled in the tub, taking a bath in his own blood. His grey suit had gone red. The blood not in the bath had apparently been hosed over the tiles. Ballard had been cut up all over the place, his clothes were slashed to shreds. His face criss-crossed like someone had etched it with a razor blade.

Time must have passed (maybe I screamed) because Hoover was next to me saying, 'What the fuck did this?' That seemed about right. The attack appeared inhuman. It looked like it had been done by a wild animal in a frenzy. The room stank of effluent and body parts. It was impossible to reconcile the mass of violated flesh with the man it had once been.

Ballard was wearing his glasses. They were smeared and spattered with blood and hid his eyes. Hoover said we had to check if Ballard still had his phone because there would be a record of calls. We frisked him with averted eyes, hands turning sticky with blood.

Hoover talked as we looked, trying to sound calm: 'Listen, nephew, this is what we're going to do. We are going to help ourselves to as many of Manny's bills as we can carry, then we're going to walk out of here.'

The phone was in the last place we looked, tucked in Ballard's top breast pocket. I felt giddy and faint with nausea.

Ballard had several unanswered calls logged from the same number, which turned out to be the Hotel Astoria in Budapest. Hoover asked the desk to put him through to Mr van der Valden. Someone picked up. Hoover said he was Bob Ballard, returning Mr van der Valden's calls.

Afterwards Hoover looked thoughtful and eventually said, 'Mr van der Valden is expecting Mr Ballard. Well, nephew, how do you feel about a trip to Budapest?'

Hoover, Zürich–Budapest

Beate had been drunk and bitter and angry. She said she should have insisted on our leaving that afternoon. I told her I would be back. She said: 'You're as bad as the others.'

The station was crowded with drunken revellers, still unaware of what had happened downtown. We got the night train to Vienna. Vaughan slept fitfully. He ground his teeth and his hands twitched. The train's stop-start slowness reminded me of wartime. I hoped Sol and the others had somehow survived. I rechecked Bob Ballard's calls. Several had been placed to Carswell.

At Vienna station Vaughan decided we were being followed. Half the men hanging round wore dog-shit yellow leather jackets. We hired a rental car and, thanks to an inadequate map, drove round the ring road twice, which at least established that Vaughan was wrong about being followed. After a sleepless night I had reached the scratchy, argumentative stage.

The autobahn was a caravan of lorries heading for the border. The drive took a lot less time than the border queue. Vaughan said, 'Are we looking for Viessmann in Budapest?'

'*Que sera*, nephew.'

He told me he thought Dora might be at the website camp in Turkey.

Hungary. It had been over fifty years. I had never planned on coming back.

A few miles over the border a heavy rain started and the big lorries threw up a wall of spray, reducing visibility to a muddy nothing. We came off the motorway without meaning to, boxed in by three juggernauts, on to a busy two-lane highway which impressively reckless drivers treated as a slalom course for overtaking, avoiding head-on collisions by seconds. Vaughan tried it once and nearly got us killed.

I threw up in a lay-by and wondered if it was my illness kicking in, regular car sickness attributable to Vaughan's driving, or a psychosomatic response to being back on the death march road.

It had taken me a while to realise that's what we were on. The road itself was no reminder. It looked like any other highway. As we drove on I nursed bad memories of the marches and of Eichmann, who would return to Berlin and spend the last months of the war shunned, then travel to South America, ghosting his way down Dulles's rat-line, where he would become a nonentity, a man deprived of service. He failed to find anything noble in exile and seemed relieved when the Israelis kidnapped him to face trial in Jerusalem. He used the trial as an act of reinvention. It reminded him of who he had once been. All the old myopia remained. Karl-Heinz had been summoned as a witness but elected to stay and give his testimony in camera. The Zionist organiser, whose ransom train Karl-Heinz had helped authorise, had been gunned down in the street following a trial in which he had been accused of being a Nazi collaborator.

I had seen Eichmann once in Budapest walking the streets alone, in civilian clothes, early one morning when it was still dark, as the marches got underway. His private quarters, on a hill in Rozsadómb, weren't far from the assembly point at the brick factory. He told me later he liked to stroll unnoticed, without escort. The remark was one of the few times I ever had the notion of him as a personality rather than a unit in a chain of command. I wondered if he had ever connected this individual impulse – his own late liberty – with what he forced thousands to do to his command.

We hit Budapest in hard continental rain that felt like it was falling for hundreds of miles around. The car fogged up. We had no map. I recognised a cemetery I used to drive Dufy past, near the brickworks. Of them there was no sign. The Communists had long since turned the neighborhood into cheap apartment blocks.

I told Vaughan to turn down an old cobbled street. The area here, a combination of fringe building and scrubland, reminded me of America. You could still see the dirt out of which the city had emerged. The road twisted and rose in steep bends. The tires made that unique corrugated sound they make on cobbles, which took me straight back to my Liège childhood.

Eichmann had lived on Apostle Street, an affluent suburban road with big detached houses, and there it was suddenly, the familiar humpback of the road, unchanged in over fifty years, with the hill running down towards the city. I recognised Eichmann's house straight away from its balcony. I told Vaughan to stop. I had to support myself on the car door as I got out.

There were geraniums on the balcony as there had been in 1944. I could see Eichmann as if it were yesterday. Karl-Heinz had made a present to him of an amphibian car (requisitioned) which had stood in the drive. Where it had come from nobody ever learned. They were not friends, not even strategic allies, and Karl-Heinz required nothing in the way of favors. I suspect it was largesse towards a man he knew was bound to lose.

Standing there in Eichmann's old grounds, I realised we were down to Willi and me. I wondered if Willi had reinvented himself so thoroughly that nothing remained of his old self, or if Willi was still the real man and Viessmann the shell.

Willi would have chosen this side of the river to live, I decided, up in the hills of Buda, near where Eichmann and his gang used to have their offices. I could see him in one of those secretive roads, the houses bigger than Apostle Street, with convenient back lanes for those who wished not to be seen coming and going.

Vaughan came to find me. I had sat down on a balustrade and couldn't get up without help. The rage I felt at my own failing strength I took out on him, and he had the good grace to understand I didn't really mean it.

Pest lies on the other side of the Danube. Pest was as I remembered. The shock was in realising how such a large drama had been played out in such a small area. Buildings grown far apart in memory were all within a short distance: the Astoria; Eichmann's downtown headquarters, borrowed from the university; the Jewish ghetto. My old apartment building was there, in a broad tree-lined street with trams, up the road from the ghetto boundary. The wooden street toilet opposite the front door of my building was still there, quite forgotten by me in the meantime. At the end of the road was a giant crucifix on a church wall. Its position, facing what had been the ghetto, was provocative and tactless. Had it been there in 1944? I could not remember. There was no word to describe how I felt except 'catapulted'. I had never expected to find myself back, staring down the funnel into that particular past.

We went into the ghetto, a network of normal-looking streets now, like a lot of other moderately rundown areas in dozens of other cities. Its past was practically unguessable, apart from the synagogues and the museum. I said to Vaughan, 'Remind me. Carswell's Systemsinc has an office here, and Faraid runs a subsidiary. And there's something called the Kalona Institute which no one has managed to connect up.'

'That's right.'

'I have no idea what the Kalona Institute is but I'll bet it has something to do with Willi. A couple of blocks from here there's a street called Kalona Jozsef. Willi talked about it once. During the time of the ghetto there were mad people living at number thirty-two.'

Number thirty-two turned out to be a normal house which showed nothing of its history. The Kalona Institute wasn't listed in the book. Systemsinc had a number that rang unanswered as did the Faraid subsidiary. Neither had machines for leaving messages. I thought of Ruiz in Lisbon running his dummy company with its false paper trail.

Van der Valden was sitting in the mezzanine lobby above the Astoria's reception. He was a big man in a light suit. His skin was very pale and he was in the process of losing his sandy hair. I remembered the mezzanine space very well. Karl-Heinz had liked to sit there because it overlooked the entrance and was private, with just a couple of tables.

I met him alone, introducing myself as an associate of Mr Ballard. Van der Valden spoke good English. In spite of his corporate bonhomie, he was nervous. In the Braille-like language of our conversation's sub-text I understood we were supposed to be offering a job to Mr van der Valden. I had no idea who Ballard was in his book. He said he wanted to work in the United States, not to be shoved off into what politeness prevented him from calling 'some Third World shithole'.

Van der Valden worked in pharmaceutical research. He was a salesman of sorts, except that the delicate nature of his work made it more complicated than that. He backed off when I asked about his clients. 'Big clients,' he said.

'Let's not be coy about this,' I replied.

But he wasn't ready to talk. I figured he sold to governments, a combined package of medical aid and arms. His clients would be drawn from the emerging nations. He admitted that the 'sensitive nature' of his work was responsible for the company's relocation to places where interference was less likely.

'Meaning nobody is going to care if you kill the patient,' I said, deadpan, and watched him crack up like it was the funniest thing he had ever heard. 'Tell that to the patient,' I added, still deadpan, and he laughed till he doubled up. A man under pressure. Nothing is that funny. He smoked too much and exaggerated his importance. He had the beginnings of a drinker's nose. I asked Mr van der Valden to join us for dinner at the Kempinski.

Vaughan, Budapest

Hoover stressed that we were a young company. Van der Valden was suspicious of my presence. My leather jacket was a testament to its informality, Hoover said, my Britishness to its internationalism. Van der Valden wanted to know what I did. I blanked then said, 'Security. I make sure everybody feels secure.'

Hoover laughed and said, 'That's horseshit.' He was making a point of being in an excellent mood. We did banter. We filled van der Valden's glass. Hoover had said we needn't be specific. We were buying. Van der Valden was the one looking to move. Hoover had said keep it general and let him fill in the blanks.

Hoover mentioned van Boogaert and got points. He remarked that he had been interested in head-hunting van Boogaert during his time as chief of Verco security. He then introduced Viessmann's name into the conversation, and moved smoothly back into the past. He told van der Valden that Viessmann had been very helpful with a recruitment programme in 1945, involving the relocation of German doctors. Van der Valden got the joke and relaxed.

Our guest was a holocaust groupie. He opened up because Hoover opened up. Hoover ensnared him with tales of meeting Eichmann and a lot of Nazi shit. Van der Valden sat with big eyes while Hoover fed him Eichmann until he was sated, and plied him with wine.

It was a shame Eichmann had given the business of population control such a bad name, Hoover said, 'Given that's the business we're all in.'

The sentence lingered. Van der Valden smirked. Hoover added: 'The problem is how to avoid drawing attention to it.'

Van der Valden looked undecided. Hoover went lateral. 'I have to ask you, as we are moving into delicate areas, who you think we are?'

Van der Valden glanced at me. Hoover said I was there to look after him. I took the ambiguity with good grace. The beauty of it was that van der Valden didn't know who he was dealing with, any more than we did. Hoover announced that he represented a privately sponsored organisation, funded by a consortium of extremely wealthy Americans, which specialised in 'bringing medical aid to under-assisted areas. It is the under-assisted that concerns us most, along with virus control. A colleague of yours, whom I cannot name, recommended you to Mr Ballard, and here we are. Now, let's stop beating about the bush.'

It was show-off time. Perhaps out of deference to Eichmann, van der Valden started with sarin. Hoover told him that he was familiar with sarin. It was the nerve gas developed by I.G. Farben – out of research into organic phosphorous compounds, van der Valden added. Its efficacy had been proved in the case of millions of Jews, and more recently by Saddam Hussein on Iraq's Kurds. It had also been used by the cult responsible for the Tokyo subway attack in 1995. Leaning forward in the manner of a man warming to his subject, van der Valden noted that the same cult had earlier sent representatives to Zaire, ostensibly to aid Ebola victims, in fact to obtain samples of the virus.

We slipped into another dimension. Van der Valden droned on, in his flat Americanised English, a dangerous bore, a man in a suit talking mass death at the dinner table, happy to be in the company of like-minded men. Ever the solicitous host, Hoover offered brandy.

Cost and efficiency. The vagaries of weather. The problems of an uncontrolled environment. Ratios of termination in relation to area size. The risk of accident. Van der Valden covered them all. The price of conventional warfare per square kilometre: two thousand dollars, as opposed to eight hundred for nuclear weapons, and six hundred for a nerve gas like sarin. Cost of a biological weapon over the same space: one dollar.

Hoover told him that design and privatisation were what it came down to. The rest was just cartoons and term papers.

Van der Valden revealed himself over several brandies. He brokered research at what he called 'the sharp end of eugenic and political biology'. He wanted to know about our testing facilities.

Hoover answered with a question of his own, asking if testing facilities were a problem for Verco. In terms of remoteness and inaccessibility, van der Valden answered yes. Hoover asked if we were talking about Turkey, and van der Valden agreed.

Hoover told him what he wanted to hear. We had a secure facility under an hour's drive from an international airport.

Van der Valden asked: 'What about the human pool?'

I got it before Hoover did. I laughed and said, 'We call them lab rats. I know you're supposed to dress this stuff in cotton-wool language, but research has taught us that in a small and controlled environment irreverence is healthy. The generic name is toast, as in "Can we get more toast?"'

Van der Valden wanted to show that there was nothing that could not be laughed at. It set him off on his own comic jag. He offered to design us a nice disease to suit somebody we had in mind. It wouldn't be long before we had target diseases, he said, specific cocktails for different types. 'A guy says, "Hey, I think I got a cold coming." Forty-eight hours later, boom, dead. Just like the old saying, "you'll catch your death".'

We obliged by laughing. 'For the moment, it's bulk,' he went on. 'Soon, who knows? You want someone specific to catch it, we can fix it.'

Hoover said we should be serious a moment and van der Valden should convince us of his discretion.

'We're discreet. Stuff happens, nobody realises, not even the guy from CNN. He thinks everyone just got sick.' He motioned us closer. 'The way I see it, you have two kinds of genocide now.'

Hoover told him, no mention of the g-word at the dinner table. We clutched our sides with mirth. Van der Valden needed no further encouragement.

'You get your dictators showing off, wanting to be TV news, but there is another way, less in-your-face. A silent programme. It means you don't end up in front of the War Crimes Commission. Everything gets taken care of and nobody is any the wiser. It isn't even news half the time, just another epidemic in some country halfway round the world that nobody gives bats' shit about. Most of the time it isn't even statistics. Maybe you don't get to brag, except to your friends, but hey, Himmler and those guys would still be alive today if they could have bought our service.'

Hoover, Budapest

My dear Beate,

I don't know what the news will have told you by now. I can only apologise for the abrupt manner of my departure, which was somewhat hastened by circumstances beyond my control. Isn't it stupid, when you get to my age, and head and heart still act in contradiction? I also find I cannot put down what is in my heart, that the distance between us has grown too great, though I sincerely hope not. My one aim is to return and for us to start again. Can we agree on that? I hope in no more than a week. In the meantime, I do need your help. I need you to get in urgent touch with whomever you contacted last time on behalf of your mother and explain where we have gone and who we are seeing. I can only stress that Mr Ballard can be of no help to you in this instance. I am placing my trust in you and I have no one else I can ask. I am certain that my worst fears are being realised, that Willi Schmidt is exactly who I said he was and that he still is involved in something far worse than I ever suspected. I understand your loyalty and your reticence, and realise that the decision is yours. I would like for you, in spite of my own reluctance and what is probably best described as emotional carelessness with you, to believe in our future. I rarely if ever pray but I would ask you to, for us, if you are the praying kind.

It was Willi who met me at the airport when I first arrived in Switzerland, and not your mother as planned. It was Willi who turned up in Strasbourg, and not your mother as planned. For my own conscience, I owe it to myself to try and make one final appointment with Willi.

Yours in trust and hope

Beate von Heimendorf, Zürich

Hoover asks the impossible. Whatever I do, I betray.

I have now read all Mother's private diaries, all the journals from the war. In them she wrote a lot about Willi, sounding like a soppy teenager.

The similarities to Uncle Konny are something I have great difficulty in accepting, except for one very good reason: a case of simple mathematics.

Nine months before I was born, Mother was in Strasbourg. It is more than possible that I am Willi Schmidt's daughter.

There is no proof. Mother has never even hinted as much, either to me or in her private papers. I cling to the illusion that the man I believed to be my father *is* – but he was not tall and I fear my height is the legacy of 'Uncle Konny'.

Vaughan, Turkey

Took a plane. Hired a car. Bob Ballard's cell phone a fading signal. We were stretched from the start.

We had to dump the gun because of airport security, and carried nothing apart from the clothes we wore, a bunch of Manny's fake dollars – a trail in themselves – toiletries picked up at the airport, and a map. The plane had landed somewhere I had never heard of. We had logged a message with Maurice's number, saying where we were going and that we would appreciate any assistance.

The feeling was of a beetle crawling across an arid cranial landscape, being watched by things much bigger.

We moved through a stripped-down relentlessly physical terrain where human life was still measured in terms of survival. Petrol stations and satellite dishes were among the few signs of the contemporary world, along with the usual McDonald's and Coca-Cola shit. (Cruising Frankfurt with the Neos now seemed like another lifetime.) We traveled away from the tourist map, more conspicuous with every mile, pale and different. The military established its presence with convoys and troop movements, road blocks and document inspections. We were waved on. The protective bubble of the car created an illusion of immunity.

We stopped in some dusty place the first night, a roadside hotel used by lorry drivers who wore faded workshirts that must have been washed a thousand times. The top floor of the building was still a concrete shell.

In the dining room two men in black suits looked like they did something nasty for the government. One of the suits checked us out. He wanted to know if we were American. He spoke textbook English, and was surface chatty while his eyes calculated. He said they were doctors. Hoover bluffed, even mentioned Viessmann's name. Afterwards he said, 'Someone has us logged.'

Big trucks boomed past all night, their lights tracing patterns across the ceiling. I could hear Hoover coughing in his room. I chased an image of Dora but whenever I got there it turned out not to be her.

We drove on. The countryside grew still emptier. Now even a roadside garage was an event; smoking obligatory while refuelling. Military installations loomed up in the hills, reached by dirt roads. 'A strategic landscape', Hoover called it, a terrain as unyielding as the feuds that got fought over it, where everything was a blood sacrifice.

Inside, the car grew dusty. The radio spoke in indecipherable languages or blared keening music. At another road block we were made to get out and were questioned about our destination, warned about rebel bandits. Then we were told to wait by the car while phone calls were made and half-a-dozen soldiers watched us, weapons aslant, cigarettes to hand. Military khaki, representative of a martial law even harsher than the surroundings; the soldiers looked familiar with the notion of informal execution. Waiting for them to make a decision, it was easy to picture the last of the heart-pump, bloodstained earth, hot bullet-casings casually ejected, another cigarette lit after the shooting.

Seeing my nerves on getting back in the car, Hoover said, 'You have an overactive imagination, nephew. Those guys are at the bottom of the order-pole.'

The road climbed, narrowed and sheered away into a dizzying drop. Traffic barrelled along. Road duelling was compulsory, breakneck speed a requisite. Everyone drove with the reckless panache of men on amphetamines or alcohol or both; no women drivers. Passing vehicles left a gap of inches, sometimes not even that. There was no turnaround. Hands sticky on the steering wheel, I would have driven with my eyes shut if I could. Hoover paled when a carelessly packed open truck braked and its load looked as though it was about to dump itself in our laps.

We greeted the level road with a relieved silence, then Hoover said, 'I'm tired, nephew, I want to go home.' But five minutes later he was studying the map. 'Oil. Money. Guns. Drugs. It pretty much comes down to that,' he said. 'Dulles knew that. The Kurds know that. And water, too, in this part of the world. There are too many outside interests.'

A while later, he added, 'I can see how those guys would have enjoyed shooting up a five-star hotel. All that pampered luxury, and a taste for violent change.'

He reminded me that the hotel was one of the places where Betty Monroe and Allen Dulles had met. Dulles was quite unworldly in some respects, said Hoover. According to Betty, he had been ignorant of the details of the homosexual act. Hoover's explanation was that money didn't fuck and money was what Dulles really understood in a highly advanced, visionary way. Hoover said: 'Money can fuck with you, and money can fuck you, but money itself doesn't fuck. It multiplies by itself.'

In the late afternoon we detoured off the main road. In a village store a woman spoke some French. Hoover said he was looking for a very tall European man with white hair who ran a camp for children. We drew a blank.

We criss-crossed the region. Cheap lodgings. Variable food. We got bad stomachs and had to stop to shit by the roadside. The processes of civilisation started to break down. In one village we were stopped and questioned by a couple of probable rebels. They spoke a little English. They let us go but warned us that our presence was known in the area.

We moved into the PKK heartland. We were never sure if the men who talked to us were part of Maurice's network. Mistrust translated into procrastination. We were a curiosity at best. Hoover grew discouraged, wondered what he was hoping to achieve. The quality of his life was not going to be improved for finding Viessmann.

Twice a helicopter flew above us. Twice was still coincidence, Hoover said.

Then, after miles of rough road and what felt like pointless circling, we stopped at a café in a town square and spoke to a German engineer named Dieter who showed a drunk's lack of curiosity. He was working on the dam-construction project, he told us. He had believed it would bring prosperity to the region, with Kurds the main beneficiaries. The inconvenience of relocation would be compensated for by the better education, employment and modernisation. Safe in his European compound, Dieter had dismissed the Kurds as backward and reactionary. Now he wasn't sure. He had heard stories of how the Turkish army bought off Kurdish men and turned them into 'village guards', paying the kind of money they would not earn by other means, setting Kurd against Kurd. And the completed dam, he had learned, could have adverse climatic effects on the whole region. Dieter's unease seemed in part historical. He said he was trying to get transferred back to Germany, to head office in Frankfurt. His situation was complicated by his seeing an Englishwoman, a co-ordinator on one of the construction sites, who shared none of his misgivings.

Outside the next town we found the corpse of a young man casually thrown by the side of the road. He was young and poorly dressed, and there was a small bullet-hole in his forehead. His nose had been bleeding and flies drank the still fresh blood. It was impossible to say whether he had been shot there or elsewhere and dumped on the edge of town as a warning or some kind of power statement. A truck went past and didn't stop. The driver hooted angrily at us and gesticulated.

A mile or so later we drove through a shack-town slum. Scruffy kids stared. Skinny dogs with yellow eyes skulked by the roadside.

The old town had a wall and was large enough to have municipal buildings and a square. A terrace café was being patronised by loud men with guns, dressed in civilian clothes, some sporting well-worn shoulder-holsters, openly displayed. They were sullen and drunk and dangerous. Hoover insisted on asking in English and German if anyone could tell him why a dead man was lying in the road on the outskirts of town.

The corpse seemed to have unhinged Hoover. He was determined to report it. The men in the café had ignored him. The police station wasn't interested either. A minor municipal official with deferential manners and some English explained we would have to talk to the army. However, we should be aware that there was no formal procedure for reporting such a crime.

'All bullets and no paperwork,' grunted Hoover and walked out. He insisted on going back to the café where the men still were, drunker. He ignored them, nursed a beer and told me of an incident which had been no more than a footnote at the time. Now he wondered if it didn't connect to the final period of Karl-Heinz's life.

One of Hoover's last wartime jobs had been to arrange the transportation of a consignment of bullion from

Budapest to Istanbul, using old Red Cross connections to ensure its safe passage. It was not a job he had paid any great attention to and he never connected it, until now, to a story told by Karl-Heinz which had lain around in the back of his head.

It concerned the Grand Mufti of Jerusalem, leader of the Palestinian Muslims who had allied himself to Hitler because of shared anti-British and Jewish policies.

Hoover had seen the Mufti once under strange circumstances in Croatia in 1942. While out riding with Karl-Heinz, they had chanced across a detachment of SS soldiers, in themselves an anomaly, being both Croatian and Muslim.

Just then, one of the drunken thugs came over to advise us to leave town before dark. It seemed like a good idea to me, but Hoover said it would be more dangerous on the roads after dark. The man said there had been a lot of shootings in town and he could not guarantee our safety. Hoover thanked him, offered to buy him and his friends a round, which was accepted, then said, 'We'll take our chances.

'What you have to understand,' he went on to me, 'is how uncertain times were by the end of the war. They were superstitious days and there was much casting around. Astrologers became some of the most important figures in the last days of the Third Reich. Hitler used them. Himmler did, too – and his advisers, according to Karl-Heinz, told him something that might be connected with us being here.'

Among her future predictions, Himmler's astrologer had announced that the new millennium would see a development in the Middle East with the birth of 'A Chosen One'. This new leader would become a Kurdish warrior in the tradition of Saladin and would unite Muslims in a Holy War which would drive the Jews out of Israel.

He saw my scepticism and pointed out that what he or I believed didn't have anything to do with it. He personally retained a certain incredulity at Himmler's desperation and superstition. 'But, if you ask me, the money I sent to Istanbul was being used by Karl-Heinz, to finance that prediction.'

'Meaning that Kurdish operations are on an old Nazi budget?' I remembered Karl-Heinz's admiration for the Kurdish warrior.

'It's not out of the question.'

On her other predictions, Himmler's astrologer had been accurate on where the Russian front line would end up, less so on the Reichsführer's fate. 'She had him down as a big cheese in the postwar set-up.'

We checked into a cheap hotel overlooking the square, which was patrolled by a Land-Rover being driven by the now very drunk gunmen.

That night a bomb went off by the railway station: a thin dull *thwup* that woke us both up but didn't sound dramatic enough to be alarming. Hoover joined me in the corridor, grumbling about interrupted sleep. Everything felt weirdly low-key, as it had with finding the corpse. We joined a small crowd that had gathered in the town square. The gunmen drove up and down at high speed a few times, then later they came and arrested us in the hotel. It was something I had been half-expecting since Hoover's initial confrontation but it didn't prepare me for guns being pointed in my face.

We were handcuffed and taken off in the Land-Rover. Hoover's sticking-up hair made him look old and frail. One of the gunmen unholstered a Colt .45 and looked like he might start firing it inside the vehicle. He shouted in Turkish while I silently cursed Hoover for having drawn attention to us in the first place.

We drove to a camp with a sentry post and barbed wire, behind which stood a central stone building and a number of smaller single-storey wooden huts. By the door of the hut into which we were dragged I noticed a plate displaying the manufacturer's name: a Swiss company.

We were separated and a soldier in starched uniform and smelling of aftershave slapped me across the face – not hard, almost girlishly – and said I would be questioned about my role in the explosion at the railway station.

The smell of aftershave hung in the air after he had gone. I told myself it was mind-games and that only the cold was making me shiver. Want and dread fought for attention: please let this end; don't let anything happen. I was stuck in dead time. At some point a helicopter hovered low overhead and landed nearby.

It was daylight before anyone came – other soldiers,

politer and more deferential. They removed the handcuffs. I was taken to a canteen, given a cup of sweet black coffee, then led to a gymnasium. Hoover was there. We had no time to speak before being joined by another man whom I immediately recognised, though his hair was longer than I was expecting and, where he had previously been glimpsed in a smart overcoat, he now dressed like a bum in raggedy jeans, sandals and an old workshirt.

Hoover appeared beyond surprise. 'This,' he said, 'is Konrad Viessmann.'

Viessmann's eyes were a blank pale blue and showed no recognition of Hoover, who looked uncertain. I had no idea if this was Willi Schmidt. He looked too young and fit.

'What's going on?' I asked Hoover, but he was lost for words.

The helicopter I had heard landing was Viessmann's. To find ourselves suddenly his passengers seemed beyond any ordinary prediction. Hoover remained silent. He seemed ashamed of his frailty compared to the robust calm and technical competence displayed by Viessmann, who appeared lofty in every sense. Viessmann the mystery bird-man descending from the sky.

We took off but flew only a few minutes before landing again on the bank of the Tigris on wasteland close to the shack town, our arrival watched by a gathering crowd.

We walked up through the slums, following Viessmann. Hoover said nothing and refused to meet my eye. This was not Willi Schmidt. There was a resemblance but too much wishful thinking and speculation on Hoover's part. Viessmann wore a copper bracelet against arthritis, a very un-Willi detail, I thought. The man's charisma was undeniable. He operated in the same sort of self-contained space cultivated by the very important or very famous, as though he was always a beat ahead and in anticipation of the next move. His unblinking gaze invited nothing in return.

We spent about half an hour in the slums. Hoover and I were like strangers to each other, while Viessmann did his pied-piper act, giving his attention to the children, and talking with the adults in their own language. Hoover spoke once, in English, to ask if Viessmann knew what the new buildings were behind the slum. He replied that they were for the security forces. He pointed out another taller block built originally for refugees from the big earthquake of 1976. Compared to the cost of housing the security forces, he said it would be far cheaper to send everyone home to their villages, and restock them.

We left with two children, aged around four or five. They had no parents and would be coming back with us to be looked after. Viessmann behaved like a rich man playing Schweitzer, salving his conscience with the profits of his business. He reminded me of a sportsman, an old tennis pro, concentrated, eye on the ball, in the zone. An excellent advert for the ageing process.

As we took off again and the town seemed to shoot away from us, I spoke for the first time, saying we had a car down there. Viessmann announced that a pick-up would be arranged. He smiled unexpectedly. We were going to 'his place', he said.

'His place' involved flying over a mountain range, through narrow gorges, past snow-capped peaks. Beyond lay Iraq, he said. Against such dramatic and implacable scenery the fleeting shadow of our helicopter looked frighteningly insubstantial.

Where we landed didn't look so different from the army barracks of our departure, except this had no stone buildings. The compound consisted of half-a-dozen prefabricated huts – Swiss-made, again. After such a spectacular, vertiginous flight our destination appeared makeshift and anticlimactic until – whether spontaneous or choreographed – a crowd of thirty or forty children, their cheers just audible over the noise of the engine, ran out of the huts to greet our arrival. They were accompanied by several adults, all European, all female. None was Dora.

Viessmann gave himself over to the crowd of enthused children and introduced the new arrivals. Hoover and I stood there dazed and stupid. My head was still full of the noise of the flight. Viessmann's child-handling skills continued to look exemplary. Hoover appeared more and more sour and withdrawn.

There was an outdoors eating area, with a roof but otherwise open. We ate, more or less immediately, with the others, adults interspersed with children. Hoover and I sat together but two children wriggled between us, making conversation impossible. Lunch was rice and a vegetable stew. Viessmann was seated at another table and made no effort to join us. Afterwards we were left to ourselves. The children disappeared into one of the buildings and Viessmann contrived to vanish without our noticing.

Hoover was behaving like a man who has just discovered that his holy grail is nothing but a tin pot. When I asked him if we had just had lunch with Willi Schmidt he gave me a nasty look and I left him to himself.

Everyone was indoors. The weather had turned warmer and was nearly hot. My head was muzzy, as if I had been drinking. The solitariness of the place was emphasised by an air of self-sufficiency, with gardens and allotments. I went and lay by a stream and soon fell asleep.

I was woken by the shadow passing over my face. Viessmann was looking down at me. I had the impression he had been watching for some time. I felt vulnerable but didn't want to show it by moving. The sun made it hard to see him and I had to shield my eyes.

'What are we doing here?' I asked.

'Beate von Heimendorf said that you were making a dangerous journey and she was concerned for your safety.'

'Beate?'

Viessmann ignored me. 'Your friend is ill, isn't he?'

'I thought he was supposed to be an old friend of yours too.'

He subjected me to his disconcerting silence.

'Do you have someone from England working here called Dora?' I asked.

'Dora. Of course.'

I got up quickly. 'Where is she?'

'She moved on, last week. She was with us a few weeks, passing through.'

'Where is she now?'

'Perhaps we can find out later.' He sounded reasonable, less aloof.

'My companion is sure he knows you.'

'He is wrong. I have an excellent memory for names and faces. Besides, your friend is not well. He probably should not be travelling at all. It would be best to take him back. I know Beate would be happy to arrange a clinic. Perhaps if he has good travel insurance the medical costs would be covered.'

After what everyone had said about Viessmann, it was odd to end up talking about something as banal as medical insurance, but maybe not. He was Swiss.

Hoover, Turkey

I could not tell, I really could not. I felt it was my fault. Viessmann had admitted he was Viessmann and behaved as though our presence at his godforsaken camp was because he had interceded on Beate's behalf. It also raised the question of how she had reacted to my letter.

I tried to fit what I remembered of Willi with Viessmann. The eyes. The voice. The walk. They were the things that were hardest to disguise. Sometimes it had to be Willi. There were too many similarities. Then I would look again and decide there was nothing of him.

We were treated like guests, but there was no escape. We had nothing to do. We were given no tasks. Remoteness acted like an anesthetic while the air was so clear it stung, resulting in a state of alert torpor. Clear vision was not matched by clarity of thought. My edginess was easily countered by Viessmann's messianic aloofness. It seemed to be part of his power that he could leave one in a state of exhaustion and indecision. He was plausible, we the impostors. He was honest with his kids and they liked him. Kids are good readers of adults. I knew that from the grandchildren who had been quick to figure me for a disgruntled old fart, short of any capacity for play.

On our first tour of the camp we had been shown kids' dormitories, playrooms full of donated toys, informal classrooms, which was when I first noticed that all the helpers were female and barely more than teenagers. The office hut had computers and telephones, and was run by a couple more helpers. The technology relied on a local generator, which provided the distinctive noise we could hear, like an outboard motor. Viessmann said that we were very private and even with satellite links communications remained variable.

In one office a whole wall was devoted to mugshots of kids. Viessmann was especially proud of this display. They were the ones who had found homes, either with middle-class Kurdish families or in the West with foster parents.

Vaughan did his best to ask questions, and was met with answers that pointed out the obvious until he asked him how running a multinational business related to what he was doing at the camp. At this, Viessmann was transformed. His imperiousness deserted him and he was reduced to an enthusiastic babble: 'A young mind is a healthy mind,' he said. 'Businesses have to learn how to realign themselves for the twenty-first century, providing care as well as nurturing profit.' He advocated the study of children in group activity to promote his theory of business as play. Children were good motivators and organisers, he said, much less inclined to boredom, and up to a certain age non-exclusive. Viessmann the pedagogue: what we can learn from the little ones.

I thought of my grandchildren. Bored and whiny. Demanding. Divisive. Given to squabbling on a level that would impress the Balkans. Incapable of amusing themselves. Hostile.

Recognition was not instant, as I had been expecting. When it came it was a real shock and quite unexpected, a combination of a shaft of sunlight coming through the window and the particular angle of Viessmann's head at that moment. It was not Willi Schmidt that I read into Viessmann, but Beate. It was her I saw in him.

Did I faint? According to Vaughan, I stood up and fell over. Then I was in a sanatorium-like room with half a dozen beds and too weak to get up.

My first visitor was Viessmann, playing the concerned host. He laid a dry hand on my brow and asked if I shouldn't be flown to another place with better facilities. I wondered about that because the room I was in already had what looked like a lot of expensive medical equipment. Viessmann said that many of the children they found needed treatment.

We then embarked on a surreal conversation, starting with my asking if he was Beate's father. He didn't miss a beat. He said he had no children apart from the ones I saw here. He said the special quality of the local air made for light-headedness and poor judgement. I looked for signs of guile and found none (saw only Viessmann and nothing of

Beate now). Every question he met with expert deflection: Betty Monroe he admitted to knowing, no more; Carswell was Beate's former husband, no more; Karl-Heinz he passed on, without a pause. 'I am sorry I don't know that name.'

'Willi Schmidt,' I said. Viessmann turned and looked at me. Not a glimmer, not even a chink. 'I was pretty sure Willi Schmidt was a friend we had in common.' I said it slowly.

He repeated the name, sounding like he was saying it for the first time. 'No,' he decided.

He offered me something to help me sleep. I declined and asked for Vaughan. He told me Vaughan had gone for provisions with one of the trucks. The news scared me. He paused by the door and again offered me a sedative, then asked, 'Who was this Willi Schmidt?'

The first betrayal of curiosity. Mischief made me bold. 'Willi was the most interesting man I ever met. A pity you didn't know him.'

A truck came in the evening. Through the window I saw Viessmann in the compound talking to armed men in plain-clothes. They stayed fifteen minutes before driving off. I imagined Viessmann telling them where they could find Vaughan. I imagined Viessmann shooting me full of something while I slept to ensure I didn't wake up. Willi Schmidt's casual remark in Strasbourg as he had prepared to shoot me: 'It's making me hard doing this,' said in an offhand way, with an air of pleasure and mild surprise, that old delight in himself. 'Go fuck yourself, Willi,' I had told him and he chided me for my lack of originality.

Viessmann found me stumbling around the compound in the dark and guided me back to bed. I felt old and impotent, mocked by the memory of Willi's curiosity at his own tumescence, and tired to death. I asked Viessmann what the camp had by way of entertainment. He looked as though the word didn't exist in his book. Would he show me where he lived? I asked. Viessmann, man of manners, too polite to refuse. His living quarters included a sitting room with armchairs. I didn't think he would have any drink, but he produced a bottle of Scotch, raised his glass and said, 'Cheers!'

We asked polite questions of each other. He did not wince when I told him of my suburban Floridian background, but I sensed distaste. He had a house, as I had guessed, in the hills of Buda. Before that he had lived in Locarno. He confirmed that he was executive director of a pharmaceutical concern, based in Switzerland but in the process of relocating to Malaysia. I asked about the Kurds bombing his factory and was surprised by his answer. 'They were quite right. These are practices that must be stopped.' The First World could not continue to exploit the less fortunate in the way that it had.

Did the rebels know that he was the man whose factory they had bombed? I asked. Yes, he said. He had talked to them about it and now employed Kurdish doctors to ensure that there was no more malpractice.

We had drunk most of the Scotch yet Viessmann remained so sober that he was able to refute anything I threw at him.

I asked how he managed to look so fit and young. Diet, yoga and exercise, he said. And plastic surgery, I wanted to add. Viessmann didn't have Willi's teeth. I had expected more tension between us. I had expected him to give off something, some scent that let me know he knew I was on to him. But he looked like he had done years of controlled breathing and could take any lie-detector test.

He asked about my sickness. I said it was undiagnosed. I had run away before the tests could be done. 'It could be nothing, or it could be galloping through me. Unlike you, I have treated my body abysmally.'

'Are you afraid of death, Mr Hoover?'

It was the first time he had called me by name. I didn't like the way he placed it directly after the word 'death'.

'Foolish not to be,' I said.

Viessmann stared at me, unfathomable. The lights of an approaching vehicle moved across the room.

'That'll be Mr Vaughan and the others with the supplies,' said Viessmann.

I stood up, drunk and dizzy. Viessmann said I should get some sleep. I said we called it insomnia where I came from.

Vaughan, Turkey

Hoover was drunk and depressed. Viessmann was uncrackable, he said. He was angry with me for going off. 'You could have said no,' he said.

But my trip had given me a chance to question the two young women who had gone along with me. In fact, they told me nothing. They were unencumbered and cheerful. They got to look after children and drive around in four-wheel vehicles. Greta was Danish and Astrid was German. They were bland and middle-class, polite and without curiosity, trusting and uncritical. We had driven a hundred miles to a food depot, loaded up and come back. After forty miles we had exhausted our conversation. The girls were hazy on the nature of the local conflict. They had trouble grasping the statelessness of the Kurds and their consequent persecution by their host governments in Iraq and Turkey. 'They are like cuckoos!' Most of the helpers stayed only around two months, on account of the remoteness. Nearly all of them had ended up there through word-of-mouth while travelling.

Dora they knew of. Dora had worked in the office. I had expected to find mention of her name reassuring, but it had sounded quite alien. For the first time I understood Hoover's real dilemma. He was hanging on to something that wasn't there, something that Willi Schmidt, dead or alive, had relinquished long ago. Either way, Willi was gone.

For a long time Hoover lay staring at the ceiling, saying nothing. He seemed obscurely afraid, in some deep way he could not articulate, and was beyond consolation, afraid both of the conscious world and of his unconscious mind.

I had to wait till very late before he drifted into sleep. On leaving I checked out of the window. All the lights in the camp were off. The generator was switched off. There was a deep silence. The stars outside were the brightest I had ever seen.

Children slept peacefully. Toys lay stacked neatly in the toy room. There was a games room for the adults, with table-tennis. Beyond the games room, the kitchen. Everything was in order and made perfect sense, yet on another level none at all. Why weren't the kids being looked after by their own people? Why were no Kurdish adults present?

In Viessmann's sitting room I found a few esoteric paperbacks and books on business analysis. Two glasses and a bottle of Scotch were on a table. In the corner stood an old cabinet, with doors and a lid, which turned out to be an ancient record player, an old wind-up gramophone, the likes of which I had not seen in years. I idly wound the handle and watched the dusty turntable turning, hearing the old music. Count Basie. Billie Holiday. Duke Ellington.

Jazz records from the 1940s. *Willi Schmidt's jazz.*

I felt that old skin scrawl on the back of the neck which accompanies any unpleasant discovery, until recently associated entirely with Dora.

There in the cabinet cupboard I found what remained of Willi Schmidt.

Willi's records – old 78s that had somehow survived breakage. Konrad Viessmann had shed everything of Willi except his records. Willi's records in Konrad's cupboard.

I wanted to wake Hoover, but another clue, registered subconsciously, lurked just out of reach; not a conversation or a remark. I went back to the office. Everything was still. I drank a Scotch and stared at the photographs of the children on the wall and wondered about them. They were all the same age for a start. Why not eight or ten year olds? Why not girls?

A light went on. It was Viessmann, on the case, looking like his being there was the most normal thing in the world. He was dressed and alert. I asked what time it was. He said it would be dawn soon. I told him I hadn't been able to sleep. He regarded me with an intense and hostile irony. We both ignored the pistol he was holding.

I looked again at Viessmann and asked myself: What if they were all mad? What if Viessmann was as mad as Himmler and Karl-Heinz, not mad in the usual everyday way, but deeply, historically mad?

I turned to the photographs on the wall. Childhood

memories of early Bible stories flickered in my mind's eye. The Flight to Egypt and the Massacre of the Innocents, in which King Herod killed all children under the age of two years in the certainty that one of them had to be the Son of God. Viessmann stared at me. He looked expectant. I knew I shouldn't say anything, knew I should keep my mouth shut and look after Hoover and make sure we got out alive, walking if we had to.

I said it anyway, knowing what it meant. I turned and pointed at the wall of photographs and said, 'You're looking for the Chosen One.'

Vaughan

They buried me in a black box. With enough room to lie down. The only sound was the hoarse noise of my own panic. Terror rolled in, unstoppable. The first dull moments of consciousness giving way to a body-rush of panic.

Pushing upwards with both hands I could make the briefest chink of light appear. Buried alive, you drool and howl and cry for any form of human company: even the worst would be better than such stark isolation. You cramp. You make up stories: you are in a bunk in a dark room; you can get up and move around any time, it's just you choose not to. Before Viessmann coshed me with his pistol butt, I had asked him not to hurt the old man, because he was dying, and felt ashamed calling Hoover an old man. I remembered Viessmann's grunt as he swung his arm.

Like a surfacing dream, the images hold only a moment before you are back in fucked time. This dark box is it. Even if they let you out, you will carry the box in your head as long as you live.

They are inventive in their cruelty. I was allowed out at night. The rattle of unlocking, followed by the longest silence. I pushed the lid up. No one around. A dusty circle and darkness. A bowl of food and water some yards off. Stones uncomfortable on bare feet. The only warning, a soft scuffle before the dogs flew out of the night, savage-fanged beasts with crazed eyes.

Fear multiplies. The heart hammers. The dogs leap. Two beasts big enough to rip a man apart.

But the dogs halt, as if frozen. They are tethered. They attack relentlessly, stopping you reaching the food, a margin of inches. Their frustration mounts the more they strain. The box would be better than this, you think as you stand there, a basilisk of fear.

The first time, the dogs withdrew when someone started taking pot shots into the night, a signal that time outside was over. I grabbed the food and scurried back. The second time I crawled back in the box voluntarily. The third time I didn't come out.

Fear is not linear. It is a state that is both constant and in waiting. Fear is not articulate. It is the antithesis of words, beyond proper description. Language can only approximate fear. Language is the start of countering fear. Fear is easily taught. It is infectious. Carswell's wish: to create a virus out of fear. He told me.

Terror is not quantifiable. There is nothing to distinguish one person's terror from another. Terror is invasive and all-consuming. Terror and fear are individual to the sufferer, while negating that person's individuality. The rest, to paraphrase Hoover, is just talk-shows and ambulance-chasing.

They slowly let me join their world. We were in a detention camp. More prefab huts, barbed wire, and signs clear in any language: *Beware, mines*. The camp had the rough economy of a child's drawing. See, it said, this is all we need to break you: makeshift buildings and large, cruel open spaces, designed for a primitive malevolence. The scale of the place was not immediately apparent. The vast emptiness all around was more so – a brutal landscape under a cloudless sky, both stripped of any softening features.

I was let out of the box by two men with machine pistols, who took me into the rocky wilderness outside the camp, gave me a shovel and made me dig. The inference was obvious. I dug slowly, hoping they might grow bored or change their minds.

In a situation like this, you fail to create a distance between yourself and what is happening. You hope you will not be as afraid as you know you will be. You try and think of nothing, a blank for the blankness to come. Other times your brain struggles with a ferocious energy that reminds you of the leaping dogs.

It turns out you are there only as a punchline for their joke. They make you kneel down before the open hole and shoot you. Except they miss. Put the bullet past your head. Then they see if you are still capable of standing up and walking away.

Sometimes they did that two or three times a day. My job was not without purpose. The graves got used anyway.

Then one day the guards took me instead to another part of the camp. I tried to equate this change with hope, as much as my precarious self-control would permit. We passed into another fenced-off compound where a large building of several storeys was being hastily constructed. This rapid building programme was a combination of rickety wooden scaffolds, low-tech construction, hi-tech equipment and brutalised forced labor. Any clumsiness resulted in a pistol-whipping. The beaten prisoner would lie where he had fallen, an obvious object of contempt to everyone for having been too stupid to avoid punishment.

Our destination was an area beyond the site sectioned off by heavy security, including a network of surveillance cameras, which twisted and rotated on top of their perches like mechanical crows. Compared to the chaos of the site there appeared to be nothing going on here. The cameras supervised order and emptiness. The area consisted of a dozen or so of the ubiquitous prefabricated huts arranged in a neat grid, with paths in between. I glimpsed the occasional discreet professional presence. Two young men wearing white medical coats escorted two children by the hand. In a refuse section I saw a Chinese woman emptying slops and thought of Frankfurt.

After the degradation I had been subjected to, the warmth and order of the hut into which I was shown was almost too much. I experienced a flashback to Sol describing being escorted to see Karl-Heinz and Willi for the first time. Two men were waiting. They were in their thirties, professionals dressed in civilian clothes. I stood there, deferential, with bowed head, not daring to look up; how quickly you learned. One wore Timberlands. The boots looked like something from a lost world.

The Timberlands man spoke a little English. They needed an opinion, he said. They had been told I was English. In the background a woman worked at a console. I felt shamed in her presence, not that it mattered as she did not even look up.

The Timberlands man showed me some technical drawings which had been supplied by an English contractor. They appeared to be the wrong drawings. At the bottom the company address was Bury St Edmunds. I stared dumbly at the three words, which no longer made any sense, on their own or together.

Extraordinarily, they told me to speak to the supplier. I even dialled the number myself and there followed a disconcerting two-minute conversation where I spoke first to a nasal-voiced receptionist then an undermotivated executive named Tibbit. Here was Middle England at its most resentful; a cure for any homesickness.

The muddle over the drawings was ungraciously admitted. The ones that had been sent were meant for a heating system and two industrial boilers somewhere in Russia. No translation had been sent either.

The Timberlands man fretted in the background. He

looked afraid that someone would reprimand him for the mistake.

I was told the correct drawings would be faxed straight away for reference, with the originals forwarded by courier. As I tried to take in these mundane details I wondered if they had any idea in Bury St Edmunds where their product ended up. I asked Tibbit what the proper drawings were for.

Crematoria.

I put the phone down very slowly. A guard was summoned to take me back.

I was being led down a path between the huts when a man hurried out of a door just up ahead. At first I thought he was another of the white-coated doctors but his uniform was different. The top was tight-fitting and waisted.

Then the brief freeze-frame of the double-take: the familiar figure, for a moment out of place and time, but so recognisable and somehow inevitable.

I ran and grabbed his elbow, blathering, wanting his explanation, hoping only for some pity.

He reacted like he was being attacked, with a reflex backhand, without even a glance. As I fell, I consoled myself with the fact that I had seen Carswell's fear. More than that, when he recognised me, he committed what was probably the only cardinal sin in his book and lost his cool. He shrieked and kicked at me and called me a stupid meddling fucker who should have gone home when he was told.

Carswell's hysterics were followed by an exaggerated

iciness. In any other circumstances he could have been dismissed as shrill and camp but in those surroundings his histrionics could lead only to an authorised sadism.

He spoke Turkish to the guard and I was taken away to a windowless hut where Carswell's uniform was explained. In a gym-like room several men in fencing kit practised thrust and parry. While forced-labour gangs sweated through their shifts, and children were escorted God knows where, it seemed that Carswell indulged himself by training Turkish soldiers in the art of swordplay.

When Carswell returned he said to me: 'If you stand perfectly still you will not get hurt. We are going to conduct an experiment in reflex action.'

Someone held a bladed sword against the back of my neck, while Carswell lunged again and again at my face. The unblunted point of his épée always ended up within millimetres of my eye. His self-control, in contrast to his outburst, was fully in command again. I believed in the precision of his skills, believed in his need to indulge in his grown-up games, trusted him not to hurt me, yet let myself down by flinching – and each time the point of the sword jabbed the back of my neck, however hard I willed myself not to move. Carswell was toying with me, a man who understood the dynamics of intimacy and violence.

Carswell sardonic, Carswell superior, taunting, 'Can't you do better than that?' I stared him down. I no longer flinched. His blade stopped short and this time I did not feel the jab of the sword in my neck. In that moment I knew what the real point of Carswell's exercise was. To tell me that he had killed Bob Ballard.

I also saw for the first time his profound dislike of me and realised how tearfully hard it was – after the depersonalising regime of the camp – to be faced by someone who saw and hated me for myself. But my acceptance of his predatory nature was immediate and unquestioning. It was the absence of this knowledge that had previously made Carswell seem incomplete.

'You just missed Dora,' he said.

'Did you send her to Viessmann?'

'She needed to clear out her head. Do something, what was the word she used? "Unselfish." Now she has gone back, which is what you should have done while you had the chance.'

That night I was taken out of the box back to the secure area and put in a soundproofed room with a mirror that was almost certainly an observation window.

They fed me white noise. It was like having someone scratch your brains with a wire brush. I failed to smash the mirror with my hands. A console had been set up in the room with instructions that I transcribe the contents of a tape from a mini-recorder with headphones. I refused. They resorted to simple cause and effect. They turned up the volume in the room to ear-splitting level. Once I put the headphones on the noise went away.

It shamed me to transcribe the tape, but I lacked the will to refuse. The keyboard arrangement was different from English ones and I kept making mistakes. In the end, I just concentrated on typing the correct letter as a way of trying to distance myself from the spew of words being pulled out of van der Valden.

The tape was of van der Valden's interrogation by Carswell, who sounded arrogant and concentrated. He was accused of selling information to Karl-Heinz. He was accused of 'negotiating with third parties'. He was told he was the victim of a sting by Verco's security. Van der Valden denied and denied, then broke and agreed to everything, confessing to make them stop, any pretence at truth forgotten. By what mental process does someone decide to write, *Subject screams. Statement incomprehensible.*?

As I typed I knew that I too was being turned into someone's dossier, clean words on a page, documenting my regression from arrival to capitulation. I ceased to think of myself as an entity, only as a receptacle. I thought about the wire. I wondered if breaking me would take less time than calculated. In rare moments of lucidity, I understood that I was now so far undercover I was lost to myself. I no longer recognised the person looking back at me in the observation mirror. Somewhere in all of this I understood the secret of Viessmann's looks, a combination of surgery and whatever anti-ageing products his company was testing. Viessmann using his own body as an experiment site, in the vanguard of a new science, using tomorrow's high-street product on himself today. I told all of this to the mirror. I spoke to it as though it were a person, which in some ways it was, because I knew people were on the other side taking it all down. I felt my mind shutting down, the wiring starting to short.

I was kicked awake by two men who dragged me outside. It was still dark. Floodlights were on. Prisoners were being loaded onto two big container trucks like you see on every highway.

The scene was ghost quiet. There was no shouting or yelling orders. The dogs were out but they were silent too. Everything seemed inevitable. Everyone was docile as they were herded on board.

The inside of the containers had been adapted so we sat sideways in long rows in separate stalls. It was another kind of box, this time with a steel rod across to which one wrist was chained. Several head counts were taken and there were delays to check everyone was properly locked in. I noticed the Chinese woman I had seen round the back of the kitchens.

We could hear the other truck, its big diesel engines revving for a long time. From time to time a palpable ripple of fear went through our container. We were made to wait long enough for everyone to grow impatient for the journey to begin, whatever it might bring.

Our container was at last locked and we left. We travelled in the dark, with no light inside. The road was poor. Disorientation soon made people vomit and it became necessary to breathe through the mouth. Some started praying aloud, others began an intense keening. There was the dark, the motion of the container and the babble of frightened voices, which gradually stopped. Then there was only the dark and the motion.

The explosion seemed to lift the truck right off the ground, a tremendous bang that filled the air with screams. I braced myself, thinking we were toppling over the edge of one of the ravines I had driven along with Hoover. But the truck settled, and there was a brief lull followed by the steady stitch of gunfire on metal. The panic in the container was contagious. We all knew we were about to die, a hundred minds united briefly in the same certainty. The only question was how.

We could hear the back door to the container being worked open, even over the yelling and the gunfire. The shrieking rose to a crescendo, then stopped quite suddenly as everyone realised that this was our deliverance.

The truck had been attacked by rebels. But the joy was short-lived. A new anxiety quickly took over that the security forces would counter-attack before all the handcuffs could be broken.

Outside was still dark. The truck's cabin was burned out and twisted from the explosion. The dead driver was half hanging out and the rest of the guards were dead except for one standing with his arms in the air.

The prisoners had no hesitation in turning on the guard. Rebel soldiers stood by laughing as dozens of prisoners chucked rocks at the guard, who staggered around, stunned, arms out in front like he was playing Blind Man's Bluff, his faltering steps those of a drunk until his balance went and he lurched over.

The death seemed as manufactured in its clumsy, graphic violence as a cartoon and I half-expected him to get up so they could all do it again. Instead he lay there, like an old bundle of rags, in a widening pool of his own blood, which, in the last of the night, stained the ground black. I watched dumbly, mindful of Karl-Heinz's belief that violence would revert to a Biblical cruelty.

Nobody seemed in any hurry now despite the earlier panic of a counter-attack. The destroyed truck had become a symbol which everyone seemed reluctant to abandon, a sign of victory.

Eventually three military-type lorries came, low-sided and with metal skeleton frames for the canvas, which was missing. Everyone crammed on, hanging on to the frame for support. We drove a mile or so in convoy and then separated. We traveled for several hours. I slept standing, held up by the squash of bodies. Whenever I woke people were scanning the skies anxiously for the security forces' planes.

Beate von Heimendorf, Zürich

Mother rallied briefly and seemed to recognise me.

I took Vaughan. He had said he wanted to meet her. Hoover had explained to him how Mother had brought him to Switzerland in 1942. He looked at her a long time, then turned to me. 'What could any of that have to do with me? Yet it's all still going on.'

Afterwards we were a long time in a café, sitting outside, at Vaughan's insistence, even though it was cold. He drank wine, as always.

At least he goes out now. At first he sat doing nothing all day, staring into space. I let him stay at Mother's. He will tell me nothing of his experiences. The doctor has ordered a full rest. His spell as my guest looks like becoming an extended one. All he has asked is that I don't tell Dominic. So far I have not. But Dominic is in Basel, and suspicious. In the case of Hoover I was able to answer truthfully that I did not know.

Vaughan had called from Turkey, asking me to wire money which he would pay back. He returned looking like a man who had taken leave of himself and to whom too much had happened in too short a time. It rendered him more or less mute. He said he had nowhere else to go. For the best part of three days he slept and when he wasn't sleeping he was in tears, a silent crying unlike any I have ever seen. I think it was utter exhaustion. He didn't talk or read or watch television or go for walks. He didn't want to see anyone. I came in the evening to cook him pasta or an omelette, which he put aside after a couple of mouthfuls.

He drank instead, red wine, at first only in the evening, until he was drunk enough to go to bed, then all day, borrowing money from me. He sat in cafés at first, he told me, then started taking bottles into parks, wearing an old coat of Adam's which I had lent him. However much he drank he never got noisy or uncoordinated or made an exhibition of himself, just quieter and sadder.

A man from the American Embassy has called on several occasions, the first time to say that Uncle Konny's place had been found evacuated. Hoover's whereabouts are unknown, as are Bob Ballard's. There has been no news of him since before everyone left. Still, it was in the nature of his job to have to move quickly.

I don't know if Dominic spoke to Bob Ballard. It was one of my conditions for helping him obtain the museums contract that he did. The other was that he send Vaughan home. Now Vaughan is back. Soon I will have to tell him to make other arrangements because he is becoming an embarrassment, stumbling around town. I know he is suffering the after-effects of trauma, and that he wishes to offend my bourgeois sensibilities, but my patience and generosity are not limitless, nor are my manners. And Dominic is persistent.

Mother's house has become almost like the old days, with people coming and going. The man from the American Embassy has turned up to talk to Vaughan, and an Englishman, who says he is from his embassy. The Englishman is handsome. I was at Mother's house, ostensibly working on a paper, when he called round. My real reason for being there was to keep an eye on things. I suspect Vaughan will soon start stealing to pay for his drink. Today he stuck his tongue out at me. It is quite black. Whether he did it to show me or because he was being rude I cannot say. Such behaviour seems entirely in keeping with his present state of mind.

That night we talked more than usual. Vaughan said he had been 'debriefed by a couple of desks'. They had been incredulous and sceptical about what he had told them, though too professional to show it.

What Vaughan went on to tell me made no sense – such things don't go on today – and perfect sense: I understand the principle of vested interest. I am aware that my, and my country's, security is at the expense of others' freedom. The equation I find hard to accept, but will, if pushed. I did not expect to find myself being so thoroughly stripped of any illusions.

One reason for Willi Schmidt's change of identity at the end of the war was, Vaughan said, because he had swindled Jews by organising false escape routes. Konrad Viessmann's first job had been to provide a safe haven for Nazi doctors involved in the extermination programme, and the clinic used had been the foundation of his later empire.

I wish to talk of my own confusion but cannot. I am not ready to accept Konrad Viessmann as my biological father, and certainly not Willi Schmidt. I rejected Vaughan's link of a collection of jazz records as tenuous.

Vaughan wanted Carswell, he said, and he wanted me to get Carswell for him. I shook my head. It was unthinkable.

Vaughan wouldn't let me rest. He worked his story backwards, starting with the rivers. The enormous dam project would give Turkey control over the flow of Iraq and Syria's two main rivers. The project also allowed the Turks to move its problematic Kurdish population around at will. The Syrians were retaliating by harbouring Kurdish rebels, Vaughan said. 'The links go back to Bern and Zürich and further, back to 1942, and maybe even before.'

Turkey's Kurds were not a humanitarian issue for European governments, he said, because those governments needed Turkey to act as a stabilising force in the Middle East. 'Most of this comes out as isolated news stories. They never show you how the shadings go all the way from white to black, as a matter of course. When there is some scandal they make out it's an aberration, a one-off. They isolate. They personalise. And if we are going to get personal, Carswell and Viessmann are both way in the black as far as shadings go.'

I argued back. His stubbornness gave me a glimpse of what he had managed to survive. He had told me little of what had happened except to say that he had no real proof, other than what he had seen, and his own speculation to put two and two together. He was sure people were being killed, certain there was a secret medical programme.

I said if he could prove what he was saying I would help him in any way he wanted, though I did not reasonably see what I was supposed to do. My upbringing demanded you protect those closest to you, whatever they might have done. Circles are there to remain closed. My previous attempt to break it, with Hoover, ended in humiliation.

I don't particularly like Vaughan but we understand each other. He knows I am, essentially, without a voice. Vaughan laughed a weary laugh, and said, 'Even now your mother's dumb, look at the hold she has.' He said that what I took for love and obedience was fear.

I was forced to accept his description of Dominic as a cruel man. Tyranny in the bedroom is a good enough indication of a man's personality. Yet perhaps I still wanted him as a friend because I was intrinsically scared of him, too. It gave me a certain power to maintain civilised relations with Dominic, and as a result our collusion runs deep.

After I had agreed to help Vaughan he told me what

Dominic had done to Mr Ballard. I don't why he had held back, perhaps because he thought I would have resisted believing him. If only he knew! My instruction to Dominic had been 'to take care of Mr Ballard', and only now do the full and terrible implications of that phrase strike me.

Does Vaughan want to 'take care of Dominic'? He is not saying and I am not asking. My help is conditional upon not knowing what he intends to do. I pray this will help excuse my own role in Mr Ballard's gruesome end. As for Dominic, he would never fail to act on his desires. Once I saw him slap a woman in such a way that left me in no doubt of his murderous instincts. That woman was me, seen in the full-length mirror in front of which we were standing at the time. Afterwards he had cried – crocodile tears, no doubt – and apologised, which was probably more than he did to Mr Ballard.

Mother was a keen gardener; Dulles was not. Mother used to tend his garden for him – she describes doing so in her diary. Part of the slope had been turned over to a vegetable allotment. Mother had arranged a regular gardener for Dulles, but when she was there she liked to do some herself. The bank was sunny and included a vine which produced sweet grapes. Her diary describes how her times alone in that secluded garden were among her happiest. She writes: 'The garden is wasted on Allen, who appreciates it only for its secret entrance. He fails to see the beauty and magic of it, especially in spring, when it starts to conceal itself again after the winter. The summer view from Allen's bedroom window is of an impenetrable canopy of green.'

Mother died, at five o'clock this morning. She was gone by the time I arrived. I felt nothing. No release, relief or regret. I could not bring myself to kiss or touch her goodbye. The sceptical side of me thought that I had not heard the last of Mother. Actually, I felt rather giddy and lightheaded.

I called Dominic to tell him. My ex-husband was always sincere at condolences. He wanted me to know he was there for me should I need him. I was tempted to ask exactly how he had taken care of Mr Ballard. I was eager still to share Dominic's secrets. He asked if I needed anything. Not yet, I said, but I might do soon. The call was a test of nerve. It would have been easier to tell him everything.

Mother had been very Swiss in the arrangement of her death, organising for her letter to be delivered from the lawyer by courier on the morning of her demise.

It arrived at about eleven, as Vaughan was opening his first bottle of wine. I went to her room to read it. It was blunt and formal, and dated from the onset of her illness.

Betty Monroe, Zürich

My Dear Beate,

I shall be dead when you read this. Perhaps you will think good riddance. My illness will have been a trial for you, all the more because we have never been close in spite of the pretence.

I have no regrets except with regard to you. I know it will come as a great shock to you to learn that your father was not your real father, and that your Uncle Konrad was. I should have told you and the reason I did not was because the man you believed to be your father was the better person, and more appropriate father. I never told him either, and he never gave me any reason to suspect that he knew the truth. But truth, I have learned, is not an absolute commodity. I believed that subscribing to the lie would create a better truth than the truth itself. Besides, your father – I shall continue to call him that as that's what he became – had always wanted children, particularly a daughter, where Konrad had no paternal inclinations. I am telling you now, after much deliberating with my conscience – that somewhat atrophied item – because I feel that you have been held back by the half-truths and shadows that have surrounded your life.

I was never proud of my relationship with Konrad, which is not the same as saying I regret it. It caused me to do many wrong things. I told myself these were done in the name of some higher cause, which justified the tough moral decision. For a woman to be part of the world of men, she has to be as ruthless. I was enthralled by their power and wanted it for myself and not by proxy.

Your father was a victim of that power, and I dare say you were too. Perhaps most of all I enjoyed my selfishness at your expense because you and your father represented the kind of world everyone wanted for me, as a woman. One of obedience, fidelity and insufferable boredom.

Happiness was not a condition of my life. I did wonderful things and competed on the best of terms and, though it sounds old-fashioned now, I served my country. In spite of having enjoyed many lovers I lacked companionship. Happiness was brief and often solitary. I remember one such moment very clearly. I was alone in Dulles's garden one golden autumn afternoon, feeding a bonfire, watching its smoke disappear into a cloudless sky. On the train back to Zürich I smelled of burned leaves and, still happy, had to change into clean clothes before dinner.

I carried terrible secrets throughout my life. I have hesitated long and often, trying to decide whether you should share this legacy. In the end, I have decided that as my daughter you should. You have always thought of yourself as closer to your father when in fact you are more like me. You are tougher than you think, despite your deference to me and the men in your life.

One last thing I would ask you to do, related to the above. I leave the choice of how it is done to you.

There is a final set of papers. They are not discreet. Allen made me burn all the originals of any extra-curricular documents and correspondence before he left Switzerland in 1945, and he made sure he was there to watch me do it. But Allen was naive in a way only clever and deceitful men can be. He also remained ignorant of matters secretarial. He did not realise I had kept carbons of everything. This last set of papers details things even Allen did not know about.

My dear Beate, it is up to you whether you read them or not. What I ask is that you, as part of me, retrieve them and destroy them. I hope through doing this you will become free to move on, and that in the rest of your life you will achieve a happiness and fulfillment which – through my own fault, probably – eluded me.

There is a joke in all this, over the whereabouts of the papers. In Allen Dulles's garden is a vaulted cellar for storing wine with a secret hiding place, a false brick concealing a lead-lined box. Allen had it put there and we were the only ones to know about it. After he had left Switzerland, I returned and hid the papers there and I am sure they are there still. The cellar is halfway up the slope, to the right of Allen's apartment as you face it.

My wish is that you burn the papers in Allen's garden. If that is not possible, then do it at the house where the gardener burns the leaves. As for getting in the garden, Stefan the lawyer has the key. Allen gave me one all those years ago, and I kept it. It worked when I last tried it, not so long ago.

You shan't be disturbed. Nobody used the garden much and, if you are challenged, I am sure you will use that imperious manner to good effect.

I know I should think of a proper way of ending this letter, but I suspect that protestations of love would be rejected. Instead I shall think of you standing by the bonfire, hoping that you will remember my own brief happiness doing the same, and believe me when I write that I was and remain your loving errant Mother.

Beate von Heimendorf, Zürich

The rest was easy. I told Vaughan about the papers and gave him the key to Dulles's garden. Then I telephoned Dominic with details of Mother's funeral arrangements. I said I wanted Hoover there, and he should arrange for that, otherwise I would be cancelling his museums contract. Loss of face was the thing Dominic feared most. If he guessed I knew more than I was letting on, he hid it well, but men like Dominic are always alert to information withheld.

I also needed a favour, I said. How sweet to be ordering him around for a change! I mentioned Mother's papers hidden in Dulles's garden, and told him that they were certainly an embarrassment to her good name, about which Dominic remained sentimental. Please could he collect and destroy them? I had no wish to see them. Nor did I have any wish for Konrad to be at Mother's funeral, should he think of coming.

Whether I can face Dominic there remains to be seen.

Vaughan, Bern

In Bern I stayed drunk, as I had since returning to Switzerland, in that state of fuzzy blur that took the edge off. I had no plan for Carswell other than surprise, and a desire to see again that same skitter of fear which had crossed his face when I grabbed him at the camp. As a weapon I had a Stanley knife, bought in Zürich. Nothing but the finest cuts for Carswell. I reckoned after the first draw of blood the rest would follow.

I tried to think only of the knife making its first cut. I never considered any alternative – the due process of the law – because Carswell probably had a great big shiny, laminate get-out-of-gaol card. The rest I blanked. Hoover and Manny and Sol and Abe. Sol and Manny had died in the hotel shoot-out. Abe survived but was critical. Nobody had been charged or named.

Dulles's house looked unremarkable from the front, with rooms on the street you could look right into. It was hard to equate it with the hotbed of intrigue Hoover had talked about.

I used the key Beate had given me to open the garden door and stepped through it thinking about the times Hoover had gone this way. Dulles's garden was a small wilderness of allotments and lush plantings, with clearances for sitting. Like the area, it too was essentially secret. The cellar turned out to be more of a tunnel driven into the side of the gorge. It was vaulted, with a dog-leg, and empty apart from a stack of old wine bottles and gardener's tools. With the door closed it was completely dark. It was like being back in the box.

I drank half a bottle of wine and told myself I was there by choice.

Betty Monroe's papers were exactly where Beate had said, although the brick protecting the safe took some prising away. Nobody had touched it since Betty was last there, probably. The combination number was as Beate had said, with the papers inside protected by an oilskin wrapping. I had been expecting a fat document, but it was slim. The safe was also full of old paper money, including Nazi Reichsmarks, hastily stashed, the notes grown brittle with age. Betty's carbons were typed on thin foolscap, and in parts had been damaged. Elsewhere the typeface had bled into the paper.

I read Betty's pages and marvelled. For all her Jungian inclinations, the woman's icy clarity, her capacity for rational exposition, and her snobbery amounted to a perfect ruthlessness that was more than a match for Willi Schmidt's amorality, which seemed decadent by comparison. She was Lady Macbeth without the anxiety attacks.

Betty ran Dulles's agents and when Dulles couldn't cope she ran Dulles. She ran stuff behind his back he didn't know about. By 1945 she knew more about where the money was than Dulles did. Betty was keeping the books. Betty was also siphoning off money to set Willi Schmidt up.

Dulles was scared that his real war record would be investigated by what he called 'Jewish agents in the Treasury'. Himmler was blackmailing him into acting as his protector. It was all coming apart and for a while he entertained the idea of using the escape line he had set up through the Vatican to disappear to South America where he had a friend in Perón.

Meanwhile, Karl-Heinz was brokering his own deals for freedom with Betty among others, which tied in with her plans for Willi. Willi wanted two things. He wanted not to be Willi Schmidt any more. Betty was evasive on this beyond noting: *Willi has been too adventurous of late, and it is better this chapter of his life is closed.* Second, Willi wanted a clinic. He wanted German pharmaceutical expertise. He had no wish to go back to working his way up the family company.

Betty and Karl-Heinz came to an agreement. Karl-Heinz was in charge of dismantling the last of the concentration camps, a task which mainly involved not being seen to be killing Jews. As a result, he had a large medical staff facing redundancy and the Russians. Karl-

Heinz and Betty moved the best to Switzerland – her present to Willi.

But Karl-Heinz was not in the clear. Although she admired his brain and his opportunism, Betty needed him to be removed; he knew too much and was too clever to trust. If they were ever lovers – they should have been – she made no reference to it.

Of Karl-Heinz she wrote: 'He has out-guessed me. We met, cordially, at the Am Baur for tea, K-H wearing an impeccable suit. In spite of stricter Swiss border controls, in answer to American pressure, K-H seems able to come and go. We talk frankly. He worries that his recent good work on behalf of the Jews might be undermined by someone trying to besmirch his good name by spreading falsehoods about his earlier war record. Talk turns to Willi. K-H tells me about Willi in the Budapest ghetto, and what he calls Willi's "infectious behavior". (He has boasted of killing Jews through disease. Typical Willi, he has to tell someone.) This makes Willi's change of identity even more urgent. Only with that done, will the way be clear to remove K-H.'

Betty noted the débâcle over Hoover's non-death. She had nothing against him. There was just no body for Willi. According to Betty, Karl-Heinz had been called in to pull one last set of strings. After that, what mattered was that Hoover and Willi never met again, which Betty arranged by having Dulles transfer Hoover to Berlin where he was joined soon after by a de-Nazified Karl-Heinz.

After the Willi identity switch, Betty wrote: 'Karl-Heinz

is the cleverest swine. He has managed to acquire Allen's protection and looks to be safe. Let sleeping dogs lie. Instead Reichsführer Himmler gets his come-uppance. Allen is still prone to pillow-talk. He is just back from Frankfurt, for which he departed two or three days ago like a man stung. Thanks to Karl-Heinz's intervention, Allen has retrieved and destroyed the Reichsführer's file on him. In that crude Hemingway manner of his which he mistakes for manliness, he said, "I burned the thing and pissed on it." Now, he says, the way is clear to stab Himmler in the back. It quite outdoes *Julius Caesar*!

'Allen has long fretted about Himmler. Short of getting him to South America, Allen was in danger of being dragged down because Himmler was entertaining preposterous fantasies of his role in the new Europe. Karl-Heinz has short-circuited all that in exchange for his own safety. Allen will send him to Berlin where he can be watched by Hoover. The serendipity of this outcome is almost the more pleasing.'

A few entries later, Betty noted: 'Rumors of Himmler's death. Suicide, apparently, while in the hands of the Brits. Allen positively genial when we spoke on the telephone. Says his gout is quite cured up.'

I waited in vain the whole of the next day, sitting in the dark to preserve what little battery the torch had left. It was a strange feeling, being caught in the tailspin of stuff that had gone down so long ago. I knew more than Hoover now, knew the full extent of Betty Monroe's collusion with Willi in the Budapest ghetto experimenting with disease. No one had noticed. Even now they didn't notice. Those of us in the truck, maybe our fate would have been the same. Some fatal illness, some epidemic about which nobody cared.

Viessmann and Carswell were proof that whole programmes are supposed to remain invisible, not a conspiracy as such, more a matter of silent clusters forming around vested interests, and its investments. It was time that Carswell became part of that silence.

The dark's terrors lessened. Waiting became more a matter of worrying whether a gardener would turn up before Carswell. As the day wore on tiredness combined with the onset of a hangover. I had long run out of wine.

After sunset I risked stepping outside. It was a moonlit night. Some of the apartments had their lights on. It was very still and the sound of traffic carried from the bridge. The air tasted sharp and fresh, after the fetid cellar .

I was about to go back when I heard a rustling, then saw a silhouette moving up towards the cellar. I started sweating in spite of the cool night air. Dry mouth. Thick tongue. Racing heart, so noisy I could not believe it couldn't be heard. I was slow following and hoped I had the stomach for what was to come. I felt my way blind into the dark of the cave and stood pressed against the wall just before the dog-leg, willing myself on.

Something dropped, followed by a single expletive. A woman's voice.

I called her name without thinking.

Dora was picking up her torch. We splashed our beams over each other's faces. She didn't seem surprised. 'Dominic said you might be here.'

She sounded nonchalant, like we had run into each other in the street. Cool Dora. I felt undone. I had grown half-used to the idea of Carswell not coming. I had never dreamt, in the endless permutations thrown up in my head, it would be Dora.

Dora played Dora like she didn't care, like she was running some silly, sinister errand. She didn't share my surprise. She wasn't interested. She was doing Carswell a favour, with me a mild inconvenience to be stepped around. Stealthy Dora, stealer of souls. Maybe Carswell had taught her to exploit her difference, and turn avenger. Dora, white-faced in my beam, as pale as one of the undead, saying, 'Stop shining that thing in my face!'

Dora inspecting the money, indifferent. Dora asking, 'Where are the papers?'

Gone, I lied. I told her I had burned them. She appeared not to mind one way or the other.

Dora gave me two minutes of her life, maybe three, saying she had been in Turkey to get her head together. Dora had done a crash-course in idealisation. She denounced the hypocrisy of the club where she worked. She read Carswell as good.

'You mistake his influence for virtue,' I told her. She disagreed. She took Viessmann on his own Utopian terms. Slim-souled Dora. She saw only what she was shown and what she chose to see. She radiated hard purity.

I could see I took up no space in her life. Nevertheless, I tried to fool myself into believing she had persuaded Carswell to let her come in his place. Dora's intercession, to spare me. But she turned the metaphorical knife as surely as if it were real.

Dora is a stranger again, no relation at all, more an accident of biology. She said goodbye, stretching the word, leaving me in no doubt of its finality. I stood there after she had gone, aware of the space where she had been, the only evidence of our phantom encounter Betty Monroe's document, which I took with me.

I left through the door in the wall, locking up behind me.

Soft-pad Carswell was waiting. He played hide-and-seek in the night. Scuffling; me turning, him not there. Hide-and-seek turned to Grandmother's Footsteps: Carswell there in spirit, never when I looked. My mind ran away with itself. I was spooking myself, I thought, and gripped the Stanley knife harder.

Carswell stage-managed his entrance well, waiting until I had decided he was a figment of my imagination. I passed through the glow of a light, one of the few on the path. Ahead lay the buttress of the bridge, with steps running up the side. I thought of people in the bars up above, tantalisingly close. As I stood at the bend in the path, listening, I looked back at the pool cast by the lamp, expecting Carswell to step into it.

He didn't and I turned to make my way up the path.

He came at me from the side, moving silently and very

fast. I felt the slash of his blade as it whipped across my face, nicking the skin by my eye. Carswell was looking impressive and preposterous in a black cloak, allowing him a freedom of movement not possible in a coat or jacket. Homicidal Carswell. I shouted for help and none came. 'This is Switzerland,' he said. They were the only words we exchanged.

He had my line of escape cut off, blocking the path. The arc of his sword gave him a span of six feet. He swished its whippy foil in my face, relishing my panic. Were anyone to come across our silent pantomime, all he had to do was cover his sword with his cloak and stroll on.

I fled in the only direction available, up the rickety maintenance steps fixed to the buttress of the bridge. They ended in a small service platform high above the ground, going nowhere, except back down. Even standing on top of the safety rail, the underneath of the bridge would remain out of reach. Above me I could just make out a complex forest of metal stanchions. I was trapped. Carswell padded up the steps, utterly sure, nearly at the platform. He swung his sword low to high, to avoid the wall of the buttress, meaning to drive me backwards so that I fell off the platform. Verdict: death by misadventure, or whatever it's called here.

Fear dictated the next move. I climbed onto the rail of the platform, trying to escape Carswell's blade. He was close enough now for me to see the gleam in his eye. Perhaps I fell, or started to. I remember the giddy sense of letting go, wondering how it would end, and then I was hanging on to the underneath of the bridge, hugging it with my arms, while my legs bicycled air. I felt a thin string of pain down my thigh, and saw Carswell leaning out from the platform, glee on his face as he whipped his blade back and forward.

I hauled myself up. Soon I was lost among the stanchions. Hidden in the gridwork of metal it was possible, almost, to feel lost. The broad struts were wide enough for standing, and there was plenty to hang on to. Below was nothing but darkness. I willed myself into believing no height was involved. A stream of traffic rolled above my head, a matter of feet away and I drew comfort from its proximity. I had no plan, except to stay there, all night if necessary until I could attract someone's attention. I was sure Carswell would not take the same risk that I had.

Yet there he was, only a few yards away, on the edge of visibility. He had no need to hang on and strutted the stanchions, letting the tip of his foil drag along the metal. He had nerve where I had none. I properly understood the expression 'clinging on for dear life'. Carswell prowled the sub-structure, at home with the height and the limb on which we found ourselves. He hadn't seen me, frozen between stanchions, but he was getting closer.

The moonlight was his friend, not mine. It came out from behind a cloud, for the first time since the garden, a hanging near-full moon, casting a blue glow over the bridge. Carswell saw me and smiled. Way, way down below, I could see the river, marked by jagged lines of foam where rocks broke the surface.

Our macabre dance moved to its climax: suspense suspended, the strobe of vertigo kept at bay by the greater threat of Carswell, moving confidently forward where I could only inch backwards.

I moved out until I was above the middle of the river. The lights of the buildings on the bank looked very far away. I saw the ghost of Allen Dulles standing, smoking his pipe, looking at the bridge from his terrace. The white churn below became more violent. I would be down there soon but pretended, with what little imagination I had left, that I was luring Carswell, and it was I who was dictating the moves.

He slipped unexpectedly and I thought I saw him blanche, even by the pale light of the moon. I wondered if he was losing his nerve (where I had none left to lose). He advanced carefully, more human now, while I nursed that tiny slip as a cause for hope. The guard of Carswell's foil caught the moon. He was close enough now for me to see that he carried it looped around his wrist, to leave his hands free.

Until then we had worked the space under the middle of the bridge. The sense of enclosure had become almost reassuring. Now I saw an alternative but far more exposed: a caged service ladder hanging down over the side of the bridge, up which I hoped to climb.

But the ladder was a false escape. There was no way onto it. A locked metal door prevented entry. By then I was on the outside stanchion on the edge of the drop, with Carswell closing, going for the eyes again, wanting what, a blinded Icarus? I tried dazzling him with the torch but the battery was as good as dead – and so was I. Seeing my helplessness, Carswell laughed, not out of disdain but genuine good humor. The laugh of a man enjoying himself. Maybe his pleasure was what dragged me back. I was beyond scared, way out in some space alone, forward-projecting my tumbling release. There was no strategy or defence, just one last desperate action.

He lunged for the eyes again. I flicked my head aside, felt the blade slice the skin, and heard Carswell's grunt of satisfaction. For the first time since getting on the bridge I let go of the stanchion, grabbed Carswell's foil with my left hand and hung on in spite of the cord of pain burning my palm. I yanked forward, knowing the foil was attached to his wrist. My right hand was in my pocket. I flicked the blade-switch of the Stanley knife. I didn't have time to draw it clear, so slashed upwards through the fabric of my trousers, freeing the knife, which arced up towards Carswell's neck. Slash and away. Carswell was already starting his fall before the blade could reach his neck. He teetered then plummeted soundlessly, spiralling out into the night, watched by blue moonlight. As he tumbled, his cloak wrapped itself around his head so he would have died in darkness.

With Carswell gone, I was no longer so afraid of the height, and jumping from the bridge on to the platform was a lot easier than the other way round. There was the pleasure of freaking out two dopers who were left trying to work out where I had come from.

I walked giddily up into the street, clenching my hand to hide the blood. It still wasn't late, before eleven with bars open and Swiss people strolling around doing their Swiss thing. I saw Dora sitting in a bar opposite Dulles's house, waiting for Carswell. Did she see me? I don't know. I walked on by, counting the distance I was putting between myself and Dora and Carswell. With luck nobody would understand Carswell's death, except for me (and him). Man dead in river, foil attached to wrist. Big mystery. Death by misadventure.

Hoover, Syria

Nephew

I am glad to hear you are alive and well. Beate gave me your e-mail address. She says you are lying low and now staying with Abe, who is recovering. I mourn Sol and Manny.

My own adventure was probably less dramatic than yours. Most of it was spent in a sickbed, wondering whether Herr Viessmann was going to stick the big needle in me and finish off what he tried to do in 1945. As it was he fed me some top-grade morphine, which was hard to come off. Konrad fancies himself as a doctor. I slept with one eye open.

I have a couple of observations to make about Konrad Viessmann, apart from the obvious one that he is totally crazy. He is lonely for Willi Schmidt, lonely for the social creature he once was. He admitted sometimes that he was Willi, but denied it for the most part. He would recall jazz nights in Zürich, would remember us standing in a field watching Karl-Heinz showing off his horsemanship, but would deny categorically having been in Strasbourg on the night he tried to kill me, or in the ghetto in Budapest. He has also suppressed the truth about his escape line. In his version, anyone he helped went free. He did, however, admit to reclaiming Willi Schmidt's account in person. The fact that there had been no money was, he said, proof that it had gone to the right people. All that was left was what was in a large deposit box: his jazz records.

He played them with tears in his eyes. 'Look,' he said, pointing to the old labels. 'Victor 26536. "Ko-Ko" and "Jack the Bear". Duke Ellington and his Famous Orchestra. This was from March 1940, before any of us met. And this one from April 1939. Commodore 526. "Strange Fruit" and "Fine and Mellow" by Billie Holiday and Her Orchestra.'

There were others. Count Basie from June 1938. 'Blue and Sentimental', and 'Doggin' Around'; Decca 1965. Art Tatum solo piano: 'Gone With the Wind' and 'Stormy Weather', from 1937, Decca 1603; and Tatum again on Decca 1850, from 1940: 'Sweet Lorraine' and 'Get Happy'.

I have the records with me now. Willi/Konrad left without them. Who would have guessed they would end up in Syria of all places? And as for that Tatum title on Decca 1850: did anyone ever Get Happy? The most I can say for myself is that I rode my luck.

Viessmann came to my room early one morning, as

day broke. If he hadn't found me awake, who knows. When he saw me waiting for him he did not come in but remained in the doorway, for what felt like the longest time, saying nothing. Then he inclined his head and was gone. Straight after his helicopter revved up and he was back up in the skies. Less than an hour later the cavalry arrived, a bunch of fierce-looking rebels who rounded everyone up and torched the camp.

They knew I would be there. Maurice's name was mentioned, and they looked after me pretty well, and now I am told I am across the border in Syria. It's dry and high here, and I am being treated by a good doctor. Maybe there is more life in me than I had thought, because I feel a whole raft better since getting here. The gramophone came as well and I am trying to educate the Kurds in the ways of Duke Ellington and Billie Holiday. There are worse ways of spending one's last act.

My doctor is a civilised man and we speak French. We talk about how Viessmann's companies are well-screened from anyone wishing to investigate them, how lawyers can cushion them from any moral or legal responsibility, the same as it ever was. (Are you listening, Mr Dulles?)

My doctor says they are getting reports of epidemics breaking out in refugee camps. Some of the diseases have never been seen before. The dirtiness and unhygienic practices of the refugees are blamed.

Maybe Viessmann is still part of some black budget, and has been since 1945. Maybe that was what Bob

Ballard was investigating: an old operation that everyone had forgotten about, except the operative himself.

International protest about the fate of the Kurds has been limited because of army control and a complex web of business interests. I would hazard that the whole area is being used for a top-secret social and medical experiment. Some of this is merely 'sensitive', known to the various governments involved in the dam project. Some of it is way off the map in terms of human rights, and known about by very very few, and deniable because information is sketchy to non-existent. Turkey's role as a sponsored buffer state in global affairs is of enormous significance to Europe and the United States, which are prepared to overlook the state of its internal affairs. Given the relative inaccessibility of large parts, the country is ideal for the relocation of advanced scientific programs which elsewhere would attract unwelcome attention.

My doctor says that they are getting fed information by Iraqi Intelligence. Bear in mind that Iraq has slaughtered many of its own Kurds – to the loudly vocalised disgust of those civilised nations which choose to ignore the plight of the same people in Turkey. The dam project is a weapon: the Turks could turn off the Euphrates' supply altogether, like it did for Syria with the Tigris for a couple of weeks. But, unlike Syria, which sponsors the Kurdish rebels, Iraq's position is more ambivalent. Iraqi Intelligence says Viessmann's people acted as 'consultants' on their Kurdish problem. Through them the Iraqis acquired the chemical gases developed by I.G. Farben in the 1930s. Your old chum Carswell came up too. He sold them British security systems, with the blessing of MI6. After that they followed the genocide trail to Turkey.

I am speculating still, based on recent observation, and Viessmann's nostalgia for Willi Schmidt. If Viessmann has any regrets it is that his achievements have been invisible. The refugee camp became a surrogate for that other achievement: its acceptable legacy. He is a cult figure without the cult. He has closed the circle. Cure can't come without infection, and through that he sees himself working for a better world. He is preparing for disaster, and survival. His notebook doodles: arks, floods, barbed wire, a Christlike self-portrait with a razor-wire crown of thorns. Part of him subscribes to notions of cleanliness and health relating to the old Nazi doctrines, plus he is Swiss. Willi and the clean machine: any extermination part of his program he has learned to censor. Anyone visiting him would come away with the impression of a humane, spiritual man.

My own fantasies for dealing with Viessmann were pathetic and juvenile. I wanted him to flatter my ego for having figured him out. The point about men like Willi and Konrad (I am starting to think of them as separate) is that there is no specific dénouement, because there is nothing to uncover beyond a series of links. People like Willi and Konrad are assimilated. They are not sacrificial figures. Willi has been living in deep cover for years. No hi-tech wizardry, pussy cats or beautiful assistants in luxury redoubts; just somewhere clapped-out, way off the map, a few huts and a sense of quiet medical purpose. Perhaps he has convinced himself that he is leading a saintly life. Perhaps he really believes he is in the business of cure. Or perhaps Carswell was the truly nasty one, as you suggest. Apart from Willi's attempt to kill me he was never nasty in a one-on-one way, unlike Carswell. Willi was genocidally nasty. Willi was a dreamer.

From your cryptic account, I do not fully comprehend what happened to Carswell. Beate says he was found floating in the river with a fencing foil. The police are saying he probably jumped, except nobody saw. Tell me when you see me. I guess I will be leaving here soon. My doctor says I will be fit enough to travel after a couple more days' rest.

The truth is, I am a feted figure here, through my association with Karl-Heinz. In the crazy way of things, everything connects up, from all the way back, and the joke was that Willi and Karl-Heinz continued to move in an invisible tandem, working different sides of the fence. Willi's route took him to the Turks, and Karl-Heinz's, thanks to Himmler's astrologist, took him to the Kurds. It's still a pretty small world. Karl-Heinz offered his services to the people-smuggling industry, which was how he learned what was happening to the Kurds, which was why he got whacked.

He was a man who did many bad things but I miss him. That said, he poses something of a moral dilemma, even from beyond the grave. His latest adventure – posthumously bequeathed – is one of blood and prophecy, and raises again the spectre of anti-Semitism. I am sure that Karl-Heinz the romantic would see it only in terms of historical sweep, and destiny.

As a measure of my current standing, I got taken to meet the next warrior leader. The Chosen One. He's just a kid, several years off coming of age, but regarded locally as a new Messiah. The boy was moved to Syria on Karl-Heinz's instructions, apparently against the interpretation of the prophecy, which was nearly the cause of a civil war. (If the Kurds have no one else to fight they fight themselves.) But then, only days later, the village where the boy had been was taken over by the army, everyone rounded up and never seen again. So Karl-Heinz became the big local hero.

I am an old rationalist. I don't believe in anything. The Chosen One, I told myself, was just a scruffy kid, until I looked into his eyes. It is a bit late in life to be getting superstitious, but since the meeting I have been haunted by an overwhelming foreboding. I wonder what I should do with this knowledge. It sounds preposterous to say that I believe I hold history's destiny in my hands. Maybe the prophecy would be better for being denied. I know just from seeing the boy's eyes that they are witnesses-in-waiting to hundreds of thousands of deaths. If someone could have killed the child Himmler or the child Saddam in the certainty that it was the right thing to do, should they have done so?

There I am, looking at the boy they say is going to be the next great warrior leader come to establish the new world order. It's just one big rolling story, and maybe Karl-Heinz was right in believing that the next stage has been in place all along. Another million deaths, with millions more to follow. The joke is, I suspect it is one of Allen Dulles's slush funds that will pay for it, and Dulles, that consummate anti-Semite, will be having the last word, as usual.

I know what I want to do, which is to come back and fetch Beate and head south, like we planned, before it all slides away, sit in the sun and try and find a little peace of mind. What would you do?

Acknowledgements

Of the many books consulted, the following were referred to most:

Eichmann in Jerusalem by Hannah Arendt (Faber and Faber, London, 1963)

Hitler's Secret Bankers by Adam LeBor (Pocket Books, London, 1997)

IBM and the Holocaust by Edwin Black (Little, Brown and Company, London, 2001)

Jews for Sale: Nazi-Jewish Negotiations, 1933–1945 by Yehuda Bauer (Yale University Press, New Haven and London, 1994)

Maskerado by Tivadar Soros (Canongate, Edinburgh, 2000)

Nazi Gold by Ian Sayer and Douglas Botting (Granada, London, 1984)

The Politics of Genocide: The Holocaust in Hungary by

Randolph L. Braham (Wayne State University Press, Detroit, 2000)

The Secret War Against the Jews by John Loftus and Mark Aarons (St Martin's Griffin, New York, 1997)

The Summer That Bled by Anthony Masters (Michael Joseph, London, 1972)

The Swiss, the Gold, and the Dead by Jean Ziegler (Harcourt, Brace and Company, New York, 1998)

Thanks also to Adam LeBor, Liz Jobey, Lynn Ritchie and Richard Williams. Hoover's name was taken from my late uncle, Gustav van Hover, known to all as Hoover, with whom there are no similarities, apart from name, country of origin and emigration to the United States. Thanks also to my agent Gillon Aitken, for his patience, and my editors Tim Binding, George Lucas and Ben Ball, whose insight, thoroughness and attention to detail made this a much better book. A special thanks, as always, to Emma Matthews for her unfailing judgement, care and support.